Kathi Macias'

12
Days of
Christmas

First Edition

Published by

Helping Hands Press

ISBN: 978-1-62208-532-3

Printed in the United States of America

Table of Contents

Introduction

When I first sensed the stirrings to compile a collection of Christmas stories from various authors, I mulled over possible themes and settings, never seeming to land on the appropriate one. And then a song began to play in my mind: "On the first day of Christmas, my true love gave to me…"

If you're like me, once a song starts rolling around in your brain, it's tough to kick it out. This was no exception. It rolled around in there until it finally got my attention and I realized it might be exactly the theme I'd been seeking for the Christmas compilation.

And so I began to explore the possibilities. Might it be one ongoing story divided into twelve chapters, each written by a different author and each representing one day closer to Christmas Day? I liked that concept except for the fact that each of us approaches Christmas in a very personal way, and I wanted to give the authors freedom to write their story from their own individual viewpoint.

As a result, we ended up with a delightful collection of Christmas stories—some historical, some contemporary, some romance, some mystery, some Amish—well, you get the picture. But each story takes the reader one day closer to Christmas, which was my original objective.

It has been an absolute joy to compile these stories, and I do hope each will bless you in its own individual way. I also hope you won't limit yourself to reading this collection at Christmas time. Though that timeframe might work best, Christmas is, after all, timeless; its message calls to us all year long: Will you make room in your heart for the Christ Child? If the answer is yes, then read on, my friends!

Rules of Engagement

Kathi Macias

It was Saturday, twelve days before Christmas, and the wind howled through the Texas Panhandle as it did all year 'round—hot in the summer, cold in the winter, and with a fury that made even the natives weary with its intensity. But with nothing to hold it back but a barbed wire fence, the not quite 200,000 residents of Amarillo shrugged it off as part of the price they paid for living in the town they somehow, inexplicably loved.

Megan Bosworth was no different. She'd been born and raised in what her late grandpa had called "the best cow town in these parts or any other." Though she'd visited several states and two other countries in her twenty-three years of life, she'd come to the conclusion that her grandpa had been right. And so, upon graduating from college the previous June, Megan opted to take a teaching job just a few miles from the only home she'd ever known, remaining there to share that nearly 100-year-old, two-story house with her parents and younger brother, James, who was still in high school. Life was good.

And then she'd met Marty Givens, and it had gotten even better.

"Deck the halls with boughs of holly." She sang along with the CD playing in the background as she and her mother hung strings of cranberries and colored popcorn between wide doorways and along the staircase railing. It was scarcely mid-morning, and the two of them had stayed up late the night before, working on the homemade decorations together as they had for more than two decades. Several times through the years Megan had suggested they consider buying something a bit more modern to prepare the house for Christmas, but her mother nixed the idea each time.

"Your grandmother, God rest her soul, taught me to do this when I was a tiny girl, just like I taught you." The woman's jaw was set as she spoke, and Megan recognized it as a no-nonsense sign that no amount of pleading or cajoling would change her mind. "It's one of the clearest memories I have of her, and I intend to honor her this way every Christmas for as long as the good Lord allows me to stay on this earth."

And so, despite a few sore pin-pricked fingers, Megan now smiled at each new strand that brightened the house. Her smile widened as she thought of Marty. Talk about pleading and cajoling! Just a few days earlier he'd asked her to marry him, telling her he wanted to formally announce it to both their families—hers in person and his on the phone since they lived in Florida—on Christmas Eve. Megan, her head spinning, had protested that she needed time to think about it and to get used to the idea before springing it on everyone else. After all, they'd been dating only a couple months, and she didn't want to rush into anything.

"Megan, you know I love you, and I know you love me," he'd argued, as they sat together on the porch swing of her parents' home, wrapped in warm jackets and watching the sun go down. "You're so beautiful! You have the most incredible green eyes and red hair. I can't live without you, you know that. I need you, Megan. I need you in my life. Besides, what's there to think about or get used to? You do love me, don't you?"

His gray eyes, sparkling with passion and excitement, held her nearly breathless, as they always did. The man was just too handsome for his own good—or hers, for that matter. If her grandpa were still alive, she imagined he would have said, "Run for your life, Meggie girl! This one's up to no good." Then he would have laughed and left it up to her to sort it all out and decide if her grandpa was being serious or not.

Megan's mom excused herself to go do something in the kitchen, and Megan sighed, wrapping another strand around the next section of staircase railing. The polished mahogany seemed to shine brighter beneath the deep red cranberries.

Grandpa was so good at that—helping me walk through tough decisions without really telling me what to do. If only he were still here to help me now!

But of course he wasn't. This would be their third Christmas without him. She'd struggled through the first and second Christmas, telling herself it would get better with time. Now she wasn't so sure. Just thinking about his ready laugh and the nuggets of wisdom he dispensed so lovingly made her heart ache.

Enough of that, she told herself. *Christmas is less than two weeks away. This is no time to get teary-eyed.*

As the carols continued to play in the background, "Silent Night" faded to a close and "God Rest Ye Merry Gentlemen" brought an upbeat tempo to her movements. She smiled again. Why did she have misgivings about marrying Marty? He was a kind and thoughtful man, and quite popular with everyone at school, both students and faculty alike. In fact, that was how they'd met—in the teachers' lounge at Pioneer Elementary, just three days into her first real job, the one she'd studied and trained for and dreamed about for so many years. She'd been nervous, wanting desperately to do well with her second grade pupils. Marty, who taught fourth grade, had befriended and encouraged her—and quickly won her heart.

At least, I think he won it...didn't he? She frowned. *I know I think about him a lot, and I enjoy being with him. So why am I hesitating at accepting his proposal? After all, we have so much in common—including our faith and even the same professions. It's like we're made for each other. And yet...*

The memory returned, causing her to pause in her task. Once again she was sitting with him on the porch, stunned at his proposal yet mesmerized by the passion she saw reflected in his eyes. Didn't she share that passion, that longing to be together as man and wife? Perhaps she did, but she needed time to be certain. Why did he insist on an answer so quickly and an announcement to their families on Christmas Eve? That was less than two weeks away!

The doorbell rang, interrupting "O Come All Ye Faithful" and her decorating. She laid the remaining unstrung decorations on the entryway table, near the foot of the stairs, and turned toward the front door. No doubt her friends from church had arrived to pick her up. Saturday was their regular day to visit the shut-ins at the nearby Veterans' Home, an event she looked forward to each week. Today they would sing Christmas carols to a handful of the fifty or so men who lived there, once proud warriors who served their country with honor and who now spent their latter days in wheelchairs or on walkers. And yet, as sad as it made her to see them that way, she also came away inspired after each visit, glad she'd made it a priority to spend time with these elderly gentlemen.

Before she could reach the door, her brother, James, nearly flew down the stairs and brushed past her, lunging for the doorknob. "It's for me," he announced before pulling the door open and realizing otherwise.

Three women, all about Megan's age, stood on the porch, bundled up and smiling, though they seemed a bit taken aback at the sight of the eager young man who yanked the door open with such enthusiasm.

Megan, who now stood beside her brother, watched that enthusiasm fade from his face and posture, as his shoulders sagged and he mumbled a quick hello to the ladies before turning away.

"I thought it was Jason. We're supposed to go shoot some hoops."

Megan smiled. "I'm sure he'll be here soon."

James didn't answer; he was already zipping up the stairs back toward his room. She thought of calling him out on his rudeness to their guests but opted to let it go—this time.

Megan turned back to her friends, who stood waiting on the front porch. She opened the screen door. "Sorry about that. Would you like to come in? I just need to grab my coat and purse."

Andrea, an attractive brunette who stood slightly in front of the other two, smiled. "No problem. We'll wait for you in the car. We don't want to keep our best guys waiting."

They all chuckled as they headed back to the car and Megan went to the entryway coat closet to grab her things. In less than a minute she had joined them in the vehicle, settling into the backseat with Andrea, her closest friend. As they began to chatter about work and Christmas shopping and their favorite veterans at the home, Megan shut out all thoughts of Marty's pressure to accept his proposal. She'd deal with that later. Right now she and her friends were excited to bring some Christmas cheer to those who didn't have much else to brighten up their day.

It was obvious someone had been busy decorating the Veterans' Home for the holidays, as the pungent smell of evergreens permeated the air and the entryway was already adorned more colorfully than Megan's house, which she and her mother had only begun to prepare for Christmas. A floor-to-ceiling Douglas Fir, sparkling with lights and tinsel and all sorts of colored ornaments, stood in the far corner of the main assembly hall, where the "few but faithful," as Megan and her friends often called them, gathered for whatever event might come along. Today it was the four ladies from Redeemer Community Church, here to lead the men in singing carols and then to talk and pray individually with those who seemed open. Even those who weren't would usually stick around anyway, since that's when the punch and cookies were passed around.

The crowd was a bit larger than usual today. Megan imagined it was in anticipation of Christmas, which seemed to affect nearly everyone in a positive way. Looking out on the twenty or so men who had gathered at the round tables scattered around the room, she smiled in greeting. Most of them had been involved in conversations when the ladies entered, but the buzz died down quickly as several pairs of rheumy eyes sized up their entertainment for the day.

"The one in green's the prettiest one of the bunch." The loud announcement, made by a gray-haired gentleman sitting at a table near the front, echoed through the room and brought a ripple of laughter, not only from the other vets but also from Megan and her friends. George Thompson was a familiar and popular face in the little crowd, and each of the ladies from the church understood that he was not only hard of hearing but also quite outspoken, and quite possibly in the early stages of dementia. Since Megan was the one wearing green, her cheeks flushed a bit deeper than anyone else's.

Within moments the ladies had thanked everyone for allowing them to come, Andrea had settled in at the piano by the wall on the entrance side of the room, and Megan asked for requests. The gentleman sitting next to George asked for "Jingle Bells," which Megan imagined was a good one to get them started, as nearly everyone knew it. But after they'd run through several verses of it and she asked for other requests, the same man raised his hand and asked for "Jingle Bells" again.

Megan smiled. "Thank you so much for your request. You must really like that song."

He nodded, his face expectant.

She smiled again. "Maybe we'll sing that again later, but first let's sing something else, shall we?"

The man's face fell, but he nodded. When no one else made a suggestion or request, Megan announced, "How about 'Joy to the Word'? Does everyone know that one?"

Quite a few nodded their heads, and Andrea played the intro. In moments they were singing again. All went well until they closed with "Hark the Herald Angels Sing" and Megan announced that it was time for cookies and punch. Most of the group seemed more than happy to make the transition, but the man next to George raised his hand again.

"You forgot 'Jingle Bells.' You said we could sing 'Jingle Bells' again."

Megan's face flushed. She had indeed said that, and so she glanced at Andrea, who had already gathered her music and stood up from the bench. She nodded back at Megan and returned to her seat. One last rousing rendition of "Jingle Bells" rocked the room, and the music was over. Even the man next to George seemed happy and content.

Two aides quickly began to pass around the cookies and punch, as Megan and her friends worked the room, patting receptive shoulders, laughing at jokes, listening to lonely stories, offering to pray.

"That's because you don't understand the Rules of Engagement."

The loud announcement reverberated from the front of the room, interrupting all other conversations. Megan and the others turned to the source. It was George, explaining something to the man who so loved to sing "Jingle Bells."

"If you understood the Rules of Engagement, you wouldn't ask such a silly question."

One of the aides moved quickly to the front of the room and sat down in the vacant chair next to George. Her words and gestures were soothing, as she no doubt worked at settling the issue between the two men, and Megan breathed a sigh of relief. It was nearly Christmas, after all. The last thing any of them needed was a confrontation, even if it was between two elderly vets who might not even realize what they were doing.

That settled, she pulled up a chair beside a heavyset man, seated on a chair with his arms raised slightly, resting on his walker directly in front of him.

"Hello, David."

The man smiled up at Megan. "How ya doin', sweetheart? I knew you'd come and visit me. You always do."

She lowered herself into the chair. "Of course I do. I enjoy seeing you and catching up on your news."

David's dark, heavy eyebrows shot up toward his bald head. "News? You think I have news? What kind of news could I have in here?" He leaned forward and lowered his voice. "It's not like they let me leave here and go out and do things, you know." He chuckled as if he'd told a great joke.

Though she knew he hadn't meant for the words to cut her heart, they did. Why hadn't she realized how desperately these men longed to be out and about, enjoying life the way they once had? It was true they were probably grateful for a safe and inexpensive place to spend their last years, yet it didn't make up for the isolation and boredom they experienced on a daily basis.

"I hadn't thought of that." She hesitated, searching for a safer direction. "But what about news from home? Your family, maybe? Anything new with them?"

David shrugged. "Probably. But they don't tell me about it. I haven't heard from any of them in nearly a year. They come by at Christmas and bring me neckties and fruitcake and tell me how much they love me and miss me. Then they disappear again until next year. Guess they'll be by for their annual visit soon. If you like fruitcake, come back after Christmas and you can have all of mine."

Megan felt her cheeks redden, but before she could respond David laid a hand on hers. "I didn't say that to make you feel bad. It's just the way things are, that's all. But hey, it's almost Christmas, right? Whether the grandkids drop by or not, there's still reason to celebrate." His smile warmed her heart. "It's the greatest celebration of the year, you know. The greatest Gift ever given. And that's why I don't mind spending my last years here with these other old coots." He chuckled. "I'm nearly home now, and if God can use me to help take of few of these guys with me before I check out, then it'll all be worth it."

Tears bit Megan's eyes at the sudden memory of her beloved grandfather. Though he was no longer here with her, David's words had reminded her that he was "home" and that she would see him again one day. His words were also a clear reminder of why each of them was here on this earth, regardless of age or circumstance. And without realizing it, he had given her a clear reminder to stay focused on what Christmas was really all about.

"Thank you," she said. "I needed to hear that."

He nodded. "We all do. Often. Now, since I don't have any news to share with you, why don't you tell me yours? A beautiful young lady like you is bound to have a lot going on in her life."

The thought of Marty danced through her head, but she shoved it away. Much safer and definitely more comfortable to talk about her wonderful students at school. And so she began to share about their antics, quickly bringing a smile to David's lips and a light to his eyes.

Megan was surprised at how much decorating her mom had accomplished while she was gone. Apparently James had even pitched in a bit before Jason finally picked him up for their scheduled basketball practice.

"It looks great, Mom. You're nearly done."

Marilyn Bosworth laughed. "Oh, not by a long shot! We've barely gotten started. The big thing is the tree. Your dad wants us all to go out together to pick one out when he gets home from work this evening. You know how he is about finding just the right one."

Megan smiled and nodded. No doubt her dad had inherited that talent and passion for picking out the perfect tree from his father, who used to lead the pack in its annual search for such a treasure. Once again her heart constricted. *Grandpa, I sure wish you were here.*

But of course he wasn't, and Megan forced the thought away. "So what do you want to do next? It looks like most of the cranberry and popcorn strings are up."

"They are. I was about to climb up into the attic and find the manger scene so we can set it in front of the tree once it's up."

"I'll do that, Mom. Just let me change first."

"Thanks, honey. I'd appreciate that. And while you're changing, I'll finish making lunch. You must be hungry by now."

Megan smiled again. "I shouldn't be after sharing cookies with at least five different vets, but I have to admit, I'd like something a bit more substantial—and slightly less sweet."

Marilyn shook her head. "I think it's wonderful that you go visit there, honey, but five cookies? Sounds like you'll be on a sugar high for hours." She turned toward the kitchen, and Megan watched her walk away. She was so blessed to have such a wonderful family, but it still wasn't the same without her grandpa.

Her cell phone buzzed then, and she pulled it from her pocket and peered at the text message: *Are you back yet? I miss you. Why haven't you called me?*

She sighed and headed for the stairs, determined to change clothes, have lunch, and then climb up into the attic and find the crèche for her mom. Most of all, she was determined to ignore Marty's demanding message until she'd had a bit more time to think. *And pray*, she reminded herself. *Definitely need to pray!*

Lunch was over, and the two women lingered over a cup of lemon spice tea before getting back to work on the decorations. Their current topic of discussion—baking—was a pleasant one, not only anticipating the baking to come but reflecting on what they'd done in years past.

Megan smiled, her mind wandering to one of its favorite memories. "Remember how Grandpa always tried to sneak into the kitchen and steal the cookies before they had time to cool?"

Marilyn Bosworth chuckled. "I sure do. How many times did I tell him to leave them alone so we could put the icing and sprinkles on?" She shook her head. "He was just as bad when your grandma was alive. I can remember her scolding him about that very thing when I was a little girl. That grandpa of yours had a serious sweet tooth."

Nearly three full years had passed since her grandfather's death, but Megan still struggled at hearing him referred to in the past tense.

She opted to change the direction of the conversation before the tears stinging her eyes won out over her efforts to hold them back.

"James is just like Grandpa when it comes to sneaking cookies, and I've seen Dad snitch one or two himself."

Marilyn nodded. "Oh, that's for sure! This family doesn't lack for cookie monsters. We'll just have to plan our baking when they're not around."

"Any time after this coming Friday works for me. I'll be out for two weeks."

"I still can't believe it's nearly Christmas again. Where did the year go?" Marilyn sipped her tea and set the mug back on the table. "Is Marty going to join us for our traditional Christmas Eve celebration?"

The many thoughts Megan had been trying to push from her mind now flooded back in. More than once she'd come close to inviting Marty for Christmas Eve—which included a light supper at home, a candlelight service at church, and then hot cocoa and caroling around the tree. But his insistence on announcing their engagement that same evening held her back.

Rules of Engagement.

The words drifted back to her, and she frowned. Where had she heard them?

"Megan? Did you hear me? Is Marty joining us for Christmas Eve?"

Megan started, jarring herself back to the present. "Sorry, Mom. I…I haven't really asked him yet, so I don't know."

Marilyn's eyebrows rose. "You haven't? Well, why not? Christmas is less than two weeks away, honey. Don't you think you should give him some time to plan?"

Time to plan. Time to decide. That's what I wish he'd give me. If only he hadn't blindsided me with the proposal, I would have invited him long before this. She shook off the thoughts. "You're right, Mom. I'll do it soon."

Rules of Engagement.

There it was again. She frowned, trying to snag the memory.

Marilyn reached across the small kitchen table and laid her hand on Megan's. "Is everything okay, sweetheart?"

Megan blinked. "Sure. I just…"

"You were frowning. Is something wrong?"

The scene at the Veterans' Home flashed into her mind. *Rules of Engagement.* Of course! That's where she'd heard it.

"No, I'm fine. Really. I was just remembering something that happened today when we were visiting the vets."

Marilyn's concerned expression disappeared in a smile. "I'm so proud of you and your friends for going there. What a blessing it must be for those men."

"It's a blessing for us too. Some of them are real characters, but most give us more than we give them."

Marilyn withdrew her hand and picked up her tea for another sip. "It's always that way with ministry, isn't it? I feel the same way about working with the pre-schoolers at church on Sunday."

Megan laughed. "I can relate—sort of. My students are older than pre-schoolers, but I adore them."

"I know you do. And Marty seems to feel the same about his students."

There it was again, that stab of misgiving that seemed to come out of nowhere each time the subject of Marty Givens popped up. Marty was a great teacher; the children all adored him. Megan's parents and even James had taken to him right away, and she herself was drawn to him in so many ways. So what was it that held her back from moving the relationship forward to the next stage?

"Mom, have you ever heard the expression 'Rules of Engagement'?"

Her mother looked nearly as surprised at the question as Megan was. She certainly hadn't planned to ask, and couldn't imagine what it had to do with anything they were discussing. They were just three words spoken by an elderly gentleman who was hard of hearing and didn't always make a lot of sense when he talked.

Now it was Marilyn's turn to frown. "Why would you ask? That's not a common phrase."

"I know. One of the vets said it today, and for some reason it's just stuck with me. So I'm curious, that's all."

Marilyn nodded. "It's funny, but I first heard it years ago, from your grandpa. He was an old military guy, as you know, and one time when I was about eight or nine and I had a big blow-up with one of my friends, he found me pouting in my room. He asked me what was wrong and I told him that Karen wasn't a very good friend. He asked me why I thought that, and I told him that I wanted to do something and she didn't want to do it with me. The harder I tried to convince her, the more she resisted. In fact, I never could talk her into it, and I just couldn't figure out why."

"So...how did the Rules of Engagement figure into that discussion?"

Marilyn smiled and got up to take her cup to the sink. She rinsed it out as she spoke. "I wondered the same thing at the time. Didn't figure it out until I had a little more maturity, but you know how good your grandpa was at doing that—giving advice in a way that let other people work through it in their own time and way."

Megan nodded. "I sure do. And I really appreciated it." She lowered her voice as she picked up her cup to join her mother at the sink. "That's one of the things I really miss about him."

"So do I." Marilyn sighed, reminding Megan that she wasn't the only one who missed the beloved patriarch of their family.

"Anyway," Marilyn continued, "here's the basic gist of what he told me about Rules of Engagement. It's basically a military term that defines circumstances, conditions, degrees, and the manner in which one country, or even an individual, can exert pressure on another before it's considered provocative and unfriendly—in other words, quite possibly no longer in the other country's or individual's best interests. There's a lot more to it than that, of course, but that pretty much sums it up in a nutshell. I hadn't really thought much about the term until you brought it up, but I've always tried to remember the heart of it so I can apply it when I deal with others. In fact, Grandpa's advice to me about the Rules of Engagement helped save that friendship years ago when I nearly destroyed it with my pushiness."

Megan nodded, as she finished rinsing her cup and placed it in the dish drainer. Interesting concept, she thought, and one she sensed she needed to meditate on a bit more. But for now, there was a manger scene waiting to be brought down from the attic, dusted off, and placed on the hearth in the family room to await the Christmas tree that would be its backdrop for yet another holiday celebration.

She'd just come down from the attic when her phone buzzed. Cradling the crèche carefully in one arm, she used her free hand to fish her cell out of her pocket. It took only a quick peek to confirm her suspicions that it was Marty, wondering why she hadn't responded to his previous text.

Helloooo! Everything okay? I haven't heard from you, and I'm getting worried. Don't you love me anymore? Answer me this time or I'm headed over there. LOL!

She smiled, sighed, and slipped the phone back into her pocket, her emotions a jumble. She appreciated his attentiveness and concern, but for some reason questioned his motives. Was his concern more about her well-being or his need to have her respond?

She went into the family room and set the manger scene down on the hearth, near where it would rest once the tree was up and decorated. Then, because she had the room to herself, she sat down in the rocker to answer Marty.

Sorry. Been busy. Went to the Veterans' Home, just like I do every Saturday morning, and now I'm helping Mom decorate. All is fine here. Talk to you soon!

Even as she hit send, she sensed he wouldn't be satisfied with her response. She chided herself for not telling him she loved him. Should she have? Probably. But then he should already know that...shouldn't he? And if he didn't, why not?

The questions nagged at her as she once again placed the phone in her pocket, but she hadn't even had time to get up from her chair before Marty responded, this time with a call rather than a text. Settling back into her seat, she answered.

"Hey," she said, hoping her tone sounded natural. "How are you?"

The irritation in his voice, though subdued, was evident. "I'm fine...I guess. But I was hoping you'd call me instead of sending a text. I enjoy hearing your voice, you know."

She did know that, and wondered herself why she had texted instead of called.

"Sorry. I thought you might be busy, and I didn't want to interrupt—"

"It's Saturday. I'm not working, remember? I'm off. Home." His voice lost its irritable edge. "Wishing I was with you."

Her heart softened. "That's sweet. And I'm sorry. Really. I should have called. I just got caught up with all that's going on today."

After a slight hesitation he responded. "I understand. And I'm sorry to be so pushy. But I miss you."

"I miss you too." A dart of doubt flashed through her mind, but she pushed it away. "Do you...do you want to come over this evening? It seems we're all going out to get a tree after Dad gets home from work. It's kind of a big deal around here."

Marty's chuckle warmed her heart. She appreciated his ready laugh.

"Sure. You bet I would. What time?"

"Dad's usually home by five. We'll go right after that—won't even wait to eat. We'll just have something later while we set up the tree and start decorating it. What do you think?"

"Works for me." His voice dropped a notch. "But we really need to snag some alone time before the night's over. We have things to discuss, Megan. Christmas Eve is less than two weeks away, you know."

She was only too well aware of that fact, and she knew why he'd brought it up. He wanted to convince her to accept his proposal and to agree to announce it to their families on Christmas Eve. That was his idea of a discussion. Suddenly the anticipation of picking out the tree that evening diminished, and she wished she hadn't invited Marty to come along. But it was too late now.

"I have to go," she said, adding "See you then" just before disconnecting the call.

Megan sat in the rocker, unmoving, as she stared at the crèche and contemplated her conversation with Marty in light of their overall relationship. He was, for the most part, a kind man, thoughtful when it came to things like bringing her flowers and opening doors for her. He was a wildly popular teacher, with loyal students who adored him. And though he attended a different church than she and her family did, he shared her Christian faith.

She smiled, thinking of his dreamy eyes, chiseled features, and broad shoulders. *Not hard on the eyes either*, she reminded herself. But her smile faded as she tried to push herself to the next step of imagining herself married to him.

Why do I always get stuck here? Am I afraid of getting married? Is that it?

She shook her head, as if she could convince herself otherwise. After all, her parents had a wonderful relationship. They'd been married nearly a quarter of a century and still enjoyed being together. She couldn't have better role models. And yet…

"Oh, there you are!"

Her mother's exclamation cut into her thoughts, sending them flying in several directions. She lifted her eyes from the manger scene. Marilyn Bosworth's smiling face came into view, along with the memory of their earlier conversation regarding Rules of Engagement.

"I've got to go out for a few minutes," Megan said suddenly, rising from the chair and heading for the entryway to grab her coat and purse. "I won't be long."

Marilyn's smile morphed into a puzzled frown. "But…where are you going? Will you be back in time to go with us to pick out the tree?"

"Don't worry," she called over her shoulder as she slipped into her coat and then headed out the door toward her car. "I'll be back in plenty of time."

Megan knew she'd gone off "halfcocked," as her grandpa used to say, but all she could think of as she drove toward the Veterans' Home was that she had to ask George why he'd used the phrase "Rules of Engagement" when she'd been there earlier. As she parked her car and made her way toward the main entrance, she realized her lack of planning could be a problem. What would she tell the receptionist when she asked the reason for her visit?

Shooting a quick prayer for wisdom heavenward, she stepped up to the reception desk where she knew she'd have to sign in. The same smiling face she'd seen when she'd come with her friends earlier now greeted her once more.

"Hello again. I'm surprised to see you back so soon. We don't have anything scheduled, do we?"

Megan shook her head. "No, not at all. I'm not here with the group—just by myself. I…" She hesitated. Might as well just plunge in. "Would it be possible to visit with George Thompson for a few minutes? I don't know if he remembers me, but he always comes to our gatherings on Saturday and sits toward the front."

The young woman, whose nametag read Lisa, chuckled. "Oh, believe me, he'll remember you. He forgets a lot of things, but not the Saturday gatherings you ladies put on here. It's the highlight of his week—and for many of the other men too." She shook her head. "George is a bit outspoken at times, but really quite lovable."

Megan nodded. "Yes, that sounds like him, for sure. So…can I visit him?"

She shrugged. "I don't see why not, but let me buzz his room and make sure he's okay with it." She leaned forward as if she were letting Megan in on a secret. "We have his buzzer and the volume on his intercom turned up to max. He's a bit hard of hearing, as you know."

Megan nodded again, and in moments she heard the brief conversation.

"This is George. Who are you, and what do you want?"

"George, this is Lisa at the front desk. There's someone here to see you."

After a brief pause, Lisa raised her voice. "George, did you hear me?"

"I heard you. I'm just trying to figure out who would want to see me…and why."

The two women exchanged smiles and suppressed giggles. Then Lisa whispered. "Can you remind me of your name?" Megan whispered the answer, and Lisa turned back to the intercom.

"It's Megan Bosworth. She was here this morning, leading Christmas carols. May she come to your room, or would you prefer to come down here?"

A brief chuckle preceded his answer. "Tell her to come down here. I'll be waitin' for her. I haven't had a good-lookin' woman in my room in years."

There was no holding back their laughter this time as Lisa nodded permission and gave Megan the room number.

George greeted her with his nearly toothless grin when she knocked on his door before nudging it open. He was seated in a recliner in the corner, the only piece of furniture in the room besides the bed and a small chest of drawers.

"Well, what do you know?" he asked in his too-loud voice. "It's the good-lookin' one from this morning." He winked. "I was hopin' it'd be you. But you're gonna have to remember to speak up. I don't hear too well."

Megan reminded herself to speak loudly, even as she felt her cheeks warm with the lighthearted compliment. "Thanks for taking the time to see me, Mr. Thompson. I know I should have called ahead, but—"

He cut her off with a wave of his hand. "Come in and sit down." He pointed. "There's a folding chair there by the headboard."

Megan hadn't noticed it when she stepped into the doorway, but she quickly grabbed it and set it up beside George's chair.

"Like I said, I appreciate your seeing me on such short notice."

"Not nearly as much as I appreciate you comin' to see me. Do you know how long it's been since I had a visitor?"

Megan lifted her eyebrows. "I'm afraid I don't." The memory of David's comments about how no one came to visit him except to bring fruitcake and ties at Christmas darted through her mind.

George leaned toward her, and she caught a whiff of Old Spice after shave. She wondered if he wore it all the time or had just managed to splash it on before she came in.

"Too long, if you ask me. But of course, they don't ask me 'cause they don't care. Some of 'em used to drop by and visit me and the missus once in a while, before she died and I came here to live. That's when they found out I didn't have any extra money to leave behind, so now all I get is a box of candy from my daughter. She lives back East, in Massachusetts somewhere, so I suppose that's the best she can do, but you'd think she'd stop sending me the nuts and chews, since I can only eat the cream-filled ones."

He chuckled again, but Megan saw the light dim in his once lively brown eyes.

"Mr. Thompson," she said, hoping to change the subject, "I overheard a remark you made earlier today, when I was here with the ladies from the church, leading the singing. Do you remember that?"

The old man raised his bushy gray eyebrows "Course I remember. You're the prettiest one of the bunch—and none of 'em was bad lookin', if you know what I mean." He chuckled. "Besides, you were wearin' green, my favorite color. But please, stop calling me Mr. Thompson. George will do."

Megan's cheeks warmed again. "All right, George. Thank you. But actually, I meant, do you remember the comment you made? About Rules of Engagement?"

George's eyebrows shot up even higher, and Megan imagined if she surprised him anymore his brows and hairline would meet.

"Rules of Engagement? Sure, I know about that. Don't know why I would have mentioned it when you were singing, though." His eyebrows relaxed and he winked. "I should have been concentrating on you."

"No, it wasn't while we were singing." She smiled, hoping to help him focus. "It was afterward, when we were visiting and having cookies. You were talking with the gentleman next to you."

George nodded. "Ah, that explains it. I don't like the cookies they have here. Too sweet if you ask me. Not like my wonderful wife used to make." He leaned toward her and winked. "That woman's raisin-filled chocolate chip cookies were the best in the world."

Megan took a deep breath. This was going to be harder than she'd expected. "Mr. Thompson—I mean, George—I'm wondering about your comment regarding Rules of Engagement. What were you referring to at the time?"

He frowned. "What time? I'm not sure I understand your question. And if I don't understand it, I can't answer it, now can I?"

She sighed. It was obvious this conversation was going nowhere. She offered a weak smile. "It doesn't matter. I've just been thinking about something you said after we finished Christmas caroling, but—"

His eyes lit up. "Ah, Christmas! Now there's a topic I like to talk about. I love Christmas, don't you?"

Her smile broadened, and she nodded. "I do, yes. Christmas is my favorite holiday."

George's toothless grin widened. "Mine too. It's when Jesus came, you know."

"I know. That's what makes it so special."

He nodded. "Exactly. That's why I don't like it when people try to turn it into something else, like it's all about buying stuff. You know what I mean?"

She nodded again. "I do know what you mean, George. And I agree."

His forehead drew together. "Rules of Engagement, eh?"

Megan felt her eyes widen. Where had that come from?

"That's what Jesus and Christmas are all about, you know—Rules of Engagement."

Now she was nearly as confused as poor George. What was he talking about?

George laid a hand on Megan's arm as he once again leaned close. "The Father sent His Son to engage us. To confront us, sure, but to engage us too. It was His way of re-establishing relationship with us. The only way, really. By giving." He nodded, his eyes focused and sincere. "The Rules of Engagement are all about giving, not getting. Do you understand, pretty lady?"

Megan nodded and answered "yes," though she wasn't really sure if she did. Still, she realized it was probably the only explanation of Rules of Engagement she was going to get from George. Now she'd just have to see if she could sift through what he'd said and make enough sense of it to apply it to her own situation.

The wind seemed angrier than ever when she finally reached home and pulled into the driveway. Her dad would be home in a couple of hours; that meant Marty would show up too. When they first started dating, she'd looked forward to his arrival. When had that changed? Was it when he began pressuring her to say yes to his proposal? She imagined it was, but why? What was it about his marriage proposal that sent red flags flying and her heart racing—not *toward* Marty, but *away* from him?

She dragged herself into the house. From the muted sounds of music drifting down the stairs, she deduced that James had come home. She smiled at the thought of her little brother. He wanted to be so grown up in so many ways, including hanging out with his friends nearly to the exclusion of associating with his family. But she knew he wasn't about to miss their annual trek to the local tree lots to pick out just the right tree to set up in the corner next to the fireplace.

Megan was about to climb the stairway when the vision of the crèche floated into her mind. Drawn to it, she turned back to the family room and went straight for the hearth where she'd left the little manger scene. It was waiting for her. In fact, she had the distinct impression that it was purposely doing so. She picked it up and sat down in the rocker.

"What is it, Lord?" she whispered, as she gazed at the tiny baby in the manger. "What are You trying to tell me?"

The memory of George Thompson, with his bushy eyebrows and beleaguered grin, drifted through her mind as she considered the words he had spoken to her.

"The Father sent His Son to engage us. To confront us, sure, but to engage us too. It was His way of re-establishing relationship with us. The only way, really. By giving…. The Rules of Engagement are all about giving, not getting. Do you understand, pretty lady?"

And then her mind drifted to 1 Corinthians 13, one of her favorite passages of Scripture, one her grandpa used to read to her often. The verses seemed to float in and out or her consciousness, settling at last in her heart.

Love is patient, love is kind. It does not envy, it does not boast, it is not proud. It does not dishonor others, it is not self-seeking, it is not easily angered, it keeps no record of wrongs. Love does not delight in evil but rejoices with the truth. It always protects, always trusts, always hopes, always perseveres. Love never fails.

Still gazing at the manger scene, her heart jumped at the realization that she was staring at a representation of love itself. *Love is patient. Love is not self-seeking.*

In a split second, she knew that she really did understand what George had been trying to tell her—even if George himself did not. Jesus came to give, not to get! That's what love was really about, and who modeled it better than the Savior Himself?

"No one," she said aloud. "Absolutely no one."

"No one, what?"

Her mother's voice snagged her attention, and she turned to look up at her. Marilyn Bosworth stood in the doorway between the hallway and entry room, dressed in red slacks and a Christmas sweater—no doubt picked out just for their Christmas tree venture that evening.

Megan smiled. Though her mother had never said as much, Megan knew it was really her father who enjoyed traipsing through the rows of trees at various lots each year, looking for just the right one to bring home and set up in a place of honor, where the family would gather around to remember the birth of Christ. Megan's mother would prefer to stay home, out of the wind and the cold, preparing dinner while the rest of the family went on their outing. Yet she cheerfully accompanied them every year, dressing up for the occasion, smiling, and *oohing* and *aahing* over each tree until her husband had chosen the one he believed was marked out just for them. "This one has our name on it," he'd announce, and everyone would agree that he was absolutely right.

The Rules of Engagement are all about giving, not getting.

She understood now what she needed to say to Marty when he arrived shortly. She just prayed he too would understand. Either way, she knew there would be no announcement of their engagement any time soon—if at all.

"I was just thinking out loud," Megan said, setting the crèche aside. "About...about the One who came at Christmas to give everything." Tears stung her eyes. "Everything, Mom—including showing us what love really is. And I'm so grateful that He did."

Marilyn smiled in return and crossed the room to bend down and hug her daughter. "As am I, sweetheart." She kissed Megan's forehead. "Merry Christmas."

Megan lifted her gaze until their eyes met. "Merry Christmas, Mom. And thanks...for everything."

The Plain Unexpected Gift

Kathy Bruins

Evie Sternberg could feel a change already as she drove across the threshold on Highway 66 into Amish country. Even through the snow, a simpleness in lifestyle could be felt. There were very few cars or any "toys" that the world feels it must have to survive. It felt like driving through an old movie from the early 1900's.

She drove while eating her fast-food burger, fries, and diet cola. Even though it was snowing a little harder, she wanted to make it to the Steinke Resort before lunch time, and it was already 11:00 in the morning. After taking another bite of the burger, she put it on the paper on her lap. She flipped the wiper command to fastest speed, making the blades work harder in the storm. Turning up the heater the highest it would go, she blasted warm air on the windshield, hoping to clear it. The storm was not going to let up, making her travel slow and miserable. The radio kept her company with the good classic songs but also chanted warnings of staying inside tonight. That was her destination … inside her cottage.

Evie was anxious to get out of town since her mother was throwing one of her Christmas parties for all her "friends" … some her mother hadn't even met yet. It was all about promotion and networking with her. Evie found these parties and the people attending them to be fake. She had to get out of town before the "Christmas spirit" began. The gathering of onlookers during these parties was pretty much like the filming of a Hallmark movie … all matching sweaters, baking cookies together, decorating the tree with Christmas music playing and lots of laughter. After the filming of a movie, everyone goes home to their reality that more than likely looks nothing like the movie. That's how it was in her family anyway.

Turning on Bonham Street, Evie brushed her wavy auburn hair away from her eyes. She saw lights in the distance. This gave her hope, for she was ready to get out of the car and take a nice hot shower. She would check her cell phone, lying on the seat, for messages when she got there. It was outside of her purse in case she had to answer it. Reaching for her coffee, she saw something dart in front of her from the corner of her eye. The deer that ran in front of her stopped for a second, seeing her headlights, and then continued running into the field. Instinctively, she grabbed the steering wheel and hit the brakes, which sent her car spinning on the ice. The last thing she saw was a branch crashing through her windshield.

When Evie opened her eyes, she realized she must have been unconscious for a moment. Her head hurt, and she had no idea where she was … wait, she just turned on Bonham. Maybe she could get some help by calling someone on her cell phone. She didn't see it lying anywhere.

The car had landed on its side, and she was lying on the passenger window. It was hard to see anything outside the car because of the storm and the wind still whipping. The seat-belt had broken, which allowed her to ease herself to the other side of the car. She moved her limbs and found her arms and legs were free but sore from the tossing inside the car. She spotted blood on her shirt. Picking up her purse, she found a mirror and saw she was hurt. The blood on her shirt came from a nasty looking wound on her forehead. Touching it, she winced.

She looked up at the driver's side window and jumped when she saw a bearded face looking inside.

"Are you all right?" the man called.

"Yes, I think so. I just need to get out."

"Daddy, how are we going to get her out?" Evie heard another voice of a young woman and realized the man wasn't alone.

"We'll use the horse to turn the car back on its wheels. I'll be back with the horse."

Evie then saw the young woman as she walked around to the front windshield. She wore a dark coat with a dark-colored scarf. Her mittens were also dark in color. Evie wished she had put her coat on earlier … she was getting cold. She found it more comfortable to drive with it off though. She reached to the back seat and grabbed the purple coat and put it on, zipping up the front.

"Hello. I'm Katrina, and my dad has gone up to get the horse. He will be back in a moment."

"Thank you, Katrina. I'm glad you stopped to help me. My name is Evie Sternberg."

"It's nice to meet you, Evie. We were coming back from town when we heard the crash. He saw where your car lost control on the ice before the snow covered the marks, and he leaned out of the buggy and saw the lights of your car. We slid down the hill to the car and found you."

Her father, also dressed in darker colors, quickly returned with their horse and tied a rope to the rear-view mirror of the car. He looked in the window at Evie and said, "Hold on."

She braced herself inside the car while it began to move back to its normal position. It didn't seem difficult for the horse to do at all. The car landed on its four wheels, bouncing her around a bit. Katrina then tried to open the passenger side door, and found it jammed. However, her father was able to open the driver's side. When the interior light came on, she saw that Katrina's father had dark hair and a beard although it had streaks of gray throughout it. The snow covered his black hat and scarf. *They must be Amish*, she thought.

"Are you able to get out and stand?" he asked.

"I'm sure I can." Evie started to slide to the driver's side of the car. She grabbed her purse but still couldn't find her cell phone. *It must have fallen under the seats*. For a moment, she looked for it, but no luck. She turned her legs to the outside of the car and began to stand up. She felt dizzy, and both the man and his daughter grabbed an arm to help steady her. Katrina appeared younger than Evie, maybe in her late teens. She was wearing a dark coat that Evie assumed covered her Amish dress. The hood covered the white cap she wore, evidenced by the edge of white Evie could see. Her blonde hair peeked out of the bonnet.

Evie looked back at the damage to her silver Camry. *That's going to be expensive. Merry Christmas to me! It's possible that it may be totaled.*

"Daddy, this is Evie Sternberg."

"Glad to meet you, Evie, even under these trying circumstances." He steadied her as they climbed. "We're almost there … good job. By the way, my name is Jacob Rocke."

"Thank you, Mr. Rocke, and it is a pleasure to meet you, too."

They finally reached the top of the embankment. It wasn't that it was so deep, but with all the snow and the storm, it was difficult to maneuver. Evie was glad they stopped to help her, for it would have been a lot more difficult by herself. Her feet felt frozen. It was a bad choice on her part for choosing dress shoes rather than boots.

They all stood for a moment to catch their breath.

"How are you feeling?" Katrina asked.

"I'll be fine, Katrina … thank you."

"Your feet must be freezing. Let's get you in the buggy to warm up. I have a blanket in there that will do the trick." Katrina led her towards the buggy and opened the door.

Evie had been told that the Amish pretty much kept to themselves and spoke with a German or Dutch accent, using terms like "dat" and "gut." These two didn't seem to speak that way. They spoke like she did. Maybe other Amish communities used more of that dialect.

Katrina helped Evie into the closed-in black buggy, and her father hooked the horse back to the front. The horse whinnied from the petting of his nose by Jacob, and poked at something in his master's pocket.

"You know I have a treat for you, don't you, girl. Okay, you earned it." He took the carrot from his pocket and gave it to the expectant horse.

Once Katrina got Evie settled in the buggy, she covered her lap with a soft burgundy-colored blanket and sat next to her to help keep her warm. She was freezing as the wind and snow whipped around them. It was nice with the door shut to keep the weather out. Evie snuggled under the blanket. She didn't remember much about the buggy ride, but when she opened her eyes, she realized her head was resting on Katrina's shoulder. She also saw her father up front driving the buggy. There was no window there, so it must have been a lot colder for him.

Evie sat up. "I'm sorry to have inconvenienced you this way."

Katrina spoke. "No inconvenience at all."

"Your shoulder did make a nice pillow."

Katrina laughed. "My pleasure. We are almost to our house, and you can get warmed up and rest a bit. I'm sure Mama will have something warm for us to drink."

"That sounds nice. I lost my cell phone in the car. Could I please use your phone to call home?"

"No phone at the house," Katrina's father said from the front of the buggy. "In the morning, we will get you to a phone in town, if possible. Storm's pretty nasty."

"Thank you, sir."

"Are you visiting someone from the area?" Mr. Rocke asked.

"No, I was driving towards the Steinke cottages where I have a reservation, when a deer darted in front of me. I slammed on the brakes and spun out and down the embankment. I was hoping to reach the cottage before the storm got any worse, but that didn't happen."

"What brings you out here?" Katrina asked.

"I'm working. I'm a writer and sent to do an article on the Christmas traditions of the Amish."

"We could help you with that, couldn't we, Daddy?" Katrina asked.

"No pictures," he stated.

"No, of course not. I wouldn't take one without your permission." Evie looked out of the buggy and saw a lot of white houses.

"There's our house, Evie. It's the one with the large barn," Katrina said.

Evie saw the sign on the road they turned onto … Marsh Street. A few minutes later, Jacob pulled into the dirt drive and up to the house. "Katrina, show our guest inside, and I'll park the buggy by the barn."

"Yes, Daddy."

After they got down from the buggy, Katrina wrapped the blanket around Evie's shoulders and led her to the front door of the house. They stepped up onto the porch, and the door opened by a woman that must have been Katrina's mother. She seemed older as she stepped towards them on the porch and took Evie's other arm. She wore a conservative blue-colored dress and white cap. The blue brought out the blue of her eyes. Her hair was blonde like her daughter's.

"What happened, Katrina?"

"Mama, this is Evie Sternberg, and her car slid off the embankment about a mile from here on Bonham. Daddy and I climbed down to the car and helped her get out."

Closing the door behind them, Katrina led Evie to sit in a beautifully made rocking chair by a warm and glowing fireplace. The artistry on the chair was eye-catching. Evie almost was afraid to sit in it for fear of scratching it,or getting it wet.

A little girl appeared and brought her a pink flowered quilt to put on her lap and a blue shawl for her shoulders. Evie put her black purse on the floor next to the rocker.

"Thank you," Evie said, smiling at the girl. "These feel so good. My name is Evie … what's yours?"

"My name is Ruth Ann. I'm eight years old."

"It's nice to meet you, Ruth Ann. Thank you for taking care of me."

Ruth Ann had darker hair than her sister and mother. She smiled at Evie's comment and took a seat next to Evie. Katrina took off her coat, revealing the pretty burgundy-colored dress she wore.

Katrina's mother walked over to Evie and handed her a pretty red mug of tea that warmed her hands as she held it. "I'm so glad you had no worse injuries. My name is Rose. I'm married to Jacob and these girls are my beautiful daughters. Now I'm going to get a bandage and clean your head wound. It doesn't look like it needs stitches, so I think we can take care of it for you." She went to the cupboard and pulled out first aid supplies.

Evie sipped the tea. "Thank you, Rose. This tea is wonderful. It makes me feel warm inside."

"Chamomile … it should help calm you after such a scary time."

"It's a lot more excitement than what I planned. I was trying to reach Stienke Cottages before the storm got too bad. A deer ran in front of me, which made me slam on the brakes. The car spun out and landed on its side in the ditch. I am thankful that your husband and daughter were there to save me."

Katrina put her hand on Evie's. "I'm glad, too."

"Did you come here to visit someone?" Rose asked. She dipped the washcloth in the warm water she had brought out in a small tub, squeezed out the water as much as possible, and wiped Evie's brow with warm water to remove the dried blood. Then she added alcohol to a cotton ball and dotted the wound, which made Evie wince. Rose then applied some ointment on a bandage and taped it to Evie's forehead.

"No, I am a writer for a local paper in Grand Rapids, assigned to do an article on how Amish families celebrate Christmas. Would you mind if I asked you a few questions?"

Rose thought for a moment. "That shouldn't be a problem. Why don't we talk after dinner? It's almost done. Are you hungry?"

"Yes, I am, and it smells delicious." Evie heard her stomach grumble at that moment. She couldn't seem to control its eruptions.

Katrina laughed. "Yes, I would say that your stomach agrees with that."

Her father came through the door then, covered in snow. Some of the flakes blew inside before he shut the door behind him. He rubbed his hands together and blew on them. "It is freezing outside." He looked at Ruth Ann and said, "I almost froze out there, Ruth Ann. Frozen, I could have been made into a bird bath for your feathered friends."

"Daddy, I'm so glad you didn't freeze." She ran up and hugged him.

"Thank you, Daughter. I'm glad that I mean more to you than a bird bath. Although I would have been a good one." He made a silly pose that made everyone laugh. He took off his coat, hat, and scarf and hung them on a hook on the wall.

Rose interrupted. "Don't start posing now. It's time to eat."

"Thank you, my dear Rose, you have saved me from starvation," Jacob said. He took a seat at the head of the table.

It appeared to Evie that this was his place at the table all the time. This seemed to be an honored position in this house. Evie looked around and everything seemed simpler than what she was used to, but it was very nice and clean. It had a calming effect on her.

Rose set a large white plate with a great smelling roast on the table. There were roasted vegetables surrounding the meat. "Okay, everyone … let's gather around the table. Evie, you can sit here." She indicated a seat near Katrina.

Evie sat down and looked at the table filled with different kinds of salads, potatoes, rolls, and more. This feast put her fast food to shame.

Jacob looked at Rose. "Thank you, my dear, for this lovely meal you have prepared."

Rose smiled. "You're welcome."

"Now let us thank the Lord for providing for us today." Jacob held out his hands to grasp Rose's on one side of him and Katrina's on the other.

Evie took Katrina and Ruth Ann's hands, bowed her head, and listened while he prayed to show respect. She wasn't talking to God.

After they dined together, Jacob reached for the Bible. He opened the book and said, "I'll be reading from Psalm 68:1-5." It seemed so important to him, Evie thought. He ended with reading, *"A father of the fatherless..."*

This seized Evie's heart so hard that she didn't know how to react. She almost felt like crying. This did not resonate with her experience of a father's love at all. Her father did not care for her or protect her ... ever! She felt like she was screaming from inside herself.

Jacob closed the Bible and set it on the table. He led everyone in a prayer and after he said, "Amen," he stood up from the table. "Thank you, Evie, for joining us at the table this noon."

Trying to act as if nothing was wrong, Evie calmly said, "It is you I should be thanking. It was delicious." She stood up and began to clear dishes.

Ruth Ann placed a hand on her arm. "Thank you, Evie, but it is my job to clean up. You may go sit and relax with the adults."

Evie laid the plate in her hands back on the table. "Okay, thank you, Ruth Ann."

Katrina led her back to the family room and the rocker she sat in before. "Tell me more about the article you are writing."

"Well, like I said, it will be about how the Amish celebrate Christmas and why." She saw that Katrina's mother and father were nearby listening. "So what can you tell me about your Christmas traditions?"

Katrina picked up some sewing and sat in a chair nearby. "I love Christmas. It's one day that none of us work, and we spend time with each other eating wonderful foods and playing games."

"Let me get my recorder from my purse so I don't forget the information you give." She stopped and looked at Jacob. "Is audio recording okay? If it isn't, I can write it down."

Jacob smiled and said it was fine.

Evie picked up her purse and dug through it for her small recorder. The pen-size instrument was easy to operate. She clicked on the record button. "Okay, I'm ready now. Thank you."

Ruth Ann walked up to the recorder and bent down toward it like a microphone as Evie held it. She said in a loud clear voice, "I love Christmas! Daddy reads us the Christmas story, Mama makes my favorite cookies and I get to help frost them, and Katrina and I play lots of board games."

"Thank you, Ruth Ann, but you don't need to talk loud right into the microphone. It will easily pick up your voice with you speaking at a normal tone. So tell me, do you get any gifts for Christmas?"

"Yes, I usually get a wonderful toy, like a doll or game. Sometimes I get a pretty new dress or slippers."

"Wow ... that's nice, Ruth Ann. I can see why you love Christmas."

Ruth Ann sat back down on her chair. She looked excited to be part of the interview.

Evie turned to Jacob and Rose. "As parents, what is it that you stress to your children on Christmas?"

Jacob smiled at his daughters. "These girls are God's gift to me, and I am responsible in helping them grow in their faith. Outside the community, there is a lot of focus on decorations, gifts, Santa Claus, etc. In our community, our focus is Jesus ... that's it. It might sound simple to you, but we may light a candle for a decoration ... that's all."

Evie looked around and saw a few Christmas cards from friends and family, and a simple red candle, about three inches in diameter, which was nestled in the center of some evergreen branches. She found it simple, yet very peaceful and calming.

Jacob continued. "For gifts, we either buy or make something that will be meaningful and useful to the recipient. The family part of Christmas is important to me ... being together and enjoying all the things in which God has blessed us."

Evie was so touched by the love Jacob showed for his family that she wanted to cry. How could God allow her to be in a family where everything else is more important than family? Perhaps God was not in the equation … it could be just a crap shoot in life. Some have loving families and others don't. There must be something wrong in this family, she thought.

"Are there things you do not allow on Christmas?" Evie asked him.

"Anything that would bring focus on ourselves rather than on Jesus is prohibited. We observe rather than celebrate Christmas."

Rose spoke up. "Although it may sound uneventful, it is a time of great peace and joy."

"I imagine it is, Rose. It sounds very appealing to me, if I celebrated it at all."

The room went silent.

Katrina said, "Evie, you don't celebrate Christmas?"

Evie looked at the solemn faces staring at her. "Well, I wouldn't say that. I meant that I just don't get into all the religious stuff connected to Christmas."

Jacob stood up. "This interview is finished. Turn the recorder off." He walked out of the room.

"Looks like I said the wrong thing," Evie said as she put the recorder in her purse.

Rose started embroidering. "I must say that we didn't expect you to have strong feelings against Christmas. It almost feels like you are not taking us seriously in our tradition with yours being so different."

"I'm sorry. I can see how you could think that, but I would never feel that way about all of you. There just hasn't been much evidence of God in my life, so why celebrate?"

Ruth Ann walked over to her and took her hand. "Evie, God loves you a lot. He made you." Her sweet innocent voice spoke to her heart.

Jacob came back into the room. "Ruth Ann, you come over here." He gave Evie a disapproving look. "She doesn't need to hear your heresy."

"Jacob!" Rose cried.

"Great. I was fine as long as I think just like you, but if I have a mind of my own to think with, that's bad." Evie could feel her anger getting out of control.

"You need to show some respect, young lady," Jacob cautioned.

"I think that needs to go both ways," she retorted.

Jacob looked like he could have said more. His face red, he put on his hat and coat and opened the door. "I'm going to check on the animals." He then walked into the snowy weather, closing the door behind him.

Rose looked at Ruth Ann, who appeared scared. "Ruth Ann, would you like to help me do some baking for Christmas?"

Her eyes lit up again after the stress-filled exchange doused her excitement. "Yes, Mama, that would be fun." Ruth Ann followed her mother to the kitchen.

Katrina took Evie by the hand and said, "Come on. I want to show you my room."

Evie stood and followed her. She felt bad for the way she behaved. Why couldn't she keep her mouth shut? She decided she would apologize to Jacob when he returned.

When they entered her bedroom, Evie sat on her bed and hid her face in her hands. "Katrina, I don't know what came over me. I am so sorry. You have all been so good to me. I had no right to say those things."

"Evie, it will be okay … you'll see. We all say things that we don't mean or that we regret."

"I will apologize to your father when he comes back. You must all think badly of me, and I wouldn't blame you."

"That's good that you will apologize to Daddy, but please don't think we don't like you anymore. I think my father's heart gets hurt when he hears things that he feels are an insult to God. That's why he seemed so upset. I'm sure he is praying for you right now, because he cares about you."

"I doubt that very much. My parents don't even pray for me." Evie realized she just opened a window into her life.

"I'm so sorry, Evie. Do you want to talk about it?"

"There's not much to say. My parents had priorities, and I was not one of them." Evie put her head down, feeling shame of her upbringing.

"I'm sure you were, Evie. They must have loved you." Katrina looked like she might begin to cry.

There was a pause in the conversation. Evie wasn't sure whether to go on or not. She had kept it so deep inside of her for so many years. Her life was good now, and she sent that message in acting like she had it all together and didn't need anyone. *I'm a successful journalist, have my own place to live, and I am free to come and go as I like*, she thought.

Evie stood up from the bed and looked around Katrina's room. She admired the simple items, the beautiful quilt on the bed, and how everything was so neat and clean … the Amish way. "You have a pretty room, and you keep it very nice. I was never good at that. I hardly knew the color of the floor in my room."

"Thank you. I have always been kind of a neat-nick." She opened the door. Turning to Evie, Katrina said, "Listen, you can sleep in here tonight, and I will sleep with Ruth Ann."

"I can't put you out of your room."

"I insist. There are bunkbeds in Ruth Ann's room, so I will have my own bed to sleep on. If you like, you can rest awhile in here."

"I think I will … thank you." Evie desired to have some time alone and gather her thoughts.

She lay on the bed after Katrina left and was surprised when she woke up from a nap. It was still light out, so it couldn't have been too long, she thought. Sitting up and bringing her legs off the bed, she stood up and went to the door. It sounded like the cookie baking was still going on as she heard Ruth Ann's giggles. Evie still felt bad about the heated exchange earlier, but she decided to re-enter their family space. Walking downstairs, everyone greeted her like nothing happened before.

"How did you sleep?" Rose asked. She was smiling, and it didn't seem forced. She wiped the frosting from her hands on the white apron she wore.

"I slept fine, thank you. I didn't realize how tired I was."

"Well, you've been through a lot today. Sometimes sleep is the best thing," Rose said. "Would you like another cup of chamomile tea?"

"That would be very nice. Thank you," Evie responded. She was watching what she said because she didn't want to blow up again at this nice family.

Ruth Ann had a book in her hand and walked over to Evie. "Would you read this to me please?"

Evie seemed to melt whenever this little moppet would speak. *She is a doll*, she thought.

Katrina was putting dishes away, and she turned to Ruth Ann. "You already know how to read."

"I know, but sometimes it's just nice to hear a story from someone else."

Evie grinned. "I would love to read you this story. Would you like to sit on my lap?"

Ruth Ann nodded and looked at her mother to see if it would be all right.

Rose smiled and nodded. Ruth Ann climbed into Evie's lap right away and got comfortable with her head on Evie's shoulder.

Evie felt a deep warmth at the love the little girl freely gave to her. It made her eyes well up, but she pretended something was in them and wiped away the tears. "Okay, are you ready for this?"

"Yes, Ma'am!" Ruth Ann acted giddy at the prospect of being read to.

Jacob walked in from outside and saw Ruth Ann in Evie's lap.

Evie was afraid of what he might say, considering their last encounter. Evie smiled at Jacob and tried to show in her face that she was sorry.

Jacob must have picked up on the message because he smiled back and said, "What great adventures will you be reading, Miss Evie?"

"*Love You Forever*. I have not read it before, so I look forward to seeing what it is about."

"One of my favorites. You girls have a grand time." He then walked into his room to do some work.

As Evie read the book aloud, she was surprised to see how a mother gave so much love to the little boy she loved. Every time she read the words, "She'd rock him back and forth, back and forth, back and forth," Evie would rock Ruth Ann. It felt surreal to Evie, and she wondered, *Can family love be like this? I never experienced it.*

Towards the end of the story, Evie choked up. She didn't want the moment to end. When she read "the end," it made her sad. Ruth Ann looked up at her and said, "Miss Evie, I didn't mean to make you cry."

Evie hugged her tight. "No, honey, you didn't make me cry. The story was so good, it touched my heart. That's all."

"Thank you for reading it to me. You read very well," Ruth Ann said as she got down off her lap and went to put the book away.

Katrina came up to her and said, "That book makes me cry, too. It shows the kind heart you have for children. That's the kind of heart I want for my children when I have them some day."

Evie sniffled. "It made me realize what I never had." As soon as the words came out of her mouth, she wondered what she had just done. She revealed something deep inside herself. This was something she never allowed herself to do. Her mask of having a perfect life was slipping.

Rose looked up from her sewing. "Evie, I'm sorry for your pain."

Feeling panicked at these new feelings, Evie responded, "Thank you … it doesn't matter anymore. It's history."

Katrina looked at her. "Of course, it does matter. Everyone wants to be loved like that.

Evie felt uncomfortable with the discussion. "Okay, let's change the subject, or I won't get any work done." She did not want to be pitied. *They must think I'm a nut case*, she thought.

"You know what would be great for dinner tonight? Haystacks," Rose said.

Katrina looked surprised. "Now, Mama … eleven days before Christmas?"

"Oh Mama, I love them. Could I please help you make them?" Ruth Ann pleaded.

"I think we can all have a hand in it. What do you say, Evie … are you up for the challenge?"

Evie felt her heart grow warm. They were including her in this family tradition. "I could try."

"You'll do just fine. This will be great information for your article. Each of us will choose what to prepare for the haystack," Rose said.

"I'm sorry, but what is a haystack?" Evie asked.

Katrina wrapped an arm around her shoulder in a teasing manner and said, "Just one of the best meals you will ever eat. It's kind of like a tostada, but more like a layered salad. You will love it!"

"Okay, let's get started." Evie rolled up her sleeves.

Ruth Ann said, "I'll get the cheese ready by shredding it." She was already pulling a block from the ice box.

Katrina said, "I'll cut up lettuce and break up some crackers." She started tearing lettuce leaves and putting them in a bowl.

"What should I do?" Evie asked.

Rose put a bowl and spoon on the counter in front of Evie. "Why don't you mix up the cooked meat and salsa? I think that will taste good." She went to a cupboard and pulled out a blue apron and gave it to Evie. "But first, why don't you put on this apron so your nice outfit doesn't get stained."

Evie took the apron and put it on. "I will do that. Thank you!"

Rose said, "I'll get the rest of the vegetables cut up and make some ranch dressing."

"So this is a Christmas tradition … haystacks?" Evie asked.

Rose explained, "It's a dinner that is fun and feeds a lot of people. That's why we make it on Christmas because a lot of visiting happens during the week. It makes it easier to have food ready for guests."

"I see. Plus, they get to make their meal the way they want it … right?"

"Yes, Evie, people make their best meal imaginable. Some can get quite creative." Katrina continued to break up crackers.

Jacob came out of the back room. "Something is smelling pretty good out here. I can't be sure, but it looks like it may be haystack night."

Ruth Ann said, "We're showing Evie how to make haystacks, Daddy. She's doing a good job, isn't she?"

Jacob put his hand on Evie's shoulder and said, "I think she is doing a great job. I think you will enjoy this meal."

"I think so, too," Evie said. She was so relieved that Jacob didn't seem angry at her any longer. Evie had never been in a loving family experience like this before. Her mind kept telling her that they were just putting on a show and didn't care about her. *Why should they care about me? I'm a stranger to them. I just showed up today.* Her mind was battling to discern what was true.

When all the different foods were prepared and lined up on the table, they all took a seat and once again held hands. Ruth Ann was on one side of Evie, and Katrina on the other.

Jacob began the prayer. "Dear Lord, You have blessed us this day with all your goodness. You always give us more than we deserve. Lord, we pray that we can use what You have given us to be a blessing to others and give glory to You. Thank You for the wonderful food before us, for this Christmas season, and for our new friend, Evie. I pray that You will bless her as she will be leaving us soon ..."

Evie didn't hear any more of the prayer. Her mind stopped at "she will be leaving us soon." *They want me to leave. They are looking forward to me leaving. I knew this niceness was fake.*

"Amen."

Evie lifted up her face when she heard the end of the prayer. Everyone seemed excited about eating the haystacks. She had lost her appetite. She stood up from the table. "Excuse me."

Katrina looked at Evie with a worried look on her face. "Evie, where are you going? We are just beginning to eat this wonderful food that you helped prepare."

"Quit being so nice to me," Evie said in a tone that expressed how upset she was. "I know that you can't wait until I'm gone. Fine, I'm going to get my purse and leave."

"Evie, what brought this on?" Rose asked.

"You know."

"I do not know. I have no idea why you want to leave us."

Jacob stood up. "Evie, please have a seat. The food is getting cold."

"You never wanted me here." Evie could no longer think straight. "You hate me!"

Ruth Ann was crying. Katrina tried to comfort her. "Evie, please stop."

"Don't worry, I'm out of here." She grabbed her purse and coat. Walking to the front door she opened it, went outside, and closed the door behind her. She began to run, although she didn't know where she was going. She heard Jacob calling her name from the house. The wind and snow beat against her as she ran, as if for her life, to the road. When she arrived there, she looked to see if anyone was coming down the road that could give her a ride, but she saw no one.

Alone and cold, Evie began to cry. The exploding emotions swept through her as the contrast of the Rocke family and her own dug at the scars in her soul ... and it hurt. Pain coursed through her heart and mind. What was real? She couldn't seem to get control of herself. She fell in the snow and began to cry, hitting the snow around her. When her energy was spent, she looked up and she saw a covered bridge where she could get a little shelter from the storm. It would be no great loss if she froze to death either, she thought.

She traipsed through the snow to the bridge. Looking inside, she spotted a little corner she could sit in to collect herself before going on. She made her way into the corner, and found a little warmth just by being out of the wind. She sat down inside the wall of the bridge.

"Evie."

She looked up and saw Jacob. "Leave me alone!"

"You're upset and not thinking right. You will freeze out here."

"I don't care … and I'm sure no one else does either."

He spoke loudly to be heard over the wind. "Will you please come back with me to the house to get out of the weather?"

She shook her head. Through her tears, she said, "I just want to die … the pain is too much." She wrapped her arms around her knees and rocked back and forth.

Jacob picked her up, and although she fought for a moment, she couldn't continue. She laid her head on his shoulder as he carried her back to the house, where Rose was waiting to wrap her in a quilt. "Girls, would you please make Evie some nice tea, while your mother and I take care of her?"

"Yes, Daddy. Is she alright," Katrina asked.

"She'll be just fine. Don't worry."

Entering Katrina's room, Jacob walked to the bed and laid Evie down.

"Can't you please just let me die? It hurts too much," Evie cried.

Jacob brushed back the hair from her eyes. "How can you say that, Evie? We want to take care of you. God has brought you here for a purpose. I believe that."

She spoke through her tears. "God? There is no God in my life … there was no God that protected me as a child. I wasn't worth His time. The only value I had was the clients I could bring to my father." She stopped talking for a moment, trying to grasp the horror that rose to the surface after being buried so deep in her memory. "My father allowed men to do what they wanted to me in exchange for getting their business. He would say I was so pretty that I could help the family by pretending to like his clients. When they hurt me, he said that I shouldn't worry because next time would be better."

Both Rose and Jacob appeared stunned at what they heard. Then Jacob said, "Evie, no father has the right to treat a precious gift of a child given to him with such evil. You are worth far more than any amount of money your father received. It is sad that he didn't see he had been deceived by the evil one. That was not God's plan for you, but He is faithful and will bring beauty out of these dark ashes in your life. He loves you so much, Evie, and will not ever leave you alone."

Rose held her hand. "Evie, dear, you are a treasured gift. God made you, you are His, and His love for you is a real father's love that goes beyond any human experience."

"I feel so dirty and worthless. No one can ever love me. I am trash," Evie cried.

"God never considered you to be trash. You are His daughter … that makes you a princess to the King of Kings," Rose said while she rubbed Evie's arm.

"A princess … me? Hardly," Evie responded, but did smile a bit as she calmed down.

"It's true." Rose then turned to Jacob and said, "Dear, do you think we could break tradition tonight and read the Christmas story? I think it would help us all to focus on the love God has for each of us."

Jacob smiled. "I think that is a wonderful idea. Even though it is still eleven days before Christmas, this is a perfect way to prepare our hearts for His coming."

There was a knock on the door. Rose opened it and saw Katrina and Ruth Ann. Katrina was holding the hot tea, and Ruth Ann brought a plate with a ready-made haystack.

"I thought she might be hungry," Ruth Ann said. She walked over to the bed and gave Evie the plate. "I didn't want you to miss trying haystacks, Evie. I'm so sorry you're not feeling well, but we are going to take care of you."

This made Evie start to cry again, and she held out her arms to get a hug from Ruth Ann. As they embraced, Evie said, "Thank you, dear Ruth Ann. You are precious."

As Jacob stepped out of the room and Katrina set the tea down on the end table, Evie dried her tears and put a fork filled with the cheesy mixture of the haystack in her mouth. "This is wonderful! I love how all the flavors mix together. I will make this a Christmas tradition of my own."

"I told you," Katrina said. "I knew you would love them. Is there anything else you would like, Evie?"

"Just a hug from you, too," she said. As they embraced, she whispered, "You are a dear young lady. Thank you!" Evie finished the haystack and set the plate down on the table.

Jacob came back in with the Bible in his hand. Rose lit a candle, and Jacob sat in a chair while the others sat on the edge of the bed. Ruth Ann snuggled against Evie's shoulder, and Katrina held Evie's hand. Rose sat at the foot of the bed.

"Inasmuch as many have taken in hand to set in order a narrative of those things which have been fulfilled among us, just as those who from the beginning were eyewitnesses and ministers of the word delivered them to us, it seemed good to me also, having had perfect understanding of all things from the very first, to write to you an orderly account, most excellent Theophilus that you may know the certainty of those things in which you were instructed." He continued through John the Baptist's birth and the announcement of Jesus' birth to Mary. Evie felt some of the readings being branded on her heart. *"Through the tender mercy of our God, With which the Dayspring from on high has visited us; To give light to those who sit in darkness and the shadow of death, To guide our feet into the way of peace."*

Evie thought about the words she had heard. *Was God saying that He knew I was in the darkness where evil occurred and felt like I was dead, or wished to be? Was He sending a baby to help me find peace?*

Jacob continued reading in Luke 2. Evie learned about Mary and Joseph like it was the first time she had heard it. Her heart felt grasped by something ... or Someone. She wanted to hear more. The thirst inside her was being quenched. She imagined what it might have looked like in the sky with all the angels celebrating the Christ's birth. Was it filled liked the snowflakes that now filled the sky?

A man named Simeon, a devout man, held the baby Jesus in his arms and said, *"Lord, now You are letting Your servant depart in peace, According to Your word; For my eyes have seen Your salvation Which You have prepared before the face of all peoples, A light to bring revelation to the Gentiles, And the glory of Your people Israel."*

Jacob closed the book and they all sat in silence for a moment. The candle helped each of them focus on the words in the story. It seemed as if a special presence came into the room and gave peace to everyone.

Evie was the first to speak. "This has been the best present I have ever been given. My heart is full from the love you have shown me, and feeling the Lord's love through the Bible. I never expected to be loved in such a real way. Thank you."

Ruth Ann nuzzled closer to Evie, "I love you, Evie."

"Thank you, Ruth Ann, and I love you."

Katrina hugged Evie. "I love you, dear sister."

Evie smiled. "I love you, too."

Rose hugged Evie. "You are a beautiful child and welcome in this family anytime."

Evie teared up a little with the statement. "Thank you … Mama." They both laughed through tears.

Jacob then stood up and held his hand out to Evie. She got off the bed and walked up to him. He placed the Bible in her hands. "Our family Bible is now yours, Evie. Carry it with you wherever you go and remember this day, the eleventh day before Christmas. Remember how God told you of His great love for you. Remember that you are a part of this family always."

Jacob gave her a hug like a father would who loved his child. "Merry Christmas, Daughter."

Evie held onto Jacob, weeping like a flood was escaping from the deepest place in her soul. She was amazed that Jacob allowed her to cry on his shoulder and that he softly rocked her while she wept. When she emptied the tears out of herself, Evie felt cleansed. Hope, rather than hurt, filled her mind.

She stepped back from Jacob, smiled, and said, "I will cherish this moment for the rest of my life. Thank you for showing me about a father's love. The hole in my heart has been filled."

Christmas suddenly meant so much more to her. It wasn't about jazzy decorations, expensive gifts, or Santa Claus … it was about Jesus. She hugged her new Bible to her heart in response to the love experienced … a plain unexpected gift.

If You Believe

Jessica Ferguson

Ten days until Christmas and tonight held the big event—the first ever wedding extravaganza sponsored by Lonna's *Everything Wedding* and hosted by the Chicory Women's Club. South Louisiana had never experienced anything so spectacular—with the exception of Mardi Gras, of course.

Bretta Richert wiggled in anticipation and gripped the steering wheel as she maneuvered her car through the crowded streets of Chicory.

At the edge of the city, beautiful white tents waited beneath massive oaks. Each tent would be a showroom to help brides and their parents plan elaborate weddings. Tonight creative photographers would exhibit their talent with framed photos of brides and grooms, while jewelers displayed their bling. Chefs and caterers would share tasty morsels to tempt potential customers. Wedding planners would offer tips and advice. Lonna had even brought in ball room dancers and an orchestra to tutor fathers and daughters in their first waltz together. It might be the *sweetest* extravaganza ever witnessed.

And then there's that ice artist.

Bretta eased her car through the festively decorated cottage shop district, searching for the artist's address. According to her friend and employer, Lonna, ice artist C. A. Lee set up shop in the cottage district somewhere. He'd purchased an old garage and renovated it to accommodate his artistry. Why on earth would an ice artist set up shop in South Louisiana? Wouldn't the southern heat put an end to his small business? It was almost seventy degrees today—in December!

Hiring an ice artist for their wedding extravaganza had been a huge mistake. After all, if the temp was warm enough for her to show skin in ankle pants, what would it do to a block of ice? If she'd lived in Chicory when the event had been planned, she would have pointed out the negatives of hiring this guy.

Oh well, if he was a flop, they couldn't blame her.

"There it is," she mumbled, turning onto the gravel parking lot. The artist had put a lot of thought and elbow grease into the renovation of his building, but it still looked like an old service station.

She parked and climbed out of the car. *Lord, Lord, help me deal with this guy. If he'll just let the wedding bands have the huge tent he reserved, we'll all be happier.*

Her footsteps crunched as she hurried to the front door of the shop. She pushed it open and entered the coolness of the room. She glanced around the slightly cluttered area then called, "Hello, anybody here?"

No answer.

A metal door with a painted-black window beckoned. She walked toward it and turned the knob. Locked. What's with all the secrecy? Books and paperwork covered the counter to her right. Photographs of elaborate ice sculptures decorated the walls. She squinted at the pictures. No doubt he was talented but still ... What was the life span of a couple of carved ice champagne glasses?

She heard movement behind the locked door.

"Hellooo?" she called. "It's Bretta Richert from Chicory Women's Club." She heard a crash. Then another. It sounded as if someone had kicked a bucket. "Are you okay in there?"

Finally the door with the black window pushed open. Slowly. Ever so slowly.

Hesitantly—or maybe menacingly—a man with a chainsaw in his hand entered the room. His entire head was covered by some kind of helmet. Safety goggles hid his face. Bretta held her breath, hoping he'd remove them. He didn't. He stared at her through the black tinted goggles. Creepy.

"Help ya?"

His deep voice clipped the words he shot at her. A masked man holding a chain saw. Wasn't there a movie about this? She darted a glance to the front door, her only exit. If she could add an inch or two to her five-feet-four frame, maybe he wouldn't be quite so intimidating. She took a breath and stood straighter.

"I'm Bretta Richert, the new marketing assistant for Lonna's *Everything Wedding* and here on behalf of the Chicory Women's Club. I came to confirm a few things."

She waited for him to respond but he didn't so she took one step backward and tried again.

"You signed a contract to furnish quite a few items for our Christmas wedding extravaganza which is tonight." He looked like a man from another planet, contributing nothing to their dialog. She waited, tapping her foot. She wouldn't utter one more word until he responded. After a few seconds of silence, she realized if she wanted answers she had to ask questions.

"Are they finished?"

"Yes."

Obviously a man of few words. Or *no* words.

"Good, but I noticed that in addition to what you agreed to create for us, you reserved a large tent—the entire tent. You didn't want to share it with any of the other vendors. I can't imagine why you need it."

"Your point?" He jiggled the chainsaw up and down.

Was he threatening her? She took another stiff-legged step away from him, swallowed, and forged ahead with her thoughts. "We could use that tent for something else."

"The woman I talked with seemed excited about my work. I haven't dealt with you. And I do have a contract." He jiggled the saw again.

Bretta inhaled deeply. Or tried to. Her nose clogged, and her throat constricted. "Yes, well, do you suppose you could put down your weapon so we can discuss this?"

Did he just chuckle?

He walked to the counter and placed the threatening tool on top of it before he turned back to face her. What was his problem? Was he *the man without a face?*

"And really, Mr. ... Mr. ..." Her mind blanked. Odd. She knew his name when she walked in.

"Lee. C.A. Lee."

"Of course, Mr. Lee. Well, do you think you could just remove the goggles and talk with me for a moment? I'm concerned about your art and our Louisiana heat, and that extra tent you require. It seems quite large and honestly—"

She caught her breath mid-sentence as he reached toward the paraphernalia that covered his face. He hesitated, tugged at the contraption—in slow motion—but finally, finally it came off.

Beneath that weird helmet was ... "Cory!"

Before she could say more than his name, he put his hands on her waist and lifted her in the air, exactly the way he used to do. "I'm so glad to see you, Brett, I might bust a gut."

Glad to see her? Five years ago he'd left her standing in the street with tears streaming down her face while he drove away. The memory overwhelmed her and she bopped him on both sides of his head gear. "Cory Anderson Leland, put me down this instant. Is this some kind of joke?"

"Hey, no call to get violent, Brett." He plunked her to the floor where she backed away, eyeing him from head to toe. Every argument they'd ever had, every wish and dream that had crashed and burned exploded in her mind. The conglomeration of memories and emotions overwhelmed her. She wanted to double over in pain and sob. She wanted to giggle wildly, hug him, kiss him... hit him again. Getting punched in the emotional gut was every bit as horrific as the real thing.

It was truly Cory, her ex-fiancé. He'd come back.

"What kind of game are you playing? And why all the stupid headgear?" Her voice sounded as weak as a novice runner after her first marathon—out of breath, yet ecstatic. She clamped her teeth together and waited for his answer.

Cory removed his headgear and placed it beside the goggles. "The headgear was for you, but I'm not playing any kind of game, Brett. I'm the man you're looking for."

"It was silly! And no, you're not the man I'm looking for. C. A. Lee is an ice sculptor."

"At your service." He bowed flamboyantly. "I shortened my name. It has a ring of maturity, don't you think?"

She had to agree. C. A. Lee gave the impression of an older man with salt and pepper hair. A man who might have intense, beady eyes and thin lips. Certainly not the handsome pain in the neck from her past. Cory Leland, with his thick unruly hair and teasing blue eyes was anything but mature. When did he come back to town, and if he was so glad to see her, why hadn't he contacted her immediately? The questions tumbled around in her head but she pushed them away.

"Well, this certainly makes things a lot simpler. I don't have to be on my best behavior, do I? Cory, there's no way I'll let Lonna and the Chicory Women's Club be taken in by some pretend artist who stacks ice cubes. Now I know why Margot Mathis—the president of the club—was so excited. You charmed her off her feet, didn't you?"

"That's mean, Brett. I'm not that kind of guy and you know it."

What he really meant was that he wasn't anything like his father. And he was right. Cory had never been a charmer, at least, not the kind of charmer who knocked women off their feet—loved them and left them.

But wasn't that exactly what Cory had done to her? No, not exactly.

She jutted her chin forward. "For all I know, you've changed."

He ran his hand through his thick, unruly hair. She'd always loved his hair. It was the color of caramel and it had always looked as though he hadn't combed it. For sure, that hadn't changed. She ground her teeth together. She hated her memories, especially the ones that set her heart to pounding.

"You're holding a grudge, aren't you, Brett?"

She wanted to revert back to her teen years and scream a big fat, "Well, duh!" at him, but she didn't. "Why would I hold a grudge when I'm the one who broke off the engagement? I'd do the same thing today. I made the right decision. And quit calling me Brett!"

"It wasn't you; it was your mom. She didn't want you marrying the likes of me after the way my dad treated her. I heard you moved to Florida with her."

"I did, but Gram died in November and left me her Condo so I moved back."

"Your mom move back with you?"

"Of course not. She loves Florida. And what does that have to do with anything?"

He grinned. "Because I came back to marry you—just like I said I would."

Bretta gulped. Her heart pounded. "Just like that? After all this time?"

He looked so like the old Cory that she wanted to run into his arms and sob with gladness, but why on earth did he think they could pick up where they left off?

47

"I told you I'd be back and here I am."

"Five years later!" She squinted. "Who do you think you are, Cory Leland? Why do you think I'd just up and marry you with no questions asked?"

He shrugged, but that careless movement took her back to the day her mother said, "Why can't Cory speak intelligently instead of shrugging all the time? He's like his father—there's not much to him."

In spite of her mother, Cory had been her life. They had watched old movies, ate popcorn, and studied together. They'd shopped for Christmas gifts and volunteered their time at Foley's Christmas tree farm. Cory had taught her how to wrap gifts like a pro, and decorate with elaborate bows. He was much more creative than she was, and had always known how to make Christmas special.

She tried to conjure up a less attractive memory and succeeded. Her widowed mom had dated his divorced dad, and things didn't go well. Her mom had been desperate to fall in love with the handsome contractor, but he had nothing more on his mind than a fling. Their relationship didn't end well. Cory and Bretta would never be able to share holidays with both of them together. Why would he think it could ever work?

He interrupted her thoughts. "I know what you're thinking. They have nothing to do with us. Dad is in California doing what he does best—chasing women and breaking hearts. Your mom is in Florida." He reached out to touch her but she drew away. "Don't you remember the last thing I said to you?"

"Five years is a long time to wait."

"I said I'll never quit loving you and I'd be back someday to marry you. I said … just believe in me, Brett. Just believe."

She turned away from him, blinked hard to counteract the burning behind her eyes. When she had her emotions under control, she turned around. "Look, I don't want to talk about us. Just tell me if you're ready for the show. We have nine hours, and I want everything perfect. I doubt it will be. Your icy objects will probably melt and ruin the whole production."

"You're still a worrier. You still second-guess yourself and look for failure."

"I'm not second-guessing myself, Cory. I'm worried because it's not cold outside. How can your little ice goblets survive our southern weather?"

"I promise you a cold front by noon. You'll be wearing a coat by tonight—though I hope not."

For a moment she lost her focus. Why would he not want her to wear a coat? That didn't make sense. Of course, Cory had always teased and confused her with things he said. She brought her attention back to his work. "Let me see what you've done."

"No."

"No? You're telling me no?"

He grinned. "That's what I said, but I promise it's spectacular. Trust me, I'm good."

She grunted. "Of course, you are. Anyone can be spectacular after five short years of training. How did you learn this unusual trade anyway—and why would you want to?"

"It's a God-thing, Brett. He gave me the talent. And I learned from the best, a guy out in California. It only took him five years to learn it too. All you have to do is immerse yourself and—"

She made a run for the black windowed door. Cory was too fast for her and blocked her way. Just as quickly, she cut to his left, grabbed the knob, and shoved, only to bang her shoulder against a structure that didn't budge.

"I had a feeling you might try something like that. I pushed the lock before I closed it.

She made a face at him. "You know me too well."

"And I thought you knew me." He moved to the counter and leaned against it. "Do you ever regret not eloping with me? If you'd gone with me, we would've been married five years. Can you imagine?"

"No, I can't." Trouble was—she did imagine. She'd imagined it every day of every week of every month of each year.

She remembered exactly what he'd said, the tone of his voice, as he stood there, facing her and her mother. She even remembered his expression—so sure she'd say yes. Incredibly hurt when she didn't.

Let's just get married and go. I feel like God's got something really special for us, Brett.

She'd wanted to believe him. She never doubted him, yet when she'd looked into her mother's wild eyes, when she saw her fear, she knew her mother needed her. She couldn't run away with Cory. She just couldn't.

She shook her head, scattering the memories, feeling her handsome ex watching her. She tried to speak, but the words wouldn't move past her lips. Instead, an image danced in her head. She saw a blue Mustang convertible flying down the highway and her wedding veil blowing in the wind.

Bretta returned to Lonna's *Everything Wedding*, sizzling like a skillet of blackened redfish. Cory hadn't changed a bit. No, he had changed. He was more handsome, more mature looking, and he was a lot braver when it came to dealing with her. He used to let her have her way when she placed her hand on her hip and stomped her foot. It hadn't worked this time. He just gave her that hot blue stare and told her to quit worrying.

She threw herself into her chair and bent her head into her hands with a prayer on her lips. *Lord, Lord, don't let Cory do anything to ruin this special event tonight. It's so important to Lonna. And give him good sense about using that extra tent. We had to turn wedding bands away for lack of room. Surely Cory doesn't really need it.*

The phone interrupted and she expelled a breathy amen before she answered. "Hello, this is Bretta Richert, how can I help you?"

"Hey Brett, C.A. Lee here."

She switched the phone to her other ear. "Oh Cory, that sounds hysterical. C. A. Lee indeed."

Giddiness overtook her. She wasn't sure why. Was it because Cory was home and calling her or because God had answered her prayer? Cory was probably calling to tell her he didn't need the tent after all. She loved it when God sent quick answers to her prayers. Excited, she stood, stumbling over her purse she'd plopped on the floor. She bent to untangle its strap from her rolling chair. "Cory … I'm so glad you've come to your senses. You're giving up the big tent, aren't you? I knew you would."

Deep laughter vibrated from the receiver she clutched to her ear. "Whoa, Brett girl, I'm not calling about the tent. I'm calling to ask you to lunch. Want to go to that new restaurant that opened up last week? I hear they've got some mean Cajun food."

She couldn't help herself. She sputtered into the phone. "Why would I want to go out with you? We have an unhappy past. We really aren't friends anymore."

Total silence drifted through the phone. She didn't know why she was making it so hard for him. Maybe she wanted to hurt him the way he'd hurt her.

"Well, are we?" she challenged.

"I love you, Brett. I'm home to marry you. I want to talk about our future. And, I'd like to know what you've been doing the past five years."

"Existing," she mumbled.

He lowered his voice. Soft. Intimate. "C'mon, have lunch with me. I'll even let you try to talk me out of that tent."

Now there was a good idea. Incentive. She had to admit she was curious to know what Cory had been doing the last five years too. "Okay, I'll meet you at The Cajun Beanery. Is that the restaurant you're talking about?"

"Sure is, but why don't I pick you up?"

"I'll just meet you there at noon."

"We need to be there earlier because of the lines. People have been standing outside the doors every evening since they opened."

He was right, but his words reminded her that he'd been there for several months and had done nothing to contact her. Of course, she'd only returned to Chicory three weeks ago.

"Okay, you win. I'll meet you at eleven thirty."

"Great! I'll pick you up at Lonna's at eleven." Before she could respond, he disconnected. Bretta held the phone away from her and glared at it. Cory really worked hard at being C. A. Lee.

Eleven came too soon. Walking beside Cory across the parking lot toward the massive glass doors of The Cajun Beanery, she couldn't help remember another place and another time. A time when she and Cory went everywhere together, shared secrets and fears and dreams. One of her favorite memories was when they laid head to head in the grass, looking up at the sky. They talked about getting married, raising a family, how they would teach their children to value God and home and family. And holidays. They both treasured holidays.

How could Cory expect her to just pick up where they left off? Fall back in love with him. Of course, she'd never fallen *out of* love with him but that was beside the point. And while she hadn't waited for him exactly, she hadn't met anyone she wanted to share her time with either. Still, wasn't he taking a lot for granted? Or was she wrong?

"Do you like working for Lonna?"

Bretta nodded. "It's as good a job as any. Chicory is so small, there's not much else to do here."

"What did you do in Florida?"

Was he interested or just making small talk? What was he *really* asking—if she'd been happy, successful without him? The answer was a resounding no, but she wouldn't tell him that. "I worked for a small publicity firm. When Gram died and I came back for the funeral and learned she'd left me everything, I met Lonna and she offered me a job if I wanted to stay. It seemed like a good time to come home."

Before he could respond, the doors sprung open and two pretty hostesses smiled at them— or smiled at Cory. They eyed him appreciatively, but his eyes were on Bretta. She flashed him a smile, then slipped her bottom lip between her teeth. She was flirting with him! And for the sake of these two young women.

His grin broadened. Had he noticed? He seemed more perceptive than he used to be. Apparently, that was the C.A. Lee side of him.

Once seated, they searched the menu and ordered. Cory took a sip of his water with lemon, then sat back and stared. Finally, he shook his head. "Brett, you haven't changed a bit."

She poked her chin out defensively. "Yes, I have. I'm five years older and have a degree in general studies."

He nodded. "So you went to college."

"Yes, but not fun college. I worked part time and went day and night. Graduated in three years. All I wanted to do was get out and start making my own way."

"I promise you, five years, the hard studying, and the degree in general studies have made very little difference You're still headstrong and opinionated. And you're still beautiful."

A lilt danced its way into her spirit. Was it because he thought she was beautiful? She had no idea, but she did her best to ignore it. She had to be careful. She had to activate her common sense and keep it that way. Looking into his eyes, watching his lips move as he spoke, remembering how he would tug at his right ear when he planned to discuss something unpleasant—all those things played on her emotions. She didn't want to know him so well. She didn't want him to know how messed up her life had been since the day he left town. He would never know because she never confided it to anyone—and she wasn't about to tell him. She'd done a pretty good job of telling her friends she'd never wanted to marry Cory Leland. Whether they believed her or not was another story.

It was a lie. It had always been a lie.

When their food arrived, Cory said grace and Bretta prayed God's will be done and that Cory wouldn't screw up the wedding gala. When she looked up, his eyes were on her. She'd always loved his eyes. Her face heated and she looked away. He was going to say something sweet. She knew it.

He leaned toward her, making the table tilt slightly. They both grabbed their glasses of water to keep them from spilling.

"Don't do this, Cory."

"Don't do what?"

"You know what. We can't pick up where we left off. This is a business meal only. Don't act like we've never been apart."

He picked up his fork and jabbed at his bowl of gumbo. "Before we talk business, I need to know something."

Her eyes widened, then squinted suspiciously. "What?"

"Why didn't you stand up to your mother that day? Why didn't you tell her you loved me and wanted to marry me?"

A lump formed in her throat and she swallowed several times. "I was scared, Cory. And … and when I looked at my mother, I saw that she was scared too. I just couldn't."

For the first time, she'd told him the truth.

He sat back in his chair. He seemed satisfied with her answer.

"Traveling all over the country was fantastic, Brett. It would have been perfect if you'd been with me."

She wiggled in her seat. The shrimp salad lost its taste. She wasn't sure she wanted to listen to his good time, but still wanted to know how he'd spent those five years without her.

"What made it fantastic? What did you do? I can't imagine traveling to one city after another and having no one."

He leaned forward again. "But that's just it. I wasn't alone. Every place I went, I felt like I was supposed to be there. For the first time in my life, I felt I was exactly where God wanted me to be. He guided my every move. Honestly, I've never felt so close to Him."

A sudden longing filled her spirit. How she wished she could say the same thing. She couldn't. Her first year in Florida, she didn't go to church or even pray. She'd been as angry with God as she'd been with her mother, and Cory ... and herself.

"I missed you, and I missed our church too, but I learned a lot. I met some great people. They shared everything they had with me. Who knew there were people out there who'd really give you the shirt off their back?" He shrugged and shook his head, looking so much like the teenager Bretta had loved with all her heart.

"Did you sleep under a bridge?" She couldn't keep from tormenting him.

"Sometimes."

Her heart skipped a beat. "Oh, no!"

He laughed. "If you'd been with me we wouldn't have slept under bridges. I wouldn't have put you through that. My plans changed when you didn't go. I did odd jobs for all kinds of people. Lots of little churches needed work done but couldn't afford to hire anyone."

"And you did it for free?"

"Don't sound like my dad, Brett. I usually worked for food and a place to sleep. It felt great."

"Guess working for your dad's construction company paid off. You had the know-how."

Cory's face changed. "He wouldn't give one measly nail away for free. It felt good to do things for people—things that needed to be done. It felt good to care for complete strangers."

"How do you know they couldn't pay you?"

For the first time, he looked impatient with her. "That didn't matter to me. Don't you get it, Brett? Are you one of those people who believe the homeless shouldn't be given money because they'll buy dope or booze? What if they need a pair of socks or band-aids? And you buy them a fish sandwich instead?"

She found herself nodding. Where was the old Cory Leland? This new Cory took a stand was vocal about his beliefs. He'd never been that way with his father or her mother. Or her. He'd kept silent and let them have their way.

But no matter how exciting and interesting this new Cory was, Bretta didn't want to know him any more than she wanted to remember the old Cory. She would never let Cory Leland hurt her again. She would never watch him drive away from her again.

She tossed her napkin on the table and pushed her plate away. "Back to business."

He held out his hand for her to take. She didn't.

"There's no *back to* business. Everything on my end is completed. All I have to do is deliver it one hour before the event begins. My people will set it up."

"Your people? That's hilarious." Her meanness brought tears to her eyes.

He pulled his hand away. "Please trust me, Brett. I love you. I'm sorry I hurt you. I'll never hurt you again. That's a promise."

She only nodded. If she opened her mouth she would reveal all kinds of pain and disappointments.

His voice became a whisper. "Have you gone through your grandmother's things yet?"

She frowned. "No, I haven't had time. Why?"

He didn't answer her question. He picked up the ticket the waitress had delivered, stood and pulled out his wallet. "Come on. Just seven hours until show time."

The moment Bretta entered *Everything Wedding,* a flushed-faced Lonna met her. "Remember how we couldn't get on TV because they were booked? They have a cancellation. They're filming me as soon as I can get there. It'll show at five. After that, I'm running over to the Oaks to see how the set-up is going."

"Good luck!" Bretta called as Lonna ran out the door, her red hair flying.

As soon as she sat at her desk, the bell jangled again, indicating a customer. "Package for Bretta Richert."

"I'm in here." She met the young man at the door. He wasn't a mailman or UPS guy—he was just a kid. "Who do you work for?"

"C.A. Lee."

"Cory?" Bretta took the package, then searched her desk drawer for a few quarters to tip the boy.

When he left, she stood at her desk to unwrap the brightly colored paper. She opened the flaps on the box and peered inside at a crystal clear rose, sculpted from ice and sitting on an illuminated display of some kind. It was beautiful. A gold charm dangled from one of its petals, inscribed with the words, *Marry Me*.

C.A. Lee was showing her his talents and wooing her.

She smiled. She'd never been pursued. She and Cory had known each other since middle school, but this handsome C.A. Lee was someone else entirely.

She folded the flap down in her attempt to get the rose out of the box and saw one more item inside. A letter addressed to Cory, but it had her grandmother's return address—the condo she'd willed to Bretta. Should she read it?

Of course she should. Cory had obviously put it inside the box especially for her. She unfolded it. It was dated five years earlier.

Dear Cory,

You're a good young man—responsible and considerate. You know I have always liked you. However, Bretta and her mother have moved away. I'm sorry, I can't forward your letters to my granddaughter. I've prayed about it and I don't feel it's right. At least, it's not right at this time. You need to find yourself. So does Bretta, and she needs to go to college. Here's what I will do. I'll save every letter you write to her—whether you write one, five or a hundred—and someday, she'll have them all, along with my belongings since she's my only granddaughter. Cory, you both need distance and maturity before you embark on this tricky thing called marriage. If and when you return to Chicory and plead your case with her, you'll have the letters to prove you always cared. If by chance you don't follow through or she falls in love with another, then it was never meant to be.

Forgive me, Cory, but trust me as I trust God's will for your dreams. If you believe ... and pray ... you two will be together again.

I wish you the best in your travels.

Sincerely,

"Gram"

Bretta stared at the letter. Why hadn't Gram hinted at such a thing? Why would she keep this secret? Because they'd needed distance and maturity and college? Anger bubbled inside her. Would it have made a difference if she'd received letters from Cory? Yes, of course. She would have understood. She would have ... what?

The bell over the door jingled, and Cory entered. He stopped short of approaching her desk. "You read it?"

Not trusting herself to speak, she nodded. She didn't know whether to be happy or angry. Uplifted or sad. Had their future been manipulated by her seventy-five-year-old grandmother, or had she been wise to keep Bretta and Cory apart? How was Bretta supposed to feel?

She focused on Cory. He didn't look quite as confident as he had earlier. He looked as sad as she felt. She shook the letter at him. "I can't deal with this right now. I can't think about you, us, or any of this until after the wedding show tonight."

He crossed the room and propped on the edge of her desk. "What's to think about? We fell in love the moment we laid eyes on each other. Eighth grade. I don't know how I feel about what your grandmother did. Maybe she was right. You read her reasoning. But there's one thing I know for certain. It's meant to be. You came back to Chicory from Florida and I returned from California. God brought us home, Brett. We're meant to be together."

She blinked her eyes in an effort to beat back the tears.

"You didn't fall for someone else, did you?" His tone of voice told her he dreaded her answer.

She shook her head. "No. But I wanted to. I wanted to fall in love every day but you were in the way—always in the back of mind."

He touched the gold charm dangling from the rose he'd carved for her. "Not in the back of your mind, Bretta. In your heart."

When Cory left the store, Bretta shoved him out of her mind so she could concentrate. She spent the next two hours tying up loose ends as well as giving a telephone interview to a Southeast Texas newspaper. After that, she talked with delivery men, florists, and people calling to ask if the event was free.

Finally, Lonna returned from doing her television segment and running her other errands. She threw herself into a chair. "This is such work! I never dreamed it would be such a hit."

"Yes, you did. That's why you wanted to do it. You're the most creative, innovative person I've ever known," Bretta said. "And finagling a connection to an already successful event like 'Christmas under the Oaks' guarantees success. Our wedding event will bring many more people from across the state.

"I hope so."

"I know so. Where else will parents, brides and grooms meet wedding singers, planners, photographers, jewelers? All they need to plan the perfect wedding?"

Lanna sighed. "Thanks. I couldn't have done it without you. This is your first big event. Hopefully, it won't be your last."

"I'm just doing what I'm told, boss-lady."

"That and more." Lonna kicked off her shoes and stretched out her legs, wiggling her ankles. "Every woman in the club, with the exception of Heather Fontenot who has pneumonia, has turned out to participate. Thank God some of them can still get into their own wedding dresses. I called every consignment shop, Salvation Army, and Goodwill within a fifty mile radius, buying used dresses."

Bretta laughed. "Your idea about the women's club members wearing wedding gowns is brilliant, Lonna. All your hostesses will be easily identifiable. And opening the store next door with second-time-around wedding dresses is a fun idea too. You'll recoup what you've been out on the used ones. I wouldn't have thought of that."

"We'll see just how brilliant it was *after* the fact." Lonna looked at her watch. "Are you getting ready here or at your place?"

"My place. I guess I'd better be going, but Lonna, can I ask you something and you be honest with me?"

"Sure, I'm always honest, or at least I try to be. What do you want to know?"

Bretta hesitated. She couldn't bring herself to ask all she wanted to know—that might be forcing Lonna to fib a little. But she would ask about her grandmother. That couldn't hurt.

"I know you and Gram got close at church before she died, but did she ask you to give me this job?"

"Your grandmother never said a word about you other than she missed you, that you were too far away. When she found out she was ill and had so little time left, she took care of her business. She was a wonderful woman with such insight into life. She was a blessing to me. That's why I wanted to meet you. I knew you'd be a blessing too—and you are." Lonna tilted her head. "And if you're wondering about Cory, I met him at church too. He'd just moved back and everyone was so glad to see him. I didn't know you two had dated—until today."

"Today?"

"Yeah, Cory asked me if you were going to be a hostess. When I said yes, he asked me to put you in the most beautiful wedding dress I have in this shop. And that's exactly what I plan to do. So come on!"

Cory's cold front arrived. Bretta shivered as she unlocked the door to Gram's condo. The wedding dress was draped over her arm. It was heavy and would be warm ... and way too beautiful to be traipsing around under a lot of oak trees. She hung the dress on a hanger over the door, shed her sweater and kicked out of her shoes. She wanted to find those letters before she did one more thing.

Hurrying to Gram's bedroom, she tiptoed inside, much like she did when she was younger. One just didn't invade another's private areas—at least that's what Gram had taught her. But now, it was really hers—even if she didn't sleep there. She hadn't been ready to go through Gram's belongings or dispose of anything. Every night when she crawled into her own bed, she pretended her grandmother was just down the hall.

She looked around, not surprised by its neatness. Her grandmother had always been organized. She opened a closet. Two flowery hat boxes that should have been on a shelf sat in the middle of the floor. Gram and her hats. She'd always been so beautiful in them. Bretta flipped the tops off each.

Letters. Hundreds of unopened letters. All were addressed to her, in care of Gram.

Could Cory have written her several times a week for five years? Obviously.

Gram had tied each month of letters with blue ribbon. Bretta plopped down on the floor, searching for the first letter he'd written her after he left. She had to know how he felt that day.

My Sweet Brett,

I'm sending this letter in care of your grandmother. I hope she'll give it to you. I could hardly stand to look in my rearview mirror and see you in the street crying, staring after me. That made me cry too. I almost turned around to come back to you but turning around just didn't feel right. I hope you'll forgive me. Still, right or wrong, if you want to join me at any time, I'll send you a plane ticket. Just say the word. I won't ever quit loving you, Brett. You have to believe me. I promise you we're going to be married one day. If you believe in us, it'll happen. And I promise you the most beautiful wedding imaginable.

I'm spending the night in Jackson, Mississippi. My first stop. I'll look at a map and see where to go next. I'll let you know where you can write me. I should have had a plan, but I didn't because I pictured you with me, and that we'd make plans together. I miss you, Brett.

I love you. Wait for me.

Cory

She let the tears flow as she reached for the next letter, then the next. It was almost a month before he made reference to the letter he'd received from Gram. Maybe he didn't have a return address until then.

Dear Brett,

I heard from your grandmother today. I was surprised she hasn't been giving you my letters. Or forwarding them to you. I got really angry for a minute and called her. That was when she told me you were in Florida—that you and your mom moved a couple of days after I left. I can't picture you in Florida. Every time I write, I picture us walking through town together, or laying in the

61

grass talking about our hopes and dreams. I'm still going to write you a couple of times a week. It'll be harder now that I know you're in Florida.

Don't fall in love with anyone else, Brett. You're mine. God gave us to each other a long time ago—I know that without a doubt.

Believe in us. Please.

Cory

Through her tears, she glanced at her watch. She was using up valuable time. She needed to shower, make her face, do her hair, and get to the Oaks. If only she didn't have to go. Then she could read all Cory's letters.

Just one more ... the last one he'd written before coming home. She tore it open.

Hey Brett,

I'm coming home. It's time. And you're the first person I hope to see when I get there.

I love you, Brett. I've never quit loving you. Will you marry me?

Cory

Bretta shrieked, then shrieked again. He'd always loved her. His letters proved it. After laughing and crying and dancing little jigs across Gram's bedroom floor, she looked at her watch. "Oh, no... much to do and so little time!" She raced down the hall to her own bedroom. She wanted to be the most beautiful wedding hostess Chicory had ever seen. She giggled. Good practice.

Two hours later, dressed in the elegant white velvet wedding dress Lonna had chosen for her, she stepped out her front door. The slate-gray sky promised a chilly night. Would it snow? Of course not. Not in South Louisiana.

How could she get in her car, much less drive, with the full, lush skirt, and long draping sleeves?

A sleek white limo pulled up to her curb resolving the problem. *Cory to the rescue?*

A driver, dressed in a white suit with a red hankie in his breast pocket, emerged.

"Ms. Bretta Richert? I'm here to take you to the Oaks weddin' grounds."

Bretta couldn't do anything more than smile. Cory had wooing down to an art.

Nestled in the warm car, she settled her skirts around her. What might the night bring? Cory had something up his sleeve. No doubt about it. That huge tent he'd reserved wasn't for nothing. She couldn't wait to see what he had planned. Was Lonna in on it? She'd approved every single display—why not his? Why were they keeping it from Bretta? After all, she was the entire marketing department—except for Lonna. She should have promoted whatever they were hiding from her, sent out press releases if there was something unusual and special going on.

When they reached the edge of town where the wedding extravaganza was taking place, she gasped at the scene before her. The trees were wrapped in twinkle lights. The white tents looked glorious and romantic. Valets stood at attention, waiting for people to arrive. A young man opened the door and helped her out.

"The bride hostesses are in the first tent, there, meeting with Ms. Lonna."

Bretta looked at her watch. She'd been so lost in Cory's letters, she was fifteen minutes late, but if she had her way, she'd be back home reading them all, one right after another.

When she entered the tent, Lonna quit speaking and everyone turned. They oohed and ahhed and circled around her as if she were a *real* bride. For the life of her, she didn't know why. They were all just as beautiful. Even old Mrs. Breaux who usually wore comfy polyester sweat suits looked gorgeous in the wedding dress she'd worn fifty years earlier. Someone had told her that Mr. and Mrs. Breaux were scheduled to renew their vows in the near future.

Lonna interrupted her thoughts. "Okay, ladies, let's continue. It's your job to make sure every visitor finds what she's looking for. Don't let anyone be lost or left behind. And keep a smile on your face. We want this affair to be unique and memorable. And thanks to C. A. Lee, our lighting design illuminating each tent is spectacular. In about twenty-eight minutes—" she looked at her watch. "Correction, in twenty-three minutes, we'll open the front gates and begin our wedding extravaganza."

Bretta turned to leave the tent, thinking Lonna was finished, but her friend called out to her.

"I'm sorry I was late," Bretta said when Lonna came toward her. "I got involved with another chore."

"No problem, I needed to cover some things with the other ladies anyway."

Bretta frowned. "And not me?"

"We added something to the show that I didn't tell you about. In fact, C. A. Lee added it and I have to admit, I'm a little envious that I didn't think of it myself."

"What?"

"C. A. Lee—"

"Lonna please, call him Cory. I have a hard time thinking of him as C. A. Lee."

"You won't when you see what he's created. It's the most beautiful crystal cathedral I've ever seen."

"Crystal cathedral? But how? Why?"

"For anyone who wants to renew their vows. Isn't it a marvelous idea? The chapel or cathedral—whatever you want to call it— is carved out of ice. It's so incredibly beautiful—it seems so spiritual. Just wait until you see it, then you'll call him C. A. Lee."

Bretta laughed. "I doubt it, but why wouldn't you tell me? We could have really played this up."

"I mentioned it on TV today. We don't want *everyone* to come just to renew their vows; it would turn into a circus. It has to be special."

Bretta agreed. She was proud of Cory for being so forthcoming with creative ideas. He was certainly more creative than she was. He always had been.

"Where is he?" She'd looked around the tent thinking he may have shown up for their meeting.

"Final touches on things. I want you two to be in charge of the big tent, okay? But first, I want you to walk through each tent—let everyone see how beautiful you look in that fantastic velvet wedding dress. It came straight from New York—the only one I ordered."

Bretta marveled at how perfectly the dress fit her, wondered why, but she could broach that subject later. "You don't want me to mingle and help people find their way?"

"No. You need to be in the big tent at exactly seven-thirty, so just wander through the various tents and let people know about the dress and what we do at *Everything Wedding*."

Bretta left Lonna, happy to be moving. She felt antsy for some reason. Walking through the tents, she visited with a lot of people. Everything looked so perfect. The scent of fresh flowers on silk table cloths drifted through the crisp air. Across a lighted walkway, mistletoe dangled from an overhang. Christmas music played softly. Bretta stopped to inhale the beauty around her. Passion roses with greenery and berries dotted tables. A hand-tied posy of white roses surrounded by a collar of white feathers took her breath away. The night—the event—was storybook perfect.

At seven-thirty p.m. Bretta entered Cory's tent. A stunning number of people were already inside. Most of them she knew—including many of the bride hostesses. Why weren't they working? Her eyes tore away from them to the center of the tent. She pressed her fingers to her lips to keep from looking foolish when her mouth fell open. Spectacular didn't begin to describe what Cory had created.

A silver carpet had been rolled to the entrance of the ice chapel. Three ornate columns formed the structure on each side, with elaborate trusses crossing from one side to the other. The roof peaked into a cross. It was large enough to walk inside but who would dare to do so? She felt like it would have been a violation of something pure and perfect if she had. She shook her head. Cory was right. He'd been gifted.

"Brett?" When she turned at the sound of her name, she faced him.

"Cory, I'm ... I'm so sorry. I had no idea you could create something like this. It's breathtaking."

"You're breathtaking." When he kneeled on one knee, everyone in the tent gasped and murmured. Bretta held her breath. What on earth was he doing?

He flipped open a small, velvet box and held it toward her.

"Cory, is that Gram's wedding ring?"

"It is. She left it with Corbello's Jewelers in my name. She had it cleaned and made sure the diamonds and emeralds weren't loose. She believed in us, Brett. She prayed for us."

"Oh Cory—"

"If you believe, if you just believe in us—we can do anything—anywhere. You, me, and the One who made us for each other."

Tears formed behind her eyes and she blinked them away with laughter. "Of course, I believe. I love you, Cory. I was hurt when you left, when I never heard from you. I didn't know about all the letters. As hurt as I was, I never quit loving you."

"Then you'll be my wife today?"

"This very minute! But Cory—the marriage license."

He grinned. "All taken care of."

Lonna and several bride hostesses rushed forward and hustled Bretta away. "Entertain the crowd, Cory, while we add some last minute touches to your bride."

"Oh, this is so exciting!" one of older women said. "You'll have the first wedding at our very first extravaganza. Do you have something old?"

Bretta touched near her neck. "My grandmother's stick pin. It has seed pearls and a real emerald. In fact, it matches her wedding ring. Gram loved emeralds."

"Something new—that's your dress," Lonna explained.

"And something borrowed. Here take this." Patti Benoit pulled a handkerchief out of her purse.

"No, no, child, take this from me." Old Mrs. Breaux stepped forward waving a small perfume bottle in her gloved hand. "Dab it at the pulse of your throat and on your wrist. My Benjamin loves this scent. I've worn it all our married life—even when we dated. Our marriage has been strong and God-blessed, as I know yours will be." She laughed. "Of course, the perfume had nothing to do with that, but it helps."

Bretta bent down and kissed the old woman on her cheek. "Thank you, Mrs. Breaux. Will you allow your husband to give me away? I have no one."

"He'd be honored, my dear, honored." She dug into her clutch and pulled out an iPhone. "Just let me ring him. I think he's in the photography tent. He wants to learn a new hobby—though I'm concerned about it being photography. Taking pictures can get people in trouble these days."

Some of the hostesses were sniffling, as if their very own daughter was seconds away from walking down the aisle. Suddenly, someone shouted, "We forgot—something blue!"

"I don't have anything," one woman muttered.

"I don't either. All I have is green," said another.

"Wait... wait, will this do?" Bretta kicked off her shoe and wiggled her toes. "I painted my toenails yesterday. Blue!" When no one spoke, she added, "It's really not me. It was just an experiment."

Their laughter embraced her and she realized she was happier than she'd ever been in her life. She had friends. Cory was home, and they were going to be married.

The Christmas music shut off and the wedding march began. Old Mr. Breaux appeared out of nowhere. He smiled and offered Bretta his arm. "You smell beautiful," he whispered.

She could barely remember walking down the silver carpet. Within seconds she stood inside the ice chapel facing Pastor Kevin who had baptized her and Cory when they rededicated their lives as teens. He smiled at them both.

"I've been waiting to join these two in holy matrimony for a number of years. Today is a blessed day."

He read from The Book of Common Prayer, asking the traditional questions of the bride and groom. When he asked who would give this woman in matrimony, Mr. and Mrs. Breaux spoke up.

Then Pastor Kevin addressed the people crowded into the tent. "Will all of you witnessing these promises do all in your power to uphold these two persons in their marriage?"

Affirmations and murmurings resounded.

The vows had never sounded more beautiful. Cory and Bretta repeated each heartfelt word as if they'd been written just for them, and when the pastor pronounced them husband and wife, they had one thing to add:

"I believe in you—always."

They whispered the words to each other, and their lips touched.

"Hey, it's snowing!" someone shouted. "It's actually snowing outside."

Tiny perfect flakes dropped from the Louisiana sky, dusting the bride and groom as they left the tent. Bretta giggled and Cory pulled her close. "You know... sometimes everything really does come together when you believe."

Heavenly Haven

Christine Lindsay

A stiff cake of snow formed on the peaks of Steven's Pass in the Washington Cascades. Snow crystals, unsteady and shifting like white sand, sparkled in the moonlight. Steep cliffs covered by these tiny diamonds, beautiful and treacherous, waited silently for the next big wind, the swish of a ski, the thrust of a snowboard, any movement to disturb the cold and uneasy layers of snow beneath.

But in the ski village below, Jack Burke wanted nothing more than to warm up the cold front gathering in his own kitchen, specifically the coldness emanating from his wife's slender back.

Jack leaned over the kitchen table, pressing his knuckles to its spotless surface. He infused his voice with all the softness he could drum up. "Avalanches happen, Angel. It's my job—I've got to go."

"Keep your voice down—you'll wake the kids." His diminutive wife tossed her ponytail off her shoulder with the flick of one flour-dusted wrist. With the fluid movement of an athlete she slipped an envelope from her jeans pocket into her purse on the counter. Only three a.m. yet she was dressed for the day in jeans and a green sweatshirt, her feet toasty in a pair of his extra thick socks. Adorable as usual, but the only time Shaina baked in the middle of the night was when she was upset enough to spit nails.

"Our two little monkeys never stir 'til the crack of dawn." He hoped his reference to the kids would loosen a smile from her. "And I've got to get to work."

"Yes, I know—you've got to get out there and save lives while I stay at home all day and reorganize the cutlery drawer. Maybe for extra excitement I'll restack the bathroom towels according to size instead of color." Shaina couldn't have shown more anger if Genghis Khan had traipsed into her cookie-scented kitchen. "But just don't make me out the bad guy here, Jack, as if I didn't care about people on the slopes. You promised that this year—this year finally—we were going away overnight for our anniversary."

"There's three guys sick with the flu, Stan already booked the entire day off, and I'm the designated rescue coordinator for my crew."

With two hands she lobbed a small mountain of gingerbread dough on the counter and began to pulverize it with a rolling pin. "All I asked was one full day—twenty-four hours—just the two of us in December at a nice hotel."

"Right, December…winter…the busiest time of the year for me. Well, it wasn't my idea to elope a mere nine days before Christmas." He forced a chuckle. "I wanted to get married in summer, a big wedding where I could show you off in church and on the dance floor, not elope as if you were ashamed—" His lame attempt to lighten the mood landed like a pile of slush. Shaina's blue-green eyes welled. *Dear God, save me from being a jack-ass.* "I'm sorry, Angel, I didn't mean that."

"Ashamed?" she said in an undertone he barely caught. "I wanted to be your wife before…before you left for Iraq. I didn't want you going into combat without knowing how much…how much I love…" Without another word she washed her hands at the sink and left him.

He followed her to the living room. Outside, sleet hissed at the windows and held the room in a cold grip. He ought to turn on the gas fireplace for her, but he couldn't seem to move, couldn't seem to breathe properly. Did she think he'd purposely chosen to work today's extended shift instead of spending a romantic night alone with her?

Shaina sank into the easy chair closest to the bay window. The street light illumined the outline of the front yard, all straight edges softened and rounded by the ever increasing inches of snow. There sat the rough shape of the bench he'd set beneath the maple tree at Shaina's request two years ago, the white picket fence he'd built, the wagon wheel at the end of the driveway set at just the right angle for her climbing roses to grow on in the summer.

It was a far cry from summer now. And this three-bedroom rancher was a far cry from the upscale house she'd grown up in.

And he completely got it—that she wanted to go away somewhere fancy for their anniversary. He'd not had the heart to tell her though, that they couldn't quite swing it financially this month. But there was something else. What was in that envelope?

Hooking his thumbs at the back of his belt, he turned to her. A quilt of Christmas penguins she'd sewn one year covered her favorite chair. Each evening she'd sit there while he watched hockey on TV, and she read or completed a craft. But this morning her back was as straight as a ski pole. She folded her hands in her lap while the sheen of her amber hair caught the twinkling lights of their Christmas tree. Was it only two nights ago they'd played with the kids and together strung the lights? Afterward, he'd sat in his recliner, Scottie in one arm, Zoey in the other, munching on popcorn and watching his beautiful wife smile.

Like every year, Shaina fussed with the gold ribbons on the tree to make them turn and twist. The ribbons shimmered, reminding him of ski runs at night when the speed of light slowed on the freezing air. Like the way the rest of the world slowed to a stop when he'd first laid eyes on Shaina. He'd been out with a work crew grooming the slopes when she, a guest at the ski lodge, schussed down the mountainside and become the reason for his heart to keep beating.

Now this morning she sat there looking anywhere but at him. He'd been a good husband, hadn't he? A good provider? Not like her dad, but good enough, hadn't he?

They'd known the risks, especially when so many of Shaina's old friends said their marriage would never last the first year. She'd come from such a wealthy family, and he was just a guy who'd grown up in the foster-care system. Because of the differences in their upbringing, they'd entered marriage prepared by taking a marriage course. They went to a couples' Sunday School class and attended church each Sunday.

Casting his memory back to their pre-marital counseling, he searched for the right principle or any wisp of wisdom he could use. Nothing came. "I didn't mean what I said, Angel. I didn't want to wait 'til I got back from Iraq either. I wanted a December wedding too."

She placed the back of her hand to her lips for a moment, as if that would keep her emotions under control. "But you meant something." Her words came out soft. Too soft, a soft puff of snow before an avalanche.

The wedge of ice in his stomach widened to a field. He'd thought they were fine as a couple: now all of a sudden a chasm opened between them.

She raised that perfect, stubborn little chin while her unshed tears shimmered as much as her ribbons on the tree. "You think I'm ashamed of you." Her voice rose. "After ten years together you still don't know me."

A cry pierced the pre-dawn silence, of eighteen-month-old Zoey from her room down the hall.

Shaina started to rise to tend to Zoey, and he stopped her. "I'll tuck her in."

Down the hall in Zoey's room, he found the toddler standing in her crib. The glowing nightlight showed her little face screwed up with tears, her strawberry blonde curls all awry with sweet baby sweat. He picked his little girl up and cuddled her against his flannel shirt as he rubbed her back, and she hiccupped. He sang her favorite lullaby in a whisper until the sobbing eased and stopped. "I'm going to put you in bed now, snookums."

"Noooo, Dadda." She clung to him tighter.

"Have to, snookums: it's too early for you to get up, and I'll see you tonight like always."

"Swed, Dadda, swed."

"Sled? Is that what you're saying?"

She nodded, and his sigh ruffled the curls on top of her head. His tiny child had the memory of an elephant—a baby elephant supposedly. He'd mentioned offhand last week that he'd buy her and her big brother a sled. "All right, baby girl, tonight I'll bring you a sled. I promise. Now you get into bed."

He laid her down and covered her with her favorite quilt, one that Shaina had made, with forest critters hopping all over it. Never having sewn before, Shaina had taken a quilting course the first year they were married. While her mother would hire a team of decorators to embellish their grand Seattle mansion, Shaina—as elegant as her mother—tapped into home-made crafts to grace their home. Everything Shaina did, she did to perfection, but she'd given up so much to be his wife.

His chest tightened with the need to release his own emotions. But he was a man and he had a job to go to, though he never left home without checking on Scottie too.

In the other bedroom, his three-year-old son, wearing his cowboy pajamas, lay flat out on his back, a soft snore coming from him as regular and triumphant as a small Sousa marching piece. A fringe of brown hair fell over the child's brow, which Jack brushed back. Scottie didn't wake, even when he sat down on the side of the boy's bed. Nor did his son stir when Jack leaned down to kiss his cheek, still sticky with last night's toothpaste.

In the hallway outside the living room, Jack geared himself up to face Shaina, grasping for the right things to say, but when he entered the room it was empty. Only their smiling faces in their wedding portrait above the fireplace greeted him. In the picture Shaina stood in his embrace, wearing a simple white dress, no extravagant gown or veil like her mom and dad had preferred. And there'd been no fancy reception at the yacht club.

Still, to him, Shaina had looked like a snow angel that day.

He'd been wearing his Class A uniform, a full head taller than Shaina, his brown hair in a military buzz. After their elopement, her parents had not bothered to mask their disappointment that she'd married an enlisted man. If she had to marry a soldier in such a fashion, couldn't he at least have been an officer? He'd never measure up to their standards.

Only then did he notice the door to his and Shaina's bedroom was closed. He should go in and clear the air with her, but at the moment he didn't have the strength to argue with that closed door. Had she at last begun to think her parents were right?

The garage swung closed behind him as he drove his truck over the mounding snow in his driveway and the road. Department of Transportation plows would be out on the suburb streets anytime now, having spent the entire night keeping the freeway clear.

Through his rearview mirror he looked back at his little house that Shaina worked hard to dress up for each season. For Christmas she'd created a winter wonderland on the porch draped with red ribbons and bows. White cotton batten on the floor sufficed for snow. And animated bears, chipmunks, bunnies, all stood on small wooden skis that she'd cut, sanded, and painted in the garage.

All the silly critters waved their paws goodbye to him, while above them twinkled green and blue Christmas lights. But the little myriad of festivity seemed to fade on this cold, blue winter dawn. That envelope Shaina had stuffed into her purse—though he'd only got a glance, he'd seen the quality of the paper, something embossed on the front. His gut sank. That envelope was something her parents would send. And if it was, why was he out of the loop?

He stomped on the gas and snow spun under his back wheels. Right now Christmas and its warmth felt a long ways off.

In their ten years of marriage Shaina couldn't remember ever closing the bedroom door on Jack. That sort of emotional coldness happened to other people. Not to them. Still, she was glad he was gone to work, leaving her alone with her thoughts. She curled up in their bed and tried to sleep, but the aroma of ginger, nutmeg, and cloves called her back to the kitchen. She might as well finish baking the gingerbread slabs for the house she was building.

Having won the local contest last year, the competitive spirit had risen in her again. Nothing wrong with that. Mom was always winning golf tournaments, boating races, summer garden shows, and getting mentioned in the paper for her spectacular Christmas décor.

Shaina had to admit, there was a lot of her mother in her, her need to compete, to embellish her surroundings. Last year she'd won the village's gingerbread contest with a simple log cabin. But creating gingerbread houses and going all out to trim her home was not all she shared with her mom.

Like her mother, she enjoyed sports. Not just sports, but surrounding those sports with a touch of chic-ness, a certain…savoir faire. For Shaina there was nothing like swishing down the slopes with an arc of cold powder rising around her, caressing her waist in a cloud of white. She could ski with Jack here in Steven's Pass anytime, but for this anniversary she wanted to retire to a five-star hotel in Seattle after a day on the slopes. For dinner and dancing. Jack in some nice dress casuals, she in a slinky black number…Jack caressing her bare back.

Her sigh came out heavy. This year she'd wanted the kind of establishment she used to enjoy with her parents, but as usual Jack had to work. So she might as well sink her pent-up energy into that gingerbread house. Her plans for this year's competition were more ambitious—a rendition of the Stimson-Green Mansion, one of

Seattle's finest landmarks, complete with wooden gables and pointed arches. Her mother might even be impressed.

But the way she and Jack had parted left her cold even in the oven-warmed kitchen, and she added an extra pair of his socks to her feet. If Mom could see her morning ensemble she'd probably shudder.

After Shaina removed the slabs from the oven, she still couldn't summon any interest, and pushed them aside. Outside, the snow still fell. She watched it fall until the sun rose at last, but it remained hidden behind heavy clouds. It was true what Jack hinted at. Today for the first time she was disappointed that he couldn't provide for her what her father provided for her mother, that monetary provision to take off whenever they felt like it.

Thankfully, the children woke at their normal time of seven and yanked her back to her real life. She loved her parents, and they could traipse around the world like first-class tourists with her blessing. She wanted only what Jack provided. Or did she?

Zoey woke first, as usual, banging her teddy on the side of her crib. Her little girl's chubby arms reached for her when she entered the room and nearly strangled her around the neck with exuberance. Oh these hugs, they were the stuff of life, not five-star hotels and her father's yacht. Shaina grinned at her little girl and strained to decipher that string of garbled words issuing from Zoey's mouth. She got two—Dadda, and something that sounded like sled.

She'd finished changing Zoey's diaper and plopped her into her highchair in the kitchen when, like a drunken sailor, Scottie staggered down the hall, rubbing sleep out of his eyes. As if he were a world-weary man of forty he held a hand to his head. "Juice, Mama: I need apple juice."

"And the magic word, my good sir?"

"Please."

She handed him the kiddy-size container and he gulped it down. "Thanks, Mama, I needed that."

"Anytime, son." But the laughter that her children always drew out of her failed this morning to lift the cloud. This unceasing snow was burying the town. She was suffocating under its weight. All she wanted was to get out on top of the slopes. Feel the cold tingle her cheeks. Be the first to make her signature on a run of virgin powder. And then, of course, return to the hotel for a professional massage and some private time in a hot tub with Jack.

She poured milk into bowls of cereal for the kids. Scottie started to devour his while Zoey winked at her as if Shaina had provided her with a steak and lobster dinner. Oh to be so easily satisfied! But that envelope in her purse wouldn't let her.

She pulled the itinerary out and spread it open on the counter. Two full days at one of Seattle's finest, and fun on the slopes of Mount Rainier.

Blowing frustration through pursed lips, she started to tuck the itinerary into her purse but pulled it out again, smoothing it repeatedly with her hand. She could change their booking to another date, but there was no way she wanted to sit home today. Not after scrimping for months to save for this get-away. She'd take the kids if Jack couldn't come. They'd have a good time. And Jack would understand. Of course he would.

She punched in his cell number but couldn't get an answer. He must be somewhere in the folds of the pass, out of range. She'd have to call him later. So much for her original surprise. Stuffing down a twinge of guilt she glanced at the still falling snow. It would be bad in the pass today, but she was heading to Seattle. The roads would be fine. Jack would understand.

And if she kept telling herself that, maybe she'd eventually believe it.

From the pump station in the pass, Jack looked down two thousand feet to the valley. Winter populated this little ski village. Skiers and snowboarders from Seattle, California, New York, from as far away as Europe, came to play. Then there were those permanent inhabitants who ran gift shops, waited on tables, operated lifts, sanded and plowed the roads, and those who kept the mountains safe. Folks like him and Shaina called the village home year round. So too did the crews he worked with on the Washington Avalanche Control.

Jack's supervisor, Stan, strolled toward him from the make-up shed where inside they prepared the explosives. Stan's orange safety vest matched that of every other man on the mountainside. "You're looking a bit down in the mouth, Jack. Not coming down with the flu too?"

He sent his supervisor a reassuring grin. "Nope, so off you go for your day as planned. Everything's under control."

Stan removed his glove to rub an eyebrow. "I'm not so sure." He glanced up at the peaks. "Those deaths last week, so unnecessary. The warning was up, danger high to considerable. Those skiers should have known better than to ski out of bounds."

"Looking for fresh snow." Jack shrugged. "Experienced and well-equipped as they were, they thought they could handle anything that came their way. That's what people think—avalanches always happen to other people."

Stan's eyes narrowed. "And the snow buried them."

Jack placed a hand on the older man's shoulder. "We're saving more lives than before."

"That's some comfort at least." Stan put his glove back on. "How's Shaina and the kids? You've been talking about taking your wife away for your anniversary. So what date is that again? Louise and I are happy to babysit."

He glanced away, feeling Stan's gaze, and was about to answer when Carlton from his crew strode over to them. "Just got the word. The snowpack up there's pretty weak, not enough support for the tank."

Stan gestured to Jack. "You're the blaster. It's your call."

Jack drew his shoulders back. "We'll have to use the old recoilless rifle to take off some of those layers. Plus I'd like to add a few more kill zones to the plan I drew up yesterday."

With militaristic procedure he entered the shed and retrieved ten of the four-foot long bullets, and after logging his plans he strode to the workshop to warm up the ammunition. The crew knew their jobs. Soon the roads would be blocked off, disallowing traffic, and Jack was going to have to shoot to trigger an avalanche.

By ten-thirty Jack's crew reached the first of the areas on the mountain that he'd chosen, and hoisted the eleven-foot rifle onto its mounting. Stan, who'd insisted on coming along to help instead of taking his day off as planned, stood back as Jack adjusted the sightings. Stan knew the lion's share about avalanches, but Jack was the expert on anti-personnel weapons from his service in Iraq. When those bullets slammed into the mountain's sweet spot they would detonate 4.5 pounds of TNT.

Jack shouted clearly into the radio to the crew a thousand feet below. "Clear to the front!"

His radio crackled. "All clear."

"Clear to the rear?"

"Ten four. All clear."

Stan and Carlton pressed their ear protection close to their heads as Jack prepared to fire into the first of the kill zones, a twelve foot crown of snow.

"Ready to fire." He took a breath and held it.

"Fire!"

The force of the shot brought the usual blow to his chest, and he jerked back a bit. Seconds later, a puff of smoke rose from the face of the mountain two hundred yards away. But it was only that first soft whisper. A second later came the dull report of the explosion. A fracture appeared in the crust. Slowly the slope began to give way. The white mountainside moved downward. Silently, it built and tumbled, crashing into trees, throwing trunks and branches of tall firs into the air like sticks, and a pillar of snow billowed.

Jack prepared the second round. More layers needed to be peeled back in strategic spots before they could allow the graders to enter the roads far below to clear the freeway.

Reports from the crews confirmed all was well. He and his men were safe. They had their escape route planned in the event of the avalanche reaching them. Shaina and the kids were tucked up at home in the valley. No doubt Scottie and Zoey were helping to decorate the gingerbread mansion much like the house Shaina had grown up in. And tonight when he got home, he had to make things right with his wife.

But before igniting the next charge he lifted his eyes to the mountains. The avalanche's downward slide struck him with awe. What power, this remarkable and silent force of nature. God was speaking.

Shaina pulled her lower lip between her teeth. Nothing had gone as she'd planned after leaving the house. She and the kids had gone only fifty feet on the freeway in the direction of Seattle when the traffic controllers flagged the cars to stop. One of the crews must be causing the delay, and that meant it would be a while. Not Jack's crew. According to the schedule he'd shared with her last night, he was working in an entirely different area of the pass.

She laid her head back against the headrest. Nothing to do but wait in the Jeep. Wait…and have patience. Patience she should have used this morning while talking to Jack. Sure, she'd been disappointed, but taking the kids to Seattle without him was sounding dumber all the time. Not to mention wrong.

Her cell phone rang. *Oh, please let it be him!*

She dug her phone out of her purse to hear Elaine from the women's Bible study group. "No study today, kiddo. It's a snow day."

"No surprises there." Shaina swallowed her disappointment that it wasn't Jack. She'd forgotten all about today's study anyway.

"Yep, stay in," Elaine continued. "Bake cookies, make hot chocolate for the kids, and only go out to build a snowman in the backyard. If you can get this fluffy stuff to stick. Too bad really. We were just getting to the good part in the Book of Job, but we'll start up again in January."

She kept the fact to herself that she and the kids weren't in the house but out on the freeway, and injected a smile into her voice. "There's a good part in Job, Elaine? Shocking. I know that I haven't read that far yet, what with Job's family being wiped off the face of the earth, losing all his worldly possessions, and painful boils covering his entire body. Forgive me, but in my opinion Job doesn't have the makings of a feel-good movie."

Elaine's laughter peeled. "Don't forget the well-meaning friends, their unwanted advice, and his nagging, bitter, acid-tongued wife who only spoke to tear her husband down."

Shaina's throat thickened. This very morning she hadn't just made a dumb decision: she'd been the acid-tongued wife.

Her friend took a breath. "Seriously, I used to think that about the Book of Job. Oh my...talk...about...depressing...with a capital D. Then I read the parts where God starts to talk." Elaine's sigh came through the phone. "Doesn't it give you goose bumps when God starts to speak?"

"Uh huh." She couldn't have answered if Elaine had asked her a direct question. Not after the way she'd shouted at Jack that she'd wanted a December wedding because she wanted him to know how much she loved him before he'd shipped out to Iraq. Loved him! Yet today, with coldness like icicles dripping from her, she'd sent him off to work—work that included rifles and ammunition just as dangerous as combat. She'd been ready to steal away with the kids for a few days. Her tight throat grew painful. This was no way for a wife to act.

Elaine hung up with warm effervescence, no doubt to phone the rest of the group.

Shaina tucked her phone away and sat back, unable to move. Falling snow drew her gaze. With her words this morning she'd cemented Jack's fear that he'd never measure up in her parents' eyes. By closing their bedroom door on him, she'd belittled him. As she reached for a tissue, she caught Zoey staring at her in the rearview mirror. Her daughter's blue eyes were as round as saucers, as if at eighteen months she knew how silly her mama had acted.

Her little boy undid himself from his car seat and reached over to pat Shaina on the shoulder while she blew her nose. "Mama, why are you sad?"

She gulped back the desire to fully weep. "Because, sunshine, I hurt Daddy's feeling this morning."

"Can't you say sorry?"

She nodded through fresh tears. "Yep." She reached for the phone, but pulled her hand back. Words weren't enough. She wanted to wrap her arms around her husband and tell him that she loved him with all her heart. That the affluent lifestyle she'd grown up with could never compare to the life she shared with him. Their marriage was the real thing—the real prize.

She swung around to face Scottie. "How about we go up to Daddy's work, surprise him for his lunch break?"

"Yay!" Scottie did his favorite Ninja moves in spite of being trapped in the Jeep. He never needed convincing to go up to the Department of Transportation work yard.

She checked the time. They could be there soon if only the roads weren't blockaded in that direction too. But she knew this area like the back of her hand. She'd skied here as a kid, and this was where she'd met Jack. This was their mountain.

Her fingers drummed the steering wheel. There was that back road up to the camp. It would be safe enough. She knew which areas to avoid since Jack wasn't triggering slides near here.

Out of sight of the traffic controllers, she drove her Jeep Wrangler on to the shoulder of the road. If they saw her they'd stop her for sure. The driver of the car in front glared at her. Somewhat embarrassed, she ignored him. Most of these travelers had no idea this rough opening in the trees led to a fairly good forestry road.

Her winter tires grabbed the snow, and the Jeep made good headway through the woods. Snow draped the evergreen boughs, while in the backseat the kids chattered. Dressed in their snowsuits, toques, boots, scarves, and mittens, they had the same rotund shape as well-dressed snowmen.

Zoey knew a smattering of words, but hung on to everything Scottie said, as if she considered his commentary with all judiciousness. She adored her big brother, and he basked in that adoration. But his one-sided conversation on Ninjas possibly repelling down the mountainside and attacking their vehicle grew boring after a while. Soon Scottie was asking to stop for something to drink.

Waving her hands encased in scarlet mittens, Zoey added her own request in a jumble of words which Scottie translated. "She wants a coffee break, Mama."

"It won't be much longer, kids. Daddy's camp is about two miles aw—"

Her words were cut off by the muffled echo of a rifle shot.

The sensation of ice trickled down her spine. Dear God, surely she wasn't in the area that Jack was actually working!

The snow on each side of the Jeep was a foot deep, nothing the vehicle couldn't handle. Still, she craned her neck to stare out and upward through the windshield.

At the first sign of the white cloud wafting over the treetops, her heart and soul froze. Sickening knowledge filled her mind with cold clarity. It was happening.

Any second now.

Stay in the car. Stay in the car.

The snow landed on the vehicle's hard top and from the front, engulfing them in a heartbeat. Cutting off all light. Something slammed into her face. She couldn't breathe.

The Jeep rocked. Then came to a solid stop. Her befuddled mind took in Zoey's screeching, Scottie whimpering, "Mama?" and the pain in her face.

The airbag deflated and she could breathe. That was what had punched her in the face. "It's all right, babies, we're going to be okay—don't be scared." Thank God they'd remained upright on the road, and the avalanche hadn't sent them careening down the mountainside.

She wiped a smear of blood from her nose and reached behind to check the kids. Their car seats had kept them safe. They seemed fine, but Zoey cried out, "Dadda! Dadda!"

Had the slide fully ended? She prayed it had. Suffocation was the major reason for death during an avalanche. Her brain clicked into the list of procedures Jack had gone over with her time and again. Conserve air and energy. Don't jeopardize your air pocket.

The remaining air inside the closed Jeep would keep them alive for a while. But how deeply were they buried? They were now at the mercy of others to rescue them.

Was anyone nearby? Don't shout. Shouting wastes your air supply. There was nothing she could do but wait. Stay calm, and wait. And start honking the horn.

But when she started pushing on the horn, Zoey let out another howl, and Scottie began to sniffle too. She reached behind to touch their legs. "It's okay, my sweeties. Don't you think this is funny, Mama honking the horn?"

She faced the windshield again. *Come on Shaina, think.* Between her and Jack they kept both vehicles equipped for any situation. The emergency kit contained shovels and probes as well as food, water, blankets, and so much more. There had to be something else she could do.

Setting her face in a smile, she turned around to the kids. It would be easier to unhook Scottie from his car seat and give him the flashlight. With her own heart thumping she watched him climb into the back to retrieve the items she needed.

Her phone couldn't get a signal where they were currently stranded. She'd been an idiot to take such a risk by going off-road, but there was a cabin not far from here. It sat on a rise overlooking this low spot where the snow had filled. She might get a signal there. That was, if she could dig her way out. Her stomach turned to ice. Her worst nightmare had come to pass, and she knew the statistics only too well. Few avalanche victims could dig their way out. But she had to try.

For good measure she switched places with Scottie, putting him in the front seat to play with the horn. He could honk it as much as he liked.

"I know you missed coffee break with Daddy." She worked hard to produce a soothing tone. "But here's your favorite apple juice—just a box to share between the two of you for now—and a granola bar." The kids settled down with their snack as if they were out on any of the picnics she and Jack had taken them, while her heart battered against her chest.

It was then she noticed that the darkness wasn't quite as dark as she'd first thought. She switched off the flashlight. A grayish light filtered through from above. *Oh, Lord, please let this mean we're not buried deep.*

Her eye landed on the snowshoes sticking up in the back muddle of items that Scottie had disturbed. If she could get out of the Jeep....

It was Jack who'd introduced her to snowshoeing. Coming from a family of skiers she at first thought his interest in that old-fashioned form of travel as weird. Grudgingly she came to admit that snowshoeing was quaint. Now she wanted to kiss him for teaching her how to walk in them, and for insisting they stay in her Jeep all winter. There was even a small pair for Scottie. If she could get them out, she would carry Zoey.

She peered again at the snow through the window. It was pressed hard as cement against the left side of the vehicle. But on the right side there were large scattered air pockets. It was much lighter here too. In fact...yes...a beam of light intensified. The sun must have broken through the morning cloud. It shone bluish through the looser snow. It had to be only a foot or so deep. Only a foot, yet twelve inches of snow was enough to snuff out a life. Still, it was a chance.

Zoey would be safer on the left side of the car in Scottie's car seat. Her little boy would be fine in the driver's seat, pressing repeatedly on the horn. She reached across to the steering column, turned the key to start the battery only, and lowered the automatic back right window, praying she was making the right decision and that the Jeep would not fill with snow.

Some of the snow plopped into the backseat, cold and wet, but her nerves sang with relief. The snow remained packed outside the vehicle, and the first of the air pockets was surely within easy reach.

She got through the window and began to shove the snow aside into the larger pocket of air. It was much less compact than she'd feared. With the small shovel she worked her way through the first pocket, and on to the next. Sunlight glittered through a layer of snow above her, like the ceiling of a ballroom. She strained, reaching upward, pressing with her feet to push through when a load of snow landed on her face, sucking the air from her nose and mouth. Suffocating her.

In her panic, she dropped the shovel. It took a heart-stopping moment for her fingers to find it again, and she began to flail with her arms. As if swimming, she burst through the last few inches of snow and gasped for breath.

Her woolen toque and hair were soaked by the time she poked her head completely up through the opening. Her eyes blinked in the blazing sunlight. The depth covering this side of the vehicle was as she'd surmised. Still, they could have died in that depth. But the other side of the Jeep was buried in as much as three feet.

In a shaking voice she called down to the kids. "I made it. Coming back for you."

It was easier to dig her way down to them. By the time she widened the opening, Scottie released Zoey from the car seat, and helped her scramble up and out to Shaina's waiting arms. With a kiss and a hug for each of them, she returned to the car to bring up the snowshoes and emergency gear.

Her limbs shook as much as her voice did, but she'd get her babies to safety now.

The radio crackled with a message as Jack and his crew climbed into the truck for the return trip to the depot. One of the crew below practically yelled, "We've got a problem. A horn's sounding off. Coming from the co-ordinates at the outer edges of the slide."

Jack's insides twisted. That area was a summer spot with a few cabins. At least from their last confirmation it was supposed to be vacant and cordoned off. To make matters worse, that last explosion he'd fired an hour ago had unsettled more snow than he'd liked, creating a wider slide.

A few minutes later, the news came through the radio that the horn had stopped. An emergency helicopter had lifted off and was on its way. Jack could hardly breathe. Who had slipped through their safety net? How had they got trapped inside the kill zone? He'd never forgive himself if he'd inadvertently caused someone's death.

Shaina's snowshoes crunched on top of the snow. Scottie was a brave little man, keeping up to her strides while she carried Zoey through the forest. Rounding the mountain to the leeward side, they finally came upon the cabin. Its logs the color of warm gingerbread almost disappeared in the nearly all-white surroundings. The summer abode sparkled in the noon sun. With the sky above a cerulean blue, and holly bushes adding a dash of evergreen and crimson, the place looked like a Christmas card.

Still though, snow brought the ground up level with the front porch. The slide had added a fresh layer, half burying the front door.

Shaina carried the emergency kit on her back, and Scottie the sack of juice boxes and granola bars. "Please forgive me for this," she said to the absent owners as she used her shovel to break the front door lock. "I'll pay for it later," she said to the kids as they entered the cabin.

The little ones heaved sighs as laden as hers when she slumped down on a worn corduroy couch in the middle of the main room. From down here she could see a few beds up in the loft. The walls inside this cabin were the same reddish cedar logs as outside and rose up to the roof that had remained intact during the slide. Smooth stones from the frozen river outside framed a deep and welcome fireplace.

Snow melted from their boots to dribble on an old-fashioned rag rug. Zoey looked around her while Scottie dangled his feet as he cuddled next to Shaina. "Nice place, Mama. We'll be safe from Ninjas here."

"Dadda," Zoey added, plus another word Shaina couldn't make out. It still sounded like sled.

She slapped her hands to her knees and stood. "What we need, guys, is a fire to warm up, some more juice and granola bars. And someone will come soon. Maybe even Daddy."

She still couldn't get a signal with her phone, and pushed her damp hair back from her face. What on earth would Jack say when he did see them? He was sure to be fuming. Her heart sank. Or worse still, what if he had come home late tonight and found them gone? With those terrible things she'd said this morning, she wanted to wash her mouth out with snow.

The owners had winterized the place, plastic over the windows, covers over the furniture, as well as containers of crystals to soak up dampness, but they'd left stacks of firewood, canned goods in the rudimentary kitchen, and cooking utensils. She could get a fire going and prepare a meal until help arrived.

As she moved toward the kitchen the sound of a helicopter's blades whirred nearby. She and the kids ran outside as the chopper hovered over the cabin, sending evergreens into a whipped frenzy. There was no room in the dense forest for the aircraft to land, but a man leaned out and spoke through a bullhorn. "Are you okay?"

She gave him the thumbs up.

He peered through his binoculars. "Shaina Burke, is that you? And the kids? Were you honking that horn?"

Again she gave him the thumbs up, and the man returned the affirming gesture. "We'll send people in by foot to bring you out. You need anything?"

She shook her head, and satisfied with her answer the helicopter moved off. Oh brother, Jack was really going to be mad. The cost of that emergency flight was going to eat up their next five years' of anniversary dates in fancy hotels. And this time, there was no one to blame but her.

The scuttlebutt filtered through the radios to all crews that it was Jack Burke's wife and kids stranded but safe in a cabin near the edge of the slide.

Stan insisted on remaining behind at the depot after Jack got the news. "I had a feeling this morning when we talked that I'd messed up on the dates. I'm sorry, Jack. You should have had this day off with your wife for your anniversary. And now they're stuck. Safe, but stuck. Go on now, and I'll cover things back here. If there's anything you need, just radio. We'll get a team of people in tomorrow to bring you all out."

According to another avalanche crew, the snow in the vicinity where Shaina had taken shelter was steady, but not steady enough for vehicles or snowmobiles. He'd have to hike in part of the way.

Between the guys at the depot and the chopper pilot, they loaded Jack's backpack with provisions and treats. The pilot set down in a wide open meadow a couple of miles from the small clearing Shaina had gone to. By the time Jack snow-shoed it to the cabin, the sun shone at an angle through the glistening trees.

As he approached the cabin, the warming temperature thrust up a mist so that the snow particles shimmered in the air like the gold ribbons on Shaina's Christmas tree at home.

He stopped and a chuckle escaped.

Someone—as if he didn't know who—had adorned the snow-covered porch with green fir boughs and red holly berries. Leading from the cabin a series of footprints trampled the snow. One set had been made by a narrow adult foot, another set much smaller, and another made by very tiny boots. The tracks swirled in concentric circles as if made by a bunch of tipsy sailors. But in the center of that maze of footprints sat a snowman of sorts. Scottie's green toque, Shaina's blue scarf, and Zoey's red mittens completed the snowman's outfit.

A wine-like fragrance of burning apple wood smoke trailed from the chimney. When his gaze landed on the front door of the cabin, there stood his beautiful wife and children. God had carved this haven out of an avalanche to keep his family safe. And God who'd created these mountains would do what Jack couldn't do— He'd help him keep his marriage to Shaina solid and happy.

No words transpired between her and Jack when he first came into the cabin. Shaina hung back against the wall. She couldn't meet Jack's eyes. Between Scottie and Zoey she and her husband couldn't have squeezed a word in anyway. Their son described the avalanche in full detail with all accompanying sound effects and full Ninja body moves to heighten the effect. Zoey added a few of her own sounds, but mostly her speech was a lisping jigsaw puzzle of half-formed clauses.

Finally, Shaina lifted her eyes to Jack's. Over the hubbub, he looked down at her, deep lines between his brows. She couldn't sustain his gaze and looked away. He had every right to be angry.

Scottie, still in full newscaster mode, clung to his father's leg, and Jack cupped the back of the boy's head. With his other arm, Jack lifted Zoey up to his chest. The next thing Shaina knew, his hand captured hers and drew her into a four-person embrace.

As the children chattered like chickadees looking for suet and seeds on the snow, she felt Jack's lips on her forehead and his sigh melding with hers. "Thank God you're safe," he said against her hair.

Later, after Jack heard her version of the avalanche, he kissed the tip of her aching nose that still hurt from the airbag. He then helped her make the cabin warmer for the night ahead, while the kids lay down for a long overdue nap—more like a temporary coma from today's excitement.

Though death had brushed by close today, the prosaic aspects of life continued. There was dinner to be made. Jack's backpack contained a canned ham and carton of macaroni and cheese, and she'd purloined a can of peas and peaches from the cabin's pantry. As she set out these items, she listened to Jack moving around in the shed outside.

She should be happy. She and Jack had a good marriage, but what Elaine said in that early phone call tapped at her mind. It felt so long ago, yet it was still only ten years since she'd got married on this ninth day before Christmas. And she'd yet to tell Jack about the hotel reservation—and if she were honest, that she wanted more from their marriage.

She'd seen a Bible on the bookshelf earlier, and now found the Book of Job and flipped through its pages. Where was that place in the story that excited Elaine so much? Shaina too wanted to hear God speaking.

Then in the last few chapters she found, "Have you entered the storehouses of the snow or seen the storehouses of hail…?" A little bit further, "From whose womb comes the ice? Who gives birth to the frost from the heavens when the waters become hard as stone…?"

God had spoken to her earlier, through Elaine and then through a very controlled avalanche triggered by her husband. Yes, there was much to be thankful for. But she'd been taking Jack and their marriage for granted, just like she'd been taking God for granted. She wanted more from God too. To hear His voice on a regular basis, to involve Him in every aspect of her life.

Dinner could wait. Not bothering with her wet ski jacket, she wrapped a woolen afghan around her shoulders and went out to the shed in search of her husband. The sound of tinkering on metal renewed the sense of security Jack always gave her. As usual he was building or repairing something.

He looked up when she entered. "Hey, Angel." She sat next to him at a bench where he hammered out a long, one-inch strip of metal. He slanted a look her way. "I'm sorry, Shaina, for the dumb things I said this morning. I should never have insulted you by insinuating you were ashamed of me. You are so far above that sort of nonsense."

"You better believe it. But I've got to apologize for being a spoiled brat this morning. The way I spoke to you was so full of acid; the memory of it makes me cringe."

He didn't answer right away, but focused on shaping that piece of metal. When he did speak, his words came out soft as powder. "Avalanches always happen to other people."

She touched his arm. "So do unhappy marriages."

The metal landed with a clink on the workbench as he set it down. His head sank to his chest. "Not us—surely that would never happen to us."

"We may think we're far from that, Jack, but today I had a glimpse of what could happen if we're not careful."

"Yeah, me too. Even though we both know the risks, one wrong decision and it could happen to us."

The floor drew her gaze. "And I have a confession. I had a reservation for us at the hotel where we spent our honeymoon."

His face softened. "So that's what that envelope was." He grinned at her. "I was so scared…well, never mind. We can still go even a day late."

"That's what I want to do too. But, Jack…" She could barely lift her gaze to his. "I have more to confess. I was on my way there this morning…with the kids." Tears stung the backs of her eyes. "I'm so sorry. I got carried away. I never want to go anywhere like that without you."

He reached to enfold her in a tight hug. "It's all right, Angel. Just know that you and the kids mean everything to me. I can't live without you. And I'll make whatever changes you want."

She spoke against the warm flannel of his shirt, and heard his heartbeat. "I don't want much to change. All I want is to spend more time with you. Really listen to each other."

"Let's start right away then. How about we go to Seattle day after tomorrow? Stan and Louise offered to babysit. You and I, skiing, then dinner and dancing."

Ecstatic tears weren't far off, but she held them back with a smile. "Sounds good, but let's skip the dancing. I'd like to just hold hands and talk long into the night."

The seriousness melted from his face, and his lopsided grin shot a fizzle of electricity through her. "As for this evening, I can't offer you any elegant fare, Mrs. Burke, but I'm willing to start on the romantic stuff."

Heat shot down to her toes, warmer than several pairs of Jack's socks. She tipped her face upwards to within an inch of his, her voice breathless. "What do you suggest? Because in all honesty, Jack, all I want is you, no matter how plain the establishment might be."

His eyes widened and his breath fanned her hair. "I was thinking…tonight when the kids are asleep, you and me curl up in those moth-eaten sleeping bags with broken zippers that I found. I called ahead to the Maître d' and reserved a spot for us directly in front of a roaring hot fireplace."

"Promise?" She placed her lips against his.

His answer brushed her mouth, then deepened, taking her back to those kisses they'd shared during their engagement and on their wedding night, until Zoey's cry broke the silence. They drew apart reluctantly and smiled the same bemused smile.

Jack held her loosely. "Speaking of promises, I have another one to keep."

She sent a questioning glance to the bench where he lifted that long strip of metal. It was some kind of casing off a crate.

"Go on inside, Angel. Warm up the hot chocolate and get the kids dressed. I'll meet you all outside in twenty minutes."

"Okay, lover."

His answering smile sent her tummy into warm somersaults thinking of later tonight, just her and her husband and his promise to her alone.

In the cabin she told the kids about the surprise, and Scottie did his Ninja dance. Ripples of anticipation zipped through Shaina's bloodstream too, thinking of the fun they'd have as a family.

Only Zoey seemed to take the mystery in her stride. Fully dressed in her snowsuit, she turned to her brother with her spare set of mittens dangling from her sleeves. A stream of consonants and vowels sputtered from her mouth. The flush on her cheeks added to the impression that she insinuated Scottie should know very well what the mystery was all about.

Shaina and the kids rushed out of the cabin just as Jack came out of the shed. She slipped into her husband's strong embrace and walked at his side. She was blessed to have such a man.

He'd tied a set of old skis together with leather straps, creating a flat base. A wooden crate sat on top of that, and on the bottom of the skis he'd attached those long strips of metal. In his hand he held a rope attached to the front of the homemade contraption.

First he lifted Scottie into the crate and then Zoey into the space between Scottie's legs. Their little girl looked up at Jack, her eyes crinkling with smiles as she clapped her hands encased in red mittens.

As they walked, together pulling their children in a home-made sled, her husband slipped his hand beneath her ski jacket and caressed her about the waist. Above them, an early evening moon waned, lending a shade of blue to the snow-covered peaks of Steven's Pass. On those steep cliffs, the snow sparkled like white sand in the moonlight.

An Unexpected Glory

Marcia Lee Laycock

The call came early in the morning. I sat in stunned silence as Linda told me we would have to cancel our main fund-raiser that was scheduled to happen that night, eight days before Christmas.

"But we can't cancel now! We've sold over three hundred tickets. Even the mayor is coming."

"I'm really sorry, Pastor Steve; there's nothing we can do. Two kids have come down with measles and some of the adults are showing symptoms. We're quarantined."

"Measles? I didn't think that existed anymore."

"Apparently it's trying for a comeback."

"What about the orchestra? Can we at least still get the orchestra to come?"

"I'm sorry, no. The orchestra was with us for our last rehearsal. The public health people have quarantined us all until the incubation period is over."

I groaned into the phone. *God, this can't be happening.*

"I'm truly sorry," Linda said again, "but I'm sure everything will be on track for next year."

Next year? And what about this year? What about tonight?

"Thank you for letting me know." I knew my voice sounded morose but I couldn't keep my despair from showing. I hung up and put my head in my hands. I'd been running New Life Shelter for Men for the past ten years and we'd always had tremendous success with the Christmas pageant. Five churches banded together to perform a pageant that was a spectacle to behold. It was the highlight of the Christmas season for the whole city. Everyone expected it to be on the eighth day before Christmas. Everyone expected it to be amazing. It was also our main fundraiser. Without the pageant we would be in danger of having to close our doors.

"Trouble, boss?"

I lifted my head to see Stanley standing in the doorway, his shaggy red head cocked to one side.

"I'm afraid so, Stanley. Big trouble."

He stepped closer. "What's up?"

"We have to cancel the pageant."

"What? We can't. It's tonight. And we've sold every ticket."

I shook my head. "Linda Thomas just called. A bunch of their kids have measles. Everyone else is under quarantine. The orchestra from Grace Community too." I held out my hands, palms up. "We have nothing."

Stanley slumped into the chair opposite my desk. He stared at his scuffed work boots for a while. Then he straightened and his head came up. "Not true, boss," he said.

I frowned.

"We've got everything we need right here. The residents. Yup, yup. The residents can do it."

I shook my head. "Stanley ..."

He stood up, his shaggy head nodding. "Most of them have seen it a gazillion times. They have the lines in their heads. Yup. Yup. All we have to do is get them going."

I grinned at my unflappable assistant. Stanley had once been a resident here, a man down on his luck, trying to find the solution to his pain in a bottle of cheap wine. He'd started coming for the free meals, started listening to the messages I preached about the love of Jesus, and slowly began a long road to recovery. He'd been my right-hand man for five years, and aside from a mildly annoying habit of saying "yup, yup" a lot, he was always a welcome help. I couldn't run the place without him. He stood before me now with such hope in his eyes I almost believed what he suggested was possible. But I shook my head.

"Maybe if we had a month, or two ... but it's supposed to happen tonight, Stanley. There's no way we can pull this together in one day."

Stanley's eyes clouded for a minute. "We have to, boss. We have to."

He was right. The alternative was unthinkable. My head sank into my hands again. Stanley chuckled, making my head jerk up.

"We've seen miracles here before. Maybe this is just another opportunity for God to show us how much He loves us. You always say that's what He's all about, right?"

I couldn't help but grin at him again. Then faces started flowing through my head, as though they were stored on some kind of mental database. The faces of all the men who depended on us to feed them and give them a warm bed and a chance to get their lives back. Some of the faces started to appear with headdresses on them ... the three wise men, Herod and Joseph. Charlie One-note appeared with a white halo around him. I let out a loud guffaw at that. *Really, Lord? Really?*

Stanley was leaning toward me, his eyebrows raised expectantly.

I took a deep breath and glanced at the clock on the wall. 7:30. Breakfast would be served in half an hour.

"We'll have to recruit them at breakfast," I said.

Stanley leaped in the air and clapped his hands together. "How many?"

I went down the list of characters in my mind. "Ten at least." I frowned. "Do you think we can find ten able and willing to do it?"

"Let's go find out." He turned for the door.

"Stanley." He turned back to me.

"Like you said, this is going to take a miracle. So maybe we should start with prayer."

"Yup, yup. You got it, boss. You pray and I'll recruit." He strode through the door as though he were going on stage himself. Another face suddenly appeared in my mind with Joseph's striped towel around his head. I laughed out loud again, then knelt beside my desk to pray.

I joined Stanley in the dining hall a few minutes later. He waved a sheet of paper at me.

"Fifteen names so far," he said. The gleam in his eyes was infectious.

"Really?" I scanned the list.

"Well, I sort of told them if they signed up they could stay inside all day. They'd have to anyways, right? To rehearse?"

I sighed. One of our strict rules was that the men had to leave right after breakfast to look for work in the community. They were allowed back in for the noon meal but had to leave again until five in the evening. On cold days like this they usually grumbled about having to leave and I usually felt guilty, but it was the rule. But not today.

"Right," I said. "It's going to take all day to get them organized." *Not to mention a major miracle.*

"Milly said she'd check on the costumes."

Milly was our kitchen supervisor, a sixty-something woman whose head barely reached to my shoulders but who had the energy of the Energizer Bunny. I knew I could count on her. I tossed up a prayer that there would be no snag with the costumes. They were professionally made by a local theatre company and one of the big attractions of the performance. We had to have the costumes.

I glanced again at the list Stanley had given me. I guess I was frowning because he clapped me on the back like a football coach.

"It's going to be grand, boss. You'll see."

I watched the men lining up for their breakfast. Most of them were dressed in grubby clothes; some looked like they were living in a perpetual state of hang-over. A few wore stocking caps on their heads, and I knew it was to hide the stringy hair underneath. Maybe grand wasn't the right word, but I began to feel that maybe we could pull it off. I just hoped the people attending wouldn't be so disappointed at not getting the usual performance that their generosity would be affected. We needed that offering desperately.

I took a deep breath and went into the kitchen. Milly was busy keeping her volunteers moving, but I stepped up behind her. "Can you check on the costumes as soon as breakfast is over, Milly?"

She tossed me a look over her shoulder that said go away and don't bug me, but then she smiled and nodded. "Just don't ask me to be Mary."

Mary! Oh Lord. Where were we going to find a Mary? I guess I had a pleading look in my eyes because Milly turned to face me and spread her arms. "Seriously, Pastor Steve, you weren't thinking..."

I shook my head. "No. Truth is, I wasn't thinking at all. I have no idea what to do about a Mary."

"I'll get on the phone and call a couple of my volunteers. I'm sure I can find someone."

I let out a sigh and nodded. "Let me know as soon as you do."

I returned to my office and started searching on the computer for Christmas pageant scripts. There were a lot of them, and it took me a while to find something I thought might work. Something really simple. I'd just finished printing off copies when Stanley showed up in the doorway again.

"Any idea where the backdrop is, boss?"

"Backdrop? You mean the blue curtain?"

"Yeah. I can't seem to find it."

I frowned. "Should be in a bag in the back storage room."

Stanley shook his head. "Nope. Looked there."

"Maybe it got put under the stage?" We both headed for the gymnasium where the performance would be held. Our building had once been a school. The gym was still full of cots and sleeping mats, but tonight it would be transformed. At least, I hoped it would. The curtain we were looking for had been used for several years. It was huge and heavy, a dark blue velvet that made an elegant backdrop for the pageant. Stanley opened the storage area under the stage and crawled in with a flashlight. I waited impatiently.

"Got it!" he hollered, then exited the compartment backwards, bent over and dragging the huge drapery.

I frowned again. It should have been folded carefully, wrapped in plastic and stored in a better place. As Stanley dragged it out after him I groaned. It was covered in dust and, worse, full of holes.

Stanley poked his finger through one of them. "Looks like the mice got at it." He pulled at the material, spreading it out on the floor. "But it's not too bad. We can mend it."

"Mend it? When are we going to get time to mend it?" I stared at the curtain. My optimism was hitting bottom again.

Stanley chewed his lip. Then his head snapped up. "Stars!" he said.

"Stars?"

"Yup, yup. We can get some of the guys cutting out cardboard stars and covering them with tinfoil. Yup, yup. Then we just attach them over the holes."

I sighed and started to fold the curtain. "Okay, Stanley. Go recruit some star cutters."

He grinned and strode off with purpose in his step. I hefted the curtain and dragged it up onto the stage. Tinfoil stars. Well, maybe it would work but, again, it wouldn't be anything like what the audience was expecting. A nervous flip in my stomach made me say another prayer. It was a short one. *Lord, please help.*

Milly was on the phone when I got back to the office.

"It's okay," she was saying, "I understand. Yes, see you on Monday."

She hung up and sighed. "Not having much luck with a Mary, Pastor Steve. I'm down to my last female volunteer." She picked up the phone again. "Pray," she said.

I did, earnestly, but the answer was no. Milly shook her head. "I can't believe I can't find a single person to do this."

"Keep trying, Mill. We have to find someone, and soon. Did you call the theatre about the costumes?"

Milly nodded as she picked up the phone again. "They're on their way over."

Finally, a bit of good news.

I noticed Reg Dawson, our accountant, sitting at his tiny desk in the corner, hunched over a litter of papers. He jumped when I put my hand on his shoulder.

"How's it going, Reg?"

He sighed and shook his head. "We're in a bad way, Pastor Steve. The income from the tickets doesn't quite cover our overdraft. We're going to need a really good offering this year."

I nodded and said another prayer.

Stanley poked his head in. "We're set to go, boss. Everyone's in the gym."

I asked Reg to give me a report on the offering right after the performance and scooped up the copies of the script.

I stopped in the doorway and surveyed our cast. Most of them were middle-aged or older men, and most of them very scruffy. Some of them smelled like a brewery. I sighed. Charlie One-note was there with his wooden recorder in hand. There was another man I didn't know slouched by the stage. He was tall and extremely thin, his dreadlocks matted under a baseball cap. He was holding a battered saxophone. Stanley winked at me, took the scripts from my hands, and gave them out. He chose four men, got them on the stage, and arranged for the first scene: the wise men visit Herod.

Herod had to hold the script so close it almost touched his nose. "Lost my glasses," he told Stanley.

I made a mental note to find him some reading glasses. One of the wise men insisted on squatting on the floor, another read his script so softly I couldn't hear a word, and the third kept missing his cue, even with the script in front of him. I prayed that short prayer again.

Stanley had them run through their scene several times, then called the shepherds and angels to the stage.

Charlie One-note had a look on his face I knew well: don't try to tell me what to do. Great. This was going to go well.

"Okay, Charlie," Stanley said, "this is where you play 'Hark the Herald Angels.'"

"Haven't played 'You Are My Sunshine' yet," Charlie said.

"Um, well, maybe you can play that some other time. It doesn't really fit in a Christmas pageant."

"Sure it does. Won't play nothin' less I can play that first."

Stanley sighed and looked at me. I shrugged.

"Okay, Charlie. 'You Are My Sunshine,' then 'Hark the Herald Angels.' You know it, right?"

"Course I do." He raised the recorder to his lips. It was high-pitched and squeaked several times, but he got through both songs.

Stanley took Johnson by the arm. He was another regular, and I wasn't surprised to see him among the volunteers. He hated the cold and complained loudly about having to leave each morning. "Okay, Johnson," Stanley said. "You're the angel, so when the carol is over you step forward and say your lines."

Johnson nodded, took a purposeful step forward and read his lines perfectly, telling the shepherds their Messiah had been born and could be found in a stable in Bethlehem.

"Wonderful!" Stanley clapped his hands. "Okay, now you all go off, stage left."

Some of them went left, some went right. Stanley herded them together and off the stage, then asked someone to carry the manger up.

When it was in place Stanley looked at me. "We'll need some straw, boss."

"Right," I said, making another mental note. Reading glasses and straw. What could be easier?

Stanley called Joseph and the wise men up and then motioned me onto the stage. "We need a Mary," he said.

"Can't you?"

He grinned. "I'm the stage manager."

"Right," I mumbled and made my way onstage, crouched down by the manger, and made another mental note. Find the baby Jesus.

Stanley positioned the wise men. "Don't forget, you don't want your backs to the audience," he said. "Okay, Peter Jolly, you speak first."

Peter Jolly – I never did find out why he was always addressed by both names, or even if it was his real name, but everyone seemed to know that's what he was called. He was one of our regulars too, a man slowly getting his feet back under him. He'd gone into a bit of a tail spin recently, but seemed to be doing his best to get back on track. He hiccupped a couple of times, something he did when he had to talk for more than a minute or two, and stared at Stanley for what seemed like twice that.

"Maybe I'm not the right person...*hic*...to be a wise man," he said.

Stanley put an arm over his shoulder. "Yes you are. You're perfect for this role. Just read the lines good and loud, okay?"

Peter Jolly stared at his script for a while longer, hiccupped a couple more times, then looked up at the ceiling. The page started to shake in his hands. I held my breath and let it out all at once when he started to speak, his voice like a megaphone. I saw Stanley's eyes widen.

"Wow," he said. "Where'd that come from?"

Peter Jolly grinned. "Used to be a radio announcer." He lifted his chin and opened his mouth, the words booming out. "This is CRWB radio, coming to you from the heart of downtown Chicago."

Stanley laughed. "Amazing! See, I told you you'd be perfect."

Peter Jolly beamed. I sucked in my breath. It was the kind of look that was rarely seen around here. It was a look of pleasure, yes, but more, it was a look of hope. I let out my breath with another prayer. *Thank you, Lord. Thank you.* That single moment had given me hope too.

The rehearsal continued until lunch, and by the time Milly rang the gong everyone was ready for a break. Stanley sat across from me and dove into his stew with relish.

"So, what do you think, boss?"

"I think this was a good idea, Stan."

He put another scoop into his mouth and nodded. "Yup, yup."

I just hope everyone else thinks so too. Then something occurred to me. "Do you think the guys can memorize their lines? Or should we just let them read from the script?"

"Read?" Stanley blinked. "No way. They can do it. Yup, yup. We'll get right back at it after lunch."

I took a deep breath and picked up my sandwich. The lines they each had to say weren't long or complicated. Maybe ... "Okay, Stanley," I agreed. "You're the stage manager."

He grinned. I swallowed my sandwich in a few hasty bites and headed for a nearby pharmacy. Goal number one, reading glasses. The straw was going to be a little more difficult to find, but I had an idea.

The streets looked refreshingly clean after a newly-fallen snow. I noticed a couple of our regulars loitering in front of the coffee shop across the street, their shoulders hunched against the cold. I knew it was a favorite place to pan-handle. If they were lucky someone might even invite them to go in for a cup of coffee. I said a short prayer for them and reached for the door of the pharmacy. And stopped dead. The poster was hard to miss, placed in a prominent spot. It showed a picture of last year's pageant, the orchestra prominent in the front, the huge choir robed and beaming in the back, the rest of the cast resplendent in their costumes. I groaned. That's what everyone would be expecting when they walked in the doors of our converted gym. I got that flutter in my stomach again. *Lord, please help.*

The reading glasses did the trick, and Herod was grateful. Stanley had recruited some of Milly's volunteers to help everyone learn their lines. Second rehearsal was due to start in one hour. I headed for my office and looked up the number for the city zoo. Surely they could spare a bale of hay or two.

Or not. Seems there was a shortage of hay in the city at the moment. Maybe an old blanket would do. Maybe I could find a yellow one. As I stood up to go in search of something that might work, Milly burst in.

"Have the costumes arrived?"

I frowned. "Haven't seen them yet."

She frowned too. "They should have been here a couple of hours ago." She whirled around. "I'll call the theatre again."

I headed for the storage area, remembering I still needed to find the plaster baby Jesus as well as a yellow blanket. After pawing through the shelves of bedding, the best I could come up with was a ragged green blanket. I figured the ragged edges would simulate the look of straw, even if it wasn't yellow. But my search for the baby Jesus turned up nothing. Maybe it was under the stage. I grabbed a flashlight and headed back to the gym. As I got to the door I heard loud voices. Two of our residents were nose to nose.

"The gold is mine! I had it first!"

"So what? You ain't got no first dibs."

Stanley put his hand on one man's arm. "C'mon, Ben, it's okay. I'll see if I can find some more gold foil for you. How about cutting out another cardboard star? We still need a few more."

Ben grumbled and pulled away but sat down and dragged a piece of cardboard toward him. I caught Stanley's eye as he puffed out his cheeks and let his breath out. He headed toward me, but another ruckus broke out. It seemed they were sharing the scissors and glue, and someone was getting impatient. Stanley rolled his eyes and turned back to the table.

I pulled open the door to the storage area under the stage and crawled in, flicking the flashlight on as I went. There wasn't much under there. A few old chairs, a few boxes. I hauled the boxes out and pawed through them. No baby Jesus. I looked in the next bin, but the result was the same. Where could it be? I was standing there scratching my head when Milly arrived.

"We've got another problem, Pastor Steve," she said.

"What now?"

The theatre company thought the costumes were supposed to go to their sister company down south. They were put on a bus this morning.

I groaned. "Is there any way they can get them back?"

Milly shrugged. "Don't know. The manager said he'd try, but I wouldn't count on it.

I took a deep breath. "Okay. See if you can round up some bath robes and T-towels."

Milly nodded and whirled around. "Way ahead of you."

"Milly?"

She turned back to me.

"Any idea where the baby Jesus might be?"

"Wha ... oh, you mean the plaster one they used last year?"

I nodded. "I've looked everywhere I can think of."

Milly shrugged. "Sorry, no idea."

Another argument erupted from the men cutting out stars. I stood there with the ragged blanket in my hand and watched Stanley get them back on task. *God bless the man*, I thought. I made my way on stage and draped the blanket over the manger. It didn't look anything like straw but it would have to do. I joined Stanley and his star cutters just as they were pulling the huge drapery across the table.

"Okay," Stanley said, "Now all we have to do is sew the stars over the holes."

He handed out needles and thread and tried to demonstrate what he wanted them to do. A man I'd never seen before stood up and put a hand on Stanley's arm.

"You'll want small stitches," he said, "so they won't be visible from the audience." He took the needle from Stanley's hand and bent over the curtain. "Like this, see?"

Stanley leaned in. "Perfect!" he exclaimed.

The man grinned. "Used to be a tailor." He glanced around at the others. "Just leave me with one or two of these guys and I'll get it done for you."

Stanley heaved a sigh and nodded. He named two of the men and told the others to get ready for the next rehearsal. They shuffled off to retrieve their scripts.

I asked Stanley if he knew where the baby Jesus might be, but he had no idea either. "Could we do it without it?"

I shook my head. "He's kind of the main attraction, Stanley."

"Oh, yeah, I guess." He scratched his head. "Maybe we could find a doll somewhere?"

I nodded, hoping they made big dolls these days. "Right. I'll have one more look around, then go see if I can buy one."

"Did Milly find a Mary yet?"

"Not yet. Improvise for now."

"Right," he said and grinned. "That's kinda the order of the day isn't it?"

I sighed, thinking again of the professional polished performance everyone would be expecting. Stanley must have read my mind because he clapped me on the shoulder.

"Don't worry, boss. It'll all come together in the end."

I smiled at the twinkle in his eyes, then went in search of the baby Jesus once more. As I pawed around in the storage room, the plaintive strains of a saxophone filled the building. I stopped to listen and quickly recognized the classic carol, "Silent Night." Maybe I was imagining it, but though it wasn't exactly sweet and clear, it was somehow perfect. It made me think Stanley might be right. And maybe the Lord did have a reason for all that was happening.

I was on my way to the office, thinking of calling the theatre company to check on the costumes and ask if maybe they had the baby Jesus, when Milly stopped me. A family had knocked on the front door, looking for a place for the night.

"I know we don't take in families, Pastor Steve, but I think maybe you should talk to these folks."

I was about to repeat what she already knew, but something in her eyes stopped me. I agreed and told her to bring them to the office. I was slumped in my chair when the knock came and Milly ushered them in. They were young, looked barely out of their teens, but they had a little boy, maybe three or so, and the woman, who said her name was Stacey, was holding a baby, fussing in her arms, that looked like it was less than a month old.

I opened my mouth to tell them we couldn't house them, but Milly's eyes were sparkling, her eyebrows arched with expectancy. I could almost read her mind – *Are you thinking what I'm thinking?*

I glanced at the young woman again. "You may be an answer to our prayers," I said.

Stacey quickly agreed to be part of the pageant, and her husband, Randy, agreed to watch the kids while she was on stage. We had our Mary. Now all we needed was a baby Jesus. I considered asking if we could use the baby too, but just then he started to cry. He had strong lungs. I decided not to push my luck, or rather, blessings.

"Put them in my apartment, Mill."

Milly smiled and led them out of the room.

I picked up the phone and finally got in touch with the prop director of the theatre company, but he had no idea what had happened to the baby Jesus.

"We left all the props there," he said. "Like we do every year."

I thanked him, hung up, and prayed that small prayer again. I was on my way out the door to find a store that sold dolls when Peter Jolly stopped me.

"Stanley said to get you, Pastor. He needs some help hanging the curtain."

I followed him back to the gym. The curtain was spread out on the stage, the tinfoil stars sewn over every hole.

Stanley scratched his head. "Uh, so, how do we get it up there?" He poked his finger toward the high ceiling. I followed his gaze.

"Our ladder won't do it." I sighed again. "We'll need another one. A tall one."

"Yup, yup," Stanley said.

Wondering how much it was going to cost, I spun on my heel. "I'll head over to Hector's."

I loved Hector's Hardware. It was in an old building with creaky wooden floors and too much stock, the kind of place you could wander in for hours if you liked that kind of thing. I did. And Hector was always there with a smile and a willingness to help. He'd done some carpentry work for the shelter on several occasions, and his wife, Bonita, often volunteered in the kitchen. He had also often extended us credit. Hector greeted me warmly.

"What can I get for you today, Pastor Steve?" he said, his dark Mexican eyes dancing. I was about to tell him when I saw his son Alberto peering out from behind him.

"Hey, Alberto, what's up?" I smiled down on the boy.

He dropped his eyes and pulled back, hiding himself behind his father. Hector frowned and turned, pulling him out to face me. "Alberto, mind your manners. Say hello to Pastor Steve."

Alberto did not raise his eyes but said a soft hello. Hector was still frowning and cocked his head at the boy.

"What's the matter with you, Alberto?"

The lad flashed a look at me, then turned and fled.

Hector apologized for his son. "I'm sorry, Pastor. He's been acting strange lately. I think maybe it's because of his grandma, yes?"

I knew Alberto's grandmother had been quite ill, and I knew the boy was worried about her, but I didn't understand why he was reacting that way with me. He often came to the shelter with his mother and was always friendly, flashing his father's wide smile.

I shrugged. Maybe he was just having a bad day. I followed Hector down the rows toward the stack of ladders. He pulled a tall one out and offered to bring it over himself right way. I thanked him and headed for the door. As I pulled it open I noticed Alberto peeking around the corner of one of the display racks. I let the door swing back and started toward him, but he dashed back down the aisle and didn't look back even when I called his name. Strange. I made another mental note to try and talk with him later. After the pageant was over.

Stanley and his cast of characters were halfway through the second rehearsal by the time I got back. I stood in the doorway and watched for a while.

Charlie One-note was still insisting on playing "You Are My Sunshine" and his recorder still sounded awfully squeaky, but the look on his face when he played made up for it. Peter Jolly's voice seemed to be getting stronger, but that seemed to make the others even more timid. I made another mental note to tell Stanley to suggest he tone it down a notch. Just as I turned to go, Peter Jolly let out several loud hiccups. I headed back to my office as Johnson started to recite his lines.

"This will be a sign to you: You will find a baby wrapped in cloths and lying in a manger."

Right, I thought, as long as I can find one. Better go do that right away. I headed for the front door and almost got there when one of the residents approached. He was holding his pants up with both hands and looking at his feet. They were soaking wet. A rather foul odor preceded him. I was about to ask him if he was okay when he blurted, "It's the toilet. Couldn't get it to flush. Then the water and, uh, other stuff, kinda overflowed."

I groaned and headed for the men's washroom. The floor was covered in a thin layer of brown sludge. I closed the door again and posted a man there to keep everyone out until I could get my rubber boots.

I was about to barge into my apartment when I remembered there was a family staying there. Randy answered my knock and let me in without a word, mostly because it was hard to hear over the baby's screams.

"Is he okay?" I asked, leaning in close so he could hear me.

The young man looked worried. "I think he's coming down with something, a cold maybe."

I glanced at Stacey, trying to soothe the baby as she rocked him in her arms on the small couch.

"Anything I can do?"

Randy shrugged, glanced over his shoulder, then looked at me with pleading in his eyes. "We don't have medical insurance."

I frowned. "Maybe I can get something that will help from the pharmacy."

I found my rubber boots and left, promising to return with something for the baby as soon as I could.

Lord, I prayed, *could we have a little less drama, please?*

It took me over an hour to get the toilet unplugged and the bathroom cleaned up, and by the time I was finished Stanley was complaining that they needed Mary on stage, but the baby was still fussing and she didn't want to leave him. I headed for the pharmacy.

Max was another one of our neighbors who'd been a big support to the shelter. He was also a good pharmacist and gave me a mild dose of over-the-counter medicine for the baby.

"This will make him sleep," he said. "But they should take him to emergency if he gets any worse." I assured him we'd watch him closely. Then I asked if he sold dolls.

"Dolls?"

"I need a big one," I said.

He shook his head. "Sorry."

I ran back to the shelter, gave the medicine to the frazzled parents, and asked Stacey if she would make her way to the gym as soon as she could.

As I opened the door to leave, Milly just about fell into my arms. "Oh, I was looking for you, Pastor Steve," she panted. "Stanley wants to do a dress rehearsal right away, but we're still short a few bathrobes. I was wondering if you could dash over to the Carson Hotel. They said they've got a few they can loan us, but I have to get back to the kitchen."

I nodded. "I'm on my way." As I drove I wracked my brain trying to think of a store close to the hotel that might sell dolls. I came up blank so settled for collecting the bathrobes and getting them back to Stanley as soon as possible.

He wasn't too happy that they were all white but handed them out to those who still needed a costume. I was glad to see Stacey on stage. She looked even more tiny and vulnerable when she snuggled into the large fluffy white bathrobe Stanley gave her. She smiled when I asked about the baby.

"He's doing better, sleeping," she said.

I thanked the Lord and started to head off the stage when Hector arrived from the hardware store with the tall ladder. Everyone clustered to the side of the stage and watched as we set it up. Stanley stared up its length, then glanced at me.

"I'm not so good with heights, boss."

Hector stepped forward. "I am."

We unfolded the curtain, stretched it out across the stage, and drew a heavy wire through the top hem. Hector grasped one corner and started to climb. About halfway up he stopped, shifted his position, pulled on the heavy drapery, and mumbled something in Spanish. I called on our "actors" to lift the rest of the curtain as high as they could to try and take some of the weight. Hector almost had the corner attached when Charlie One-note, who was lifting the curtain with both hands, turned his head and gave a loud, juicy sneeze. The man behind him reacted by staggering back, bumping into the man behind him, who did the same. The domino effect moved down the line until everyone was staggering back. But no one let go of the curtain. What happened next seemed to be in slow motion. I saw the ladder teeter as the curtain was pulled taught. I saw Hector's eyes widen as he realized he was going to fall. I saw him and the ladder crash into the others below, the blue curtain billowing as it flowed over them all.

Stanley and I scrambled to help and were relieved to discover that the other men had broken Hector's fall. It seemed no one was hurt. We got everyone back on their feet and spread the curtain out again. Hector reached down to heft a corner of it again, but pulled back, wincing and grabbing his wrist. I took his arm in my hands and examined it.

"I don't think it's broken, but we should get it checked."

Hector pulled back. "No, Pastor, it will be all right."

I knew he was thinking of the cost. So was I, but I didn't want to risk that his wrist was worse than it looked. I could almost see it swelling as we stood there.

"The shelter will cover the bill, Hector," I assured him, imagining the look on our accountant's face when I had to explain about that. I glanced down at the curtain. "Leave it for now," I told Stanley. "We'll deal with it when I get back."

I left Hector in the emergency room, after making him promise he'd have it looked at, and hurried back. I was stunned to see the curtain hung.

"I had six guys holding the ladder this time," Stanley said.

"But who ..."

He grinned and shrugged. "It's not as high as I thought."

I clapped him on the back. "You're a hero, Stan."

He grinned, then clapped his hands and called the cast together.

"Okay, guys, this is it, our last rehearsal." He looked each one in the eye. "I know we can do this. I know God wants us to." He glanced at me. "But maybe we should pray and ask him to help."

I nodded and watched as they all bowed their heads. It was one of those moments for me - the kind when you recognize your own weakness and know there's only One who is able to help. "Lord, Jesus," I began, "we thank you for this day. It's been crazy, Lord, but it's been good. I thank you for the things you've been showing us, for the way you've been blessing us in the midst of it all. We ask that you help Hector's wrist heal. And we ask that you help us now to do a good job, not just for our sakes, but for yours. We want to glorify you, Jesus. Help us do that right now in this rehearsal and then tonight in the performance. Amen."

The amens the men said were strong and echoed through the gym.

Stanley clapped his hands again. "Yup, yup. Let's do this."

I stood back to watch. The only one who managed to get through all their lines without prompting was Johnson. You'd think the man had been born to act. Stanley was getting pretty frustrated with the others, but at least the announcement of the birth of Christ from the lips of a not-so-perfect angel would be perfect. The man with the saxophone was nowhere to be found, and the star-studded backdrop was starting to sag in the middle. The rehearsal ended just as the dinner gong sounded. Stanley and I stood back and watched the men trudge off the stage, shedding their robes as they went.

Stanley shot me a look that told me he wasn't nearly as optimistic as his usual buoyant self.

"I dunno, boss," he said. "Doesn't seem like the Lord heard you. Maybe it would have been better to cancel after all."

It was my turn to encourage him. I put my hand on his shoulder. "It all comes together in the end, remember?"

He sighed. "Sure hope so, boss. Yup, yup. Sure hope so."

I gulped down my supper and looked at my watch. One and a half hours till show time. Stanley was urging his cast to eat fast and get back on stage for one last run-through. The chairs still needed to be set up in the gym, and I still needed to find a baby Jesus. I called for volunteers and was gratified to see we had more than enough men to do the job. Then I went to my office, did a quick computer search for the nearest toy store, and headed for the back door.

I'd almost made it when Milly stopped me again.

"It's Bonita Ramirez, Pastor. She says she really needs to talk to you. I told her it's not a great time, but ..."

"Is Hector's arm okay?"

Milly nodded. "Yes. Bonita said he called her from the hospital and should be home soon."

I sighed and almost told her to tell Bonita to come back tomorrow, but then that check hit me, the one that often comes when I'm about to go against the Lord's will. I reminded myself I was a pastor, and a pastor tends to his flock. "Tell her to come to my office," I said, and headed back in that direction. I could hear a slight hum of people already arriving for the performance. *Lord*, I prayed, *please make this a quick counselling session.*

Bonita arrived, her left hand clutching a large plastic bag and her right wrapped around her son's arm. She was almost dragging the boy behind her.

I opened the door to my office and ushered them in.

"Hector's wrist is going to be okay? Not broken, I hope?"

Bonita nodded. "Si," she said. "It is only a sprain."

"Good." I noticed Bonita's eyes refused to meet mine.

She stammered a bit and stared at her feet as she spoke. "I ... I am so sorry, Pastor Steve. After all you have done, I hope you can forgive us."

"Forgive you? What for, Bonita?"

She pulled her son in front of her, handed him the bag and put both hands on his shoulders, shoving him toward me.

"Tell the pastor what you did, Alberto."

The boy was almost in tears. He stared at the floor and said nothing. The buzz of people arriving for the performance was getting louder. And I still had no baby Jesus. I put my hand on Alberto's shoulder.

"It's all right, son," I said. "Don't be afraid."

He flashed a glance up at me, handed me the bag and hung his head again. "I took the baby Jesus," he said.

I opened the bag and, sure enough, it held the plaster baby we'd been hunting for. I put the bag down and dropped to my knees in front of Alberto.

"But why, Alberto?, Why did you take it?"

He chewed his lip. His mother nudged him and he finally looked at me. "Last year, at the end of the pageant, you said the manger contained the only solution to all our problems." He dropped his eyes again. "*Mi abuela*, my granny, has been really sick, so I thought ... I thought maybe if I put the baby under her bed she'd get better."

I glanced up at Bonita. She was smiling a bit but had tears in her eyes too.

"Look at me, Alberto." I waited for him to do so. "What you did was wrong. You know that, right?"

He nodded.

"But what you wanted was right, Alberto. You wanted your granny to get better. But it isn't the plaster Jesus that helps us; it's the real Jesus."

Alberto looked at me, and I saw the question in his eyes.

"Can he make her better?" he asked.

"Yes, I believe he can but sometimes he doesn't do exactly what we want him to do. He knows what's best for all of us and we have to trust him to do the best thing. Can you understand that?"

Alberto frowned. "I guess so."

"It's kind of like if you asked your dad for something you really wanted but your dad knew it wasn't the best thing for you right then or the best thing for others, so he said no. Maybe it would make you mad at first, but you know your dad loves you and would always do what's best for you, right?"

Alberto nodded. I put my hand on his shoulder. "Would you like to talk to the real Jesus and ask him to help your granny?"

He hesitated. His mother nudged him again, but he shrugged away and looked up at her. "But we already prayed, and we still don't have the money for the medicine."

I looked at Bonita, but her eyes shifted away.

"Maybe God has something special in mind," I said. "Let's pray and see what happens, okay?"

He looked right into my eyes. "You pray," he said.

So I did. Fervently. And I prayed as I watched them walk away that the Lord would show that little boy that he loves him and his grandma. Then I headed to the gym to put the baby Jesus in his manger. I could hear the buzz of the crowd, louder as I got closer.

I was almost there when Milly rushed down the corridor toward me.

"The costumes," she panted and leaned against the wall.

"What about them?" I asked, wondering what on earth could go wrong with T-towels and bathrobes.

"They're here!" Milly beamed. "The theatre manager drove them back himself, bless his heart!"

"Praise the Lord!" I almost did a Stanley-like leap in the air.

I arrived backstage just as he was digging into the boxes and handing out the richly ornamented clothing. I stopped and watched, the scene before me making goose bumps rise on my arms. Herod was there, strutting in a fine red robe, the shepherds were testing out their crooks, and Charlie One-note was pacing in a flowing cape, his recorder held up as though it were a golden scepter. Our saxophone player was back, standing to one side in a long white robe trimmed with silver. The hood almost totally hid his dreadlocks. His instrument had been polished and gleamed at his side. Then I saw the wise men. Peter Jolly was resplendent in a rich purple mantle, the crown on his head a perfect fit. The others were just as dazzling. I stood with my mouth hanging open. The transformation of the men was astonishing to behold.

Stanley was giving them all last-minute instructions and they were all attentive. An air of expectation filled the room. And it filled my heart. I made my way to the side of the stage and placed the baby Jesus in the manger. His arms reached out to me, and I knew it was crazy but I could have sworn his tiny eyes twinkled, just for a minute. I tucked the blanket around him and prayed. But this time it wasn't a plaintive prayer for help. It was a heart-felt thank you.

The buzz of the audience was really loud now. I peeked out from behind the curtain. Almost all the seats were filled. The mayor and his entourage were in the front row, and I noticed several more important people, all decked out as though they were at the opera. I took a deep breath, then glanced down at myself. I was still in jeans and a T-shirt. And they weren't exactly clean. I dashed to my apartment and changed into the only suit and tie I owned, praying all the while.

I got back to the stage just as the lights were dimming. A hush slowly fell. The men stood behind me, quiet, waiting. I gave my tie a tug, parted the curtain and walked out into the middle of a spotlight.

"Welcome, everyone, to New Life's annual Christmas pageant." I couldn't see the faces of the audience because of the bright light, but I could feel their expectation. I prayed again that God would open their hearts, and their pocketbooks. I told them they were in for a special treat this year and explained that the cast was made up entirely of New Life's residents. I thought I heard a soft intake of breath at that, but kept going. "So sit back, relax, and enjoy the retelling of this ancient but oh-so-significant story, the story of when time began and our Savior was born."

I stepped out of the spotlight, crossed the stage, and nodded at Stanley. The front curtain swept back as he nudged Herod forward and waved at the three wise men to make their entrance. I scooted down the stairs to take my seat. I was impressed with how they all strode across the stage to take their places. Herod really did look like the imperious ruler, and the wise men looked like royalty too. But then Peter Jolly grinned and squinted out at the audience. I squirmed in my seat as the silence continued. Then I heard a loud stage whisper. Peter Jolly glanced over his shoulder, then turned back and opened his mouth.

"We're seeking the King of the Jews," he said. "Tell us where we can find him."

Herod's head jerked up. "The King of the Jews? What are you talking about?"

Not exactly according to script, but the audience didn't seem to notice.

"Haven't you seen the star?" Peter Jolly let out a loud hiccup, then gave a grand sweep with his arm up toward the backdrop, which was still sagging. But the one large star was catching the light and gleaming.

"We've been following it, and it has led us here," Peter Jolly continued.

Herod shrugged. "I don't know where this King is," he said, "but when you find him, come back and tell me so I can ..." Herod frowned and turned his head toward the side of the stage. Then he gave his head a shake and continued. "So I can honor him too."

The wise men made their way offstage on cue, and the lights went up on the angels, already in place. Stanley had dressed several of them in the long flowing white gowns trimmed with gold ribbon, and they looked almost ethereal in the soft light. The shepherds cowered in the shadows as Charlie One-note stepped forward and put the recorder to his lips. There were a few titters from the audience as he squeaked through "You Are My Sunshine," but not a peep as the piping reed sweetly played "Hark the Herald Angels Sing."

As the last note hung in the air Johnson stepped forward. I saw his Adam's apple bob as he swallowed, but no sound came out of his mouth. The stage whisper from the back was a bit louder this time. Johnson blinked and nodded. He looked over his shoulder at the others standing behind him, shifting the large gossamer wings attached to his back.

"We're all ..." He hesitated. "We're all angels. And, and I have good news. We're a sign for you that the Messiah has been born, your Messiah. That means Savior." He raised his arm and pointed. "So go and find him. He's in a cradle--no, I mean a manger, in a little town called... called Bethlehem. That's David's hometown." He waved his hand at the shepherds. "So go on; go find him."

I put my hand over my eyes. He'd done it so perfectly in rehearsal. My head jerked up as he continued.

"And you, too," Johnson's voice boomed out now. He swept his arm out toward the audience. "You go find him too."

The other angels stepped forward and boomed out their line: "Glory to God in the highest and on earth peace to men on whom his favor rests."

Another loud stage whisper and the shepherds started to move off the stage. Stanley had set up a large white sheet that now lit up as the shadows of the wise men and camels flowed across it, then the shadow of the shepherds who seemed to be jostling one another for a minute but then got sorted out and flowed from left to right. The spotlight fell on the manger just as the shepherds stepped out onto the open stage and knelt beside it.

I sucked in my breath. Mary looked perfect, her petite face a picture of sweet holiness as she peered down at the baby in the manger. The green blanket looked okay, and when Johnson stepped out, his long arms upraised, his white gown glowing, I was suddenly transported back 2,000 years and stood in that stable, watching. It wasn't until Peter Jolly spoke that I realized I'd been holding my breath.

"We have brought gifts for the child," he said, "because he is God's gift to us, our Messiah, our Savior."

The three wise men placed their gifts before the manger. Mary's smile was radiant. Peter Jolly turned to the audience and used his best radio voice for the last lines of the night.

"Now we must go and tell the world about this night, for to us a child is born, to us a son is given, and the government will be on his shoulders. And he will be called Wonderful Counselor, Mighty God, Everlasting Father, Prince of Peace. Of the greatness of his government and peace there will be no end. He will reign on David's throne and over his kingdom, establishing and upholding it with justice and righteousness from that time on and forever. The zeal of the lord almighty will accomplish this" (Isaiah 9:6,7 NIV).

He stepped back, and the spotlight brightened on the manger. Then a saxophone began to play the sweet plaintive notes of "Silent Night." After a few bars the audience started to sing softly. When it was over there was silence. Total silence. Then the room went black. I was glad because it gave me a moment to wipe the tears from my face.

The house lights came up, and the audience stood to its feet, applauding. Stanley ushered his cast back on stage, and they all took an awkward group bow. Then Stanley was standing there alone. The audience quieted and sat.

"Most of you know about the work we do here at New Life Shelter. I think you've just seen some of the result. I know this pageant wasn't exactly what you were expecting tonight, but then, the tiny baby born in a manger wasn't what the Jews were expecting either. They wanted a King. They got a baby. They wanted a military victory. They got a man who preached about loving your enemies. You might say what they got was an unexpected glory and an invitation to everlasting life. The kind of new life that is happening, literally, right here, because of our Messiah, our Savior and Lord, Jesus Christ. But it takes a lot of effort too. Just ask Pastor Steve. He's had kind of a stressful day." He grinned at me as the audience chuckled. "And it takes a lot of money," he continued. "So we're asking you to help. Some of our guys are going to hand out pails and baskets. I think you know what to do. Thanks for coming, and Merry Christmas."

I rushed backstage to shake the hand of everyone in the cast. And I gave Stanley a big bear hug.

"It was amazing, Stanley, amazing."

"Well, it wasn't perfect," he laughed. "But I think it did all come together in the end, right, boss?"

"Oh yes, Stanley." I chuckled. "It surely did."

The crowd was moving steadily out into the cafeteria where Milly had laid out the refreshments. We joined them, smiling as people shook our hands and told us it was the best pageant ever.

I was taking a long drink of hot apple cider when I saw Reg, our accountant, making his way through the crowd. I smiled at him. Somehow I wasn't really concerned what the total was anymore, but my jaw dropped when he told me. It was well over our needed goal. There would be enough to ensure New Life Shelter would remain open, enough to pay Hector's hospital bill, and enough to make sure Alberto's grandmother got her medicine.

I was still in shock when the mayor approached and pumped my hand.

"Well, done, Reverend, well done. It was, um, a bit unconventional," he said. "But it was, well, like the man said, it had a certain unexpected glory to it, didn't it?"

I nodded. An unexpected glory. Yes. Exactly.

A Carol of Light

Marcy Weydemuller

"**T**en minutes," the stage manager bellowed, just as Kat painted on her last whisker.

A shadow across her flimsy curtain said that Sam had taken up his protective stance. She shivered a little with excitement. Only two more performances today disguised as the boy known as Kat. Then tonight at the candlelight worship she could become herself again, except with short hair.

"Maureen Katrina Sokolov." She whispered her long buried name, but she knew she would keep to Kat as Katrina. Maureen belonged to her old life, the one she lost a year ago when her parents' ship sunk and she had to run for her life. Now she only wanted to stop hiding and hopefully one day be able to tell Samuel how much she loved him.

She looked over at his shadow. These past few weeks he had become suddenly distant and almost secretive, so unlike him. Did the weight of hiding her worry him as their performances became more public? If anything, they seemed to become safer as their troupe established themselves in San Francisco. With their name now recognized within the theaters, they no longer had to give a long detailed background to get a job.

A newsboy on the street below shouted out the headlines, "The Wright Brothers fly in the air." Kat paused in astonishment. Today would become a history marker. Not that she would forget it. December 18, 1903, seven days before Christmas.

Sam coughed a warning. She heard a clatter of footsteps coming up the rickety back staircase, and then giggles.

"Mrs. Calder, hello," Sam gasped. Her little girls must have plowed into him.

"Samuel, good day. Is Kat still here?"

"Come in," she called. "I'm dressed."

Nia Calder hesitated half-in, half-out of the curtain.

"We'll watch them," Cameron and Benjamin, already in their costumes, growled at the little ones.

Kat laughed.

As Nia came in, Ben leaned up to the curtain. "Kat, you laugh like a girl."

She and Nia looked at each other. "Did you decide to tell him?" Nia whispered.

"No, I wonder why he said that," Kat murmured as she stood to give Nia a hug.

"Hmm." Nia looked Kat over. "You're finally filling out, so I'd suggest a little more stuffing."

"Two minutes, Kat." Sam said. "We're taking the girls down, Mrs. Calder."

"Thank you. Iain is in the second row, holding our seats." Nia helped plump out Kat's waist to hide any curves. "Here's your dress for tonight." She handed Kat a flat package wrapped in brown paper.

Kat caressed the package, forcing back tears. "I can't thank you enough." A dress. She could go into worship tonight wearing a dress. And play her cello music openly as herself before the Lord.

"And I have a surprise for you. Do you remember the woman I told you about who works with Donalinda Cameron to rescue the Chinese girls from the Yellow Slave Traders? Well, she's here today at this performance. At the break, I'll quietly point her out to you. She's already checking to see if there are any more safety measures that need to be taken. But she doesn't know who you are yet. Only that as far as they know you are the only non-Chinese girl ever taken."

"I don't think they intended to take me. I think my imposter guardian forced them in an attempt to make me disappear. He has a lot of influence in the crime community, and their paths must cross when convenient."

"Nevertheless, they want to hear your whole story as it might help them save other girls."

Kat sighed. It was one thing to become herself for Samuel and her friends. She didn't know if she could share the details of her escape with strangers yet. A whole year of silence would be hard to break. Only Samuel and Cameron knew, since they had found her beaten, unconscious, and fevered in the Cascade Mountain foothills. They didn't even know that Nia had guessed just a few months ago. But the relief of sharing with another woman had broken open her heart's desire to truly stop hiding as a boy. Now today—on her eighteenth birthday—seven days before Christmas. Her blessing birthday, her parents always said. A week of light breaking open the darkness before Jesus' birth.

She swallowed. What if she should wait longer? Would her beloved rescuer leave her when she lit the candle tonight undisguised? Fear crept inside. No. Christmas caroled faith, her parents used to say. Time to live now by its light and hope again.

A few minutes later as the curtains opened, she practically leapt onto the stage in her cat costume, swishing her tail and playing her fiddle.

"Joy to the World!" The audience sang along to their quick tempo. Then they quieted as the Christmas play began with all four "animals" trudging through a dark night looking for a place to sleep. Benjamin as a tired hound puppy playing his spoons as only a ten-year-old could, Cameron as a red-winged blackbird humming his notes, Kat on the fiddle, and Samuel as a brown bear playing his shepherd's flute.

At first they had played music to keep their spirits up on the lonely dark nights walking to the Pacific coast. Then they tried to find work as a traveling troupe once they reached California. When they began doing an American version of the Bremen Town musicians, suddenly they were in demand as they made their way to San Francisco. Together they wrote scripts, and Kat wrote the music although everyone else thought Sam did.

Kat loved this particular play they had worked so hard to write. This would be one of a few places the children would hear the Christmas story. And many of them lived in cold, plain rooms with not enough coal to warm them. They needed to know hope too.

As the story ended, Kat rolled across the stage in a somersault and froze at the edge. The Imposter, her so-called guardian whom she refused to call by name, leaned over the shoulder of Nia's friend, looking at their play sheet. She tried to take a breath and force herself to move. She barely managed to look down and hide her distinct aqua eyes.

Instead of picking up a violin for the first act finale, she spun around and gave three sharp whistles, the danger warning signal they'd copied from the Sandpipers whistles and used in their months trekking down the Pacific coast from Washington to San Francisco in California.

She saw Samuel and Cameron go on instant alert.

Ben looked confused but played along to the change and chased Kat until she scampered through the curtains and raced for the boys' dressing closet. There she pulled the tabby cat costume over her own gray cat, along with a black mask, and she waddled back onto the stage, keeping to the shadows.

"Oh, a new cat," the children in the front row murmured, as she managed to play another Christmas carol on the psaltery, hoping to give the illusion of a new troupe member.

At first, the Imposter tried to leave his seat but couldn't as the children came close to the stage, ready to receive the hoped-for candy.

Kat kept pressed against the back curtain. Finally the front curtain lowered, and the boys headed straight to her.

Samuel drew her shaking hands in his. "Tell me. Who is he?"

"My guardian."

"The one who sold you." Cameron slumped next to her.

"Who is he sitting with?" Samuel's grip held her.

"A…a friend of Mrs. Calder's." Kat shook all over as the fear took hold. The law didn't even try to stop him in Washington State. Would California be any different? Besides, he knew how to sidestep the law. He hired others to do his criminal deeds for him.

"Ben, get to Mrs. Calder as quick as you can and warn her to stay away from that man and her friend. Then meet Cameron back here on stage. Don't go to the dressing rooms. We're doing the second act without Kat."

Samuel lifted her up and carried her down the back stairs to a room with a hidden storage closet behind damaged old sets. "Oh, Kat, what have you done?"

Her shaking began to ease in the comfort of Sam's arms. "A few months ago Nia guessed, and I only told her a little part with no names. She decided to check on ways I could become me again."

Sam put her down next to the huge closet. "If you hear any footsteps, hide in here. We'll use the signal if it's one of us."

He glared at her and she wilted. Sam had never looked so angry, at least not at her. "You had no right to keep that a secret. You put us all in danger. Why would you take such a risk after all this time?"

She swallowed a gulp. "I wanted to surprise you. I wanted to be a girl again."

"Do you want your life back so badly? To leave us?"

He turned away, and she clutched at the fur of his costume. "No, no, never leave you. Just be a girl." She hesitated. "A woman."

He looked back at her, and his face softened a little. "I guess I forget how hard it must be. But, Kat, all of us are at risk, not just you. Cameron and Ben can still be claimed as runaways until we find a solution." He awkwardly patted her on the head like he did to Ben and headed back to the stage.

She crawled into the closet and curled into a ball. That's how he saw her, like Ben, a child who needed his protection. Shards of pain split into her heart even stronger than the whiplashes her abductor had cut across her legs when she first tried to run away.

Oh, Lord, have I done wrong for selfish reasons? Kat sighed. *I thought I just wanted to live in Your light again. Live true. But maybe I have done it all backwards and should have told the boys first. Please keep them safe.*

A double note whistled down the corridor, and Kat shook herself awake, surprised she'd fallen asleep. Still she waited inside the closet.

"Kat, you still in here?" Ben's anxious whisper sounded faint.

She pushed open the door.

"Oh, you had me there." Ben lifted up a small basket. "Cameron got us some meat pies and apples from the vendor down the street. Says we have to stay here until the afternoon show."

Kat didn't think she could possibly eat anything, but her grumbling stomach disagreed. "Where did he get the money?"

"Samuel gave it to him before he left."

"Left?" Kat stared at Ben. "Sam left us alone?"

"Yep. Said he had some important business that couldn't wait and he'd be back for the second show. Said to tell you to keep wearing the tabby cat and the black mask to hide the color of your eyes and to sit next to the oak tree. I'm doing your part." He handed her a hot pie and sat down next to her. "Oh, and don't play the fiddle. Said to keep on like you finished last time."

"So, he thinks it's safe for me?"

"Don't know. Just said we have to finish."

Another whistle sounded, and Cameron came in carrying three sarsaparillas. His face was flushed as if he had been running, but he shook his head at Kat as she tilted her head in a question.

They ate quietly. As quietly as when they'd hidden off the coast trails every time they heard hunting dogs. The two weeks in Oregon after Kat found Ben unconscious by a stream were the worst. Ben insisted they wouldn't spend the time hunting a kid just to put him in the workhouse, but Samuel didn't agree. Sending orphanage kids to a workhouse for pay sounded like too much money for them to risk losing, if Ben ever found someone to believe him. Which would be hard enough for him as shunned by both the white and black communities, neither willing to accept him as their own. Now he belonged with them and they were determined to keep him safe.

Her eyes puddled again. For months she had been able to keep her emotions hard and eyes dry, but today the floodgates were wide open.

"I gotta say, Kat, you do pretty good as a boy, 'cept when you laugh." Ben took another bite of his pie and chewed with a look of pure satisfaction.

"So, you've been warning me all along. You knew?" She looked over at Cameron's stunned expression.

"Sure, from about a week after you took me on the road with you."

"Why didn't you say anything then?" Cam said.

"Figured you would trust me one day."

"Oh, Ben, we've always trusted you. We didn't want you to have to lie." Kat put her arm around his shoulder. "You might be the youngest, but you are just as brave."

"Really?" He broke into a big grin.

"Yes. Lies have a way of becoming easy and making dark choices seem okay. We felt we would be wrong to put you in that position. Samuel and Cameron knew because they found me, like I found you. Then a few months ago Mrs. Calder guessed. No one else knows."

"So, you were protecting me too. Like Sam protected that man in the summer who got stabbed. And never told us his real name."

"Well, we were trying."

"So, if I kind of lied once to protect you, it would be okay?" Ben's voice got a little quiet. "Kind of like that Bible story when the bad guy hid in the tent, and when he fell asleep the woman killed him. She kind of lied, didn't she? By not saying she was on the other side?"

Cameron made a choking sound.

"Well, I'm really glad you are remembering our Bible stories, but for now maybe you should tell us what you did or did not do." Kat's fingers shook a little as she stroked his curly black hair. Something she had wanted to do since they had scooped Ben up off the ground ten months ago, so famished he had passed out near a stream. She would do anything to keep him safe.

"Sam said to warn Mrs. Calder, and I barely did when that man came right up to her face and demanded she tell him where Maureen was. The little girls started to cry and Iain started to move in front of her, but she stood her ground and looked him straight in the eye.

"Then she says, 'I have never heard the name Maureen for anyone of my acquaintances, and how dare you speak to me in such a tone?'

"The man took a step back and then saw me and tried to grab me, but Iain pushed me behind him and stood next to his mother. 'Where's the girl?' he said. 'What girl?' I said. 'That cat,' he said. 'That's not a girl, that's a cat,' I said.'

"He got all stiff-like and pointed his finger at me. 'Are you addle-brained?' he asked. 'I don't know,' I said. 'What does that mean?'"

Kat forced back her laughter but Cameron could not. He buried his face in his arms to dim the noise. "Well done, Ben," he muffled between breaths.

Kat took Ben in her arms. "Yes, well done, but I don't want you to mess with him at all if he comes back."

"He's really dangerous, isn't he, Kat? He's got cold eyes. Just like the man who tried to send us kids to the workhouse instead of another orphanage when the old lady died."

She remembered those cold eyes. For a little kid, Ben could really see people's hearts accurately. Kat hugged him a little tighter. Although they fed him as much as possible, he still felt too skinny.

Oh, Lord, please protect him, she prayed. *And Cam, and Samuel, and the Calders.* She knew what her guardian was capable of. She had seen him in action as he coerced her grieving aunt to marry him, shipped her twin cousins off to an unheard of boarding school, and set her up for a kidnapping all in a month after her parents' death. Which now Kat sincerely wondered about. Yes, it had been a terrible storm, but not as bad as others her father had safely navigated them through many times.

Kat looked over at Cameron. "Why were you running?"

"I think he left someone to watch and follow us. When I went to get our meal, I saw a Pinkerton-like man across the street. After I handed the basket to Ben, I went down a block and he kept coming, so I ran through the alleys till I lost him."

"And Sam had already left."

Cameron nodded. As if prepared for her next question, he stood up and brushed off the crumbs from his costume. "He only said we had to finish today's play."

"No matter what," Kat said.

Cam's face tightened. Just as other times they had faced unknown danger.

"Kat, you're not going to leave us now that you are a girl, are you?" Ben leaned a little closer.

"Not if I can help it. You are my family now."

Footsteps sent Kat into the closet as a stagehand came in and tossed what sounded like a crate into the corner. "What are you doing down here?"

"Looking for a board strong enough to jump off," Cameron said. "Can we use anything in here that we find?"

"Sure, pretty much all junk down here. Take what you want. If you see Kat, tell him a lady said she would deliver the package on her way home." He hummed a Christmas carol as he left, and Kat cracked open the door.

"So what do we do now?" Ben said.

"Look for a board," Cameron muttered. "I'm thinking we can make a spring as a diversion if we need to."

Kat watched them scouring the room. They were all in danger now because of her, and she still hid in the closet. *I need Your strength and wisdom, Lord. Please show me what to do.*

Sam arrived a few minutes before curtain call, a little out of breath, and stern. "Listen carefully. This is going to be one of the most difficult days we have had to face, and we cannot use our usual survival tactics. Today, no matter what happens, we stand and we do not run and hide. Everything comes out into the open today. We will trust in the Lord."

They looked back at him hesitantly, but one by one they nodded their agreement. As they joined hands for prayer, Ben let go of Kat's hand and wrapped his arm around her instead, leaning into her shoulder. She could feel him shaking and wondered if she shook as much too. Sam looked at them and rocked back on his heels, a sure sign of his stress.

"Lord, You have carried us through many dangers this past year, and we ask once again for Your protection and to break the power of evil that continues to hunt Kat. Give us wisdom for the choices before us today. Give us courage to be faithful to You."

"Amen," they said together. Kat realized he had not prayed that they stay together. And he would not look her in the eye. Her lunch suddenly felt like rocks in her stomach. If he forced her to leave him, leave them, her heart would break forever.

He bent down to ruffle Ben's hair. "Stay as close to Cameron's side as possible. Stick to him like a starfish. Understand?"

Her heart lurched. Sam had to choose between them, and Benjamin needed him more. She would not be able to protect him as a woman. But surely she could still be a part of his life. She gasped at the possible cost.

Then he looked at Kat. "Stay strong today. You are no longer the beaten, bedraggled girl dying on the mountain. You survived a whipping many could not and five days of fever. Every time we thought you were gone, you fought your way back. And you are whole again and wiser. You will get through this too."

Perhaps not on the inside, Kat reflected as they prepared to bounce on stage, but her heart still struggled to believe. She inhaled the opening words as Cameron read from a scroll, *"And this is the message we have heard from Him and announce to you, that God is light and in Him there is no darkness at all."*

All along they thought they had written this Christmas play for the children when it seemed they themselves needed it more.

Despite the tension, they gave one of their best performances ever, and there were no shadows lurking in corners or hunkering near the stage.

Not until the crowd began to leave and Kat saw Imposter make his way to the stage with a sergeant. Two police stood at each of the side door exits, and another two men dressed plainly waited near the front entrance.

"Arrest them," the Imposter demanded.

Kat and the boys automatically stepped backwards. Kat looked anxiously over at the stage exit, but Sam shook his head. No running. His instincts were always right. She needed to trust him. *"And you, Lord."*

Then Edward, the theater owner, stepped closer, followed by a distinguished clean-shaven gentleman who seemed vaguely familiar to Kat, except that they didn't know any highbrow people. "On what grounds?"

"Runaways," Imposter sneered.

Edward opened the paper the sergeant handed him and then passed it on to the gentlemen who replied, "This is from the State of Washington. It has no authority here in California. It also has no legal stamp."

"It's none of your business. Your judges have granted me authority." Imposter waved at the officer who stayed stopped before the gentleman. "What are you waiting for?"

"My approval," the gentleman answered.

The police came down the aisles. The troupe could not run even if they wanted to. Yet Samuel looked as if the weight of the world had just rolled away.

"And who do you think you are?" Imposter swaggered a little.

The sergeant gasped. "He's Judge Campbell."

"So what? I've already got a judge's signature."

"Your Honor, is this man harassing you?" one of the policemen asked.

Her guardian grew still. "The Judge. My apologies. I didn't think you would be bothered with such an insignificant matter."

"Actually, I'm here on another legality. But I will be happy to check your legitimate credentials when I'm finished." He turned back to Edward. "Somewhere private, please."

"Officers, please wait here and keep our Washington guest company. Sergeant, please come with me." His Honor waved to the two plain-dressed men to join him as well.

Inside the office, Kat and Ben stayed behind Sam and Cameron at first, but when Edward and sergeant went back outside to wait, Ben stepped forward.

"It is you, Mr. Brown. Didn't recognize you right away without your beard and long hair. Except I guess that's not your name. And you're not a broken-down miner that got stabbed for his gold nuggets."

"Well I did have gold nuggets, but they were part of my undercover investigation, which as you all saw took a bad turn, if not for Sam."

Kat remembered the evening he brought the wounded "miner" to their encampment. That week Sam and Cameron were working on a farm and they actually had a wood hut to stay in. Good thing because it took a week before Mr. Brown could hobble on a makeshift crutch. Then just as suddenly as he arrived he left, and Sam would not talk about it.

"How are you, young Ben? I think you're grown three inches at least." Judge Campbell turned around. "Hello, Cameron and Miss Katrina."

Kat gasped. The man whose life Samuel saved in the summer was a judge, actually *the* judge, and the one who consistently worked to clean up the city. He knew her real name. She thought back to the week they nursed him back to health. Nothing happened that would have given her away.

"When you all patched me up last summer, I told Samuel that if any of you were ever in need, he could contact me. A few months ago he gave me your details, Katrina, and my legal team has been investigating the whole situation. Then today, he came to tell me of your immediate danger."

Kat looked at Samuel. "A few months ago. And you chose not to tell me."

He flushed.

"First, though, I want to bring some legal documents for Benjamin and Cameron. You both need to make an important choice. Now that Samuel is twenty-one, he is offering to become your legal guardian until you each become eighteen."

Oh, Samuel, not only my rescuer. Lord, You have gifted him with Your own care for the lost. Kat's heart ached with love. He had no ties to any of them, yet he loved as if they were his own.

"Cameron, since you are already sixteen, you could probably manage on your own, but with Sam to stand for you, there will be much more opportunity for education or an apprenticeship." Cameron's face shone with delight.

"Benjamin, as an orphan, you are always in danger of being forced into an orphanage or, as you already know, a shady workhouse."

Tears poured down Kat's cheeks. Ben would be safe. No matter what.

Sam leaned down to Ben. "There's a new Quaker school opening in the new year and a place for you. Cameron, we can look into tutors if school is not what you want."

Cameron turned to the judge. "I know it doesn't make a whole lot of sense for me with only a few years between us, but is it possible for Sam to adopt us instead?"

"Why adopt?" Judge Campbell asked quietly.

"Well, neither Ben nor I even know our last names. It would be nice to have one."

"Maybe you want to know what it is first," Sam said. His face had turned beet red.

"Doesn't matter," Cameron answered. "You've been more than a brother, father, uncle, than any I've ever seen. I don't care how bad it is. We're family now."

The judge looked over at the two men with folders. "Is it possible?" They nodded yes. "Samuel?"

"I'd be honored."

Benjamin looked up at Sam. "So, just how bad is it?"

"Reader."

Despite the day's tension Kat, Cameron, and Ben all started laughing. Kat explained. "Every moment he gets, Sam reads. Always from the Bible, but pretty much any books he can borrow too."

"Sign the papers, then, and an early Merry Christmas." Judge Campbell grinned.

"What about Kat?" Ben said. "Can Sam adopt her too?"

"No, Katrina is eighteen today, now an adult, and when her so-called guardian comes in, I will go into detail about her inheritance."

Kat stared in confusion.

"Sam," the Judge said. "It's time."

Sam ruffled Ben's head and patted Cam's shoulder. "I have to go. I'll be home late tonight." He turned to Kat. "You'll be free now to take back your name. To go home, or to go to Europe and study your music."

How could she make him understand she didn't want to leave? Everything and everyone she loved was in this room. She looked at his tight expression. Did he want her to go? "Am I also free to stay, Sam, if my heart is here? If God says I should stay?"

He took a step backwards as if she had slapped him across the face. "I have to go."

Cameron turned towards the judge. "She can't be alone with her guardian or whoever he is. We'll stay too."

A chill went down Kat's spine. "No. He must not see what you look like. He's too dangerous. I'll meet you back at the house. We have to be ready by seven for worship tonight."

"The sergeant will see her home safely. You have my word." The judge opened the door. "Go out through the back exit. Sergeant, bring our impatient guest here, please."

Ben turned back to Kat, "You aren't going to leave like Sam said, are you?"

"I don't plan to or want to. We will need to pray. I don't think I can live with you all after today. Not once everyone knows I'm not a boy."

"I know. You need to marry Sam. That will fix everything."

"Marriage needs to be based on love, Ben, not on convenience. Not a marriage that we make before God."

"Hmm. You'll see. Thanks, Judge."

As they left, Kat began to tremble again. How could she face the Imposter as anger and fear battled within her? Either one a potential weapon in his hands. He used words to manipulate. Samuel used words to heal.

"Remember, there is someone mightier than all of us here," Judge Campbell said quietly as they heard him blustering in the hall.

She looked at him with surprise.

"I guess all those prayers and Bible reading you all did every day I spent with you made a dent in my darkness."

"And the light continues to burn," Kat whispered, hearing her ballad echo within. She turned to face her enemy.

As the Imposter and the sergeant entered the room, Kat felt a rush of heat flow through her just like when she played her cello, dormant now for so many months. Was it the Holy Spirit comforting her?

The Judge began. "I have more important matters to attend to, so I am going to make this quick. Your charges are bogus. We have been investigating you for a few months now for fraud and embezzlement, false witness, and coercion. We didn't even know about the kidnapping charges, which at this time cannot be proven, but we will keep looking."

Kat's hand flew across her mouth to stifle her gasp. They had evidence of what he had done to her aunt.

"Last year, before Captain Sokolov returned home, he unloaded his cargo here in San Francisco and set up his will and estate. It was his last voyage, and he had already sold his ship. The new owners were due to take possession a few days after his return home. Although they still collected on insurance, imagine their surprise when rumors of its sabotage arose.

"You bore false witness to trick his widowed sister into marriage, which has now been annulled, and used deception to assert guardian rights over Maureen Katrina Sokolov."

Sabotage! He had her parents killed. Red-hot hate sizzled in Kat as the Imposter stood there, implacable. He knew they would never find that evidence. He glanced at Kat. She clenched her fists, and he smiled. *Oh, no Lord, keep me from this desire for revenge. Or I will become cold and heartless too.*

"As it stands now, the family home is owned by both Maureen and her aunt. And each has a small, separate yearly allowance from the estate that cannot be touched or borrowed against by anyone else for any reason. Their dual signatures are required for any changes to the property."

Samuel knew. That's why he said she could go home. An allowance. She could stay in San Francisco, even if Sam asked her to leave the troupe. Would he really do that? Would they still have a troupe if Ben and Cameron were in school? They all still needed work. She forced herself back to the conversation.

The sergeant pulled Imposter's hands in front of him and tied his wrists with a rope. "You are under arrest for embezzlement against the banks you defrauded. California can enforce these charges since all the headquarters are here in this city." Judge

Campbell paused to look at Kat with a gentle smile, and then continued.

"If after your jail time you go anywhere near Maureen Katrina Sokolov, you will be re-arrested. Get him out of my sight."

Imposter turned away from the sergeant and laughed at Kat. "Looks as if I will need to correspond with my associates."

"I will trust in the Lord's light," Kat said.

He laughed again as the sergeant pushed him out the door.

After they left, the judge took Kat's hands in his. "It is over. He should be in prison for about ten years. Your allowance is enough for you to continue your education and rent a modest house, if you choose not to return to your home in Washington. We do have evidence that the ship was sabotaged but cannot yet link beyond the person hired to actually cause the damage."

Kat felt as wrung out as a dishrag by the time she reached their lodgings. No sign of the boys, which she thought odd given the circumstances of the day.

A twinge of worry crossed her heart. How could so many emotions collide at the same time? What would be the point of the Imposter continuing to threaten her? Revenge? What could he possibly gain now?

When she reached her room, she immediately pulled out the borrowed cello and began to play. Gradually her relief and joy and sorrow all poured into the notes, and she relaxed. Whatever happened she would get her aunt to send her cello. Free now to play whenever, wherever she wanted. Free to soar. Is that what the Wright brothers felt like when their flying machine took to the air?

Then she noticed the brown paper package on the floor. Her dress. Nia had delivered it. She hung it over the door and pressed down the creases. Her fingers lingered over the lace bodice. Although she admitted wearing boy's clothes had many advantages, she missed dresses. Maybe wearing them would help Samuel see her in a different light.

She washed her hair and wrapped what small pieces she could into rag curls. It wouldn't be much, but still a little more feminine.

No more weekly sheering to keep her bouncy tufts under control, which Sam would have done tomorrow.

She climbed up to the attic room to see if Ben had fallen asleep there. No, not there either. She curled up in the windowsill next to the hollow wall where sound carried up from the porch. She could hear their landlord's dog Thunder snoring lightly. And yawned herself.

Next she knew, Thunder growled and the sky had a darker hue. Must be almost sunset.

"Get off my property," her elderly landlord, Mr. Trent, said. "Or I'll sic my dog on you. I told you I don't know what you are talking about."

"Old man, I don't have time for games." Kat heard the click of a gun. "Tell me where she is or I'll shoot the dog first and you next."

How could he be here? The judge put him in jail. She looked out the window and saw a hefty man standing on the road behind the Imposter. She saw Benjamin coming up the street. He stopped at the Eucalyptus tree and reached in his pocket. He couldn't take them on with his slingshot.

Kat ran into Sam's room and searched his trunk. *Thank you, God!* Sam hadn't taken the gun today. She clicked open the barrel to be sure it was loaded and raced down the back stairs and crept around to the side away from his hefty companion.

Just as she arrived, Imposter reached up his arm to strike her landlord, and Thunder bared his teeth, ready to charge.

Kat took careful aim and shot next to his feet.

He jumped.

"Move away from them, now," Kat said.

"Well, well, you really did turn wild, didn't you? You can't take us both on. I wonder how good a shot you are."

"Not very," Kat said. "I was aiming for your shoulder. I'm still learning, so I tend to be a might fidgety. 'Sides I only need to get one of you, and Thunder will take on the other."

"Or I will." A quavery voice spoke from the front window. Mrs. Trent had a rifle square on the hefty man. "Kat might still be learning, but I came out with the wagons and I'm still a crack shot. Now move away from my husband."

The hefty man took off running straight past Ben, who tripped him, then smacked him on the head with a thick stick. The neighbors had come out at the gunshot, and two seamen bound the fallen man.

Imposter took the opportunity to turn his gun straight on Kat. "Then we both go down."

They all stood as if frozen in a painting Kat had once seen. A part of her wanted to think of the humor. Another part just wanted to stay alive. *How, Lord?*

A movement to her right caught her eye. The sergeant and two policemen, plus several neighbors closed in. Then came the whistle tweet, chitter, chitter.

With a prayer, Kat crumpled to the ground as the men rushed him.

The shot grazed past her hair. Thunder raced over to her and licked her face.

"Good boy."

Ben charged into her, sobbing. Cameron came up behind him, his face so pale his red hair looked on fire. "Kat, we thought you were safe. We never would have left you alone."

"But I wasn't. God protected me."

"Fidgety, huh. I've seen you hit a bull's-eye," Mrs. Trent said. "Thank you, Kat. Dinner's ready, so you boys come in and catch us up on what just happened."

The sergeant came over. "I'm sorry, Miss Sokolov. We laid a trap for him once he got to the prison, but he got away from us when a cart overturned a few blocks away. Pretty sure he had set it up just in case. However, now we can charge him with attempted murder. He won't get out on any bail, and he won't be going anywhere."

He turned to Ben. "Well done, young man. His Honor said you were clever and brave, and he is right."

Ben finally calmed but kept a grip on Kat. "What's that stuff in your hair?" He and Cameron helped her stand up.

She hesitantly touched her few rags. "I thought I'd fix my hair up a little."

Cameron wrapped his arm around her shoulder. "Things are sure going to be different with you as a real girl."

They washed their hands at the pump outside the kitchen and trooped into the room, rich with fresh-baked bread and stew. After they served up and prayed, they began to explain the day.

"Why isn't Samuel here then with all this going on?" Mrs. Trent asked.

"We were out looking for him. We figured something really important had to be going on for him to leave Kat."

"Or he's in some kind of trouble too?"

Cameron nodded.

"Don't think so," Mr. Trent said. "Elsewise his Honor wouldn't have let you all sign those papers." He looked over at Kat. "You know you cannot stay with the boys now, starting tonight. It wouldn't be right."

"We'll fix up the extra room while you all go to worship, and tomorrow we'll figure it out, so Samuel is here too to help decide," Mrs. Trent said. "Go get yourselves ready. It's after six o'clock."

When Kat came down the stairs, Ben and Cam stared at her in amazement. "You are beautiful," Ben said. "Sam better get smart quick."

A loud knock made them all jump. Cameron cautiously opened the door, where a sailor from their congregation stood along with Iain Calder. "For some reason, my parents thought you guys needed a wagon tonight. Oh! Kat. Is that really you?"

Even though it hardly ever snowed in San Francisco, the night air had that smell of crispness just before a fresh snow. They appreciated the Calders' thoughtfulness as they wrapped up in the thick blankets.

Kat leaned back against the rough wood and gazed up at the sky shining with stars. She tracked the star course her parents would have taken last year to sail home by. From the time she reached ten, her father had carefully taught her how to navigate by stars and by nautical charts. Their last trip had been the only one she ever missed being on. Without the knowledge he taught her, the sky would just be a jumble. Beautiful and awe-inspiring, but still a jumble. Only God knew every name and every course point. Every voice and every note.

He had seen the course her path would take this past year, the intersecting paths of all their lives. Sam and Cameron finding her. She finding Ben. Samuel saving the judge who saved them today. Samuel making the Scriptures and faith real to her and to all he met. Before she had faith, of course, but more because she believed her parents and she rode their faith, especially when in danger on the sea. But this year she had lived faith day to day. Because Sam had shown her how in concrete prayer. She did love him for that knowledge, but also because she loved him for himself. Maybe he thought she loved him as only her rescuer. Or he didn't love her the way she loved. All a jumble. And only God knew their course.

So she had to let go and trust, no matter the pain if he rejected her permanently. But she could stay in the city and find a mentor for her music. She could still be friends and remain in Ben and Cameron's lives, in the church, and their fellowship with the Calders. *If.* If God gave her affirmation.

Tonight she would praise. Praise for new hope and new music and new opportunities. Praise for friends and praise for the Lord's ongoing protection.

She pulled out of her reverie as Iain gave a whoop. "We'll be in the same school. Great!"

She smiled. Iain had shot up this summer, almost as tall as Cameron, but as skinny as Ben. Although two years older, he and Ben became friends right from their first meeting, and now they would be in school together. Another course planned. Both boys had gone through hardship, and they knew kindred spirits.

"Miss Katrina," Iain began a little shyly.

"I'm still Kat, Iain."

"Oh, good. How long have you played the cello?"

"From the time I could hold one up. And before that my mother told me that as a baby I would go and sit next to one whenever I saw one. She used to say God created me with cello music written on my heart. And in some ways it's true. When I write music for the cello, it sings words and thoughts I don't know how to say."

"That's exactly how I feel when I draw. Then how come you haven't played all these months we've known you?"

"If anyone looked for me they would expect me to be playing the cello. So I had to give it up and let them think the kidnappers had succeeded."

The wagon pulled up before the meeting hall, and Kat took a deep breath before taking Ben's arm. Cameron went around the back with Iain to set up the cello for her. As they walked in, several people called out to Ben and looked at Kat curiously. They didn't recognize her. She smiled a little at the irony of a reverse disguise. But still no sign of Samuel.

Worship began, and the meeting hall filled with happiness. After the short sermon, Kat slipped up to the chair behind the podium.

The hall quieted as Pastor Ahlberg came to the center. "What a blessed worship, and we still have one more offering and a welcome before communion. Many of you know The Sandpiper Troupe, as they have worshipped with us since the summer. What you do not know is that Kat is actually Katrina, and after a year of forced disguise, she takes back her true identity tonight. She is also an acclaimed cellist and closes our worship with a ballad she has written, 'A Carol of Light,' to give welcome to this week before our Savior's birth. Also today our council has approved the examination and interviews for our new associate pastor who will begin a year's training with us before his ordination. He will close us in prayer." He lifted the podium and stepped away from in front of Kat, and the lights went out.

"To You, Lord, be the glory," she prayed in a whisper and began to play. The mournful strings danced under her, and she felt her heart soar free. Tonight she'd play the music only as she had no one to sing the lyrics. Maybe one day, Samuel would see her and accept her. She knew she had to let him go and trust God for both their futures.

As she lowered the volume for the vocal part, a deep baritone rang out from the side, and a man walked toward her in the dark. "'Racing the waves the merchant ship, sped eagerly for child and home, a Christmas day to embrace, as the light continues to burn.'"

Samuel sang beside her in the darkness. He knew her lyrics by heart. Her tears flowed again as she looked up into his face and realized he wore a pastor's collar, the new pastor. *Oh, Lord, thank you.* Is that where he had rushed off to, to take his examination? As they finished the ballad, the congregation remained in a hush, the best kind of response.

Samuel took her hand in his and squeezed lightly. "Lord, thank you that in all circumstances Your light burns away our darkness. We cannot always see, yet may we always trust Your grace to carry us through. To You be the glory. May we wait upon Your birth with hope and expectation and courage. Amen."

Then he held her in his arms. "Katrina, I have loved you from the first day I saw you. When I heard that I almost you lost today, I realized that without you my life would forever have an emptiness. Will you marry me, my Kat?"

"Oh, yes." Even though she had stopped playing her cello, music soared even higher within her, stretching towards the heavens with pure joy.

Cameron and Ben ran forward and wrapped their arms around them.

Samuel stepped back. "My family," he said to the smiling congregation. Together, all four knelt hand in hand for the communion blessing.

Ballad *The Carol of Light*

by Kat

Racing waves the merchant ship
Sped eagerly for child and home
A Christmas day to embrace
As the light continues to burn.

Seven days away
Storm clouds near, sabotage within
Plan evil intent
As the light continues to burn.

In darkness sailor slid away
Left damaged ship no escape
Heaven's hearth their resting place
As the light continues to burn.

Steadfast through the night
Their daughter watched horizon
Church bells rang at dawn
As the light continues to burn.

Submerged in grief did not see
Danger standing on her doorstep
Buried sorrow in her music
As the light continues to burn.

Guardian set trap
Bound and sold into slavery
Heaven intervened
As the light continues to burn.

Beaten, broken, untied her ropes
Crawled through Sierra hills
Shepherd prince found her, bound wounds
As the light continues to burn.

Hidden as a boy
Four now all gifted with music
New traveling troupe
As the light continues to burn.

Seven days away Christmas
She remembered His gift of grace
Pierces darkness, hope brings truth
As the light continues to burn.

Leaves disguise behind
Chooses life, love, no more shadows
Will he take her hand?
As the light continues to burn.

Historical Note

Although this is a work of fiction, there are two historical facts mentioned within the story. Donalinda Cameron is a real missionary who battled for social justice almost forty years (1895-1934), in San Francisco and throughout California, to free young Asian girls, mostly Chinese, from slavery as indentured servants and forced prostitution. It was often referred to as the "Yellow Slave Trade." Cameron became the Superintendent of the Presbyterian Mission Home at the age of twenty-five.

Also, only a few theaters survived the 1906 earthquake and ensuing fires. Only the best known were rebuilt. However, before the earthquake, there were so many theaters throughout the city that some journalists referred to San Francisco as a city of theaters. Almost every immigrant community had a theater in their neighborhood, some giving shows and performances in their native languages.

CECILE'S
CHRISTMAS MIRACLE

Ruth L. Snyder

Living in the desert at Christmas time is so depressing, twenty-four-year-old Cecile thought. She sat cross-legged outside a San Bushman hut made of a semi-circle of branches tied together and then covered with tufts of bushveld grass. The smoke from the fire she was sitting beside drifted up into the sky and disappeared. Branches from thorn trees and moretiwa bushes provided a windbreak and fence around the courtyard. She pasted a smile on her face. Cecile still had her quiet time every morning, but lately the Bible seemed dry and unappetizing, like cold cereal with no milk. Time to get in the spirit of the season, she told herself. Her hostess, Naisa, chattered on, oblivious to Cecile's inner turmoil. Cecile swatted at the flies that plagued her. If she tried hard enough, perhaps she could imagine their continual cacophony as an exuberant chorus of Christmas carolers she wished she were hearing. Cecile watched as a dung beetle rolled a ball of cow dung across the sand. She had become familiar with many bugs and insects she had never seen in North America.

Living and working here was nothing like she had imagined it. In many ways, Cecile felt like she'd been plunked into the middle of a movie set for *The Gods Must Be Crazy*. The calendar said 2002, but these people lived like early settlers in North America. To top it all off, she was hearing rumors about the government relocating the San Bushmen and closing clinics. Something to do with a major discovery of diamonds in the area. She had poured her heart and soul into ministering to these people. Was it all going to come to a sudden ignoble end, like a puff of dandelion seeds being blown into the air? Wasn't right supposed to win? Was her contribution to the San Bushmen just a bunch of smoke that would disappear into nothingness without any lasting impact? *Maybe Dad was right. Maybe I should just pack up, go home, and leave these people to fight their own battles.*

As she sipped her cup of Rooibos tea, Cecile allowed her thoughts to transport her back to childhood memories of Christmas in rural Alberta. She could almost hear the melodious jingling of sleigh bells, accompanied by carefree laughter and the snorts of the horses pulling her father's sleigh. She saw cherubic faces, tinted pink from the cold, peeking out from a melee of toques and scarves. Voices combined in colorful harmony to scatter Christmas carols across the snow-blanketed prairies. After neighbors were treated to the annual round of caroling, people from around the whole community gathered in the local hall. Cecile's mouth watered as she thought of the traditional turkey dinner, which was served complete with dressing, cranberry sauce, and a host of other tasty trimmings. Cecile always looked forward to the first luscious bite of her Grandma's fruitcake. No matter how hard others tried, they just couldn't get their fruitcake to taste like Grandma's. She smiled as she thought of the Christmas tree decorated with a combination of handmade ornaments and candy canes. It was a yearly tradition for all the school children to contribute at least one ornament. Teachers were always looking for new ideas to make the tree even more beautiful than it was the year before. Cecile almost laughed out loud as she remembered her grade two teacher's professed indignation as she was kissed under the mistletoe.

Cecile's heart clenched as she thought of the kiss she had received under the mistletoe just the year before. She pictured Colin's dark wavy hair and his mischievous eyes. She remembered his gentle, questioning kiss and could almost feel the shivers of pleasure tingling right down to her toes even now. Colin was the most eligible bachelor at the party that year. He had graduated with honors from the medical faculty at the University of Alberta and was setting up his practice. Colin asked Cecile to marry him and work with him as his nurse, but she told him no. She felt God was calling her to serve people in a third world country. Her desire to follow God and tell other people about her amazing Savior had been stronger than wanting marriage and a family of her own, so she had turned her back on everything familiar and safe and had ventured to "the end of the world," as her dad called it. She still remembered the pleading look in her father's eyes as he begged her to reconsider her decision and stay in Alberta. A year later, Cecile was beginning to wonder if she had made the right decision. Was following God supposed to be this hard? If she was meant to be here in the Kalahari Desert, then why was her heart begging her to go home to Alberta? Was her life really making a difference to the people around her? Maybe her dad had been right when he commented that she'd never make it on her own in the middle of the desert. Maybe she should just forget it all and go home to Colin, if he still loved her.

Naisa's gentle tap pulled Cecile from her reverie. "Come, go work!"

Colin Dumont parked his Lexus in the stall, which had a placard with his name marked in shiny gold lettering. He opened the door and shivered as a gust of wind whooshed snow into his face. He stepped out into the cold, crisp morning, sputtering while he brushed away the flakes. The snow crunched and squeaked under his feet as he walked up to the clinic, his clinic. As he unlocked the door, he sighed. It was six days before Christmas. He should be excited, but he wasn't. Here he was, doing what he'd always dreamed of doing, in a clinic he'd designed, staffed with people he handpicked . . . well, except for one. Cecile. He wondered what she was doing. How she was doing. If she ever thought of him. He could still imagine how she felt in his arms with her silky blonde hair caressing his cheek. He remembered the pain in her sky-blue eyes as she looked up at him and told him what he never wanted to hear.

"Colin, I do have feelings for you, but I can't marry you. God has placed a burden on my heart for the San Bushman people in Botswana. I have to go. I'm sorry."

Colin swiped at moisture in his eyes as he stomped his feet and entered the clinic. Removing his boots, he slipped his feet into his black oxford shoes. He shook his head to clear his thoughts. Why couldn't he forget about Cecile and get on with his life? After all, there were plenty of other beautiful women willing to spend time with him. His nurses constantly teased him about the flirting that took place in this clinic. But he didn't want to spend time with any other women. He wasn't attracted to any of them. Colin walked into his office and hung up his winter jacket. He paced the floor. This is ridiculous!

"Oh, ya? So what are you going to do about it?"

Colin stopped pacing and looked around. There was no one else in the clinic yet, but he had just heard something, as if someone was talking to him. Was he going crazy?

"Why don't you go join Cecile?"

"Hmmm. Now that's an idea I could go for." Now he had really lost it. Not only was he hearing a voice, but he was also listening to a ridiculous suggestion. Why would he leave everything behind and travel halfway around the world?

"Because you love her AND, more importantly, you love Me."

Wow, this was getting really weird. Was God actually talking to him? Or was his imagination just getting the best of him?

Colin plunked down in his leather office chair. "OK, God, if this is You, show me. I'll need someone to take over my clinic for at least six months, a ticket to Botswana, Africa, and support from my family."

Colin's cell phone chirped. He flicked it on and read the text message.

"Hi, long time no see. Do you know of any clinics looking for a dr? Looking for change." It was Eric, one of his classmates and friends from medical school. Someone he'd trust with his life.

Colin drew his breath in sharply and tapped a reply.

"Hi yourself. Just so happens I need a dr. When can u start and how long u staying?"

"Sooner the better. At least 6 months"

Colin shook his head and chuckled. "How soon can u be here?"

"Tomorrow soon enough?"

Colin couldn't help himself. He let out a loud guffaw. "Sounds great. Call when you arrive. Lodging included in deal."

"Great! Ttyl"

"OK, God. Step one on project Cecile. You've got my attention. Show me what's next."

A sharp rapping on his office door interrupted Colin's thoughts. Eva, one of his "more mature" nurses poked her head around the corner. "Good morning, Dr. Dumont. Sounds like you're in a great mood this morning. Ready for your first patient?"

"Good Morning, Eva. Yes, I'm ready. Thanks. Let's get started."

Cecile followed Naisa out of the gap in the fence and carefully blocked the opening with a jagged piece of tin and some logs. It was only eight in the morning, but already the sun was beating down. It may be December, but that meant it was the middle of summer in the Kalahari. The only ice or snow Cecile would find here would be in the propane freezer she had insisted on bringing with her. Cecile pulled her felt hat tighter onto her head to protect herself from the assault of the sun. Even though the hat was hot, her fair skin didn't fare well without it. Her long-sleeved cotton blouse and loose-fitting, floor-length skirt also provided much-needed protection. In the past few days, the temperatures had hovered between 30 and 40 degrees Celsius during the day. Nights would "cool down" to between 10 and 20 degrees in the summer, only plummeting to the freezing mark occasionally during the African winter months of June and July.

Cecile clambered into the driver's seat of her rickety Land Rover and gestured to Naisa to sit in the passenger seat. Although infrastructure was progressing well in other parts of Botswana, in large part due to the diamond industry, here at the village outside Mabutsane, the dirt trail roads were still impassible unless you had a four-wheel-drive. The monster rumbled to life and grumbled as Cecile shifted into gear. Cecile was making good use of the mechanical knowledge she had gained growing up on her parents' mixed farm. It was a good thing she knew the basics of maintenance like changing oil and checking transmission fluid. If there were major issues, the closest mechanic was hours away. Out here she was considered the expert at many things, because she was the only white person who lived in the village. She still shuddered to think she was regarded as the medical expert in this area. She only had her nursing degree. The nearest major hospital was only 300 kilometers away in Gaborone, but with the roads the way they were it took almost five hours to drive there. Flying Mission provided the only ambulance service (by airplane) in the area, and Cecile had been instructed to use the service only for extreme emergencies due to the cost. The local language was a fascinating combination of clicks, strange vowels, and tones that still left Cecile muddled. That's why Naisa was her translator. Naisa was one of the few women who had been outside the village and had learned rudimentary English.

A cloud of dust announced their arrival at the clinic – a bare mud-brick structure with simple glass windows and a tin roof. Government officials had indicated a brand new clinic would soon be built, but that was before talk of resettlement. A long queue of people waited at the clinic door. Babies wailed and children with runny noses and coughs clung to their mothers. They were kept company by people with tuberculosis who came every day for their medication. The blank looks bothered Cecile the most. These people didn't seem to understand that each of them was a unique individual created on purpose by a loving God.

Do you? Her conscience taunted her. Cecile gritted her teeth. "Yes, I do!"

Naisa gave her a puzzled look. "You do? What you mean?"

Cecile chuckled. "Sorry, Naisa. I was just talking to myself."

Naisa shook her head and opened the door of the jeep. Cecile grabbed her purse and followed suit. Judging by the long line of people, it was going to be another exhausting day.

Cecile's first patient was a toddler, a little girl no more than two years old with second and third-degree burns on her left shoulder and arm. Through Naisa, Cecile caught the broken story:

"She put daughter close to fire. Keep warm."

"It's not that cold at night yet. Why didn't she just give her daughter a blanket?"

Naisa sighed. "She no have blankets."

Tears formed in Cecile's eyes as she gently cleaned the burns. Every time Cecile touched the toddler, the little girl winced and whimpered. Cecile spoke in a soft, soothing tone, even though she knew the girl couldn't understand what she said. Hopefully her body language and tone would communicate what the little girl needed to know. Naisa and the girl's mom held the toddler still while Cecile worked. When the burns were clean, Cecile applied some antimicrobial cream to the red, weepy wounds and then wrapped the shoulder and arm with non-stretch roller gauze. Cecile handed a bar of soap and a tube of cream to the girl's mother.

"Tell her she needs to wash the burns every morning and put cream on in the morning and at night."

Naisa nodded. A heated discussion ensued between Naisa and the mother.

"Why's she arguing with you?"

"She says no water in home. I say she needs get some."

Cecile grimaced. "Why can't she get some from the borehole?"

"She says men come in trucks and destroy borehole. She says they empty tank of water onto ground. They tell people must move."

"Move where?"

"I tell later. You have water we send? If not, no washing."

Cecile retrieved her canteen and handed it to the mother. *I'm not sure how many gifts I'll be getting this Christmas, but I can share what I have.* Looking directly into the mother's eyes she said, "Here, take my water. When you need more, come get some from the clinic rain barrel." Naisa translated. The mother accepted the canteen with two hands and dipped her head in thanks. Then, with tears dripping down her face, she shook Cecile's hand and left.

Cecile glanced up at a plaque on the wall.

"Matthew 25:35-36 'For I was hungry and you gave me something to eat, I was thirsty and you gave me something to drink, I was a stranger and you invited me in, I needed clothes and you clothed me, I was sick and you looked after me, I was in prison and you came to visit me.'"

"Thank you, Lord Jesus, for the reminder that I'm actually serving You every time I bind up a wound. Give me wisdom and strength to be a servant to these people."

Colin finished dictating notes for his previous patient into his Dictaphone. Even though he had been attentive to Mrs. Andrews and had provided information so that she could learn everything she needed to know about the upcoming delivery of her first child, his mind had been thousands of kilometers away with a certain young, slender nurse. Sitting down at his desk, Colin dialed the local travel agent.

"Good morning, Mr. Yachurski. I know this is short notice, but is there any way you could get me to Botswana by Christmas?"

Colin winced at the reaction. "Yes, I know I should have planned ahead more, but could you see what you can do for me? I'd really like to surprise Cecile Amyotte by arriving on Christmas day."

Colin tapped his pen against his desk while he waited. "There's no openings? Are you sure? There must be some way I can get there."

Colin heard more clicking noises. He didn't realize he was holding his breath until Mr. Yachurski came back on the line and asked if he'd be willing to go standby. "Yes, I'm willing to go standby . . . as long as you can guarantee I'll be there for Christmas. What's that? You can't guarantee arrival date on standby? Tell you what. Keep your eyes open for flights. If you can find me something other than standby, I'll throw in an extra five hundred dollars."

Colin blew out his breath. "God? If this is supposed to happen, You will have to make a way. You parted the Red Sea, and you can get me to Botswana, Africa, if You want me to go. Help me trust You . . . and show me if this is my idea or Yours."

Colin sighed as he took the next patient's chart out and reviewed it. Mr. Howard didn't come to see him very often. He was a very healthy senior who enjoyed travelling. Maybe Mr. Howard needed some updates on his immunizations. Colin placed a smile on his face and knocked on the door, then opened it and walked into the check-up room. Mr. Howard greeted him with a half-hearted smile.

"Good Morning, Mr. Howard. What can I do for you today?"

"Morning, Dr. Dumont. I'm hoping you have good news for me, but I think I may have to cancel my next trip. I have a rash that's very painful and it's driving me crazy."

"I'm sorry to hear that, Mr. Howard. Let's take a look, shall we?"

Mr. Howard cringed as he pulled up his shirt. "It started out with pain, and then this morning when I woke up I had this." He pointed to a large red rash on the left side of his torso, which was starting to blister.

Colin nodded. "Unfortunately, Mr. Howard, you have shingles. I'm assuming you had Chickenpox as a child?"

Mr. Howard nodded.

"I can prescribe some antiviral cream which will help prevent the rash from spreading. Usually the cream helps the rash disappear sooner than if you don't use it. Shingles can be very painful, so I'd advise you to use the cream. Otherwise you may not get much sleep for a few days. Other than that, you'll have to let it run its course."

Mr. Howard groaned. "Just what I didn't want to hear. And so close to Christmas! What about my travel plans?

"When were you planning to leave?"

"In three days."

Colin placed his hand on Mr. Howard's shoulder. "I'm not going to tell you what to do, but I'd advise against travel for at least a couple of months. Shingles is not contagious per se, but you probably won't be sleeping like you usually do, and stress will cause the shingles to flare up and get worse."

Mr. Howard hung his head and said something so softly Colin couldn't hear what he said.

"What was that? I didn't catch what you said."

Mr. Howard looked into Colin's eyes and said, "So much for my safari in Botswana."

Colin was incredulous. "You mean you have a ticket to fly to Botswana? That's great!"

"What do you mean, that's great?" Mr. Howard's eyes were dark and cold.

"Oh, sorry. It's not great for you, but you just may be the answer to my prayers. You see, I'm hoping to go to Botswana to visit Cecile Amyotte. The only problem is, I only decided to go this morning, and there are no tickets available, and if I go standby there's no guarantee that I'll arrive before Christmas, and . . ."

Mr. Howard chuckled. "Slow down there, young man. I would be delighted to give you my ticket. Merry Christmas!"

"Are you sure, Mr. Howard?"

"Of course I'm sure. There's no way I'm standing in the way of love, especially at Christmas. Thank you for solving my dilemma."

"Let me write you a check then. How much do I owe you?"

"Are you getting deaf, Dr. Dumont? I said I would GIVE you my ticket."

Colin grabbed Mr. Howard in a bear hug. "Thank you, thank you!"

Mr. Howard pushed free of the hug and looked at Colin dubiously. "You're welcome, I think. Save your hugs for that young lady you're going to visit."

Colin felt his face flushing. "Oh, sorry, Mr. Howard." He reached out and grabbed Mr. Howard's hand, pumping it up and down. "Thanks again."

"Don't thank me yet. You don't even have the ticket in your possession. I'll drop it off this afternoon." With a grin and a wave, Mr. Howard eased himself out of the office.

Colin watched him exit and then sat down at his computer. "Lord, is it okay if I give Cecile a heads up?" He waited for a few seconds and sensed no check in his spirit. He opened his email and found Cecile's address. It took several tries before Colin was comfortable with the wording.

Hi Cecile,

Sorry I haven't communicated with you for a while. I think the last time I wrote was just after the clinic opened. I have been busy, but that's no excuse. I want you to know that you are still very important to me.

It looks like it may work out for me to come see what you're up to, as long as that's OK with you. I can't believe how things are falling into place to make the trip possible. It may be as soon as Christmas. When I have all the details, I'll write you again.

Until then, take care and God bless.

Sincerely,

Colin

Colin clicked on the send button. He felt like he was going to burst if he didn't share the news with someone. He ran down the hallway and spied Eva closing the door to another check-up room. Colin grabbed Eva's hands and spun her in a circle.

"Guess what, Eva! I'm going to Botswana for Christmas . . . to see Cecile."

Eva laughed. "My, my, aren't you in a giddy mood today. I'm happy for you, but you'd better stop spinning me around before I get dizzy, land on top of you, and break one of your bones. Then you won't be going!"

Colin stopped and steadied Eva before he let go of her hands. "Sorry, I don't know what's come over me. You wouldn't believe it if I told you everything that's happened today. Oh, excuse me. I need to phone Mr. Yachurski and let him know I have a ticket already."

Colin heard Eva's chuckle following him as he returned to his office and dialed.

"Hello, Mr. Yachurski, I won't be needing that ticket after all..."

Cecile smiled as she greeted the next patient – a young teenager who had large bruises and welts on his arms and legs. Looking closer, Cecile noted the boy's left leg projected out at a strange angle. Cecile waited as Naisa questioned the teen, noting that her voice increased in volume as the query continued. The boy's speech was slurred and he tottered on the chair as if he was going to fall over. After a few minutes, Cecile placed her hand on Naisa's arm.

"What's up?"

"This boy hurt by men."

"Why?"

"Men they take away pump and pipes from borehole. Boy try stop them. Family need water."

"So they attacked him?"

Naisa's eyes were hard as flint. "Yes. Use pipe to hit. Boy have to be carried here by family."

Cecile felt the blood rushing to her head. No wonder Naisa was angry. "OK, well let's help this boy. We'll have to deal with the men who hurt him later."

The boy flinched when Cecile touched his arm.

"Tell him I'm not angry with him. I'm angry with the people who hurt him." Cecile watched the boy relax as Naisa spoke to him. Cecile calmed her breathing and steeled herself for the task ahead.

"First, I'll do a thorough exam. It looks like he has a displaced fracture in his left leg. Maybe there are other injuries too. Tell him to let me know if something hurts when I touch it."

The boy nodded his understanding, but in the typical San Bushman way, he sat stoically as Cecile performed the exam. She had to rely more on her observations of wincing and quick intakes of breath than his verbal response to determine if there were any other serious injuries. The left leg appeared to have taken the brunt of the beating.

"Now I need you to tell him we have to line his leg up so it will heal properly. It's going to hurt."

When Naisa began to talk to the boy, he exclaimed and argued. However, as she continued to talk, he nodded at Cecile and bit his lip.

"He ready," Naisa said.

"What did you tell him?"

Naisa smiled. "I say he mighty hunter."

Cecile grinned back. "Smart thinking."

When Cecile had been in nurse's training, she never thought she would be setting a broken bone. That was a doctor's job. "Lord, guide my hands and heal these wounds. This young lad has enough invisible scars. He doesn't need visible ones too."

An hour later, the leg was straight and had a cast on it. Perspiration stood out on all three foreheads. The boy dipped his thanks as his family members carried him out.

Cecile turned around to see her next patient had already taken her seat – a young mother. Just as Naisa was providing details about the woman's condition, Cecile heard the roar of a vehicle and was startled to see a tall, thin African man dressed in a white shirt and three-piece suit push his way into the clinic. She didn't have long to wonder what was going on.

"Who's in charge here?"

Cecile stepped forward. "I am."

The man stepped towards her, waving some papers as if they were a weapon. "My name is Nathan Baboloki. I have here papers telling you to shut your clinic down, effective immediately."

Cecile put her hands on her hips, "I will do no such thing."

"Then you'll be deported for rebelling against the government."

"What are you talking about?"

"You need to close this clinic. If you comply, you will be provided with finances to build a clinic in an area designated by the government for resettlement."

"So you're bribing me." Cecile felt heat rising to her face.

Nathan had not closed the door when he came in. Naisa and the woman had slipped out the door. Outside, the patients were all quiet, watching and listening to the confrontation.

"I'm going to close the door and then we'll finish talking about this. These people don't need to be dragged into the conversation."

Nathan laughed a dry, humorless laugh. "Oh, but they're already part of the conversation. You see, they've been told to have all their belongings moved by this afternoon. We will be taking their houses apart, twig-by-twig, starting tomorrow morning. That is, we'll take care of the houses after we deal with the clinic."

Cecile stopped mid-stride, mouth wide open, just like the door. "What kind of monster are you? I just finished treating a teenaged boy wounded by one of your men. His only crime was trying to protect the borehole that means the difference between life and death to him. These people have nothing. It's six days before Christmas. And you're going to strip them of everything they DO have?!"

"I apologize for the timing, but I do not apologize for my actions. I know it will soon be Christmas, but I am under orders to make sure the people of this village and all the surrounding areas move to the outskirts of Gaborone as soon as possible. We are harming them by allowing them to maintain their hunting and gathering lifestyle here in the desert. Our world is changing and we must help them catch up, or they will be destroyed by their own backwardness."

Cecile slammed the door shut and turned. She folded her arms and clutched them tightly against herself. "I cannot believe you just said that. What's wrong with giving people choices about where they live and what they do? This is not about protecting people from their backwardness. This is about greed . . . and money." Cecile took a breath and tried to calm herself so that she could think clearly. "If you have money to relocate people, then certainly you have money to help them experience new things. Instead of stopping up wells, why don't you build them, so that these people don't have to work so hard to eke out an existence? Instead of chasing them away from the animals, which provide their food and clothing, why don't you teach them how to herd animals and grow crops, so that they become self-sufficient?"

Nathan strode towards her, "We WILL teach them those things, but it will be where we decide, not here. Our whole country is being held hostage by them. We, as the government, need to have the ability to develop the wonderful natural resources we have in this country."

Cecile intentionally softened her tone. "You CAN develop the resources you have. Look at all the tourists who come to see the elephants, giraffe, and the other big five in the game reserves."

"I can see I'm wasting my time," Nathan said. "Our government is ready for progress. In order for new game parks AND diamond mines to be built, these people need to move out of this area. We have discovered a mother lode of diamonds here, and we have diamond mining companies waiting to set up their equipment as we speak. Tourist groups are also waiting to set up hotels and take people on those game drives you referenced. But first, these people have to go. Remember what I said. You have to close these doors immediately and start packing for your move. Tomorrow I will be closing the doors for good. Be ready with all the supplies packed in boxes at 8:00 A.M."

Cecile stood with her mouth gaping as Nathan turned on his heel and marched out the door.

Colin was just finishing up his roast beef and vegetable wrap when the phone rang. The ladies were out of the office for lunch, so Colin answered the phone after the second ring.

"Good afternoon, Dr. Dumont speaking."

"Hi Colin, this is Mom. Sorry to bother you at the office."

"Mom, is something wrong?"

"Wrong? No, I'm just in the middle of answering invitations to Christmas events, and I need to know what you want to attend with us."

"Uh, Mom, there's something I need to tell you."

"Oh? Is it something to do with a female? Did you meet someone?"

"Well, yes, it does have something to do with a girl." Colin pulled the phone away from his ear as his Mom screamed.

"I knew it! What's her name? Where's she from? How long have you been seeing her?"

"Uh, Mom, you need to calm down and listen. You know her very well. We grew up together."

"Well, why are you keeping me in suspense? Who is it?"

"It's Cecile."

"Cecile? I thought she was in Africa?"

"Well, she is."

"Then how are you going to bring her home for Christmas?"

154

Colin sighed. "Mom, I'm not. Cecile is still in Africa, and I'm going there to see her. Eric is coming to take over my practice for a few months."

The line was deathly quiet.

"Mom, are you still there?"

"Yes, I'm still here." His mother's voice was quiet. Too quiet.

"Is there a problem, Mom?"

"Is there a problem? He asks if there's a problem. I'm at home making elaborate plans for Christmas so my son can meet and marry the girl of his dreams, and he's taking off and going to Africa to spend time with the girl who dashed his dreams. Not only that, but he's leaving behind the clinic he worked a decade to get set up and throwing away all the training his parents paid for. Is there a problem? WHAT DO YOU THINK?"

Colin sent a quick prayer up for wisdom. "Mom, I'm sorry. This all came about rather suddenly. That's why you haven't heard about it. In fact, I just decided this morning . . . " Colin jerked the phone away as he heard the receiver slam into place on the other end. "...that I would go, as long as three things fall into place for me," he said to the silent receiver, which rested in his hand.

Colin hung up the phone and then closed his eyes and bowed his head. "Oh God, what am I doing? Is this Your will, or mine? From everything that's happened, I thought it was Your will. But Father, I can't go against the wishes of my parents. Show me Your will. I leave it all in Your hands."

"Are you OK, Dr. Dumont?"

Colin looked up and saw Eva standing beside the door to his office. "Oh, hi, Eva. I'm fine. Just a bit confused."

"You, confused?"

Colin chuckled. "Yes, me. It seemed like everything was working out for me to go see Cecile for Christmas. But I told God to show me it was His will by making three things happen. The first two are in place, but the last condition looks like Mount Everest right now."

Eva entered his office and closed the door behind her. "You want to talk about it?"

"Well, I guess that couldn't hurt. This morning when I was thinking about Cecile, I told God that if this was His idea I needed someone to take over my practice for at least six months, I needed a ticket for Africa, AND I wanted my family's support. My friend Eric is coming tomorrow to work in the clinic – I was going to let the staff know this afternoon. Mr. Howard is bringing my ticket by this afternoon. He booked a ticket to Botswana for a safari, but as you know, he has the shingles and is not feeling up to going. He wouldn't even let me pay him for the ticket, he is so tickled about me going to see Cecile."

"So the last condition is that your family supports you? And they don't?"

"That's correct, Eva. I just finished talking to my mom a few minutes ago. She was livid when I started telling her about my plans. I thought my dad would be the hard one to convince, but even my mom is not in favor. If they don't want me to go, I guess the deal's off." Colin felt a big lump growing in his throat.

"Well, I say you should go, even if your family doesn't support you. Why would you let them get in the way of love?"

Colin shook his head. "As much as I'm tempted, I can't. I'm trying to follow God, and He says I should honor my father and my mother. I know I don't have to do what they say. I'm an adult now and perfectly capable of making my own choices. But I'm not sure if this idea is mine or God's. I know He can change my parents' hearts IF He wants me to go to Africa."

"I can't say I understand your logic, but I respect your integrity. It's not too often I see a young person honoring his father and mother nowadays."

Colin smiled. "Thanks, Eva. That means a lot. Well, I guess it's time to get back to work."

The door swung open wide and a very pregnant woman waddled in with Naisa. The mother-to-be gritted her teeth and nodded her head at Cecile as Naisa led her towards the birthing table. After the patient was on the table, Naisa shooed everyone else out of the clinic, then closed and locked the door.

Cecile sent up another quick prayer, thankful she had done her practicum in obstetrics. However, aiding with a birth and being the attending "doctor" were two different things. Especially when there was absolutely no one to call on if something went wrong.

"It time for baby."

The mother groaned in agreement.

"Naisa, heat the water. I'll get set up here." Cecile performed a quick physical examination. "Oh, no!"

Naisa came back to the table. "Something wrong?"

Cecile tried to push down the panic that was engulfing her. "Ask her how long she's been having pains. This baby is breach."

Naisa looked puzzled.

Cecile forced herself to speak in a clear, gentle manner, so as not to alarm the mother. "We have to try to turn the baby. Right now the bottom is coming out first. We need the head." As she spoke, Cecile punctuated her words with actions, trying to help Naisa and the mother understand. She gritted her teeth. Valuable time was being used up. She wanted them to know what was happening so that they could all work together, but she didn't want to lose the baby, or the mother. "I will need to push on the mother's abdomen and push the baby around into the head-down position. Tell the mother to let me know if I'm hurting her."

As Cecile started to work on turning the baby, her instructor's words came back as if there was a recording in her head. "When a baby is breach, the doctor will perform an external cephalic version or ECV. It is preferable for the ECV to be performed between 32 and 37 weeks gestation. The success rate is about 58 percent, but sometimes a baby will not move or will end up rotating back into a breech position after the procedure. If this is not the mother's first delivery, the chances of success are much greater. There are several risks associated with the ECV. The placenta may separate from the uterine wall. If this happens, the baby must be delivered quickly by way of an emergency c-section. The heart rate of the baby may also drop suddenly and not recover. This will also necessitate an emergency c-section. A doctor should always perform this procedure where facilities for an emergency c-section are available."

The baby was not turning. Cecile bowed her head. "Heavenly Father, you know this situation is way beyond me. Guide my hands and help me deliver this baby, please!"

Cecile glanced up to see Naisa staring at her. "I just prayed that God would help me. I've never done this before." Cecile glimpsed panic flash across Naisa's features before she shoved it away, focusing on her part of the task. Cecile turned her focus back to the mother, who was panting and groaning. Cecile had no way of knowing how the baby was faring. She continued to push, praying as she did. Little by little the baby rotated. Cecile performed another internal examination. She let her breath out as she felt the head and confirmed it was in the down position. Cecile gave Naisa a thumbs up. "OK, this baby's ready for birth. Coach the mother through the birth process."

There were many grunts and tears, but Cecile was amazed at how calm the mother was during the process. A couple hours later a baby landed in Cecile's open arms. Cecile smiled as she heard the squall of the newborn. Despite the odds, the woman delivered a healthy boy. Cecile knew she had witnessed a miracle.

There was a loud knock on the door.

Cecile looked at the new mother, who smiled and gestured that Cecile should open the door. Cecile strode to the door and opened it. There stood Nathan Baboloki.

Cecile put her hands on her hips. "Go away. You told me I had until . . ."

Nathan cut her off mid-sentence. "I'm not here about the clinic. I'm here to see my wife AND baby."

Cecile turned around and looked at the patient holding her newborn son. The mother was smiling broadly and waving for Nathan to come in. "You mean . . ."

Nathan smiled. "I mean you just helped make me a father, and I want to see my child. I knew my wife would have our baby soon, but I didn't realize it would be today. And I didn't know that I would need the services offered in your clinic. May I come in?"

Cecile moved away from the door and gestured for Nathan to enter. She closed the door behind him and then mouthed a quick prayer. "God, I don't know what you're up to here, but use this event to help the San Bushmen."

Nathan introduced Cecile and Naisa to his wife, Obwile. "She decided to come with me on my business trip. Her sister lives in the village over there." He gestured using his chin. "Sometime this morning she started having the pains. When the traditional village midwife checked her, she knew my wife needed more help than she could give, so she brought her here. Thank you for saving my son."

Cecile nodded. She took a deep breath. "Actually, it was God who saved your son. You see, I probably don't have as much experience as the midwife. Just more book learning. Without God's help, your son and perhaps even your wife would have died."

Nathan held the baby at a right angle to himself so he could gaze into his son's eyes.

The mother smiled and spoke to her husband.

Nathan looked at Cecile. "She says our son needs a name that reminds us all of what happened and how he came to be born. She's naming him Ontlametse, which means He [God] has protected me; He [God] has taken care of me."

Cecile swiped at the tears that were threatening to drip out of her eyes.

Nathan turned to Cecile. "Now, about closing the clinic. . ."

Cecile sighed. "I know. I haven't packed yet. I'll. . ."

"You've been busy. . .delivering my son and helping many more people. I will talk to my superiors and see what I can do to keep this clinic open. I'm not promising anything, but at least the clinic can stay open temporarily. Sorry for my intrusion earlier today." Nathan held out his hand to Cecile.

"What about the village?"

Nathan took a deep breath. "I'll do what I can. That's all I can promise."

Cecile clasped Nathan's hand and shook it. "Thank you."

The rest of the afternoon flew by for Colin. There was a steady stream of patients with the usual maladies - respiratory infections, complications from diabetes, hypertension, and people wanting an easy way to lose weight. At 5:00 P.M. Colin held a quick meeting with his staff, said goodbye, and drove home. He usually enjoyed the thirty-minute drive out of town to his lakeside property, which was surrounded by pine and spruce trees. Tonight, however, Colin wished he could snap his fingers and be instantly transported from work to home. While he drove, he made lists in his mind of what needed to be done before he left for Botswana. He kept reminding himself that he was not free to go yet, that he wanted and needed his family's support or he would not go. When he finally did make it home, he decided to spend half an hour on the treadmill to clear his mind. Colin listened to Stephen Curtis Chapman as he jogged. Some of the words from the song, "Great Expectations," seemed to jump out at him. The song stressed the importance of believing the unbelievable and receiving the inconceivable and then invited the listener to come to the Lord with great expectations.

"Yes, Lord, I do come with great expectations. I want to be open to whatever you have for me. If it's being faithful here in my practice, so be it. If it's going to Africa to see Cecile and see if there's a future for us together somehow, then even better. You know about the roadblock I have. Give me wisdom, please." Soon his jog was over and he consciously tried to relax as the warm spray of the shower pelted his back. He dried himself off, dressed, and then ran up the stairs to the main floor.

Colin stood by the counter, pondering what he should make for supper. Although his stomach was rumbling, he knew he wouldn't be able to eat until he resolved things with his mother. Sighing, he picked up the phone and dialed his parents' number. *Ring, ring.* "Come on, Mom and Dad! Pick up. A message isn't going to cut it this time." *Ring.*

"Hello, Dumont residence."

Colin let out his breath. "Oh, hi, Dad. How are you?"

"Hi, Collin! I'm fine. It's good to hear your voice again. Will we be seeing you soon?"

Colin raked his fingers through his damp hair. "Uh, I'm not sure. I take it you haven't talked to Mom about our conversation earlier today?"

"No, she didn't say anything about talking to you. Is something up?" Colin heard voices murmuring in the background and then there was a click.

"Are you both on the line now?"

"Yes, Colin, I put the phone on speaker mode so we can all talk."

"Thanks, Dad. Hi again, Mom. Listen, Mom, I've been thinking about the conversation we had earlier and I want you to know that I'm sorry for taking you for granted. I love you and Dad and want to honor you by what I do. If you want me home for Christmas, I'll be there."

"Thanks, Colin, I appreciate your apology. Let's talk this over with Dad and come to a conclusion together. Maybe I was a bit hasty with my words this afternoon."

Colin brought his dad up to speed about what had taken place that day. Both of his parents asked questions to clarify what his intentions were regarding how long he was planning to be away, and where things stood with Cecile.

"I know this sounds crazy, but I really feel I need to go see Cecile and see if there's a possibility of a future together for us. I can't get her out of my mind, and until I resolve our relationship, I won't be free to pursue any other relationship."

"Thanks for being honest with us, Son," said his father.

"Yes, thanks, Colin. I was angry this afternoon, because I don't want to see you hurt again. After listening to you, it sounds to me like you need to make this trip so you can move on with your life."

"I agree with your mother. If this is what you feel you should do, then you have my blessing."

"So you don't feel like I'm rejecting you and what you've done for me? What if Cecile and I end up getting married and stay in Africa for years? I know I'm really imagining things now, but I need to know."

Colin heard his dad clearing his throat. "Colin, we respect the young man you've become, and we know you don't make decisions lightly. If you did, you wouldn't be talking to us right now. I repeat: You have your mom's and my blessing to go to Africa and follow whatever path you choose. We can deal with the ramifications if and when we need to. Go enjoy yourself. Follow your heart. We love you, Colin!"

Colin felt a lump growing in his throat. "Mom and Dad, you don't know how much this means to me. You've given me one of the best Christmas presents ever! I'll keep you informed as much as possible . . ."

"Colin, you'd better get packing. Three days is not a lot of time to get ready to go halfway around the world."

Colin laughed, "Yes, Mom. I'll get right on it. I love you both. Bye for now."

Colin hung up the phone and raised his arms high, pumping his fists in a victory celebration. "Wow, God, you did it. You really did!"

It had been a long day, and Cecile was ready for bed. However, before they left the clinic, Cecile wanted to check her emails. The clinic was the only location in the area that had internet access and a computer. A few minutes later, Cecile cheered. Her inbox had fifty new messages. She heartily agreed with the verse in Proverbs 25:25, "Like cold water to a thirsty soul, so is good news from a far country." She read through several messages, including a couple from her parents. They were great at describing events that were taking place and keeping her up-to-date with what people were doing. Her hand trembled as she held the pointer over the next message, from Colin Dumont. Hesitating for a mere second, she double-clicked. Halfway through the e-mail, she gasped.

"Something wrong, Cecile?" Naisa hurried over to the computer.

Cecile jumped up and hugged Naisa. "Not at all! One of my friends may be coming to see me. For Christmas."

Naisa smiled. "I happy too. Good day. Now time go home."

"Thanks, Naisa. Yes, it's time to go home. Let's go."

Late that night, Cecile limped into her hut. Her legs felt like jelly, her back ached, and her arms felt like they had been squeezed through her grandma's wringer washing machine. However, Cecile's smile stretched from ear to ear, and there was nothing fake about it. She shook her head as she thought about the events of the day.

The baby's birth was not the only miracle Cecile had experienced. Cecile still missed her family. She hoped she'd be able to Skype with them if the server speed would allow it, but it wouldn't be the same as sitting around the table enjoying a turkey dinner and having animated conversations with them. Cecile wasn't going to experience the wonder and beauty of snow or the excitement of exchanging gifts and other childhood traditions she had grown up with either. But she had no doubt that God was with her and she was where she was supposed to be. And soon Colin would be coming. The primitive surroundings would help them focus on the birth of Jesus Christ and celebrate the true meaning of the season. Christmas in the desert wasn't going to be so depressing after all.

Yankee Doodle Christmas

Sheila Seiler Lagrand

"**R**uth?" Margot called out her mother-in-law's name as she darted into the library, her panic rising. Clattering down the gleaming oak floors of the hallway, she raced through the kitchen and yanked open the door to the pantry. "Ruth? Are you in here?"

Spinning around, she headed for the staircase, nearly colliding with her husband. "Paul!" she gasped. "I didn't hear you come in! I can't find Mom!"

"Calm down, Dear. Breathe." He slipped an arm around her, patting her back. "I'll help you."

"But what if she's wandered off?"

"If she's wandered, we'll find her. Everyone in Mitchell knows she's my mother."

"Shh. Listen!" A faint thumping noise sent Margot scurrying down the hall toward Ruth's bedroom. Paul followed her. He suppressed a chuckle as he stepped into his mother's room. She sat on the floor in her closet, hatboxes scattered around her. She'd tied a large, floppy straw hat onto her head, completely obscuring her wavy hair, so white now it almost glittered. Margot stood at the door to the closet, scowling. "Ruth! What on earth?"

"Help me up, now, would you? That's a dear. And don't be such a worrier! I remembered you had said you were decorating today, so I came in to get out my sun hat so I could help you. Hanging that bunting is hot work!"

"Bunting?" Margot shook her head. "We're setting up the Nativity scene, not—"

163

"Let's listen to Mom's ideas, sweetheart." Paul cut his wife off. Hadn't the doctor explained that when she was confused, arguing with his mother was pointless? Margot looked at her husband, her green eyes flashing as she bored an imaginary hole in his forehead.

He's reading me, Margot thought as her husband gazed back at her. *Once he learned to read my expression, I could never keep a secret from him. . .* "But I promised the ladies of the women's fellowship that we'd display the traditional Nativity in the parlor, just as Pastor Jacobsen's wife always did. Why, they made it out to practically be a condition of occupying the parsonage!" Margot's protest cut off her husband's fond reverie.

His mother was unperturbed. "You two chat away," Ruth chirped. "I'm going down to the basement for the bunting. We must be ready for the big Fourth of July Parade!" She strode purposefully down the hall, her enormous hat flouncing in time to her step.

Margot looked down the hallway to make sure Ruth was out of earshot. "Fourth of July? What on earth? Oh, Paul, she's all mixed up again! What am I to do? The Christmas Home Tour is tonight, and the ladies made it *very* clear when we moved in last spring that the parsonage parlor has always been the showpiece of the tour. We are to set up that large Nativity scene that's down in the basement in front of the parlor picture window. Mrs. Delsey even suggested I bake her famous butter cookies and serve them with hot cider. As if I couldn't be trusted to provide proper refreshments!"

"Honey, relax. I'll see if I can't get Mom reoriented to the right holiday. And don't you worry about Mrs. Delsey. I promise you, our congregation loves you. You're a great pastor's wife and they all see that. It's going to be fine. Just fine."

Margot watched her husband disappear down the stairway leading to the basement. Closing the door to her mother-in-law's room, she retreated to her kitchen. Glancing at the clock, she noted that it was only 8:30. Pouring herself a cup of coffee, she sat at the maple table and gazed out over the back yard.

Had it really only been nine months since they had left Los Angeles and moved to Mitchell? Somehow it seemed like much longer. Margot brushed her dark hair back from her forehead as she pondered the twists and turns the past year had brought them. For so long, it seemed their life together was blessed beyond reason: They'd met at a film screening sponsored by the University Religious Conference at UCLA, where she studied art history and Paul studied engineering. He planned a career in the oil business—until he was called to the pastorate. Following a sweet courtship, they married in her family's church on the corner of San Vicente and Bundy, with Paul's father, Mark, assisting Margot's family pastor.

As a young married couple they moved to Pasadena so Paul could attend Fuller Theological Seminary. Their tiny studio in a converted house on campus meant Margot could take their battered blue Toyota to her museum, since Paul could walk to his classes. "Her museum" was the Norton Simon. After a childhood spent roaming the Getty, the switch to Pasadena's treasure trove had been challenging.

Almost as challenging as being a pastor's wife, Margot mused. A knock at the kitchen door drew her back to the moment. It was, after all, December 20, just five days before Christmas, and she was, for better or for worse, married to a small-town pastor. Unexpected visitors, she had quickly learned, were common.

Through the sheer curtain at the window in the door she made out the silhouette of her neighbor-cum-confidante, Sue. Letting out a tiny squeal, Margot opened the door with a yank. "Sue! What a sweet surprise! How *are you?*"

"I'm fine," Sue smiled, her short gray curls bobbing as she eased herself into a chair at the kitchen table. "I brought you a coffee cake."

"Mmmmm. That smells delicious! Let me call Ruth and Paul—"

"In a minute, Margot. First, just sit down. Please."

Margot slid a steaming mug to Sue and reclaimed her seat at the table.

"What's up?" Margot asked.

Sue's gray-blue eyes searched Margot's face. "You seem really stressed out over Christmas. I came by to see how I could help. I've lived next door to the parsonage long enough to know that the Christmas Home Tour is a challenging day—most of all for the pastor's wife. Especially," she added, her left eyebrow darting skyward for emphasis, "your first year here."

"I was just sitting here thinking that it seems like we've been here forever. It's—it's hard sometimes." Margot surprised herself; unbidden tears filled her eyes, threatening to spill over and down her creamy-smooth cheeks. She blinked twice and swallowed hard.

"Not quite what you expected, are we?" Sue grinned.

"Oh, no, it's not that. It's just—well, I'm a city girl at heart. When Paul was a chaplain at the university I thought we were in heaven on earth. He loved serving the campus community, and I related to all those young, hopeful students—even as we got older I always had a heart for the kids. Then his mom came to live with us after his father died—" Margot stopped to snuffle back a tear—"And she really didn't adjust to life in the city. So when this congregation called Paul, we jumped at the chance. Ruth spent her entire life in a small town. Even though she struggles with dementia, this place is much more familiar to her than our home in the city was. She even knows how to put up bread and butter pickles! But me, well, I didn't expect to have to give up my museums and my study of sculpture. I grew up right in Brentwood, you know. I cut my teeth at LACMA and the Getty. This place?" Margot shook her head. "It's almost like we live on another planet." One tear escaped Margot's vigilance and traced a path down to her chin, where it clung like a stubborn dewdrop before falling into the slab of coffee cake Sue had slid in front of Margot.

Sue looked at her friend with sympathy. "Folks are different here," she admitted. "But they're not bad folks. Today you'll earn your place as one of them. They'll troop through and *ooh* and *ahh* at the Nativity, munching on the cookies we bake, and by tomorrow nobody will even remember the strawberry jam fiasco."

Margot smiled and wiped her face on the hem of her apron.

"Here's what we'll do," Sue continued. "It's just past nine now. Let's get the butter out of the fridge to soften up, then we'll start hauling the Nativity pieces up to the parlor. You looked them over, right? I seem to remember one of the lambs had a broken leg last year. Anyway,we'll move the furniture out of the way and set up the Nativity, then we can get cracking on those cookies. They're best fresh, you know."

"Oh, don't I know." Margot giggled. "Mrs. Delsey told me. Four or five times."

Sue paused, her short, stout frame leaning against one marble counter in the stately old house's enormous kitchen. "Don't sell her short, Margot," she said, suddenly serious. "Mrs. Delsey is a force in this town."

Margot felt her face flush. "Oh, I'm sure she is. I'll play nicely, you just watch me. Now then. Paul and his mother are in the basement. I'll call them up to have some coffee cake, then we can head down there to look over the Nativity pieces."

Before she could leave the room, voices in the hallway caught both women's attention. Margot slipped out the door, Sue at her heels, to investigate.

Ruth's sun hat listed lopsided over her right ear. Her arms full of red, white, and blue ribbons, she disappeared into the living room, followed by Paul. Dust frosted his still-full head of sandy hair as he carried an armload of bunting. Margot crossed the hallway and watched, Sue agape in astonishment beside her, as mother and son dragged the Independence Day decorations out on the broad front porch that spanned the breadth of the parsonage.

Sue looked at Margot, obviously puzzled. "Yesterday I took Ruth with me to the U.S.O. over by the Marine base," Margot explained. "We put together holiday baskets with a patriotic theme for the families of the deployed Marines. Today, Ruth remembers that we need to decorate the house, but she thinks we're getting it ready for the Fourth of July parade."

Sue opened her mouth, then closed it again as her friend continued. "And the doctor says it's Alzheimer's. It's not just grief, it won't get better, she's just going to get more and more confused until—well, until she doesn't know anything anymore. And Paul, of course, wants to honor his mother, and he doesn't want to upset her. So he goes along with her delusions. Oh, Sue, what on earth will I do? He went down to the basement to try to remind her that it's Christmastime, not July. I guess he had no luck. Oh! What will the ladies of the church say? What will *Mrs. Delsey* say?" The tears Margot had fought finally won the battle, pouring down her face.

Sue reached up and placed a hand on each of her neighbor's shoulders, taking a firm grip. "Listen here, Margot. Get a hold of yourself. We'll work it out. You'll see. And Monday—don't forget, we're leaving here bright and early Monday morning for that trip down to Los Angeles. We'll shop at the Beverly Center and eat dinner at that new bistro on Melrose. It'll be just the thing to stir up some Christmas cheer in a city girl like you."

Margot smiled at Sue, who always seemed to understand her, even to the point of suggesting a three-hour drive to see the city dressed for Christmas. "Let's get them in here to enjoy your coffee cake while it's still warm," she said. She opened the front door. "Honey? Ruth? Sue's here. She brought a nice hot coffee cake. Come on in and have a piece."

Paul turned from where he leaned over the house's porch rail, tacking bunting into place. "Coffee cake? We'll be right there! Come on, Mom. Sue brought us a coffee cake."

Margot turned to Sue. "That husband of mine. He's got a sweet tooth like you've never seen on a grown-up. I don't know how he stays so trim."

Ruth and Paul settled into the breakfast nook while Sue sliced coffee cake and Margot poured coffee. Paul sniffed appreciatively at the aromas of cinnamon and nutmeg that rose from the porcelain platter holding Sue's gift. "You two enjoy this treat," she told them. "Sue and I are going downstairs to look over the decorations."

"I think we already brought up all the red, white, and blue," Ruth called after them. Margot pretended not to hear as she and her friend hurried down the hall to the basement stairs.

"See what a fix I'm in? What on earth do I do now?" Margot exclaimed as the fluorescent bulbs blinked to life, feebly illuminating the stacks of boxes and odd pieces of furniture that filled the old house's basement.

"We'll figure something out," Sue promised. "Don't forget: I spent thirty years as a teacher. And we're experts at working magic with decorations. Just let me think a minute."

Footsteps on the staircase told the women they were no longer alone. Paul's lanky build emerged from the shadows. "She sent me to get the chairs," he explained, shrugging.

"Chairs?" Margot asked.

"Chairs. To save our places at the curb. For the parade."

"Parade? Oh, goodness! How do I decorate for the Christmas Home Tour when Ruth thinks it's July?"

"Don't worry so much. It'll be fine."

"But I promised! I promised the ladies of the congregation, *your* congregation, that we would preserve the holiday traditions of the parsonage!"

"The ladies of the congregation will surely understand. Outside, it will be the Fourth of July. Inside, the Christmas Nativity will stand at the parlor window as it always has. Look at me. Look. At. Me." Paul's voice carried a touch of sternness.

Margot raised her face to look her husband in the eye. She found a spark of steeliness there, something she'd seen only once before in all their years together. *He means business,* she realized.

"Mom's cognitive state is difficult for all of us. But I will not have her humiliated or ground down, made to feel small, in order to please the members of our congregation. I tried to bring her back to Yuletide and today, it just didn't work. And you, Margot—" his voice softened, almost against his will, when he spoke his wife's name—"I want you to worry less about pleasing our congregation and more about pleasing God. We're commanded to honor our parents. There is no comparable command about Christmas decorations and traditions."

Without another word, Paul gathered up the folding chairs, dusted them off with an old towel, and hauled them up the basement stairs. He was a controlled, gentle man, but Margot could tell by his attack on the staircase that he was close to his limits. Her eyes filled with tears.

"What will I do?" she wailed. "I have cookies to bake, guests to receive, and *two* holidays to prepare for, and now my own husband is mad at me!"

Sue took her friend's hand. "Margot, take a breath. There. Blow it out. Okay, now another. Good. Remember, Paul's heart is hurting. He's lost his father, and his mother is fading from him before his eyes. Just show him some grace. You know he adores you."

Margot squared her slender shoulders and nodded. "You're right, of course. What would I do without you? Some days I'm not sure I could withstand life in Mitchell without you next door. Time for me to cancel this pity party and get to work."

"That's the spirit! Come on, let's haul these Nativity pieces upstairs and then we can get busy on those cookies." Sue grabbed the statue of Joseph and tucked it under her arm. "C'mon, Pal," she said. "It's time for your annual appearance."

Margot giggled as she gathered the baby Jesus and a lamb into her arms. She blew at a cobweb hanging from the lamb's ear and hauled the pieces up the stairs.

The women lined up the pieces on the back porch of the stately home and armed themselves with feather dusters and damp rags. Together they dusted and polished until the pieces gleamed with the patina of their years. Margot leaned on the porch rail and inspected the set. "Well, they're certainly vernacular art, but they're nicely rendered, and the proportions are gorgeous. Someday I'd like to repaint them, though."

Sue gasped in mock horror. "You know their pedigree, right? Old Pastor Jonas, who built this house back when the church, and the town, were new, carved these pieces from trees that were felled to clear the lot. He worked a whole year to create them. They've only been repainted once—and he did the repainting himself, in his old age. Of course the good people of First Community Church would never adore idols, but these Nativity pieces are about as close as can be."

Hauling the pieces through the kitchen to the front parlor, Margot peeked out the wide picture window. Red, white, and blue bunting festooned the generous front veranda of their home. Miniature flags waved in pairs, tied to each post supporting the porch roof. Four folding chairs lined the sidewalk, facing expectantly toward the street. Ruth sat, her floppy sun hat perched down low on her forehead. Paul, dear Paul, sat beside her, holding her hand and waiting with her.

Margot saw a sadness in the set of his shoulders, the tilt of his head. He missed his father terribly, she knew. Her own parents had answered the call home after brief illnesses that made it clear their time had come. The whole family had time to gather, to say goodbye, to prepare their hearts for the separation to come. Not so with Paul. She shuddered as she remembered the phone shattering the peace of their evening quiet time together. She closed her eyes and saw again how the color had drained from his face as he listened, how he deflated in a way she'd never before seen. The unfamiliar gravelly tone in his voice on that sad night still haunted her memory of that evening, barging unbidden into her mind at the most unexpected moments. *Two years now,* she mused, *and I still hear him crying when he thinks I'm sleeping. And now to watch his mom slowly losing touch with reality—with* him—*it's such a painful burden.*

A car slowing at the curb snapped her attention back to the present. Sue stood beside her, sharing her gaze out the window. "This hurts him," Margot said to her friend.

"Of course it does, Margot. That's his *mother*. And she's fading." Sue nodded. "Look. Mrs. Delsey's here. Let's get busy on those cookies."

Margot and Sue watched as Mrs. Delsey emerged from her gray Chrysler. She wore a dull purple wool coat; a fascinator adorned with short feathers and a spotted veil perched rather precariously atop the bun in her hair. She'd died it black to cover the gray, giving her pinched features an air of stinginess. From the window the two women watched as Mrs. Delsey stopped short and stared at the veranda. Then she strode over to the chairs. Margot noticed that her head bobbed as if to emphasize her words as she spoke with Paul and Ruth.

"I wonder what she's saying?" Sue murmured.

"I'm sure we'll find out soon enough," Margot said, grimacing. "Let's head into the kitchen and beat up some butter."

Sue giggled as they slipped aprons over their heads and took up their mixing bowls and wooden spoons. Margot took her rolling pin down from its rack on the wall and scattered a dusting of flour over the marble surface of the kitchen's old counters. Squinting at the recipe, which marched across a page of vellum in Mrs. Delsey's exacting schoolmarm's script, Sue inspected the spacing of the oven racks then set the oven to preheating. By the time Mrs. Delsey made her way to the front door, both women wore faint dustings of flour.

Margot held up her dough-coated hands as a surgeon would after scrubbing in as she made her way to the home's grand entry hall. She motioned through the leaded glass in the enormous mahogany door for Mrs. Delsey to enter. "Forgive me for not opening the door, Mrs. Delsey," she said. "I'm up to my elbows in the dough for your marvelous cookies. Thank you again for sharing your recipe."

"You're welcome, Dear. See that you don't overwork the dough or you will end up with tough cookies." Sue's eyes danced. Margot turned away from her neighbor, afraid she would break out in laughter if their eyes met.

Mrs. Delsey nodded toward the Nativity pieces gathered across the hall in the parlor. "It seems that your preparations are well underway. I'm sure you'll be ready to greet your guests this afternoon. But whatever were you thinking when you decked out the veranda in red, white, and blue? It certainly doesn't look like Christmas from the street. I asked Pastor Paul about it, but he mumbled something cryptic about a parade. I didn't understand a word. Not a word."

"Oh, Mrs. Delsey," Margot exclaimed, "I'm in a pickle!" She slid two sheets filled with cookie dough into the oven, snapped its door closed, washed her hands, then wiped them distractedly on her polka dot apron. Sue stood quietly, rolling more dough and filling two more cookie sheets.

"Please sit down, Mrs. Delsey. Would you like some tea? Sue brought this lovely coffee cake." Margot set the kettle on the stove and sat opposite her guest at the kitchen table. Sue remained at the counter, working the mass of cookie dough. *Sue has a knack for making herself invisible,* Margot thought as she took Mrs. Delsey's coat.

"Well, what of the bunting, then?" Mrs. Delsey asked as Margot set a steaming cup of tea before her.

"It's Ruth," Margot explained. "I took her with me to the U.S.O. yesterday, you'll recall, when we all went to prepare the baskets, and now she's convinced that it's the Fourth of July. Paul tried to help her remember that it's Christmastime, but she is really stuck. It happens, sometimes. The doctor told us we could expect episodes like this . . ." Her voice caught in her throat as sudden tears ambushed her. *Please, Lord, give me composure,* she silently prayed. *Don't let me make a fool of myself in front of Mrs. Delsey!*

A thick silence descended over the parsonage's broad, heavy kitchen table. Mrs. Delsey appeared to be carefully studying the windowsill. Margot sniffled, struggling to stifle her tears. Sue expertly swapped the cookie sheets on the counter for the ones in the oven, sliding the delicate butter cookies onto cooling racks.

The front door banged closed and footsteps filled the hallway. Margot swiped at her eyes with the hem of her apron.

"What's for lunch?" Paul asked. "A guy works up an appetite decorating the porch." He stole a cookie from the cooling rack. Sue swatted at him playfully with her spatula. "Mmmm," he said, rolling his eyes in mock ecstasy.

His mother responded before his wife could speak. "Why, it's the Fourth of July! We always have hot dogs for lunch on the Fourth. And baked beans. We eat hot dogs and baked beans and we sit at the curb and wait for the parade. Then the band marches down the street and we all stand and cheer for Old Glory." Ruth sighed rapturously. "And," she concluded triumphantly, "we drink *lemonade!*"

"I'll light the grill, then," Paul said. "Honey, we have some hot dogs, don't we?"

Margot nodded. Mrs. Delsey, looking pale, rose from her seat at the table. "Well, I must be on my way. I have a lot to do to prepare."

"Can't you join us?" Margot asked, reflexively.

"Thank you, Child. No."

"Are you marching with the D.A.R. ladies, Mrs. Delsey?" Ruth asked.

"We'll just have to see what the day brings," Mrs. Delsey murmured. Paul brought her purple coat and held it as she slipped her arms into its sleeves. She nodded to him. "Thank you, Pastor."

Sue swapped out another round of cookies. "Well, that was strange," she said. "Mrs. Delsey looked like she'd seen a ghost!"

"It *was* odd. And she left without so much as tasting one of the cookies we baked. I was certain she would want to make sure they were satisfactory," Margot said. She looked through the kitchen window. Paul stood at the grill, cooking hot dogs as his mother sat at the picnic table. "I guess I'd better get some beans going," she said. "You'll stay for lunch, Sue?"

Her friend smiled. "I wouldn't miss this."

Margot pulled a glass pitcher down from the top shelf of the cabinet. "I have a can of lemonade in the freezer. I'll just mix it up while the beans cook."

Margot slipped hot dog buns into the still-warm oven to toast and chopped some onion to garnish the hot dogs. "Sue, I gotta say, this is not the way I wanted our first Christmas with this congregation to go. I wanted to do them proud. I wanted to honor their holiday traditions. I wanted the parsonage to feel as welcoming and familiar to them as it did when Pastor Jacobsen was still alive. And now, now . . ." Her friend nodded, sympathetic, as Margot ran out of words.

She raised her eyebrows pointedly toward her mother-in-law as she gathered a second wind. "I don't want to embarrass her, or hurt her feelings, but I have gorgeous evergreen wreaths in the garage. Potted poinsettias, too, and forced amaryllis. I ordered them from Cynthia's Florist and I'd planned to decorate the porch and the front doors. I was hoping to give that little local business a boost by featuring her arrangements in our décor. Now instead we have flags everywhere. I wanted the people of Mitchell to see that we aren't some uppity city folk, but real people, Christians, who adore our Lord Jesus and revel in celebrating His birth. Instead I've got the Baby Jesus in the parlor and the Stars and Stripes on the porch, and for all I know by the time the Tour begins, Ruth will have Paul playing Sousa marches on the stereo!"

Sue shrugged. "Margot, you know, we're never as much in control as we like to think we are. I know it's hard when our plans don't work out, but sometimes a better plan comes into play instead. We can use the wreaths and the flowers in the foyer and in the parlor. This house is a grand old lady, you know. She can carry it all."

"Grand like Mrs. Delsey?" Margot snickered.

"Shh," Sue said. "Look. The dogs are all ready. Let's eat."

After lunch, Ruth announced that she was going to nap. "Be sure to wake me up in time for the parade," she said as she slipped down the hallway. Margot scowled behind her back.

"Paul," she beseeched, turning to her husband. "Isn't there anything you can do to snap her out of it?"

"I tried, Sweetheart," he responded. "She's really, really fixated on the Independence Day Parade. I think the best we can do is prepare the parlor and hope she's not too terribly disappointed when no parade passes by. And don't worry," he added, giving her shoulder a reassuring squeeze. "These people aren't coming here to judge you. They're coming to enjoy a Mitchell Christmas tradition."

"I'm not so sure," Margot mumbled as her husband left the room.

Sue cleared her throat. "Let's go set up the Nativity. It's going to be beautiful."

Margot closed the heavy, golden velvet drapes that adorned the parlor's enormous picture window. Sue blinked in the sudden dimness. "Mrs. Delsey told me that we're to 'unveil' the Nativity when the tour begins," she explained. Sue wrestled a shepherd into place and gave Mary one last swipe with the duster. Margot fitted creamy candles into a candelabra she'd placed on the table in the corner. She arranged the cookies on a tiered Spode server and set it beside the candelabra. Sue straightened a pillow on the green-and-gold jacquard loveseat. Paul carried in the poinsettias and amaryllises, lining the foyer and hall with their showy blooms. He tied the fragrant wreaths onto the stairway's balusters.

He chuckled. "Well, it looks just like Christmas in here. Out there, though,"-- he nodded toward the veranda-- "out there it looks like we're expecting Uncle Sam."

Margot shook her head. "I'm going to be a laughingstock," she cried. "This is going to be even worse than the strawberry jam debacle. I can just feel it!"

Paul's jawline settled. "You know," he said to his wife, "this all really isn't about you. It's about celebrating our Savior. It's about opening our home to the community. It's about offering hospitality to the good people of this town. Honestly, I don't think people pay nearly as much attention to you as you seem to think they do. It borders on pridefulness." He held her gaze, waiting for her response.

Sue stepped toward the kitchen. "I've got some errands to do," she explained. "I'll be back before the tour begins, I promise."

Margot listened as her friend's footsteps faded, punctuated by the kitchen door moaning on its hinges. Then her eyes flashed. "You just don't understand! You have no idea how hard it can be to be the pastor's wife. Why, when I met you, I thought I would be marrying an *engineer!* Instead you got this silly notion to be a minister. I stood by you through seminary. I smile and nod and say all the right things to the church people. I've done my best to love you—and to love Jesus—all these years. Even when I have doubts. Oh, yes! I do!" Margot trembled as her husband shook his head. "And you know I love your mother, too. I do everything I can to make her happy, to take good care of her. But this. THIS! It's just too much. Today I was going to secure my place in this town. I was going to win them over. I even baked Mrs. Delsey's cookies instead of my traditional gingerbread and snickerdoodles. If Jesus loves us so much, why does He let your mom be so mixed up? Why does He let our hearts hurt so?"

Paul wrapped his arms around his wife, folding her into his embrace. He stroked her back, kissed the part in her glossy hair. "Margot, please. You know as well as I do that we live in a fallen world. We just have to trust Him. Someday we'll stand in His presence, and everything will be clear. And I have this feeling that God will look upon your care of Mom and say to you, 'Well done, My good and faithful servant.' I know this little town is a big change for you," he went on, talking right over her remonstrations. "I'm grateful for the sacrifice you made for us to accept this call. Now, let's get these finishing touches done. Maybe when Mom wakes up from her nap she'll be over her parade fantasy."

"My wh-a-a-?" Ruth's voice rose from the hallway. "Fantasy? You think I'm having some kind of fantasy? Well!" She turned on her heel and marched down the hallway. Opening the front door, she swept her enormous hat up from its hook on the hall tree, clamped it onto her head, and resumed her vigil at the sidewalk.

Margot dissolved. The tears she'd struggled against all day overwhelmed her. She was beyond ladylike weeping; she dredged the sobs up from some well inside her, choking and blowing her nose on the hem of her apron. Paul held her close as the tears wracked her body. She cried for her father-in-law. She cried for her life in the city. She cried for her dear, confused mother-in-law. She cried for her husband, saddled with a sorry shadow of a wife like her. She cried for her own questioning heart.

Her husband stood and held her until the storm in her soul passed. When she was quiet again, he placed his hands on her shoulders, holding her off at arm's length. "Our home is beautiful. You're a gracious hostess. You're honoring my mother. God will honor *that.* Why don't you go upstairs and get ready for our guests. It's going to be fine, just fine." His voice soothed her spirit.

Sue called out as the kitchen door banged behind her. "I'm back," she said. "I've got everything we need for wassail, or at least a bowl of hot spiced cider." She giggled. "No alcohol involved," she added quickly as Paul's right eyebrow shot up.

"Margot's just going upstairs to get ready," he said, propelling his wife gently toward the stairs.

Margot washed her tearstained face. She donned a pair of black velvet slacks and pulled on a burgundy angora sweater. Slipping a velvet ribbon into her curly mane, she freshened her makeup, doing her best to minimize the puffiness that her tearful episode had wrought. *Paul's right,* she thought. *I worry too much about what these people think of* me.

She slipped to her knees. "Father, please forgive me. We're celebrating the precious gift of Your Son. I've met my promise to the church ladies, *and* we're honoring Ruth's wishes, confused though she may be. You know it all, dear God. You know exactly why Ruth thinks it's July. You know why Mrs. Delsey blanched as she did and hurried off. You know everyone's hearts, and I commit this day, every day, to Your will. So long as I'm honoring You, God, I won't worry about my popularity with the congregation. Thank You for Your love and Your mercy. Help me to always embrace Your perfect plan, instead of my own. I repent of my pride, Father. Please soften my stony heart. Thank You for sending Your Son to save me. I pray in His name, Amen."

She started as she heard Paul clearing his throat. "How long have you been standing there?"

"Long enough," he said, "to be reminded of how much I love you and how dear you are to me. I'm so glad that you're the woman beside me in this ministry. Mom's up from her nap, Sue's got the cider simmering, and the house smells like Christmas. Now let's go downstairs. I have a feeling it will all be just fine."

Margot took her husband's hand and permitted him to lead her down the stairs. The sun was low on the horizon: the tour would begin soon enough. "Can you turn on the twinkle lights on the eaves?" she asked him. "They'll look great with—with the bunting."

Ruth nodded. She wrapped a blue sweatshirt around her thin frame—*so thin,* Margot noticed as she watched her mother-in-law.

"They sure will," Ruth agreed. "C'mon, everyone. Let's go down to the sidewalk. It must be about time for the parade."

Margot poured lemonade into acrylic glasses and handed one to Ruth, Paul, and Sue. They all trooped down to the sidewalk and settled themselves into the chairs Ruth had insisted on that morning. *The neighbors will never forget this,* she thought. *This will make the jam spectacle look like nothing!* Remembering her prayer, Margot shook her head as if to chase off the thoughts of their foolish behavior.

Ruth sat, wrapped in her sweatshirt with her straw hat clamped down on over its hood, expectantly watching the street, waiting for the parade. The breeze carried a wintery chill. *Now what,* Margot wondered. *Do we sit here until the Christmas Home Tour people begin to arrive?* Paul squeezed her hand and Sue, sitting at her other side, patted her arm sympathetically.

Margot became aware of a faint noise just as Paul turned, craning his neck to look down the street. A muffled cadence sounded in the distance. Ruth's eyes lit up. She clapped her hands together, squealing like a delighted child. "The parade! It's starting!"

Margot looked at her husband, her eyes pleading: What to do? Sit here and watch her mother-in-law's hopes crushed when some teenager's booming car stereo proved to be the source of the drumming?

"Ruth," she began, then faltered. The old woman sat there, eyes shining, waiting, certain that her parade was on its way. Margot braced herself, preparing to witness her mother-in-law's painful disappointment. She reached around behind her husband to give Ruth a gentle pat on the shoulder.

Then she noticed the muffled cadence wasn't so muffled. It was closer and clearer. It was no car stereo. No. It was a marching band.

Now the Ramirez family, who lived across the street, hurried down to the sidewalk, looking towards the corner. The Butlers who lived next door came out, too. Old Mr. Johnson, who never came outside, stood at his bedroom window, watching. Ruth, radiant, waved gaily at the neighbors as the music grew louder and louder.

Around the corner came the Ormsby MacKnight Mitchel High School "Old Stars" Marching Band. Led by a gangly seventeen-year-old drum major who stood straight as a redwood, the flutes, clarinets, trumpets, trombones, saxophones, and tubas marched proudly past. The drum corps followed behind, tapping out a smart cadence between the choruses of "Yankee Doodle Dandy," the band's signature song. Majorettes tossed their batons in the air, catching them neatly behind their backs, smiling their impossibly white smiles as they twirled down the street.

Next came the mayor of Mitchell, William Bonneville, riding in a red convertible Mustang.

Behind the mayor the local Girls Scouts and Boy Scouts marched along in ragged rows as they waved American flags. Then came the men from the American Legion.

Margot looked at her mother-in-law. Ruth fairly glowed, her delicate face stretched into a smile bigger than any Margot had seen from her since her beloved Henry had died.

Finally, the parade's lone float rounded the corner. It carried the Daughters of the American Revolution, Mitchell Chapter. Dressed in18th-century finery, Estelle Delsey waved her handkerchief at Ruth, Paul, Sue, and Margot. Ruth rose and applauded. Margot thought she caught a glistening in Mrs. Delsey's eye as the float passed their vantage point.

The marching band's strains grew fainter as the D.A.R. float disappeared around the corner. Margot tried to make sense of it all. How on earth had a parade, even a three-minute parade, been so hastily planned and carried out? By whom? And *why?*

But those questions would have to wait. The Christmas Home Tour was due to begin in minutes.

Paul gathered the chairs from the sidewalk and returned them to the basement. Ruth removed her sweatshirt and floppy sun hat, then excused herself to smooth her hair. Sue stirred the cider and filled the punchbowl, floating a clove-studded orange in the fragrant drink. Margot lit the candles in the candelabra and swept the room with her eye, performing that last-minute check so instinctive to good hostesses.

The doorbell rang before Margot had a chance to reconsider the placement of the Nativity pieces. Her husband's steady, gracious voice sounded at the door: "Mr. Bonneville. Honored to see you, Sir. Won't you come in?" A satisfied smile overtook her. However that parade had happened, Ruth was happy. Everything would be all right after all.

Margot heard the mayor comment, "I *love* the patriotic flavor you've brought to the manse this holiday season, Pastor. It's so important that we love God *and* Country." Standing beside her, Sue groaned softly at the mayor's smarmy comment "If he only knew," she whispered in Margot's ear. They snickered together.

The tour was scheduled to conclude at seven. Most of the people who worshiped at First Community Church, along with dozens of other Mitchell residents, had streamed through the parsonage, exclaiming at the floral décor in the entry hall, proclaiming the goodness of Mrs. Delsey's butter cookies, and complimenting the new pastor and his wife on their tasteful Christmas display of the traditional Mitchell Nativity.

But Mrs. Delsey had not passed through. Margot mentally reviewed the day's events, trying to pinpoint the moment when she had caused offense. Mrs. Delsey was Mitchell's *grande dame*; withholding her presence from any social event carried a clear message. If anyone else noticed her absence, it would reflect poorly—

Hold on, now. Remember the prayer? Remember how it felt when Paul accused you of pridefulness? Margot, get a grip. It's not about you. Margot was so absorbed in scolding herself that she didn't hear the doorbell. Fortunately, Paul heard it and hurried to the door.

"Why, hello," Margot heard her husband say. "So nice to see you, Mrs. Delsey. We were hoping you would come by."

Margot took a deep breath. She and Sue exchanged glances. A moment later, Paul escorted Estelle Delsey into the parlor.

"I was just leaving, Mrs. Delsey," Sue chirped. Gathering her purse, she headed for the door.

"Thanks for all your help," Margot called after her.

"Are you on foot, Sue? Let me see you to your door," Paul offered. He followed Sue out the door, leaving Ruth, Margot, and Mrs. Delsey alone in the parlor.

Ruth stood and said, "Henry will be home any minute. I must get his supper."

"Ruth," Margot said, "Henry, um—"

She watched as her mother-in-law's face fell. *She remembers now,* Margot thought. *Henry's never coming home for his supper again.*

Ruth shook herself slightly. "I must go to my room. I have some reading to do." She walked from the room like a woman overtaken by a trance. Margot watched her make her way down the hall.

Margot turned to face her guest. "Would you like some tea?" she offered, a little too brightly.

"No, thank you," Mrs. Delsey said. "That warm cider smells inviting, though."

Margot hurried to ladle a glass of cider from the punchbowl. "Everyone loved your cookies, Mrs. Delsey. Thank you for sharing your special recipe with me."

Estelle nodded, silent. Margot felt herself faltering under the woman's gaze.

"Mrs. Delsey, I must apologize," she finally said, talking too fast, avoiding eye contact with Mrs. Delsey. "You told us when we came to First Community Church that the Christmas Home Tour was an important event, and we promised to honor the town's tradition. I'm so sorry for the bunting! And I'm still mystified by the parade. I hadn't heard a thing about it! But I know between the bunting all over the veranda and the parade, the Home Tour had to share the limelight—"

Margot stopped short. Was that a sniffle she'd heard? She raised her eyes and looked across the parlor at her guest. Mrs. Delsey held a monogrammed handkerchief to her face, dabbing gently at her eyes. *Now I've done it,* Margot thought. *She's so insulted she's crying. They're going to ride us out of town on a rail. How do I fix this?*

The two women sat in silence for several long minutes, the candlelight from the ivory candles bathing them in gentle, forgiving light.

Finally, a sound broke the silence. Margot looked up and realized it was Mrs. Delsey, speaking not in her usual commanding, President-of-the-Women's-Club voice, but in a soft monotone that she had to strain to hear.

"Ever since you came here this past spring," Mrs. Delsey said, "you have always felt so cool, so composed, so, so—perfect, I suppose, that I avoided a relationship with you. It seemed that you were too guarded to truly *be* a friend, and I feared that you would see right through me with those penetrating green eyes and discover the truth."

"The truth?" Margot repeated blankly. "What truth?"

"The truth," Mrs. Delsey continued, her voice gaining vigor as she pressed on with her story, "of my wicked, selfish heart. I was a young woman when my own mother-in-law began to decline—Mr. Delsey, God rest his soul, was twenty years older than I, you know—

and she wasn't nearly as sweet as your Ruth. I didn't understand dementia the way we do today. I thought it was something shameful, casting dishonor on the Delsey family name. When she grew confused, I insisted on 'straightening her out,' explaining the reality of a given moment, never, not one time, indulging her as you and your fine husband did here today. And when she couldn't take good care of herself, I refused to take her into our home. She died just weeks after the move to the nursing home. She just lost her will to live."

Margot saw a tear developing in Estelle's eye. She wiped at it carelessly, continuing her tale. "When I stopped by today and you shared your fears about Ruth spoiling the tour, I saw the *real* you for the first time. You're not cold and composed, not at all! You're just doing your best to be a good wife, a good pastor's wife, no less, and a good daughter-in-law. I trust you are familiar with my position here in Mitchell?"

Margot nodded, noting Mrs. Delsey's familiar imperious tone returning.

"I rang up the high school band director, who's a cousin, you know, and asked him to call a 'dress rehearsal' on your street. It was easy enough to round up the Scout troops, and that blowhard of a mayor would show up for a tooth extraction if he thought he'd have a chance to press the flesh. It was easy enough to give Ruth her Independence Day Parade."

Mrs. Delsey paused. Margot saw tears streaming freely down the old woman's crepe-like cheeks. Margot rose and crossed the room, sitting next to her visitor. She slipped an arm around Estelle's shoulder, tentatively, offering comfort. To her surprise, Estelle rested her head on Margot's shoulder, relaxing into her reassuring hug.

"It's too late for me to make things right for Mother Delsey," she spoke, her voice muffled by Margot's angora sleeve, "but if that little impromptu parade made Ruth happy, then I feel like I'm honoring her memory."

"I'm not sure what to say," Margot whispered. "Thank you for sharing your story. And you know, God doesn't intend for you to carry that burden. Have you handed it over to Him?"

Mrs. Delsey shook her head. "It's too horrible. I could never expect to be forgiven for my hard-hearted treatment of my own mother-in-law."

"But that's not so!" Margot exclaimed. "God is longing for us to bring our failures to Him. It's promised, right there in First John: *If we confess our sins, He is faithful and righteous to forgive us our sins and to cleanse us from all unrighteousness."*

"I don't even know how," Mrs. Delsey groaned. "Sure, I go to church every week, and I serve on the committees, but I never dared to truly give myself over to the Lord. It felt too, too—"

"Risky?" Margot offered. "I know that feeling. I've had my doubts, too. Yes, I have!" she insisted, cutting off Mrs. Delsey's protests. "But when I stop to think about it, I realize that life is so much better when I live it for Him. He's never let me down, and I can't say that about anyone else—not even my husband, wonderful as he is. "

"Now, normally I would feel hurt to hear those words!"

Both women started as Paul's baritone intruded on their quiet moment.

"I didn't hear you come in," Margot stuttered.

"Me either," Mrs. Delsey said. "We were talking, you see."

"I've been standing here for a few minutes," Paul admitted.

Mrs. Delsey blanched. "So you, you heard me, what I said about church?"

"I heard your heart, Mrs. Delsey. I heard the yearning. Are you ready? Is tonight the night that you hand over your burdens and claim your salvation?"

Estelle Delsey nodded, tears once again coursing down her face.

"Well then," Paul said. "Let us pray."

Best Laid Plans

Peggy Blann Phifer

After several continuous loops through the short-term parking garage at McCarran International Airport, Erin finally spotted someone leaving and quickly pulled into the vacated space. She sped over the people-mover across to the baggage claim and rushed into the throng of people milling around the luggage carousels, but didn't see her tall, red-headed sister. She stepped away to position herself near the down escalator delivering a flash-flood of arriving passengers beneath the Jumbotron screen blasting out the exciting attractions of Las Vegas.

The flood dwindled to a trickle. Then dried up.

"C'mon, Sis, where are you?" Five more minutes passed and still no Larke. It was now almost 9:00 A.M. Thirty minutes past arrival time.

Okay, Erin Weyland Macintyre, time to enter panic mode.

This was squeaking things close. She'd gone ahead with her plans, even knowing full well her sister was in France with her touring dance troupe and wouldn't be home until four days before Christmas.

And the wedding.

And Larke was to be her maid of honor.

And knowing, too, that anything could go wrong. And probably would, given her history.

Well, it already had, like Clay refusing to wear purple.

"Why? What's wrong with purple?"

"Nothing. And it looks great on you, darlin'. Just don't ask me to wear it."

Honestly, men were . . . men. She'd given up. Sort of.

Oh, and then there was the issue of her "back to the 50's" idea.

But not having Larke here? Unacceptable. Unthinkable.

Erin moved away from the chaos of passengers wrestling each other to claim their luggage, narrowly avoiding being run down by a burly man lunging for his golf bag.

She perched on the edge of an inactive carousel, her over-active imagination conjuring up all sorts of horrible scenarios as to why Larke had not arrived as scheduled. She fumbled for her cell phone in her purse to see if she'd missed a call or text message explaining Larke's non-appearance and nearly dropped it when an incoming call sounded.

"Larke! Where are you?"

"Albuquerque."

"What?"

"Yeah. There was this guy on the plane who had a heart attack or something, so the plane was diverted to an emergency landing in Albuquerque to get him to a hospital."

"Wow."

"Yeah, pretty scary stuff. I watched the flight attendants grabbing emergency medical or first-aid stuff from the overhead bin across the aisle from me, and rush to the back of the cabin."

"Oh, my."

"It was pretty tense. They carried him off a few minutes ago and loaded him into the ambulance."

"Wow. I hope he'll be okay."

"Me, too." Larke paused. "Uh, you're at the airport, aren't you?"

"Of course I am! Where else would I be?"

"And you didn't verify the flight's arrival time before you left home." Larke's sigh hissed through the phone. "Of course you didn't because you overslept."

It was not a question. "Nor did you think to check the monitors at baggage claim, either."

Erin cringed and raised her head to the bank of monitors. Sure enough, Larke's flight number clearly said "Delayed." Not that seeing that after getting here would have done any good. She was tempted to point that out, but Larke had her dead to rights. Erin knew better. But with the pressure of Christmas, and the wedding—

Yikes! They had a final dress fitting at 11:00.

And Larke's plane was still on the ground.

In Albuquerque.

"Erin, you still there?"

Larke's voice in her ear brought her thoughts back to her phone. "Yeah, sorry."

"They're preparing for takeoff now so I'll be turning the phone off. They said the flight into Vegas would be about an hour and twenty-five minutes."

Erin's heart dropped. "That long?"

"Check the monitor in a few minutes. Gotta go."

Erin dropped the phone back into her purse and stepped closer to the bank of monitors. As she watched, the screen for Larke's flight went blank and then showed a new arrival time of 10:46. She groaned. No way would they make that dress fitting appointment now.

Her tummy growled, reminding her she hadn't eaten breakfast. Though Larke had been wrong about her oversleeping, Erin had fallen behind schedule because her friend Magie, who was to stay with BJ for the day, had run into traffic and arrived later than they'd arranged.

What would she do without Magie? Surrogate mother and best friend, always there for her. No matter what. Had been since Erin was four years old. It always amused Erin when Magie would defend the spelling of her nickname.

"Not Maggie, it's Magie. Stands for Margaret Ann Gifford Instrumental Enterprises. MAGIE. Got it?"

Erin chuckled as she pondered what to do next. It didn't make any sense to leave the airport only to have to drive back so soon, plus pay two parking fees, so Erin decided to grab something to eat while she waited.

At the bar and grill not too far from baggage claim, she ordered coffee and a grilled cheese sandwich, knowing full well she'd regret it later. She chose the patio style seating in front and called the dressmaker, relieved to be able to reset the time for twelve o'clock. It would still be cutting it close, but barring any further delays they should make it.

With little choice in the matter, Erin settled in to wait. Despite the numerous items on her to-do list still to be checked off, she found herself relaxing. She felt her lips curl upward in a smile as she pictured a tall, lean man in a Stetson, jeans, and cowboy boots. A face permanently tanned indented with dimples so deep she could hide a nickel in them.

Clay Buchanan. Teenage crush, then boyfriend, until he'd introduced her to his best friend, Justin Macintyre, whom she'd married, dropping Clay cold. And Clay had disappeared on the eve of her wedding, leaving Justin high and dry without a best man. And she'd hated him for that for over seven years.

Then Justin's SUV plunged off a mountain road into a ravine, killing him instantly, leaving Erin widowed and pregnant. Clay returned to Vegas, claiming Justin's death had not been an accident. It had taken months of collecting evidence to prove it, including the kidnapping of Erin and her newborn baby boy.

That had been fifteen months ago.

She smiled at life's twists and turns. In that time Erin and Clay had fallen in love again. Deeply. Forever. Four days from now, she would become Mrs. Clayton Buchanan. And she couldn't be happier. She was also sure Justin would approve.

Finished with her meal, Erin sat back in her chair and played her favorite waiting game . . . people watching. McCarran was always a great place to do this, but it was especially bustling this time of year with the huge influx of visitors for Christmas. This year's expected incoming passenger count through the airport alone was expected to be a record high. Each year it seemed the numbers grew.

Amusement mixed with wonder at the varying attitudes of the steady stream of people passing by her position. Happy greetings as the locals met their friends and family around the baggage claim area. The strained faces of stressed-out mothers wrestling with tired, cranky children after hours of confinement in a flying metal tube.

And the inevitable boisterous and rowdy folks who'd had more than their share of cheer during their flight. Erin shuddered. She'd encountered this on many trips with Justin, but it seemed peculiar to flights coming into Las Vegas. The time of day didn't seem to matter.

As always, Erin tried to imagine the lives of the constantly shifting wave of humanity coming and going past her table. One young woman pressed her way through the surge, struggling to control a pair of rambunctious twin boys about four years old. Erin's heart went out to the woman. How was she going to claim luggage and still hang on to those two?

At that moment, Erin grew aware of a gradual lowering of the noise and confusion around the turning carousels and people stepping aside, opening a path, as, in twos and threes, men and women in desert camouflage filled that widening corridor. Then, first one, then several, then hundreds of hands joined together in soaring, heart-stopping applause. Erin stood to join in.

Then, through the din, Erin heard a child shriek, "Daddy!" Another echoed, "Daddy, Daddy!"

One of the men detached himself from the others and squatted as the twin boys wrenched away from their mother and slammed into their daddy's open arms, nearly knocking him over.

Oh. My.

Erin watched the scene through blurred vision as the song "I'll Be Home for Christmas" played through her head. Only *this* time, *this* man really *was* home for Christmas. Not just in his dreams.

The little family left the airport amid laughter and happy chatter, man and wife with arms linked and two little boys dancing and darting back and forth ahead of them.

"Hey, little sister."

Erin spun with a yelp. "Larke, you're here!"

"Obviously," came the sarcastic reply, but moisture glistened on the tips of her eyelashes. "That," she nodded to the door through which the little family had left, "was a beautiful thing to see."

"Yes, it was." Erin released a breath of air. "I'm glad your plane was delayed. I'd have missed that."

"I know. You see it all the time on the Internet. All kinds of videos of our returning military heroes with elaborately set up surprises. But none of them can compare to seeing it firsthand." She paused. "I was on the plane with them. I'll never be the same."

As Larke spoke, Erin's attention was drawn to the towering man who stood next to her sister. He wore the same desert camouflage as the others who'd just passed through. *Tower* was right. The guy had to be at least six-feet, six-inches tall, if not more. A good match for Larke's five-foot, seven-inch height, though still a good foot taller.

Erin quirked an eyebrow at her sister, waiting for an introduction or . . . whatever.

"Oh!" Larke blinked, as if just now aware of Erin's stare. "I'm sorry. This is Matthew, uh . . ." She shot a quick look at his name badge "Jenkins. Matthew, this is my little sister, Erin Macintyre."

She had to check his last name?

Interesting.

"Matt," he said, as Erin's hand disappeared into his baseball-mitt-sized one. "I understand you're about to be married."

Erin could only nod, fascinated at Larke's uncharacteristic behavior. This was not the suave, woman-of-the-world sister she knew. Flustered was not part of the Larke LePaige profile.

Erin grinned. This could be fun.

"Speaking of getting married," Larke said, "we'd better get going to that gown fitting, right?"

"Uh, right." Erin tore her attention away from the tall man and back to her sister. "I did manage to get the appointment changed to twelve, but, yeah, you're right."

At five-foot nothing, Erin was used to having to look up at everyone, but this guy . . . she craned her neck nearly backward to look up at the airman. "Nice to meet you, Matt, but we've got to be going."

"Of course," he said, stepping back. "I wish you well in your marriage." His gaze, however, lingered on Larke.

Interesting.

Clay Buchanan had waited until Erin's car left her gated community before swinging his Buick Rendezvous into the *cul de sac* and parking in front of her home. Magie Gifford, Erin's best friend since forever, greeted him at the door.

"Got everything ready to go?" he asked, giving her a hug.

"Yep. Let me finish getting BJ ready and we can head out."

Clay followed her into the kitchen and laughed at the little guy's excitement at seeing him.

"Kay, up," he shouted, raising his arms. "Beej up!"

"You got it, BJ, that's exactly what I'm here for." He lifted the toddler from the highchair and lifted him high, much to BJ's delight, then cuddled the precious little boy close to his heart. Not his son, but Clay would cherish him and protect him for the rest of his life.

"I'll take him now, Clay," Magie said. "The rest of the things are in the back of my car."

"Erin didn't see them?"

Magie laughed. "Nope. She pulled her usual 'I'm late, I'm late' White Rabbit stunt and dashed out of here without a sideways glance." She wrestled the wiggling toddler into a light jacket. "Besides, I'm out front and her car was in the garage, so she wouldn't have noticed anything, anyway."

"That's my girl," Clay said. "I just hope she won't be late for our wedding." He was only half-joking. Erin did tend to be a bit scatterbrained when under pressure.

Why had he let her talk him into a wedding in such a short time? Rhetorical question. Because his greatest desire was to make her his, a woman he'd loved unconditionally for over ten years. He wanted to become a father to her son . . . and the son of his best friend. Clay would always regret abandoning Justin on the eve of his wedding. But there was no way Clay could stand at the altar and watch the love of his life walk down the aisle and pledge her life to someone else. Nor could he bear the thought of remaining in the same town as their *happily ever after* slammed his heart day after day after day.

So, he'd left. Cowardly? Some had accused him of that. He had even accused himself. But he had contacted Justin a year later to apologize. Justin had understood, and forgiven. But Clay had forbidden Justin to tell Erin. He thought he'd had good reason for that as he'd never planned to return to Vegas.

But then Justin died. And everything changed.

"All right, Clay, let's get out of here so we can be back before Erin returns." Magie led the way out the front door, leaving Clay to lock up behind her. "I'll buckle him in to the car seat while you grab the stuff from the Beemer."

"You did say Doug was picking up the tree, right?" Clay asked after stowing several boxes of Christmas decorations into the back and starting up the SUV.

"Yes, he said he found exactly what he wanted yesterday and arranged for delivery this morning." Magie chuckled. "That man is having the time of his life. Said it's not often anyone can pull off anything without Erin finding out sooner or later."

"And her habitual procrastination has worked in our favor this time." Clay shook his head in amusement. "Never thought I'd be thankful for that. She must have driven Justin nuts."

"Oh, she did, but he seldom let her delay things for very long. If she didn't do it when he thought it should be done, he'd do it himself."

"And he never got mad at her?"

"Nope. Spoiled her, plain and simple." Magie touched his arm. "But don't get the wrong picture, here, Clay. Erin never took advantage of it. She never did it on purpose, you know? It's just her way."

"Yeah, I know. And I love her with everything in me, little putter-offer or not." He felt a grin forming as a long-ago memory surfaced. "I used to tell her that the reason her hair was always so unruly was because of her constant rush to get everything done at the last minute."

"Oh, I remember that. You teased her unmercifully."

"I did. And I got bopped many times for it. The weird thing is that her crazy hair was one of the things I loved most about her. That and her beautiful purple eyes."

Magie glanced over her shoulder at the baby in the car seat behind her. "BJ got his mother's squirrely hair but his daddy's color. And Justin's blue, blue eyes."

Clay felt his heart twist. Justin had not lived to see his son. And now he, Clay, would be raising that child in Justin's place. As he'd once vowed at Justin's gravesite, he would devote his entire life and love to both Erin and BJ.

The SUV's tires crunched on the white gravel of the Macintyre driveway as Clay stopped in front of the huge house. In the months since Doug's wife, Astrid, had passed away, Doug had undertaken the massive project of changing the entire façade of the place. Much still remained to be done, but the once brick exterior now wore the more suitable stucco finish. Many of the water-wasting trees and shrubs had been replaced with desert landscaping, making the whole place fit comfortably in the sprawling golfing community.

Erin had hated it. She'd called it ostentatious and ugly. Said the place belonged in Vermont or somewhere else, not in the middle of the Mojave Desert. Clay had to agree. Little could be done about the overall structure. It would remain a blocky two-story building. But the brooding, dark-red brick had disappeared behind tan stucco over the top two-thirds of the house and the lower area covered with cut sandstone pieces fitted together.

Before either Clay or Magie could even get out of the car, Doug Macintyre was down the stairs, across the drive, and reaching in to pull his grandson out of the car seat, much to BJ's delight.

"Gappa, Beej up!"

"Absolutely, little fella. Gappa's got you now." He lifted the boy over his head and swung him in a circle amidst squeals of joy. Doug lowered the giggling baby into his arms and headed back to the door.

"Let's get inside and do this so you can get back to Green Valley before Erin gets home. This is one surprise I'm going to pull off . . . with your help, of course."

Clay grinned. Yes, Erin had a way of sniffing things out no matter how hard one tried to keep a secret. She couldn't keep a secret either, so keeping one from her was a real coup.

Once inside, Doug led them through the house to the glassed-in conservatory, the one Erin had scathingly dubbed the Astrid Dome. Clay's heart skipped a beat. Poor Astrid. Unloved and unloving, misunderstood until just a few hours before she died. He'd never forget that day and the inward beauty that shone through both women as they made peace with each other.

And it was so typical of Erin that this lovely tropical indoor paradise was the place she chose to hold her wedding. Clay shook his head. She was a mercurial elf, a sprite full of wonder and mischief.

Doug deposited a protesting BJ into a playpen set up inside the fragrant indoor garden, but the toddler quieted instantly when Doug handed him a cup full of fruity loops. "That should keep him happy for a while, I think."

He turned away from the playpen and swept an arm toward the curved end of the conservatory, now sparkling in the bright morning sun. "So, what do you think?"

"Two?" Clay stared.

"You had them painted?" Mouth agape, Magie approached two very tall, very purple flocked live Christmas trees, one on either side of an archway constructed of gnarled twigs and covered with lush, hanging wisteria.

Clay took a moment to study the conservatory. "It feels different in here, Doug. And I don't recall seeing that arbor before."

"It's always been there, Clayton. But, at Erin's suggestion, I had some of the potted plants removed or relocated so I could widen the path a bit more to create an aisle to it."

"It's lovely, Doug. I love that shade of lavender on the trees." Magie stretched out her arm to rub a hand along the curved back of an old-fashioned park bench. "Where did you get these? I don't remember seeing them before."

"No, I'd bought them at a sale several years ago, but Astrid never wanted them in here so I just stored them in the extra garage. When Erin decided she wanted to hold your ceremony here, I had them refinished and, well, there they are."

"Does Erin know about this?" Magie asked.

"The benches? No. It's my surprise to her, along with the painted trees. She wants a purple wedding, so I'll do my part to give her one."

"Doug, you're a genius." Clay walked up next to Magie and stared. "This will blow her away."

"I hope so," Doug said. "Now, let's get busy."

An hour and a half later, both purple Christmas trees were festooned with silver and purple ornaments, garlands, ribbons and bows, and hundreds of clear mini lights. Not quite sure what to do about tree-toppers, Magie decided to fashion a bow at the top of each tree from the silver garlands and drape them across to meet at the top center of the wisteria arch.

"I'm sure Erin has different plans for this archway, Doug, and she may not like this." She waved at the two garland swags. "But that's easily changed."

She gave Doug a hug and stepped over to the playpen where little BJ now lay fast asleep. "I hate to wake him up but we need to go if we're to be back to the bungalow before Erin returns."

"Agreed," Doug said, "though I have a feeling you'll be safe enough. After the dress fitting, I believe Erin intended to do a little shopping before heading for home."

"Ha," Magie laughed. "With that girl there's no such thing as a *little* shopping."

Clay grinned. "So I'm finding out. Gotta love her, though." He winked. "And I do."

After dropping Magie and the baby off at Erin's, Clay headed back into town to his office. Not that there was much going on in the PI business right now, but one never knew. The Christmas season didn't always mean peace and light in the city. Somehow, it seemed to bring out the worst in some people. Not necessarily for his line of work, but he knew his Metro Detective friend Hutch could be in for a rough few days. Not just Christmas, but New Year's Eve, probably the worst holiday in Las Vegas for law enforcement.

"Hey, Alex," he called as he entered the kitchen of his combination home and office. He grabbed a Dr Pepper from the fridge. "Anything popping this afternoon?"

"Back so soon, partner?" Alexander Hunter, long-time friend and business partner, entered from the front rooms.

"Yeah, got it all done. You should see what Doug has done with the conservatory. It's nothing short of amazing how well he knows Erin." He finished off his drink and crushed the can, tossing it into their recycle bag. "Did you pick up the vests and ties?"

"Yep, they're in the hall closet. And may I add that I'll be forever grateful that you talked Erin out of that horrid purple plaid she wanted."

"Oh, I had to work hard on that. In the end we compromised. We'd wear her purple colors as long as it was a solid purple. Dark purple. Not a shade lighter. With Doug seconding that, it was a done deal."

"Hope she wasn't too upset. I wouldn't hurt that little gal for anything."

Clay smiled at his friend. "I know the feeling, Alex. But no, she gave in graciously. And there is the fact that Larke's dress is this same shade of purple."

Clay grabbed another Dr Pepper from the fridge and the two friends walked into the office rooms across the hall.

"So, Clay, you have four more days of freedom. Are you getting nervous?"

"No, not really. Well, maybe just a little. Mostly because I'm convinced she's probably the one they referred to when they said 'if anything can go wrong, it will.' That's what makes me worried."

He chuckled. "And I'm only half joking. But I've loved Erin Weyland Macintyre since what seems like forever. Like a fool I let her go once. I don't know why, and I don't deserve it, but for some reason I'll never understand, God has given her back to me."

With two minutes to spare, Erin parked in front of the specialty bridal shop and ushered Larke inside.

"You'll love the dresses, Larke. Thank you for trusting me to choose. I think the only things Lissa will have to adjust on yours will be the hem and the waist." She smiled at her sister. "But she's good, and she's fast. Let's not worry until we have to."

Inside, they were greeted by a diminutive woman of Asian descent who bowed in the traditional manner, then, eyes a-twinkle, she wrapped her arms around Erin.

"Ah, Mrs. Erin, I am glad to see you." She lifted her eyes to stare up at Larke. "And you must be Miss Larke?" Without waiting for confirmation, the woman smiled. "Of course you are. Your amethyst eyes give you away. There is no doubt about it."

Erin laughed. "Larke, this is Lissa Chou, my inimitable dressmaker. Lissa, meet my big sister, Larke LePaige."

Lissa frowned. "What is ini-mitt-apple?"

"Close enough," Larke laughed. "It means it is impossible for anyone to imitate you."

The woman's eyes widened. "That is good, yes?"

"It is very good, Lissa." Erin looped her hand through Lissa's arm. "Now, let's see what you've done with our dresses."

Lissa led them through the exquisite showroom to the sewing room in back. "Both dresses are finished except for some nips and tucks for Miss Larke." She gestured to two curtained dressing rooms. "Please to undress and put on the robes in there, and I will bring the dresses out to you."

When the girls returned to the sewing room, Lissa was waiting with a silvery froth of chiffon draped over her arm. "Mrs. Erin, we will start with you. I want to make certain it is right. Then we will do that nipping and tucking for Miss Larke."

Discarding the robe she'd put on in the dressing room, Erin stood in front of Lissa while the seamstress slid the dress over her head, the deliciously soft yards of fabric slipping down over her body. Facing the mirror as Lissa fastened the back, Erin caught her breath.

The full-skirted cocktail dress fit to perfection. A four-inch jeweled band cinched her waist, above which more chiffon gathered into a halter-style bodice that fastened at the back of her neck with tiny loops over three crystal buttons, leaving her back bare above the waist.

Erin couldn't resist a little pirouette to make the fullness of the skirt flare in a frothy circle.

"Beautiful, Lissa." She twirled again. "I love this dress."

"Erin," Larke said, eyes wide. "Except for the color, that dress looks a lot like the famous white dress that Marilyn Monroe wore in that movie. You know, where she stood above the subway vent in New York?"

"Give the lady a gold star," Erin said. "The movie was 'The Seven Year Itch' and I fell in love with that dress. It wasn't really white, you know. It was ivory, and it was pleated."

"So you really are going to go with the 50's idea?"

"Of course. Well, partly." Erin couldn't resist another spin of the skirt. "You doubted?"

"I should have known better because I know how captivated you've always been by everything from that era." Larke shrugged. "But, yeah, I did."

Erin stepped off the little platform. "Lissa, it's perfect. Thank you."

The dressmaker smiled and turned to Erin's sister. "Now, Miss Larke, it is your turn." She disappeared around the corner and returned, yards of rich purple chiffon in her arms. "We must be careful getting this on as it is only stay-stitched in places."

Larke took Erin's spot but had to stoop to allow the much shorter seamstress to guide the dress over her head.

"Try not to move your body too much, Miss Larke. The seams are only basted, and there are some pins holding other parts together that might stick you."

"Duly noted," Larke said, wincing as one of said pins pricked her at the waist. "Ouch."

Lissa giggled, fussing with the seams as the dress settled over Larke's body. "Did I not warn you?"

Erin stood back and watched as the dressmaker fussed with her creation, a nagging feeling that something was wrong. But what? Then, as Lissa maneuvered Larke's position, pinning and tucking, one of the jewels in the waistband sparked in the light. She looked down at her own dress.

Oh, no!

"Lissa, wait!"

Lissa's head jerked up. Larke cringed. "Ouch!"

"Sorry, Sis. But, Lissa, you've got the waistbands wrong. Mine is supposed to be the one with the purple jewels. Larke's is to have the crystals."

Lissa's face showed confusion, then alarm. "Oh, Mrs. Erin, you are right," she said, wringing her hands. "I am so sorry."

Larke's gaze studied Erin's dress, then assessed her own. "But, Erin, this is lovely. Does it really matter?"

The question brought Erin up short. Was it that important? Probably not. Still . . .

"But . . . I wanted everything in contrast, you know? My silver dress with purple accents. Your purple dress with silver. Well, okay, crystal."

She stopped and shrugged, feeling juvenile. "You're right, Larke. It doesn't matter."

"I will fix the dresses, Mrs. Erin."

Erin swung around toward the dressmaker, pierced to the heart at Lissa's crushed demeanor. Yes, the error had been hers because Erin had been quite specific in her requirements for the two dresses. But now?

Erin shot a glance over her shoulder at Larke. *Follow my lead.*

As Larke stepped up on the other side of the seamstress, Erin turned all three of them to face the floor-to-ceiling mirror that filled one whole wall of the sewing area. And Erin realized that she had been wrong. The clear crystal gems did belong on her dress. Her wedding dress. And the various shades of purple were definitely meant to be on Larke's dress.

"No, Lissa. Don't change anything."

"I will give discount for mistake."

"You'll do nothing of the sort. Somehow, some way, you knew. The mistake would have been mine if you had made them my way." Erin hugged the small woman. "Thank you."

"You are very kind, Mrs. Erin. I will finish Miss Larke's dress and have them both ready tomorrow afternoon."

"That woman is a marvel, Erin," Larke said, buckling her seatbelt a few minutes later. "How'd you find her?"

Erin started the car and pulled out into traffic. "Yes, she is." She laughed. "The weirdest thing about that is Lissa was recommended to me several years ago by one of Astrid's friends."

"You're kidding me."

"Nope. Mrs. Carmichael. Remember her? She was one of the nicer ones, more genuine. She was someone I could actually talk to during my forced appearances at one of Astrid's *soirees*, as she called them."

"Oh, now I remember. Nice lady."

"Mm, hmm . . . oh, no!"

"Oh, no, what?" Larke stiffened in her seat.

"I forgot to call Magie," Erin said, slamming the heel of her hand against her forehead. "She doesn't know your plane was late and she'll be wondering where I am."

"Relax, Erin. If she was worried, wouldn't she have called *you?*"

"Well, yeah, I guess."

"Little sister of mine, you've got to relax or you're going to snap. You're acting as if this was the society wedding of the year or something." Larke jabbed Erin's knee with a long, manicured finger, emphasizing each word. "Small." *Jab.* "Informal." *Jab.* "Remember?" *Jab, jab.*

Erin willed her shoulders to come down from below her ears. How had she let herself get so tense? Larke was right. Small wedding. Family only. Why did she now make it seem like such a big affair?

"I'm being silly, aren't I?" She caught herself up short. "No, not silly. Selfish. And more than a little self-centered."

"Well, maybe just a little. But perhaps you can be forgiven after all you've been through in the last two years. But if you don't calm down, you're going to implode into a heap of rubble and there won't be anything left for Clay to carry over the threshold."

Erin giggled. "Oh, we can't have that, now, can we?"

Then she sobered. She was being a little obsessive over this, wasn't she? Why? No reason she could think of. None. Nobody to impress. The wedding wouldn't even hit the papers until after the fact. By then she and Clay would be on a cruise ship somewhere in the Mediterranean.

Snap out of it, Erin.

"Hey, where are you going?" Larke peered through the windshield as Erin turned off Stephanie and cruised the lot in front of Hobby Lobby for a parking space. "I thought we were going home."

"I need to pick up some silk flowers and ribbons for our wrist corsages and the guy's boutonnieres."

"You're going to make them?"

"Yeah, the florists couldn't come up with anything I liked."

"Wow, no wonder you're a nervous wreck."

"It's no big deal, Sis. I can do them all in a day, provided you'll keep BJ." Erin winked as she got out of the car.

Larke joined Erin in front of the car. "You'll never get over your last-minute sprints, will you?"

Erin shrugged. "Probably not."

They entered the store and Erin headed straight for the fabric department. She hadn't told Larke but she wanted to find some lengths of silver and purple tulle to drape around the twig arbor in the conservatory. She loved the purple wisteria that climbed all over it, but it needed some . . . froth. She grinned. Men hated froth. *Foofaraw,* Justin had called it. Doug called it foo-foo. She wondered what Clay would call it.

"We're not going to find any silver tulle here, Larke," Erin said after some frustrated searching, "and we're running out of time. I'll just have to make do with the lilac and purple."

They gathered the two bolts of tulle and headed to the cutting table when Erin spotted some silvery netting in the next aisle over. "Oh, look, Larke, that's perfect," she said and scooped it up.

"What are you going to do with all this tulle, dear?" the woman asked as she cut the lengths Erin ordered. "The colors are lovely."

"I'm making a wedding canopy," Erin replied, waiting for the reaction she knew was coming.

"Purple bridal colors? How beautiful. When is the wedding?"

"In four days." Erin suppressed a giggle as the clerk gawked.

"Four days? But that's Christmas Day!"

"Yup, it is." Erin gathered the stacked and priced pieces to take to the cashier. "It's going to be a Purple Christmas Wedding." She smiled. "Thank you, and Merry Christmas!"

On their way to the cashier, Erin picked up some purple and lilac satin ribbon roses, a length of silver beads, and two child-size hair *scrunchies.* "There, I think that's all."

"If you're making your own flowers, why wrist corsages instead of bouquets?"

'Now, Sis, what will you do with your bouquet when I hand you BJ after I get to the altar?"

"Hand me . . . *BJ*? What in the world are you talking about?"

"My son, BJ." Erin laughed as they loaded their purchases into the car. "You just agreed to watch him for me tomorrow, remember?"

Larke sputtered. "Of course I remember, but—" Her eyes widened. "You're going to carry the baby down the aisle?

"Oh, Larke, he's not a baby anymore. Wait till you see him. So, no, at fifteen months he's too heavy for me to carry, especially in high heels." She grinned. "Doug is going to carry him."

"But I thought Doug was to be the one to escort you down the aisle."

"Yes, that's right. BJ in one arm, me on the other."

Larke stared at her over the top of the car, saying nothing, which made Erin fidget. "I'm not sure how to explain this." Erin groped for the right words. "It's like a . . . a dedication, I guess. BJ is Justin's son. He will always be a Macintyre. Clay has accepted that, though he would adopt BJ in a blink. But Justin was Doug's only son, and BJ, as Justin's son, will carry on the Macintyre name. It just seems fitting to me that Doug be the one to turn his grandson over into Clay's care."

Erin held her sister's gaze for a moment, letting her absorb her words. "Our rings will be tucked in the pocket of BJ's little vest. He will be the ring bearer."

Larke's face relaxed into a smile. "That's adorable! I love it."

Erin slid in behind the wheel, waiting for Larke to settle her long, dancer's body into the seat and fasten her seatbelt. She wondered anew how they two could be so different yet so alike. Larke, five years older and seven inches taller than Erin, had a slim, lithesome body, all grace and fluid motion. Stick-straight red hair contrasted to Erin's gold-silver unruly curls. But both had the same amethyst eyes.

"So, tell me how you're going to work your 50's fascination into the wedding."

"Hm? Oh! Well, except for our dresses, just a little Ronnie Milsap."

"Huh?"

Erin giggled. "'Lost in the Fifties Tonight' will be playing while you, and then Doug and I, walk down the aisle."

She watched as Larke processed the idea, her body moving in time to the music Erin knew was running through Larke's head, and recognized the instant it clicked.

Larke opened her eyes to look at Erin. "You're serious."

Erin nodded, waiting.

"Does Clay know?"

"No."

Larke paused, eyes steady, as if peering deep into Erin's soul.

"Baby sister, given the history between the two of you," Larke said, reaching across the console between them to give Erin a hug, "this is absolutely perfect."

They broke their awkward embrace and Erin swiped the moisture from her eyes. "Thank you, Larke. I knew you'd understand."

"Count on it."

Erin straightened and turned the ignition, her heart lighter than it had been for the past several hours.

"Next stop, the Macintyre Mansion and . . . get ready . . . the Astrid Dome."

Larke laughed, as Erin intended. "You still call it that?"

"Yeah, it will always be the Astrid Dome, only now it has a different meaning to me. You know?"

Larke nodded. "I know."

"Clay? Hey, Clay."

Alex's shout from the edge of the pool caught Clay's ear as he brought his head out of the water in mid-stroke.

"What?"

"You've got company."

Clay swam to the edge of the pool and pulled himself up the ladder. "Company?" He looked up to see the grinning faces of Hutchinson Cooke, Detective, Las Vegas Metropolitan Police, and Paul Weyland, Erin's uncle.

"What are you two doing here?" He grabbed an oversized towel and wrapped it around himself. Though the pool was warm, the December air was chilly. He quickly led the way into the house and stopped short. The kitchen table sagged with boxes and bags of all kinds of fast-food offerings.

"What—?"

"Surprise bachelor party, Clay," Hutch beamed. "We didn't know what to bring so we brought a little of everything. Besides, we were hungry."

Clay glanced over the selection again. Chinese, Mexican, Pizza Hut, KFC, even . . . "In-N-Out Burgers?" The pungent and tantalizing aroma of sautéed onions made his mouth water. "You guys are nuts!"

"Not really." Paul, a distinguished-looking man with silver hair that belied his youthful-looking face, patted Clay on the back. "As my soon-to-be nephew-in-law, I figured you needed a good send-off."

"Yeah, right." Clay laughed. "Let me get dressed so we can do this right."

When he came back into the kitchen, the men had opened their own choices and Clay headed straight for one of the In-N-Out Double-Double Cheeseburgers and a box of fries. He grabbed a Dr Pepper from the fridge and took his meal into the front room, where he sank into his recliner, the others following.

"I called Doug to join us," Alex said, biting into a slice of pizza. "But he said he was helping Erin and Larke decorate the conservatory."

"More like watching, if I know my girl." Clay chuckled. "If he's doing anything it's running and fetching."

"Poor Doug," Hutch said, laughing.

"Wrong. There's no *poor Doug* about it. He loves her, and there isn't anything he wouldn't do for her."

"Hey, we know that, man," Alex said. "We love Erin too and would be just as willing to fetch for her as Doug is."

"Yeah, I know. Sorry, guys."

"Just a little on edge, son?" Paul's concern touched Clay, and he smiled at the familial term.

"I guess. Maybe."

The office phone rang and Clay reached for it, resenting the interruption. But it was still a business day and business hours.

"Hunter and Buchanan Investigations. This is—"

"Clayton?"

He shot to his feet at the sound of Doug's frantic voice.

"What's wrong?"

"Meet me at UMC's ER. Erin has fallen, and I think she may have broken her ankle."

"What?" Clay's mind shut down. Erin hurt?

"Just meet me there as soon as you can."

"Doug, wait—" He had hung up.

"You're white as a ghost, Clay," Alex said. "What's happened?"

"Erin's been hurt."

"What? How?"

"Doug said she fell. He's taking her to UMC."

"Then that's where you need to be, man." Alex steered him to the kitchen and shoved the keys in his hand. "Get outta here. Now."

Clay stepped through the doorway and jerked back as his bare foot met the cold concrete outside. "Whoa!" He turned to Alex. "You'd send me out in public half naked?"

Alex's mouth twisted in a rueful grin. "Sorry."

But the moment served to relieve some of the tension and Clay hurried down the hall to his bedroom for a shirt and his boots.

Back in the kitchen he again picked up his keys and snatched his Stetson off the hook next to the door. "Now I'm outta here. I'll call when I know anything."

Naturally it was the four o'clock rush hour, and Clay had to fight to stifle his impatience as images of an injured Erin flooded his imagination. How had she fallen? How bad was it? Could she really have a broken ankle?

"Hang on, darlin', hang on."

Despite the traffic, he made it to the hospital in good time. Finding no open spots close to the entrance, Clay drove into the parking garage, his patience thinning as he looped up level after level to the top floor, just below the helipad. And of course he ended up as far away from the elevator as possible.

"Figures," he muttered, pulling his collar up as a gust of cold wind swept across the open space. His impatience mounting when the elevator failed to appear, he yanked the door to the stairs and flew down four flights, emerging opposite the ambulance entrance. He raced through the emergency doors and searched for help.

"Clay, over here!" He spun around to see both Doug and Erin seated in the waiting room, along with several other miserable-looking people. He rushed to Erin and dropped to his knees in front of her.

"Are you all right?" His gaze traveled over her body and came to rest on her left foot, wrapped in a towel and propped up on Doug's knee. A plastic bag half-full of water rested atop the towel, obviously the remains of what had been a makeshift ice pack.

"They haven't seen you yet?" Helpless anger bubbled just below the surface. He tamped it down as he heard the wail of several sirens and the thumping *whop-whop-whop* of an incoming helicopter, knowing it would be a while before Erin got any attention.

"What happened?"

His heart clenched as her weak attempt at a laugh turned into a grimace of pain.

"It was stupid," she said, shifting a bit in her chair. "I was on the ladder. I thought I had reached the bottom rung and stepped off." She winced again.

"I was standing right there, but it happened so fast I couldn't catch her." Doug's face clenched in self-recrimination. "She landed hard and must have twisted her ankle. It swelled up almost immediately."

Clay stood, frustrated at his inability to fix this. He paced a few steps, shoving his hat back on his head. As he turned back to Erin, he noticed her massaging her left wrist and rushed back to her side.

"You hurt your wrist, too?"

"I-it does hurt," she admitted, "but it doesn't look swollen."

Clay reached for her hand and gently turned it without touching the wrist. It looked slightly swollen to him. "Can you move your fingers?"

She obediently wiggled them but that didn't necessarily mean there wasn't a fracture somewhere.

"Oh, sugar," he whispered, "I'm so sorry."

"Erin. Macintyre?"

To Clay's surprise, and relief, a nurse in a colorful scrub top appeared near the desk.

"Yes, here," he answered.

"Come with me, and we'll get you signed in."

Clay lifted Erin's foot off Doug's leg, and together they helped her stand and supported her across the room to the Triage-intake room.

After asking dozens of routine questions, the nurse unwrapped the towel to look at Erin's ankle, made a note, and wrapped it back up. Then she examined Erin's wrist and placed it gently back into Erin's lap.

"That's all we need from you now. Have a seat and someone will come for you."

As Clay and Doug helped Erin hobble to the door, the nurse asked "Would you like some ice?"

Erin took a quick breath. "Yes, please."

They guided Erin back to their seats, and this time Clay took Erin's foot on his lap. The nurse appeared with two emergency ice packs, popped and shook them, then handed them to Clay and left.

A few moments later an orderly came with a wheelchair. "We'll take you back now, Ms. Macintyre, and see what you've done to yourself." He smiled mischievously as he locked the wheels, waiting for Clay to help Erin to stand, then the orderly took over.

As he released the locks he turned to Doug. "Are you her father?"

Doug shook his head. "Her father-in-law, and this is her fiancé." He indicated Clay.

The curious look the orderly gave them made Clay laugh despite the circumstances, but he didn't bother to explain. The orderly shrugged and wheeled Erin away. "Wait here, please. Someone will come for you after we get her checked out."

Clay stared at the door through which Erin had disappeared. Wait. Something he was not very good at. Apparently Doug had the same issue, for he stood and paced. Clay thought that was a good idea and got up and joined him.

"I'd better call Magie," Doug finally said, returning to his chair. "It just dawned on me that she knows nothing about any of this."

"You mean she's still out in Green Valley?" It seemed days ago that he'd dropped Magie and BJ back at Erin's home.

Doug nodded as he lifted his cell phone to his ear. "I'm not going to enjoy this call," he said, then closed his eyes. "Magie, it's Doug."

Clay watched the varying display of emotions play across Doug's face as he explained what happened. At times he could even hear Magie's voice raised a few decibels, which elicited a brief smile from Clay. Magie could be a termagant if she felt she had good cause. And Erin being injured was more than cause enough.

When Doug slipped his phone back into his pocket, he grinned at Clay. "She already knew. Larke is there."

Clay raised an eyebrow. "Then what was the noisy tirade about?"

"Magie just wanted to let me know that I should have called her, not left it up to Larke to drive home to tell her." He rubbed his neck. "To be honest, I'd forgotten all about Larke. I just wanted to get Erin to emergency."

They settled back to pacing in silence until, a full hour later, a nurse came through the door. "Clay Buchanan?"

"That's me," Clay said, stepping forward to meet her. "How is she?"

"You can come back and see her now." She looked over his shoulder. "Are you Doug Macintyre?"

At Doug's nod she turned back to the door. "Come along, then."

A moment later they were ushered into a curtained cubicle and stopped dead in their tracks. Erin sat on the exam table, tears streaming silently down her face, her left arm encased in a cast from mid-hand clear up to her underarm. Her left foot sported a huge, ugly black boot that looked like it weighed more than she.

"I'm so sorry, Clay." Her shoulders shook with sobs, but no sound emerged.

"Oh, please don't cry, sugar. It's all right." In a second he was beside her with his arms around her, absorbing her sobs. "Hush, it's all right."

"No, it's not all right. I've made a mess of everything."

Doug wrapped his arm around her from the other side, meeting Clay's eyes above Erin's head. "Nonsense, lass. It's going to be just fine."

"But the wedding," she wailed. "I can't walk down the aisle with a broken foot, let alone in this ugly thing." She kicked her foot out and scowled at the black boot.

"So we'll use a wheelchair," Clay said, causing Erin's wail to increase.

"Get married in a wheelchair?"

"Well, no, but maybe just to get you to the front. Then you can stand."

This wasn't working, Clay could tell. He shot a desperate glance at Doug but was saved further efforts at reassuring Erin when a doctor walked in through the curtain.

"Ah, I see they've got you all fixed up." He smiled at Erin, then held out his hand to Clay. "I'm Dr. McGuire."

"Doctor." Clay shook the man's hand. "So, what's the deal with my fiancée?"

The doctor leaned against the foot of the bed, facing all three of them. "She has a closed fracture of the left radius." He held up his own arm and pointed to the area. "Right here."

"Broken, then?"

The doctor nodded. "She's in a temporary cast, but she'll need to see an orthopedic doctor tomorrow for a permanent one. She'll wear the full cast for about two weeks. Then they'll put her in a short cast to below her elbow for another three weeks."

"Five weeks?" Erin gasped, obviously fighting more tears. "What about the foot?"

"The ankle is a little sprained but will be fine. But you also have a closed fracture of the second metatarsal--the second toe, in other words." He raised his foot and pointed to a spot about half-way down the top of his foot.

Another gasp from Erin stabbed Clay to the core. "Will you put a cast on that, too?"

"No, but you'll be in that walking boot for about ten weeks. You'll need to get to a podiatrist as soon as you can."

"T-ten weeks?"

Clay tightened his grip around Erin as he felt her react to the news.

The doctor nodded. "I'm afraid so. But the good news is you can take it off at night and to bathe or shower. Also take it off every few hours and apply an ice pack for twenty minutes. Then put the boot back on."

Erin slumped. "I've ruined everything, Clay. The wedding, the h—oh!"

"What, darlin'?"

"The honeymoon!"

"What about it?"

"Get serious, Clay. A honeymoon . . . like this?"

"Ah, sugar, you'll be the most pampered person on that cruise ship." He grinned. "Trust me."

She tried out a grin, but it didn't quite make it. "Yeah, sure."

The doctor stood to leave. "Any questions?"

"Yeah," Erin snorted. "Can you turn the clock back a few hours?"

The doctor left, and the orderly entered with a wheelchair. "Let's get you home, young lady," he said, positioning the chair and locking the wheels. He looked at Clay. "Where's your car, sir?"

"Uh, I'm on the top of the parking garage, but it's an SUV and it will be hard to get her up into it." Clay turned to Doug. "She'd be a lot more comfortable in your Mercedes. Why don't you go get it? I'll wait at the entrance with Erin."

"Good idea," Doug said and left after the orderly gave him directions to the door to pick Erin up.

Clay walked beside the wheelchair, holding Erin's right hand as she gripped it for all she was worth. She had to be in pain, not just physically, but emotionally as she despaired over the ruin of all her beautiful wedding plans. Clay's heart broke for her. How could he convince her it didn't matter to him?

Doug's car glided to a stop in front of them, and Clay reached to open the passenger door, then stepped back to allow the orderly to get the wheelchair into position and locked.

"Now, Mrs. Macintyre, wrap your right arm around my neck and let me lift you up out of the chair. Then put your weight on your right foot so I can turn you around to get into the car."

She obeyed meekly, Clay wishing he could help, but he knew that was against the rules. Hospital liability or something. The orderly lowered her gently to the seat, guided her left arm and leg inside, and allowed her to pivot herself in the rest of the way.

"Atta girl," he said, reaching across her to fasten the seat belt. "Take care of yourself, okay?" He stepped back, rolled the wheelchair out of the way, and closed the car door.

"Thank you," Clay said, shaking the young man's hand. "It'll be interesting getting her back out, though."

"Just do what I did in reverse. You'll be fine." He smiled and returned to the hospital with a cheerful whistle.

"You will follow me, right?" Doug said from behind him. "It'll take both of us to get her inside when we get her home."

"Of course." Clay scanned the area for a place Doug could park and wait for him. "Pull over there. I'll be right down."

When Clay pulled alongside the Mercedes, Doug got out and walked over. "Clay, why don't you drive my car? I'll follow in the Rendezvous. Erin needs you right now more than me."

Surprised, but grateful, Clay made the trade.

"Hi, darlin'."

Erin rolled her head to the side as Clay got into the car. "Hi, you."

"Doin' okay?"

"The pain meds are kicking in, so yeah, I'm good." She tried to shift position, but with only one arm for leverage she gave up with an exaggerated sigh.

"This thing is so awkward. How am I going to manage for two weeks when I can't bend my elbow?" She raised her arm toward her head and dropped it back down.

"Ow!"

"Careful, sugar."

"Oh, this is impossible. I can't even touch my head! How am I supposed to wash my face?"

Clay chuckled. "I guess I'll have to learn how to wash my wife's face for her."

"That's not funny, Buchanan." She huffed again. "Five weeks of this. I can't believe it."

"Correction, m'love. Only two weeks in the full cast."

"Oh, right, that makes everything just peachy, doesn't it?" Erin was instantly ashamed of herself. "Sorry."

"I'm sorry too, Erin. I didn't mean to sound so flippant."

"It's okay. It's not your fault. I'm just so mad at myself. How could I have been so clumsy?"

"Don't be so hard on yourself, darlin'. The doc couldn't make time go in reverse, so we'll just deal with it."

She chuckled. "No, he couldn't do that." She leaned her head against the seat. "So, how do we *deal* with this? I will not roll down the aisle in a wheelchair. Period."

"Crutches? Oh, no, wait. Not with your arm in a cast."

All at once Erin saw the absurdity of the situation and started to giggle. "This is a fine mess I've landed us into, isn't it? Good thing it's a private wedding." She giggled again. "Good grief, can you imagine what Astrid would have to say?"

Clay guffawed. "I don't think I even want to go there." That set them both off. By the time they arrived at Erin's bungalow, Erin was feeling mellow, whether from the pain medications or the presence of the man she loved with all her heart she couldn't say.

"Erin, before we go in, I want to tell you something, and I want you to listen very carefully."

"Oh, dear, this sounds serious." She smiled.

"I have been enchanted with you from the first moment I laid eyes on you all those years ago, with your crazy curly hair, purple eyes—"

"Amethyst."

"Erin!"

"Sorry. Please do go on."

"My love for you never wavered, not even when you married my best friend."

Erin sucked in a breath but said nothing.

"I want you to know that nothing you could ever do could change my love for you."

He paused, and Erin waited, feeling there was more.

"Nothing. Not even breaking an arm and a leg just before our wedding."

She gasped, then laughed. "A wrist and a foot, you goof!"

"Oh, Erin, I love you so much, and I will spend the rest of my life proving it to you."

The Rendezvous drew up behind them, and Doug came around to join Clay at Erin's door.

"Hi, Doug. Would you please help my future husband get your clumsy daughter-in-law out of this car and into the house?" She giggled. "Did you see the look on that orderly's face when you mentioned our relationships? Priceless!"

Clay chuckled. "I decided not to attempt an explanation. Best to leave it alone."

"Good thinking."

Together they maneuvered Erin out of the car and up the walk, where Magie and Larke waited, clucking like mother hens.

Inside and settled into her favorite recliner, Erin realized she had another issue to deal with. "How am I ever going to handle BJ?"

"No problem, little sis. I'll just move in until the wedding."

"And I'll spell her, kiddo," Magie said. "Not to worry. Besides, I was going to be taking care of him while you were on your honeymoon, anyway."

Erin's heart swelled at the love surrounding her. How did she get so lucky?

It's not luck, dear one.

Erin smiled.

"Listen up, everyone."

All heads turned in her direction. She grinned and pointed to the ugly black boot.

"If I have to stump down the aisle four days from now in this . . . thing . . . it *will* be wrapped in the lilac and purple tulle from the leftover decorations. Not one speck of black shall be visible."

Laughter rippled among her dearest friends.

"And," she added, holding up her left arm for attention, "tomorrow, when I get my hard cast . . . ?"

"Yes?"

"Purple."

Her Best Worst Christmas

Anne Baxter Campbell

Wendy wondered if she would faint from sheer terror.

Fury masked Thelma Johnson's face. "How could you have done something so stupid?"

"I'm sorry, Mrs. Johnson. She asked, and I…."

"That's *Ms.* Johnson. You just blurted out the first thing on your infinitesimal so-called mind. We lost a valued customer, and all you can say is you're sorry. Austina Taskers probably buys more here in the Holiday season than most people do in a lifetime. Excuse me, she *bought* more. Since she says she'll never set foot in this boutique again, it's all past tense now."

Wendy studied the moss-green carpet, her armpits soaking wet. "But…"

"There is no excuse. You were warned before. You're fired." Mrs. Johnson pointed toward the door. "Pick up your check before you leave."

Fired. Three Days before Christmas, and Wendy'd been fired. She squinted at her check through the light snow and diffused bright morning light, wishing a zero or two would miraculously appear at the end of the pitifully small amount on the check. How would she find another job without a reference? Unless she lied on the next job application. No. Not that. She stuffed the check back into the envelope and winced at the paper cut on her index finger.

Wendy shivered in the light breeze at the bus stop. Her thin but fashionable coat didn't offer much protection from the twenty-degree cold. Colored lights blinked in Baroquen Basket across the

211

street, shading in red, blue, and green the quaint miniature snow-covered village and little train chugging in circles.

Baroquen Basket. Hmm. Maybe they needed Christmas help? She stood up from the cold concrete bench and had taken a step toward the crosswalk when she heard a faint whimper coming from…the trash container? Someone had trashed a puppy? Or maybe a kitten? She pushed some papers aside and saw a bundle wrapped in a green cloth grocery bag.

"What's this?" She whispered. She lifted the bag and peered inside. Blood smeared the edges of the bag and a glob of something she probably didn't want to identify stuck to the inside of the sack. And a baby girl. Wendy yelped and nearly dropped the bag when another feeble cry escaped the infant's pursed bluish lips.

Wendy reached into the alligator leather purse hanging from her shoulder and dug for her cell phone without success. She moved back to the bench and started to set the bag down, but she thought better of it when she remembered how cold the concrete bench had been. Where could she set it? On her lap would probably ruin her coat—but this baby was already shivering in the cold. She loosed the buttons and tucked the bag close to her ruffled yellow silk blouse, wrapping the coat around the bag and baby as much as she was able. "I wish I had a warm blanket for you, little one."

She stretched her free hand again into her purse and felt around the bottom and all the pockets. Where was her phone? A mental picture of her bedside table gave her cause to groan. She'd left it at home. Now what?

She lifted her eyes again to the store across the street. They'd have a phone. She trotted awkwardly to the intersection in her four-inch Jimmie Choo heels, pushed a cracked button on the light post, and waited for the walk signal. And waited. Impatiently, she pushed the button again, this time more firmly. Minutes passed, and still the signal didn't change. There were too many cars to ignore the "don't walk" direction. Some teenagers pushed the button on the other side of the street, and the walk light lit up.

She crossed the street as fast as the heels would allow, but at the curb she slipped on a spot of ice and struck her head against the edge of the post, almost dropping the baby. She stood, holding her head with her free hand. She walked more slowly into the Baroquen Basket and up to the counter. "May I use your phone?"

"The phone isn't for public use, young lady," a scrunched older gentleman behind the counter said, frowning. "What's wrong with your head?"

"Please, sir. It's urgent. I have a new-born baby...."

"You're carrying your baby in a grocery bag?"

"It's not my baby. I found it in the trash."

"You found it." Eyebrows quirked up on his crinkly face. "In the trash?"

"Please, please, will you call 911? Hurry!" She patted the bag and peered inside again. The baby wasn't moving.

The man lifted an old rotary phone from the base and handed it to her. With shaky fingers she dialed the emergency number.

"Hello? I have a newborn baby.... My name is Wendy Blessing.... No ma'am, this is not a joke. I found a baby this morning. It was in the trash.... This is a store near where I found the baby.... It's...She's not moving, and she looks a little blue. Please send someone, quick.... Yes, I'll stay on the line.... No, I don't know how to do CPR, especially on a baby." Wendy placed her hand on the infant's chest and, the baby gave a thin, weak squeak. "Yes, it's breathing. I'm sorry, Little One.... No, I didn't hurt it. My hand is icy."

The shopkeeper leaned forward and looked inside the bag. "Agh!" He jerked back. "It's covered with blood! What did you do to it?"

"I didn't do anything. It...."

A siren wailed and an ambulance screeched to a stop in front of the store. Two men and a woman burst through the door.

"Is this the place with a baby?" One of the EMTs stepped toward her. Dark hair with black eyes that pierced her.

Nice looking medical technician, she mused. "Yes. Right here." She lifted her bundle.

The guy frowned and looked into the bag, backed up, and pulled on sterile gloves. "What's it doing in a bag?" He reached his hands in and lifted the baby and the bloody clot out. "She still has the umbilical attached." He threw a glance over his shoulder, then focused on Wendy's blood-stained yellow blouse. "Is she your baby?"

"No, I..."

"How did you get the blood all over you? Jake, we need some chloramine for this lady."

"Chloramine? Any relation between that and chlorine?"

"Yeah. You'll smell a little like bleach for a while."

"No way. This is silk." Wendy held both hands in front of her when the other man, as blond as the first one was dark, approached her.

"Ma'am, that baby could have HIV or Hepatitis. You want that? Take this into the restroom and wipe anywhere you have blood on your skin. Throw the shirt in the garbage." Blond Guy glanced at her matching green and yellow wool skirt, also red spotted. "The skirt too. And that coat. Anything else get blood on it?" He turned to the shopkeeper. "Do you have a shower here?"

"No. And the bathroom isn't for the public...." The wizened clerk paled.

"It doesn't matter. She needs to wash right away. Anything here she can change into?"

"We don't carry clothing." His voice rose by an octave and wavered.

"Jennie, get a wrap from the ambulance." Dark Eyes swathed the baby in a soft-looking gray blanket. "Let's get this kid warming up. Lady, what are you waiting for? Get into that bathroom." When she turned, he grabbed her arm. "Wait. Is that a cut on your head? You'd better come with us; the back of your head is bleeding. I think you need sutures." He grabbed a package of gauze from the medical kit they'd brought in, pulled off his used gloves and donned clean ones.

Wendy put her hand to her head and winced. She hadn't even felt it or known it was bleeding until now.

Dark Eyes placed a pad of gauze over the cut and wrapped a pink stretchy band around her head several times. "That will do until we get you to the hospital. Have you had a tetanus shot or been immunized against hepatitis B?"

"Immunizations? I don't remember when for Tetanus, and I don't think so for the other one." Wendy swallowed. She hated shots.

Jennie returned with a green lab coat and handed it to Wendy.

Wendy trudged behind the shopkeeper through a cluttered back room.

He pointed to a door. "In there. I'm sorry it's not clean, but I'm the only one who ever uses it and...." His high-pitched voice trailed off as Wendy opened the door to the worst squalor she'd ever seen.

And the smell. Had it *ever* been cleaned? The toilet lid was up, of course, and the water a sickening brownish yellow. She wrinkled her nose. Wendy remembered all the times she had berated her big brother for doing the same thing. "Would you please bring me a shopping bag?" The most expensive things she'd ever owned, her early Christmas present to herself, the items she'd blown her last check on? No way was she throwing this outfit away. Not even if Dark Eyes told her to.

The shopkeeper returned with a Christmassy plastic sack, and she stepped into the tiny, odoriferous bathroom holding her breath. In a few swift moves, she'd peeled the skirt and blouse off and stuffed them into the red and green striped container, cupping her hand over her nose to breathe whenever necessary. Wendy squeezed the chloramine onto a paper towel, wiping herself off. She pushed the rag into the already overflowing trash. The smell of bleach overwhelmed the Shalimar toilet water she'd sprayed on herself that morning, but the chloramine sure improved the smell of the bathroom.

The lab coat was a hundred sizes too large, but it covered her. She chuckled. At least she wouldn't have to ride home on the bus with the lab coat. Or would she? She supposed they'd take her to the emergency room, but then what?

The mirror revealed tangled, fine but thick and curly mousy brown hair, but she had a couple of hair bands in her purse. She pulled her bloody hair back and tucked it into a band. That would have to do.

"And then what" for that poor little baby too. No mama, no daddy. If she lived. *Dear God, please let her live.* The thought squeezed her heart.

Who would dump a baby in a trash can, for heaven's sake? She was so tiny. Wendy hurried to the ambulance. Dark Eyes extended his hand and helped her into the vehicle. She stared at the baby lying so still in a nest of blankets. A mask had been taped over the wee mouth and nose, wires draped across the baby's chest and to an electrocardiograph, and something had been taped to the baby's foot.

Oddly enough, the infant seemed not to mind all the equipment or the mask. Some pink had begun to tint her cheeks, and blue-black eyes blinked as she clenched tiny fists next to her chest. Downy black hair framed a sweet round face.

"She's so tiny," murmured Wendy. "Will she be okay?"

"It's hard to say, ma'am," Dark Eyes said softly. "I hope so." He cleared his throat. "You might want to sit over there. Or lie down, if you feel lightheaded or anything." He pointed to an empty cot behind her. "We need to get to the hospital."

She sat, and the ambulance pulled out onto the street, siren blowing. Dark Eyes remained at the baby's side; Blond Guy— Jake—drove, and Jennie sat in a seat beside Wendy. Would they stay with the baby, or would they go on to another assignment?

She tapped Dark Eyes on the shoulder. "Thank you for showing up so quickly. What's your name? My name's Wendy."

"Gabriel," he said.

"Are you serious?"

Gabriel flushed.

"I'm sorry. I'd be the last one to make fun of your name. But here we are three days before Christmas, a baby shows up, and the rescuer who saves the baby is named Gabriel. It's almost like a Christmas story."

Gabriel shook his head. "My mother named me for an angel who supposedly told Mary she was pregnant. I'm not much of an angel though."

"The angel warned Joseph too."

"Warned Joseph about what? That his girlfriend was going to have a baby? Hah! I'll bet *that* was a shocker." He shook his shoulders.

"Oh, Gabe, give her a break. Wendy, don't mind him. He's the king of the scoffers. You know, the 'bah-humbug' sort. He says he doesn't do Christmas." Jennie pushed Gabriel's arm. "Don't be such a Grinch."

Gabriel jerked his arm away and scowled. "I don't know what the big deal is. It's just another day on the job. Maybe worse. More traffic accidents." His voice caught. "More abuse."

Wendy sat back. "Really? Why would people hurt each other more at Christmas?" In her home, it had always been a festive time. Food, decorations, gifts....

Gifts.

She'd lost her job just after spending nearly every cent she had on herself. How would she buy presents for her family? The rest of the conversation faded as Wendy realized what she'd so selfishly done.

Until Gabriel spoke again. "What kind of Christmas will this baby have, if she survives that long? How about her mother? But then, what kind of mother dumps her baby in the trash on a day as cold as this? If you hadn't come along, Miss Wendy, this little life would have been gone by now. Come to think of it, did you see the person who dumped her?"

Wendy thought back. "I don't think so. I was so self-absorbed at that time I wasn't noticing anything. I'd just been fired, you see."

"Oh. Tough time to lose your job," Jennie said. "What happened? None of my business, I know, so if you'd rather not say, it's okay."

Wendy sighed. "I worked at Belle's Boudoir. I was helping my boss's favorite customer choose some nightwear for her nieces, and she asked me...."

"We're here, gang." Jake chimed in from the front. "Let's get this baby in and to a doctor."

Wendy's gaze turned to the infant. "It seems a shame to wake her when she's just gone to sleep."

"Asleep or unconscious. Let's go, let's go, let's go." Gabriel lifted the baby and Jennie brought the equipment attached to her.

"Come with us, Wendy," Jennie said. She followed Gabriel out the doors.

The earlier feathery flakes had become a thick blustery snowstorm, and Wendy shivered in the short distance between the back of the ambulance and the emergency room entrance. The lab coat covered the essentials, but it certainly wasn't very warm.

She wasn't sure where to go, so she followed the EMTs. They ignored her—the EMTs, the lab technicians, doctors, nurses, clerks, everyone. She might as well have been a wall decoration. If she'd had on her new clothes, they wouldn't have ignored her, she'd bet. She looked down at the green covering. They might have thought she was also a technician.

"You—young lady, you an EMT?" A heavy man with a white coat waved her over.

"I...."

"Take the baby to Pediatrics. Tell them to put her in a NICU."

"Is she going to be okay, then?" Wendy smiled. She lifted the infant to her chest, careful of the wires. She cradled the baby and made little cooing noises like she did with her brother Hugh's baby. "What's a nickyou?"

White Coat took a better look at her. "What are you doing?"

"You said to take her to Pediatrics. What floor is that?"

"On the gurney, not in your arms. Do you work here?"

"No."

White Coat harrumphed, his double chin jiggling. "Neonatal Intensive Care Unit. N-I-C-U." He took the baby from her and put it back on the gurney. He narrowed his eyes at Wendy. "What are you doing here in the lab coat if you don't work here?"

"I can tell you that, Doc." Gabriel said. "She's the one who found the kid. Her clothes were bloody, so we had her change out of them." He smiled a beautiful white-toothed smile at her from a disturbingly close distance. "If it weren't for her, the little one would have been dead by now. And oh, by the way? She might need some stitches. She has a cut on the back of her head."

Wendy looked up at him. She hadn't realized he was so tall. He'd changed out of his uniform too.

White Coat harrumphed again. "Good for you, young lady, good for you. We'll get you sutured in no time at all, and then we need a blood sample." He narrowed his eyes. "Do you feel okay? Do you need to sit down? When did you last eat?"

Her stomach growled. "I'm fine. I haven't eaten yet today."

"You'll need to take her to the lab, Gabe," White Coat said handing him some forms. He pointed to the top sheet of paper. "She needs to fill this one out and take it to Admissions. The other one is for the lab folks. Now, sit up here, young lady, and we'll take care of that cut."

A male nurse snipped at her hair in back. Oh, fine. How would she get a job with a haircut like this? Another technician took off with the baby, and Wendy's heart left with her.

A few minutes later, Gabriel took her arm. "Come on, Miss Wendy. We'll take care of the paperwork and labs, and then I'll show you where the cafeteria is."

"Thanks for the lunch, Gabriel. For hospital food, this Salisbury steak is tasty. How's your hamburger?"

"Best cardboard I ever ate." Gabe smirked. "I saw the name you wrote on those forms. Wednesday Miracle Blessing? Your mom must have really hated being pregnant."

Wendy flushed. "After my brother was born, my mom and dad had six miscarriages—one each year—and they were so glad to have one who lived, I'm lucky they didn't name me Giddy Happy."

A lady in a red and black pantsuit walked up to their table followed by a man with a large camera. "Are you the girl who found the baby in the trash can?"

Wendy sat up straight. "Get that camera out of my face. If you show me on the evening news in this lab coat I'll sue your socks off."

The woman took in Wendy's long unruly and probably bloody hair tied back with a rubber band, the lab coat, and the Jimmy Choo shoes. She grinned. "I'm not wearing socks, but I do understand. How about if we let you clean up first? Do you have anything to wear other than that green thing?"

"Sure...at home. My clothes were bloody. Sorry, but I don't think I'll go change and then come back for an interview."

"We can do this. The camera will focus on me, and I can interview you off camera. Would that work? Or I could talk to your boyfriend? husband?" She tilted her chin at Gabriel.

Wendy's face burned. "No, he's not my boyfriend or husband. This is one of the EMTs who came to help the baby. His name is Gabriel."

"Gabriel? Like the angel? Oh, this is too perfect." Red Suit hooked a finger at the cameraman. "Focus on this guy."

"No, do *not* focus on this guy," Gabriel said, turning his back.

The woman gave him a disgusted look. "Fine. George, focus on me."

"One, two, three, you're on," George said. A red light showed up on the front of the camera.

"Good evening, ladies and gentlemen. I'm Hope Marcel, and I'm interviewing a young woman who rescued an abandoned newborn from a waste receptacle this morning. She's a little shy, so we're not showing her on camera. Miss Blessing, would you tell us exactly what happened this morning when you found the baby?"

"Uh, I, uh...I heard a noise in the trash can. It sort of sounded like a puppy or something. When I looked in the, uh, receptacle, I

saw a green cloth grocery bag. I looked in it and there was a baby."
Thank the good Lord the camera didn't focus on her.

"What did you do then?"

"I didn't have my cell with me, so I took the baby across the street to a store called, um, the Baroquen Basket. I used their phone to call 911."

"You are quite a heroine today, Miss Blessing. How do you feel about that?"

"Uh, I, uh, I don't feel like a heroine." She glanced down at herself. She didn't look like one, either. "Anyone would have done the same thing."

"Do you know if they have found the mother?"

"No, ma'am. I haven't heard."

"Do you know the mother, or did you see her?"

"No, I don't know who she is. I didn't see her, either." Wendy shifted in her seat and gazed at Gabriel.

He had turned back around to face her, and now he smiled. "You're doing great," he mouthed and gave her a thumbs up.

"If you were going to give this infant a name, Miss Blessing, what would you call her?"

Wendy thought for a moment. "I'd name her 'Merry Christmas Blessing.'"

"Blessing. Are you thinking about adopting her, then?"

"I'd love to, but I just got fired today, and I'm not married. A baby needs a mom and a dad. Real ones who won't desert her when she needs them and who can provide for her."

"Who would fire someone three days before Christmas? I mean, besides Scrooge?" Hope asked. "Where did you work?"

"Belle's Boutique."

"Do you want to share on this broadcast why you were fired?"

Wendy stared at her hands, her lacquered nails now chipped and broken. She sighed. "I said something that displeased a customer. Let's just leave it at that, okay?"

"Cut," Red Suit said. She walked to the table and sat down at Wendy's side. "We're off camera now, Wendy. You've had a tough day, haven't you?"

Wendy nodded, still focused on her hands.

"Would you let me make it a little better for you? I'd like to treat you to a new suit of clothes."

Wendy jerked her gaze up to meet Hope's. To her surprise, the newscaster's eyes glimmered with moisture. "Why? You don't even know me."

"You remind me of my little sister. She just miscarried her baby a few days ago. And it *is* Christmas, you know." Hope smiled, one tear rolling down a cheek. She turned to Gabriel. "Are you off? Would you like to come with us?"

Gabriel's eyebrows shot up. "Me? Yeah, I just finished my shift. I guess I could." He grinned at Wendy, his dark eyes mirroring the overhead lights. "Okay by you?"

"Okay by me." Wendy's cheeks warmed under his gaze.

"George, did you send the newscast?" Hope asked.

"Of course."

"You might as well come too, then."

George winked. "I'll come along to make sure she chooses something really expensive. I hope your credit card isn't maxed out, Hope."

She winked back. "It's the station's card. I'm not too worried."

Gabriel reached across the table, palms down on the surface. "Wait a minute, news lady. Does this gift have strings attached?"

Hope held her right hand up. "No strings, I promise."

"Before we go, would it be okay if I checked on Merry?" asked Wendy.

Soft Christmas music played in the background, and expensive-looking icicle lights hung from the ceiling as Wendy gazed in wonder in the full-length mirror at her new outfit. "Do you think the color is okay? I've never worn much purple before."

"That's not purple, dear. That's royal plum." Hope chuckled, gently tugging a brush through Wendy's hair. "And you do look plumb royal."

Gabriel gave a low whistle. "Um-hum-mm! I gotta say, Wendy Blessing, you look good enough to…uh, you look really nice."

George laughed. "I ditto Gabe. I'll bet if you put her on camera now, Hope, she'd almost outshine you." His eyes glowed as he looked at Hope. "Almost…but nothing quite gets there."

Hope's blush showed through her television-thick makeup. She touched his hand with hers and then returned her gaze to Wendy. "If you want to, we can do a new interview. You look fantastic. But it's not necessary. We have a broadcast."

Wendy shook her head. "Thanks, I'd rather not. But I can't begin to tell you how much I appreciate this."

"Where do you live, Wendy? We can give you a lift home so you won't have to catch a bus."

"Actually, we have her address." George said. "I looked it up as soon as we heard her name."

Wendy's mouth dropped. "How did you do that? I only have a cell, no land line, therefore no address listed in the directory. Besides, I've only been here since June, after I graduated from college."

George shook his head. "News gatherers have sources, but I can't tell you what they are."

"And Gabe? Back to the hospital?" Hope asked.

"I could take the bus."

"Nonsense."

He shrugged. "I'd be taking the bus from there, anyway."

"*I*'d like to go back to the hospital," Wendy said. "Once I pick up my cell phone that I left at home, I'd kinda like to hang around the hospital until I know the baby is out of danger."

"I guess that's kind of where I'm at too," Gabe said.

"It's settled. We take Wendy home then both Wendy and Gabe to the hospital. We need to get an update on the kid's condition too." Hope stood and made an exaggerated wave to indicate everyone should follow her.

The snow had stopped and daylight was fading when they paraded out to the vehicle and clambered in. It wasn't far to her brownstone apartment building, but an unpleasant surprise waited there. A dozen or so other news vans parked and double parked in front of the building. Cameras and mikes and tripods sprouted everywhere

"That's what I figured," George said. "Is there another way in?"

"They won't leave me alone until I talk to them, will they?" Wendy said. She pressed her lips together.

Hope shook her head. "Not very likely."

"I guess you will get your interview after all, Hope, because I won't talk to them without talking to you too. Well, let's get it over with. Gabriel, would you mind standing by me? I might not feel quite so much like I'm under attack."

Gabriel sighed. "I guess. I'd rather not talk though."

"Why not?"

"Puerto Rican accent."

Wendy shook her head. "It's scarcely noticeable. And you shouldn't be ashamed of any accent. Most people can only speak one language, and you speak English flawlessly. You should hear how bad my French accent sounds. One of my French friends couldn't understand a word I said." She grimaced. "Now, let's go face the hoard."

As Wendy and Gabriel approached the steps to the apartment, the reporters attacked from all sides. "Wait until I get on the steps, please, and I'll answer questions."

"Follow me." Gabriel stepped in front of her and physically moved the reporters aside who wouldn't move on their own, making a path for her.

When she reached the landing in front of the door, she turned. She pointed at Hope. "Miss Marcel, what is your question?"

Fifteen minutes later, Wendy coughed into her elbow and with her other hand passed Gabriel a key. "No more questions. I'm getting hoarse. We're going inside now. Please leave."

Wendy and Gabe entered her ground floor apartment and peered through the heavy blue floral drapes. The pack of reporters dashed for their vehicles, including George and Hope.

"Thank you, Gabriel. Did I act too nervous?"

"No, I don't think so. Except when they started getting a little personal."

"They had no business asking if the baby was mine or if you were my boyfriend." She hmphed. "I do think I'll change my clothes. My old coat, blue jeans, and a ski cap might be an adequate disguise, don't you think?" She took off her heels and ran for the bedroom.

"Throw in sunglasses and they'll never know it's you. I guess we'll be going on the bus after all since Hope and George left."

When she came back out, Gabriel peeked through the edge of the drapes, and he chuckled. "Hah. Sneaky reporters. They're back."

"Oh, no. All of them?"

"No, just Hope and George. Ready?"

She nodded. He grabbed her hand, and they ran at top speed for the van.

"I like that. I buy you an outfit and you just go jump into your old clothes." Hope propped one hand on a hip and then smiled. "Smart girl. They won't be as likely to recognize you now. Gabe's another story. He still stands out."

"I should dye my hair blond."

"That would work."

Hope turned around from the front seat to face them. "I have some not-so-good news. They found the mother."

"Is she okay?" asked Wendy.

"No. She's dead; from exposure or blood loss or both, they think. I'm sorry."

Wendy's eyes filled. "Oh, no. Poor Merry."

Gabriel slipped an arm around her shoulders. "Do they know who she is?"

"Not yet. No ID on her."

"How is the baby; do you know?" Wendy asked.

"I talked to one of the nurses in Pediatrics. She's doing fine. The doctor might take her out of the NICU tomorrow if she continues to do so well."

Wendy breathed a sigh of relief. "That's good. Do you think they'd let me hold her?"

Gabriel nodded. "For publicity alone, I would think. If you'll let them take a picture, that is. Even hospitals need positive publicity."

"Good." Wendy turned on her cell phone. "Oh, wow, I have…twenty calls and scads of texts. Excuse me while I weed through them."

"Go ahead and make your calls. We have at least five minutes to the hospital. Let's see, twenty calls, five minutes…you could talk to each of them about fifteen seconds." Gabriel chuckled.

"Sh." She punched buttons and listened. "Hi, Mom. You'll never guess what happened today in a billion years…. You did? Oh…. Well, yeah, I did…. Ms. Johnson told me never to say…. Yeah, right, I did it again …. I'll start looking tomorrow. You should see this little baby, Mom. She's so sweet and cuddly…. You heard that clear over in Arizona?" Wendy giggled. "Merry Christmas is just as good a name as Wednesday Miracle, isn't it? … Okay, Mom. So did you think about flying out here to spend Christmas with me? … Oh…. Yeah, I guess. Well, say "hi" to my big brother, okay? I miss him.… Love you too." Wendy pushed the talk button and sat silent, battling tears. She wished so much see could see the snow-covered hills around Flagstaff. And her family. Her dad had passed two years before, but her mom lived there and her brother lived close by in Page. He and his family would be going to Mom's. Everyone but her. She needed to find a new job.

How did news agencies get cell numbers? Fifteen of the calls were from news stations. Three more from people she didn't know. One from her mother and one from her best friend—also in Arizona. She sighed.

Most of the texts were news stations too. One from her brother who'd caught her picture on the news and wanted to know if his "famous sister" was coming home for Christmas. She sighed. This was hard.

"We're here, Wendy." Gabriel murmured.

Tears filled her eyes. "Thanks, guys."

"No, I meant we're here at the hospital. But count me as a friend too," he added softly. "I guess your family won't be coming for Christmas?"

"No."

"Could you go see them?" He held his hand out to help her from the van.

"No, I can't. I have to hunt for a job."

Her phone vibrated, and she glanced at the caller ID. Both eyebrows bounced. "Maybe I should take this. It's Mrs. Johnson, my former boss.

She followed Gabriel, Hope, and George through the hospital doors, still holding the phone to her ear. "Mrs. …um, Ms. Johnson, I'm still the same person, and I still will answer truthfully when asked the same question. I won't lie to keep a customer happy…. No, I don't think so. Thanks, anyway. Good-bye, Mrs. Johnson."

Wendy grinned and shook her head.

"Well?" Gabriel asked.

"I turned down a job offer. Am I sick or what?"

"Your old boss wants you back? Why did you say no?"

"She wants me because her favorite customer now wants me back. I was such a 'hero,' you know. A little fame sure goes a long way. But I don't want to work there. Not when I'm told I have to lie."

"I guess you're not hungry enough yet. Sometimes you have to take what you can get until you can get what you want. It's nice to have high principles, but high principles won't feed you or pay the rent." Gabriel rubbed his left arm and pushed the elevator button.

Wendy stepped onto the elevator, a curious ache in her heart. "So you think it's just fine to lie?"

"What kind of lie did they want you to tell? One that soothes the customer doesn't sound all that bad to me. When the truth is insulting, maybe it's just not necessary to say. You know what I mean."

"Yeah, I know. You mean I can't trust you to tell the truth if a lie is easier or more profitable." She stood as far from him as she could in the elevator.

George and Hope exchanged glances.

"What exactly was it you said that was so bad, anyway?" Gabriel asked.

"Nothing." She lifted her chin and forced the tears back. "Just nothing." She stepped off the elevator and strode down the hall to the large window that exhibited row after row of babies, some sleeping peacefully, some wailing and waving their fists and feet. A few stared intently at soft lights. Wendy pressed her face to the glass, trying to determine which one was hers...or rather, the baby she'd found. Not hers.

"There she is," Gabriel said. He grinned and pointed to a NICU with a name tag saying "Merry Christmas Blessing." "Look! They took your suggestion."

A woman in a hospital gown partially covered by a rose-colored chenille robe walked to Wendy's side. "Are you the lady who found her?" She pointed to the NICU.

Wendy smiled. "Yes. Isn't she beautiful?"

"Are you really going to adopt her?"

"I wish I could, but there's not much chance. There are probably hundreds of people wanting to adopt her." Wendy had to change the subject before she started blubbering. "Is one of these yours?"

The young woman beamed. "Yes. In fact, two of them...those two boys next to your Merry."

A pencil-thin platinum blonde pushed the twins' mother aside and shoved a microphone in front of Wendy's mouth. She jumped.

"Mandy Blanding? Would you please tell us what your plans are now with this baby?"

Wendy backed into George and excused herself. "The name is *Wendy Blessing*, and I have no plans."

"It's been rumored that you filed adoption papers today. Any truth in that?"

Wendy turned to her newscaster friend. "How do I get rid of this one, Hope?"

Platinum Blonde gasped. "Hope Marcel?"

"Yes. And this young lady has had a long and wearying day. How about if you leave her alone?"

"Cut that, Will. And delete it. No way am I showing Hope Marcel on our station." The blonde and Will marched back toward the elevator.

Wendy giggled. "Wow, you're *good*. I wish I had your clout."

Hope snorted. "Seems to me I remember a threat to sue if we videoed you in that scrub gown. You carry a clout or two of your own, sweetie pie. Well, I can see little Merry is doing fine." She heaved a long sigh. "I guess that's our last excuse, George. Back to the studio."

George put out an arm and gave Wendy a hug. "It's been fun, kid. We'll stay tuned."

Wendy hugged him back and then Hope. "Thanks for everything. You were exactly what I needed today. If you ever need a favor from me, all you have to do is call." She paused. "Guess I should give you my number, huh? Got a piece of paper, anyone?"

Gabriel pulled a notebook and a pen from his shirt pocket and handed it to her. "Not that you need it. They have your number," he grinned.

She narrowed her eyes at him and quickly scribbled her number, tore out the sheet, and handed it to Hope with a flourish.

Hope held out a business card to her. "May I ask you a personal question? Would you tell me how old you are?"

Wendy shrugged. "Not a problem. I'm twenty-two. No business cards yet. Maybe someday when I have a real job that fits with my degree."

Hope's right eyebrow lifted. "And that is…?"

"A bachelor's in Early Childhood Education."

"Really!" Hope paused. "I'm glad you gave me your number. I think we'll be back in touch. Our station has talk shows on both radio and TV. Would you be game for some more interviews? You might find yourself gainfully employed in no time at all."

Wendy's eyes widened. "No way!"

"Way," said Hope. "I'll call you tomorrow."

Wendy threw her arms around Hope. "Thank you, thank you, thank you."

Hope laughed and patted Wendy's back. "I haven't done anything yet. Maybe you should wait until any of this is fruitful before you get so exuberant."

"If none of it works, I still appreciate all you have done. I take back every mean word I ever said about the paparazzi. Or at least two of them."

"Well, our station's motto is 'News with a heart.' Not that it always works, but we try."

Hope and George strode to the elevators, each tossing a wave behind them.

Suddenly awkward, Wendy folded her arms and turned back to the window to watch the babies. She took in the muted colors on the walls and soft lighting, along with the cute sign in the back of the room with infant airplanes in bassinets. It read, "Heir Port."

Gabriel cleared his throat. "I'm sorry about what I said earlier. I didn't mean it was okay to lie, just that sometimes people use honesty as an excuse to hurt other people's feelings. And I haven't known you very long, but I don't think you're that kind of person."

"I'm sorry I jumped on your case. I shouldn't have made such a huge leap to a wrong conclusion. Forgive me too?" She turned to him with a one-sided smile.

"Done. Now, let's ask if we can get a little closer to Merry. They might not let us hold her, but they should let us touch her with gloves."

"I would so love to hold her. Ever since I pulled her from that trash basket, it's felt like a strong cord bound my heart to her."

They approached the desk, and Gabriel tapped a button on the tummy of a three-inch doughboy-shaped figurine on the counter. It giggled instead of chimed, but it worked.

A nurse smiled as she approached. "May I help you?" she asked, her gaze on Gabriel.

Wendy noted the pretty redhead had glanced down at his ring hand and wondered at the twist she felt to her stomach.

"Hi. I'm Gabe, the EMT who brought in the baby over there. The one with the 'Merry Christmas Blessing' name tag. And this is the lady who pulled her out of the trash," he said, pulling Wendy up next to him with a hand on her elbow. "We wondered if we could hold her for a minute or two."

Redhead's gaze brushed Wendy, and she smiled again at Gabriel. "Sure. Follow me."

Oh, goodness. Was that what they meant by sashaying? Wendy wondered if that sort of gait could throw a person's hips out of joint.

"It's almost time for her feeding. If you'll go wash in the restroom and come back to sit here in the fathers' lounge I'll bring her to you."

Gabriel nodded. He and Wendy hurried into the hands-free restrooms and back out again. He sat on a couch, patting the cushion next to him. Wendy sat, but not close enough to touch.

Redhead returned from the NICU and placed the bassinette in front of Gabriel, a white paper gown over her arm. She handed him the covering, ignoring Wendy.

He narrowed his eyes. "Would you get another one, please?" He handed the one he'd received to Wendy.

Redhead flushed, frowned briefly, and showed her teeth. "You're an EMT. I'm not sure she should be allowed."

"She washed. She has a gown. She's handled Merry before. What's the problem?" Gabriel stood. "Where's the nurse in charge?"

She turned redder than her hair. "She's on her break. Never mind. I'll get another gown. She marched into the nurse's area and brought another covering. "Here," she said, shoving the scrubs and a bottle at Gabriel. "I'll be back to get the baby in about a half hour."

Gabriel donned the gown and picked up the baby. He cradled her for a moment, smiling and giving Merry a finger to grasp. She nuzzled at his shirt, and he chuckled. "Just a minute, there, sweet babe." He kissed her head and handed her to Wendy with the bottle.

"Oh, she is so soft...no bones!" Wendy said, snuggling Merry. She put the nipple of the bottle into the baby's mouth, giggling when Merry's tongue pushed it first one way and then the other before she seemed to get the knack of it. "There you go. See, it wasn't so hard. Isn't that nummy?" She began softly humming *Jesus Loves Me* to her and then switched to singing, "...this I know, for the Bible tells me so...."

She glanced up to catch Gabriel staring at her with wide eyes.

"Is my singing that bad?"

"No. No, not at all. I suddenly remembered my mama singing that song to me. My papa was Puerto Rican, and Mama was half

Puerto Rican and half…well, probably Irish and English and who knows what else. But she sang that song to me in English."

"You said 'was.' Are they…are they passed away?"

"Last year. In an accident. Papa had a couple of drinks at a Christmas party. He wasn't even legally intoxicated, but it was enough that he missed a stop sign. The car that T-boned them, well, that driver was killed too." Tears ran down his face. "In fact, one year ago today. It was a lousy Christmas." He dropped to the couch beside her, placed his elbows on his knees, and covered his face with his hands.

Wendy maneuvered her hold on the baby to where she could hold Merry and the bottle with one hand. With the other hand she began to rub his back in slow circles. "I'm so sorry, Gabriel," she whispered.

The bottle slipped out of the sleeping infant's mouth, but she didn't seem to mind. Her mouth pursed and made sucking movements. Wendy lifted the baby to her shoulder and began patting.

"I'm sorry," Gabriel muttered, scrubbing his face with his sleeve. "I'm more of a baby than Merry is."

"Because you cried for your parents? All that says is that you loved them. Guys cry all the time. I know. My big he-man brother cried when our dad died, and he cried when each of their babies were born. Even Jesus wept."

"You're kidding me."

"He did. His friend, Lazarus, had died. His friend's sisters came to Jesus crying because their brother was gone and saying, 'If you had been here, our brother wouldn't have died.' He saw their tears, and he cried with them."

"Fat lot of good that did. Their brother was still dead." Gabriel sank back on the couch.

"Not for long. Jesus went to his friend's tomb and called for him to come out. He did."

"And you believe that."

"Yes, I do. The whole town of Bethany witnessed it," she said. The baby made a liquid bubbling sound. "Oops. Did Redhead bring a burp rag?"

"No. Guess it's good we have these gowns on." He used part of his sleeve to wipe the baby's mouth. "It's cute how she pouts her lips when you wipe them. And if you tell any of the guys I said that, I'll deny it."

"Babies are the best of God's miracles. A single-celled seed gets planted in a womb and grows arms and legs and fingers and toes. I love it. And I hope whoever adopts this miracle will allow me to watch her grow into a beautiful young lady. I'd give my right arm to be the one who raises her, but I can't let myself hope for that."

"There are other single adopting moms out there. Why not you?"

"You have a job. You could adopt her. Single guys do that too." Wendy turned her head to look at him and found his face very close to hers. "You'd be a good dad," she whispered.

He leaned a little closer, but pulled away when a door opened and Redhead popped into the room.

"I'll take the baby now."

Another woman walked through the same door, followed by a police officer. "Wait. I want to see the baby and ask some questions," she said, showing the nurse her identification badge. "My name is Deedi Lane, and I'm from Child Protective Services.

"I have a few questions, myself. Leave the baby here." The blocky, weary looking policeman walked to a chair across from Wendy and Gabriel. "I'm Lieutenant Gifford," he said, extending his hand to Gabriel and then to her before he sank into the pink and blue floral upholstery.

Ms. Lane walked to Wendy's side, peering down at the sleeping baby. "She looks comfy. I've always envied how a baby can drop off to sleep so easily." She stretched out her fingers and stroked the baby's downy dark hair. "What a sweet babe." She switched her gaze to Wendy. "I guess you must be the one who named her. I didn't see the newscast, but I heard about it."

"I suppose so," Wendy said. "The reporter asked me what I would name her, and that's what fell out of my mouth."

"I should have been here earlier, but it's been one of those days. I'm Deedi, and I'll be little Merry's case worker. The lieutenant and I need to get a few details from you. Where were you when you found her?"

"I was waiting for a bus at Beale and Second Street. I heard a noise coming from the trash. At first I thought it might have been a kitten or a puppy in this grocery bag there, but I opened the bag and it was a baby."

"What did you do then?"

"I had left my cell at home, so I went across the street to a store called the Baroquen Basket and used their phone to call 911."

"What was her condition when you found her?"

"She was bloody and sorta cool to the touch, and her cry was pretty quiet, like she was weak. She didn't have a blanket around her or anything, just the grocery bag, and it was kinda chilly out. That was at about ten o'clock this morning. I snuggled her and the bag up inside my coat while we waited for the ambulance."

"Sir, I understand you were the lead EMT in the ambulance?"

"Yes. I'm Gabe...Gabriel Cruz."

"What did you observe?"

"The placenta and cord were still attached to the baby and the cord was uncut. So I put a couple of clamps on the cord and clipped and tied it. She seemed a little small, although I didn't weigh her. I wrapped her in heated blankets, placed a couple of warm water bottles next to her, and attached the heart and blood oxygen readers." He stroked Merry's cheek. "She liked being warm. She stopped shaking and began looking around."

"Young woman, I understand you expressed a desire to adopt the baby."

Tears stung Wendy's eyes. "I only said that I wished I could. Yes, I would like to. I've really fallen in love with her. But I realize it's impossible."

Deedi's eyebrows rose, and she paused. "Excuse me. I need to make a call. Lieutenant Gifford wants some of your time, anyway." She pulled her phone from her dark blue jacket and walked out of hearing range.

He cleared his throat. "Thanks, Ms. Lane. Now, Wendy, I hear you were pretty much covered in blood."

"No, not really, although I had some on my hands and on the front of my blouse and skirt. Oh—and in my hair." Wendy touched the bandage.

Lieutenant Gifford looked up from his note pad. "Not what you're wearing now."

"No, they're at home. The lady in the ambulance, Jennie, gave me a green wrapper and the other EMT, Jake, told me I should wash the baby's blood off myself. Then a very nice newscaster, Hope Marcel, bought me a new skirt and blouse. I changed out of those clothes, though, to avoid attracting reporters."

"I'll need the bloody clothes. You haven't washed them yet, have you?" He scribbled furiously on his notepad.

"No. I mean no, I haven't washed them. May I have them back after you've seen them?"

"Not for a while, but eventually. Probably, anyway. The baby couldn't have been in that trash can very long. Did you see the mother?"

"No, sir. I'd just gotten fired, and I wasn't paying any attention to my surroundings."

He glanced up. "Why were you fired?"

"I said something that offended a customer."

"What?"

"I had wished the customer a Merry Christmas when she paid the bill. She asked me if I really believed 'that Jesus stuff.' I said yes. She started spouting off all the old arguments that it was just a myth or maybe His mother Mary was trying to cover for "a little fun on the side,' as she called it. I told her that was a terrible thing to say about the mother of Jesus, the Baby who came to save the world. She laughed and said I was naïve. I told her she was wrong and that I hoped before she died she would find Him. She got angry and told my boss."

Lieutenant Gifford grinned. "You've got guts, I'll say that much. I wish more people would speak up for Him."

Wendy smiled. "You're a believer?"

"Yes, but I'm not allowed to bring up religion, either. Did you see anything else in the trash besides the baby?"

"No. Some of the papers around the bag had blood on them, though. I remember that. Otherwise, it was just the usual stuff you'd find there. Candy wrappers, pop cans, envelopes, food wrappers, newspapers. You know, that kind of thing."

"The store manager, Mr. Bledsoe, said he suspected you were the mother and just didn't want to say so."

Wendy shook her head. "If I had been her mother, I would never have thrown her away. Anyway, I guess they found her mother."

"Yes, probably, although we won't know for sure until DNA tests are back. I hope she was the mother, because if she wasn't we'll be needing to look for a lost baby and another mother. This woman was close by, and we suspect she's the one."

He turned to Gabriel. "You were the EMT, right?"

"One of them."

"How much blood was on Wendy?"

"On the front, about the amount you might expect from, say, a significant nosebleed. Her hair had...has still...quite a bit of blood in it from a cut, and it dripped off her hair and onto the back of her coat."

The lieutenant turned back to Wendy. "How did you cut your head?"

"I fell against the edge of a squarish post, the one with the signal lights. I guess I twisted to try to keep the baby from hitting it or landing on the concrete."

He nodded, wrote something more, and turned back to Gabriel.

"How long did it take you to get to the store after the call?"

"I would say probably only two or three minutes. We had just left what turned out to be a prank call two blocks away."

Gifford snorted. "We get those too. Like we didn't have anything more important to do than to amuse pranksters. That's all I have to ask right now. I need your phone numbers and addresses in case we need more."

Gabriel wrote his on the back of a business card, and Wendy wrote hers on the back of an envelope.

Deedi walked back to them, a smile on her face. "Wendy, would you mind filling out some more paperwork?"

"No, I guess not. What are they for?"

"Well, I just talked to my supervisor. If you would consent to a background check and fill out the paperwork, we could call you a nonrelated extended family member. If we push it through, maybe Merry could at least spend Christmas with you. We do have to attempt to find the real parents and other family members, you realize, and I can't promise anything. But Merry needs to spend a day or two here for observation, and by the time they release her the paperwork should be okayed."

Wendy's mouth dropped and tears rolled down her cheeks. "That would be so...so perfect. Did you hear that, Gabriel?"

He wrapped his arms around her and the baby. "I think this might classify as a Christmas miracle." He kissed Merry's silky head and leaned in to whisper in Wendy's ear. "May I spend Christmas with you too?"

Protecting Zoe

Mishael Austin Witty

To Fran:
Your friendship has been more of an
inspiration to me than you will ever know.
This story would not have been written if not for you.

Noelle stood behind the coffee shop counter, counting the multicolored Christmas lights for what seemed like the millionth time. She knew how many there were—77—but the obsessive act of counting was a welcome distraction from the near-constant nausea that plagued her. Coffee was one of the scents that made it worse, and the coffee was extra-strong and extra-odorous when Joe was manning the machines, as he often was when Noelle was working. Since they were both still in high school, they usually had the same work schedule.

Very soon, though, Noelle thought, the deed would be done, and she wouldn't feel this nausea anymore. She fought back the flood of tears. The after-dinner rush would start any minute, and she couldn't very well ring up orders if she was blubbering like a baby.

Baby... The word brought fresh tears to the surface, and her pregnant hormones wouldn't allow her to block them this time. She sobbed and clutched the edge of the cabinet in both hands, gazing down in alarm as her knuckles turned white. She was so caught up in her sadness that she didn't hear Abby come up behind her.

"Noelle?"

The sudden hand on her shoulder startled her from her crying. She immediately straightened and rearranged the napkin holders and creamer and sweetener containers on the counter in front of her. She swiped one crisp white sleeve over her face before she turned to meet her boss's gaze, grimacing as she noticed the smudges of foundation and mascara creating scary-looking Rorschach patterns on the bright white. Her mother wouldn't like that. How would she be able to get those out?

Abby's eyes were wide with concern, and Noelle hated that. She didn't want her to worry. "Hi, Abby. I'm sorry for crying. I've just had a rough day."

The older woman frowned. "You don't have to apologize for crying. Everybody does it. I just wondered what was wrong. Is there anything I can do to help?"

Oh, if only... Noelle shook her head and forced a smile. "No, I'm fine, really. Please don't worry."

Abby removed her hand from Noelle's shoulder and stepped back slightly. "Okay, if you're sure." Her words were long and drawn out.

Noelle nodded. "I'm sure. Thanks." *Stupid hormones!*

Abby shifted her weight from her right foot to her left. "I was wondering...I know tomorrow is Christmas Eve, and you probably have plans with your family, but I really need someone to cover the early shift tomorrow morning. Donna just called and said she couldn't make it. Do you think you could?"

Noelle sighed in relief. "Yes, of course I can make it. I'll be here at 6:30 sharp." *The more time I can spend away from my family, the better.*

Abby smiled. "Great! I'll see you then."

As their boss walked away, a fresh wave of sadness hit Noelle. She tried to stifle the gasps and sobs, but she couldn't. Joe noticed, and he moved closer to her, nudging her arm with his. "That time of month?" he asked.

Noelle frowned and pushed him away. "Go back to your coffee, jerk."

He threw his hands up in mock surrender. "Okay, okay. Sorry I asked."

She felt instantly bad about brushing him off like that. Joe was an okay guy. It wasn't his fault that she'd gotten knocked up, although he had been instrumental in introducing her to the guy who did. Well, actually, he was just an acquaintance of the guy who had come into the coffee shop one warm early summer evening and swept Noelle off her feet—almost literally. They'd spent an amazing three months together, and then, on Labor Day—just before he went off to college—she'd given him the one thing she'd promised to give only to her husband. He'd said he loved her and that he wanted to marry her, but the feeling behind those words had only lasted until Noelle's first missed period, if they'd ever existed at all. Now she was pregnant, alone, and getting ready to do the worst possible thing she could imagine.

Another sob escaped her lips at the thought, and she noticed, out of the corner of her eye, that Joe turned his head to look at her, but this time he didn't say anything. Noelle covered her mouth with her right hand and grabbed a napkin from the holder in front of her, dabbing at the moisture on her cheeks and under her eyes. The first-rush customers were beginning to come in.

She pasted another false smile on her face as she recognized the person coming toward her. One of the senior choir members from her church. "Hello, and welcome to the Java Joint. How can I help you this evening?"

The old man smiled at her warmly. "Hi, Noelle. How are you?"

She shrugged and looked down at her hands, which were clasped behind the counter. "Fine."

"I'm not much for coffee, but everyone's spoken so highly of this place, I just had to come in and check it out for myself. You all wouldn't happen to serve anything besides coffee, would you? Maybe some hot chocolate?"

Noelle nodded. "Yes, of course."

"Great! I'll have one—give me the largest you've got."

"Sure. That'll be $2.75, please."

He grinned and scratched his gray beard. "Whoo! I can remember when you could buy a cup of coffee, or, in this case, hot chocolate, for just a nickel. Inflation's a crazy thing, isn't it?"

She smiled her most patronizing smile, wondering when this guy would finish jabbering. This *was* the twenty-first century, after all. *Of course* things cost more now than they did back sixty or seventy years ago. Still, she didn't want to be rude. She knew this man—what was his name? Mr. Royce?—was pretty chummy with her father, and she didn't want the news getting back to him that his daughter offered less-than-satisfactory service to her customers. Not that *that* was her biggest worry right now, but she didn't want to add to the evidence that she was, in fact, the worst daughter, and possibly the worst human, who had ever lived.

But no, Noelle thought, *I'm a really good human; I'm just a very bad Christian.*

The tears threatened to burst forth again, but she kept them in check. She couldn't very well break down in front of Mr. maybe-Royce. She pivoted ninety degrees to accept the hot, creamy drink from Joe's hand. His fingers brushed hers as he passed it to her, and she jumped, dislodging the cup's lid and spilling the hot chocolate all down her front. She gasped and fell to her knees, choking back sobs.

"Noelle? Are you okay?" Joe put a hand on her upper back to try to help her up.

She shook him off and staggered back a few paces, hand over her mouth, her body shaking all over. She couldn't look her father's friend in the face; she couldn't even look at Joe. She felt like she was going to die of embarrassment and anguish, right there on the spot.

"Abby!" Joe ran to the door and called into the back room. "Get out here, now! Something's wrong with Noelle."

She was vaguely aware of the sound of running footsteps and the touch of a gentle hand on her arm, pulling her up and leading her to the manager's office. Suddenly, all Noelle wanted to do was close her eyes and go to sleep. She sat in the chair across from Abby's desk, leaned back, and put a protective hand over her belly.

Abby stared at the girl sitting across from her. She noticed, for the first time that evening, how pale Noelle looked. Beads of perspiration glinted off her forehead in the fluorescent office lighting.

"Noelle?" she started, and the girl jumped at the sound of her voice. The hand that had been resting on her abdomen shot up into the air and landed on her right knee.

"What?" Noelle blinked. "I'm so sorry. I don't know what happened to me out there."

"Are you ill? Do I need to call your dad to come get you?"

"No!"

The vehemence of the protest alerted Abby to the fact that something wasn't quite right here. "What's the matter, Noelle? I know something's wrong, so don't try to hide it. Just tell me, and I'll try to help you out as much as I can."

The seventeen-year-old girl blinked at her, but she didn't say a word for several minutes. The silence was deafening, and it made Abby inexplicably uncomfortable. Finally, instead of speaking, Noelle started to cry again.

Abby waited until the most forceful of the tears were out, then she said, "If you're sick…We've got some Tylenol, if you think that would help, but I'm afraid that's it. Our medical supplies are rather limited. Maybe you should go on home. Or I could drive you to the after-hours clinic."

Noelle shook her head, and Abby was relieved to finally be getting some sort of response. "No…I'm…I'm not sick. I'm pregnant."

The words were spoken so quietly—almost in a whisper—that Abby wasn't sure she'd heard them at first. "I'm sorry, you're what?"

"I'm *pregnant*!" The whisper was forceful and harsh, almost a hiss, and the words and the look on the girl's face when she said them frightened Abby for just a moment.

"Do…do your parents know?"

Noelle nodded. Abby waited for her to say more, because it looked like she was going to. There was something behind the girl's eyes—something more than just grief and embarrassment over being an unwed pregnant daughter of a music minister at the state's biggest Southern Baptist church.

"Well, if they know…" Abby started, unsure of where she was going with her own thought.

The girl shot up out of her chair then and banged her palms on the surface of Abby's desk. Abby instinctively rolled her swivel chair back toward the wall. "They know! Oh, they know, and they're going to take me to an abortion clinic the day after Christmas!"

Abortion. The word hung in the air, a giant vacuum that sucked all the air out of the room.

Abby shook her head. "But your father…"

"My *father* doesn't want the whole city to know that his daughter got knocked up at seventeen when she wasn't even married. He and mom have to keep up their holier-than-thou appearance for the community, you know."

Her tone was bitter, and her eyes were cold. The words broke Abby's heart, but so did the sight of this beautiful teenage girl faced with an impossible situation. "Do *you* want…to go through with the abortion?"

Noelle sobbed and shook her head. "No. I think abortion is wrong—it's murder. How can anybody want to do that to their unborn child?"

Abby shook her head. She didn't know the answer to that. She'd wanted, and had been unable to have, a child for so long, the desire for a baby had eaten a hole through her soul. It was all she could think about, even now, and she and her husband, Gil, had stopped trying over a year ago. It was hopeless, all the doctors said, and she'd begun to believe it. She was, after all, pushing forty.

All they could do now was adopt if they wanted a child. *Adopt.* So far, they hadn't been able to find an adoptable baby, for one reason or another. Usually, the babies were already spoken for. There were plenty of older kids who needed homes, and Abby's heart ached for them every time she walked into a foster home or an orphanage to talk to someone about possibly adopting an infant, but she was set on a baby, and she knew God wanted to give her the desires of her heart. Now here, it seemed, was the answer to all Abby's prayers, except Noelle's baby was going to be aborted in just a few days.

"But if you don't want to abort the baby, you don't have to."

Noelle stared blankly up at her. "Of course I do. What choice do I have? My parents…"

Abby fumbled in her desk drawer for the application paperwork Noelle had filled out a few months ago when she applied for the job. She noted the birth date, December 25—Christmas Day. "Your parents have no say in what happens to your body after you turn eighteen, and that's just a couple days away."

For the first time that day, Abby saw a spark of hope light up the teenager's face. "They don't?"

She shook her head, fighting the sense of frustration she felt at the girl's slow understanding of her own situation. *But she's only a child herself. How could she know what to do in a situation like this, really? And her parents don't seem to be guiding her in the right way.*

Besides that, Abby realized with a shock, she was letting her own selfish desire for a child get in the way of this opportunity to truly minister to the girl sitting in front of her. Still, she couldn't stop herself from asking, "What if...I adopted your baby?"

Noelle blinked. "You? Why would you adopt my baby?"

"Because I've always wanted a baby, and my husband and I are unable to have one of our own. Adoption is the only option for us now. You can't possibly take care of a baby on your own. You haven't even finished high school yet. I've got a decent income from running this shop, and my husband is a high-powered lawyer on his way to becoming VP of his law firm. We can give your baby everything he or she needs—and more—probably the biggest thing being lots of love." Abby saw the pain written all over the teenager's face, and she felt instantly sorry that her words had been the cause of it.

The girl put a protective hand on her middle again and looked down at her fingers as they traced a nervous pattern over her slightly bulging belly. Abby knew she was weighing the options in her head—at least, that was what she knew she would be doing if faced with the same choice.

Finally, Noelle spoke. "You...you would truly love my baby?"

Abby smiled and nodded. "Yes, just as if it was my own. It...I don't like calling a baby that. Do you know yet if it's a boy or a girl?"

Noelle shook her head.

"Have you even been to a doctor for a prenatal checkup?"

Again, the girl shook her head.

Abby felt the sudden jab of panic pierce her heart, but she stuffed it down. This wasn't even her baby. Noelle hadn't agreed to the plan, and the papers weren't even written up and signed ...yet. Besides, she hadn't even talked to her husband about this. This was something he definitely needed to know about. "Then we need to get you in to see someone as quickly as possible. My friend runs a pregnancy resource center. I'll give her a call."

The girl stared blankly up at her. Her jaw muscles looked tight.

"Are you okay with this?" she asked. "I mean, will you agree to let me and my husband raise your baby? I know this is sudden..." In fact, Abby had a hard time believing that she'd come up with the idea as quickly as she had, but it felt so right. It was just the right situation at just the right time. It had to be a blessing from God—an answer to her heart's long-whispered prayer.

Noelle nodded slowly. "Yes." Her voice wavered, and Abby couldn't ignore the clouded look in the girl's sad eyes. "Yes, I guess this is better than letting my baby die."

Abby smiled reassuringly. "It is, and I'm sure your parents will see that too, when we talk to them."

Fear showed in the teenager's features. "You'll go with me."

"Of course. I'm fully invested in this now. I'll be with you every step of the way. I just need to go home for a little while and talk to my husband about our plan first. Are you okay to go back out there and help Joe at the counter? I'm sure he's feeling overwhelmed right about now--having to make the coffee and take care of customers at the same time."

Noelle looked down and nodded. Then she stood up and walked toward the door. Before she left, she turned back to look at Abby, uncertainty marring her lovely young features. "You're sure about this? This is the right thing."

Abby smiled and nodded. "This is a God thing, Noelle. He's going to make it right."

"So what's this urgent need to see me?" Abby's husband, Gil, asked with a jovial grin as he walked through the front door into their living room, although she could see the worry written all over his square-jawed Matt Damonesque face.

Abby wanted to reassure him that everything was fine, but she wasn't sure about that herself. She wasn't exactly sure how he would take the news of her plan. As calmly and normally as she could, she got up off the couch and walked over to her husband, praying that God would give her the right words to say.

She lightly kissed his cheek and let him draw her in for a more passionate kiss on the lips, but she pulled away quickly.

Gil's eyebrows rose. His jaw wasn't so rigid anymore. "So, it's not the urgent need I was hoping for?"

Abby laughed and shook her head. "No, it's not that."

"Well, you're laughing, so it can't be too bad."

She shook her head again. "I think it's going to be very, very good."

"Oh, how so?"

She took a deep breath and took Gil's hand, leading him back to the couch she'd vacated moments before.

"I...I'm not really sure how to tell you this."

Gil smiled and rubbed a hand along the back of Abby's neck. "You can tell me anything, you know that. What's going on, honey? Are you...? You can't be...?"

"Pregnant?" Abby shook her head. "No, but I know someone who is—a girl who works in my shop. You remember Noelle?"

He tilted his head to the left slightly and nodded. "Yes, I think so. She's the one who started working for you at the beginning of the summer, right?"

"Yes, that's her. She's pregnant, Gil." She stifled a sob. "And her parents want her to have an abortion, the day after Christmas."

He sat back on the couch, his hand dropping from Abby's neck to rest in his lap. "Well, that's not good, but what does it have to do with us?"

Abby seized the moment, delightedly bouncing on the seat next to him, causing the worn-out couch springs to squeak in protest. "I've talked to her about it, and she's agreed to give us her baby."

"Give us her... What? Abby, what are you talking about?"

"I'm talking about adoption, Gil. We adopt Noelle's baby so that she doesn't have to go through with the abortion."

"What do her parents have to say about all this?"

Abby shrugged. "I don't know. She hasn't told them yet. We just came up with the idea today—well, actually, I came up with the idea. But it doesn't matter, anyway, because she'll be eighteen the day after tomorrow. She can do whatever she wants, and her parents won't be able to say anything about it."

"Abby, this is crazy! You can't just take someone's baby."

"I'm not taking it. Noelle's offering to give it to me." She couldn't ignore the frown on her husband's face. His brown eyes looked sad. "What's wrong? We've talked about adoption before."

"Yeah, a year ago, but I thought we were all done with that."

His tone hurt Abby more than his words did. She felt long-buried tears coming to the surface, but she swallowed them down, wholly devoted to her mission. "Don't you want a baby, Gil?"

He closed his eyes and sighed, his hands clasping and unclasping nervously in his lap. "Of course I want a baby, honey, but this…"

She frowned and blinked. "This what?"

"This…whole situation, Ab. It's out of the norm for anyone; you've got to admit that."

She brightened. "I know. But, don't you see, that's what makes it so perfect? It's so weird and crazy and out of our ordinary, everyday experience that it *has* to be a God thing!"

"A God thing?" His next sigh was longer, sadder. "I thought God didn't want us to have any children."

Abby frowned again and leaned closer to him. "What are you talking about?"

"Well, you know…We haven't been able to have a baby on our own, and none of our adoption plans have worked out so far. I just thought that, maybe that was a sign that God didn't want us to be parents. Maybe we're not good enough."

She smiled gently at him. "Gil, I don't think that's it at all. No one's really 'good enough' when it comes to having children, and some parents are just downright horrible at it. Do you know how many abusive parents there are in the world? They didn't have to be 'good enough' for God to bless them with children, although it's a shame they don't realize what a blessing and what a precious responsibility being a parent is. No, I think God hasn't allowed us to have children of our own because He was preparing us for just this situation. He knew we'd be less likely to offer to take care of Noelle's baby if we had one of our own to care for. We needed to be childless for so long so that we could be ready to be parents when the time was right."

Gil was silent for a long moment, and Abby knew from the look on his face as he stared at the turned-off Christmas lights arranged along the fireplace mantle that he was considering her words. He closed his eyes for a second, and when he opened them again, he smiled. "All right, Ab. I'll agree with this crazy plan. What else can I do? A life might be lost."

She threw her arms around his neck and kissed him, long and hard. "Thank you so much, Gil. This will all work out for the best, you'll see. I love you."

"I love you too, Abby," he said as he pulled her in closer.

She pushed him away gently. "Uh-uh. No time for that now. I've got to go call Noelle and tell her the news."

The after-dinner rush had just ended a few minutes before, so Noelle took the time off to rest her tired, swelling legs and feet in the break room. At a quarter past eight, according to the ancient analog wall clock she was staring at to pass the time and clear her mind of all thoughts, she heard a soft knock on the doorframe behind her. She jumped and whirled around to find Joe staring at her, a confused look on his face.

"What do you want?" she mumbled, instantly sorry she didn't soften her tone before speaking.

Joe backed off slightly before stepping boldly into the room. "Abby's on the phone out there at the counter. She wants to talk to you. I told her you were in here, but that I'd come and get you."

Noelle frowned and stood, pushing the folding metal chair back under the table. "Why did you tell her I was back here? Now she's going to think I'm sleeping on the job or something."

He took a step toward her. "Hey, everybody's entitled to a break now and then."

She ignored him and brushed past him to the phone at the counter, praying he didn't follow her. She didn't want anyone to overhear this conversation. Fortunately, the only people left in the seating area of the café were so wrapped up in their conversations they didn't even notice her, and Joe didn't follow.

She brushed back a stray strand of dark brown hair and picked up the cordless receiver. "Hello?"

"Noelle? Hey, I just wanted to let you know that I talked to my husband, and he's agreed that adopting your baby is the best thing for us all. Isn't that wonderful?"

Her heart dropped down into her stomach at Abby's words, but she cleared her throat and said, "Yeah, Abby, that's great. I'm so happy." *I just hope that one day I'll truly be able to say those words and mean them.*

"Listen, I've called Donna and told her to come over to the coffee shop and finish the rest of your shift. She should be there any minute. Gil and I will be over in a little while to come and get you. We need to go talk to your parents."

Noelle's throat tightened, and her stomach churned. That was the last thing she wanted to do right now. *But it's not really the last thing, is it? The last thing I want to do is kill my baby.* She took a deep breath and swallowed. "Okay, I'll see you then."

It felt strange, standing out on the front porch of her own house preparing to ring the doorbell, but Noelle didn't have much of a choice at the moment. She couldn't very well walk in with Abby and Gil right behind her. She had to give her parents a little warning. She shuffled her feet and stared at the tiny lighted disc, glowing bright and partially shaded pink by the bright red Christmas lights overhead. Abby placed a comforting hand on her shoulder. Noelle took one last deep breath and pressed the doorbell.

She heard it ringing inside the house, so she knew her parents heard it too, but she also knew they would be wondering who would ring the doorbell at this hour, even though it wasn't unfashionably late. Seconds later, she heard their urgent, hushed voices as they questioned each other as to who could be visiting at 8:30 on a Monday evening.

The voices stopped abruptly, and the door swung open to reveal Noelle's mother, salt-and-pepper hair pulled back in a huge gold claw clip, red terrycloth robe with Christmas trees knitted into the collar, and tied tightly around her waist. Her look of surprise at seeing Noelle on the other side of the door was quickly replaced with confusion and annoyance when she noticed that her daughter was not alone.

"Noelle, who are these people? And what are they doing here?" her mother questioned imperiously, standing up a little straighter and trying to fill the doorway with her not-quite-adequate girth.

"Mom, you remember my boss, Abby?" Noelle threw her hand back over her shoulder, thumb out to indicate the older woman standing behind her.

Her mother nodded, but her lowered eyebrows betrayed her uncertainty. "Yes, of course, I do. How are you, Mrs...?"

Abby quickly leaned forward and waved a hand in Noelle's mom's face. "Please, just call me Abby. I'm sorry to disturb you like this, Mrs. Matthews, but Noelle and I just didn't think this could wait...and neither did my husband." She nodded in Gil's direction, which was just to the left and slightly to the rear of where she stood.

"All right, *Abby*," Mrs. Matthews agreed, although her facial expression showed that she didn't think it was all right at all. She took a couple steps back into the foyer. "Won't you all come in?"

"We'd love to," Abby said cheerily, pushing Noelle forward and pulling Gil behind her.

Noelle was grateful for Abby's enthusiasm and strength. She needed it right now, more than anything. Her mother hadn't neglected to give Noelle her usual withering glance. She cringed at the argument that would soon be coming, and she wondered how it all would end. She prayed that her parents would be reasonable, but she knew the cost for going up against their desire to keep up appearances. *Why did I ever sleep with that guy in the first place?* she asked herself, but she knew she didn't have time to answer her own question. Abby was already stating her case to Noelle's parents, who sat side by side on the living room's comfortable chic loveseat.

"...I couldn't help noticing how sad Noelle looked today—in fact, she looked downright sick—so I asked her what was wrong."

Mrs. Matthews turned immediately angry eyes toward her daughter. "So you *told* her?"

Noelle shrugged and looked down at her feet. "Yes, I...I didn't have much choice."

"No, you had a choice. You just couldn't wait to tell someone how terrible your parents are to you."

"Now, Gloria..." Mr. Matthews started, but he was quickly shot down by his wife's angry glare. Noelle didn't think she'd ever seen her mother look quite so upset.

"What, Sam? You know as well as I do how gossip spreads in this town. If the coffee shop owner knows now, there's no telling how many people will know by the end of the week."

Noelle glanced over at Abby then, and she saw the flames of red light up her boss's cheeks. "Now wait a minute," Abby interrupted. "I am no gossip! We don't want to make this situation any worse than it already is. In fact, my husband and I came over tonight to offer a suggestion that would improve things for all of us."

Her mother's left eyebrow quirked up. "Improve the situation? How?"

"My husband and I want to adopt your daughter's baby."

"Adopt? But that…that's not part of our plan."

Noelle sat up a little straighter in the recliner adjacent to the loveseat where her parents sat. "Mom, please…"

Her mother cast icy eyes on her. "You be quiet! This does not concern you."

Abby sprang from her chair and stamped a foot, surprising everyone in the room. "Of *course* this concerns her! This is her body—it's her baby. Two days from now, she'll be eighteen, and you can't force her to go through with the abortion if she doesn't want to. Please, two wrongs don't make a right."

"What would you know about it?" Noelle's mother snapped. Her father stayed eerily silent, staring at the intricately patterned brown-and-beige Oriental rug at his feet.

"I know that it's not right to kill an innocent baby, especially not when there's a family willing and ready to give it a home."

"You can't talk to me like that! Get out of my house!" the older woman roared, and Noelle cowered at the tone she knew so well. "Noelle, get upstairs!"

"No!" Abby shouted almost as loudly as Noelle's mother had, but her tone wasn't quite as dark. "Noelle, you can come home with us."

"Abby, are you sure that's the right thing to do?" her husband asked, breaking his silence.

Noelle looked from one woman to the other, torn between her feelings of familial obligation and knowing what was right for her and her baby. "I…I don't know what to do," she said honestly.

"You're not eighteen yet," her mother said, her voice a little softer. "You still live in this house, and you still have to do what we say. Get upstairs and go to bed. We'll talk about this more in the morning."

"She doesn't have to live in this house anymore," Abby said.

Her boss's panic was written all over her face, but Noelle couldn't for the life of her figure out why. "Abby, what are you saying?"

"Noelle, come home with us. If you stay here, I'm afraid they'll do something drastic, and that could hurt both you *and* your baby.

Please, listen to me. I've seen situations like this before. My best friend…"

"Shut up! How dare you talk to my daughter about her own parents this way! Noelle, if you walk out of this house with them tonight, you will not be able to walk back through that front door again. You will no longer be our daughter."

"Gloria, you don't mean that!" Noelle's father clasped his wife's hand in his, tears brimming in his eyes.

"I do. I do mean it!"

Noelle looked at the anger and hatred in her mother's eyes, and she saw the hurt in her father's. Then she looked at Abby and saw only love and fear for the safety of both Noelle and her unborn baby. She knew, in that moment, what she had to do. She slowly stood and walked toward the door. Her mother stood and quickly crossed the room, putting a hand on her arm to stop her, but Noelle shook her off. She heard Abby and Gil stand up and follow her toward the door.

"Noelle, don't do this. Don't destroy this family this way!" her mother screamed.

Her right hand resting on the doorknob, Noelle turned her head back toward her mother, catching a glimpse of Abby's determined, yet supportive face out of the corner of her eye. "I'm not," she said before walking out the door.

"…And this can be your room for as long as you need it," Abby said, waving a hand around the guest bedroom with the peach-colored walls.

Noelle sat on the frilly twin bed's peach-and-white bedspread, focusing on the floor. She hadn't said a word since they'd left her parents' house. She was obviously suffering intense grief at having separated from her parents in such a way, but who could blame her for doing what she'd done? Abby couldn't, and in fact, she realized with more than a little guilt, she had actually encouraged it.

"Noelle?" Abby prodded.

The girl looked up then, and Abby saw the tears streaming down her cheeks. She'd been crying silently this whole time. Abby's heart broke for the teenage girl with the new life growing inside her and very little outside support.

"Am I doing the right thing? Really, Abby?"

Abby crossed over to the bed and sat down beside her, hugging her closely with one arm wrapped around her bony shoulders. "You are doing the right thing. Your parents are the ones who are wrong in all this. Just like I told them, two wrongs don't make a right. Ending an innocent life is wrong, you know that."

Noelle nodded.

Abby continued. "It goes against everything your parents say they believe. It goes against God." She lowered her hand to the bedspread between them. "I just had a thought. You know that friend I told you about who runs the pregnancy resource center?"

Noelle nodded again, wiping the streaks of tears from her cheeks.

"Let me give her a call. I think you need to meet her."

Noelle frowned. "But it's after nine o'clock on a Monday night. The center won't be open now."

Abby laughed. "Marcy's center is always open."

Noelle stared out the window at the houses all decked and lit for Christmas as Abby sped down the road to who-knew-where. She fought back a fresh burst of tears at the knowledge that she wouldn't be able to go back to her own home for Christmas—not this year, and maybe not ever again. She squirmed uncomfortably in the seat as she tried to convince her overactive bladder to calm down, hoping it wouldn't take much longer to get to the center.

The thing that worried her most was that Abby had driven them clear out of the city, and now they were on their way down an old state highway, passing cow pastures and cornfields that were illuminated softly by the cool late evening moonlight. Where were they going? She'd just assumed that the resource center was downtown, but this wasn't anywhere near downtown—this was the country, and there wasn't even an outhouse in sight.

Finally, after what seemed an eternity, Abby steered the car left off the highway onto a narrow gravel road. Noelle winced and gritted her teeth as every bump increased her urgent need to use the bathroom. There was nothing but an old farmhouse in front of them. There were lights on, even at this late hour, including a fully lit Christmas tree glowing cheerfully through the front box window. No lights hanging from the outside of the house, Noelle noted, as she shifted her legs slightly to stretch and relieve some bladder pressure while Abby pulled up in front of the house and turned off the car's engine.

Noelle looked uneasily over in her direction. "Hey, Abby, where are we? I thought you said you talked to your friend at the resource center, and we were going there."

Abby turned toward the younger woman and smiled. "This is the resource center I was telling you about. My friend Marcy owns this house and has turned it into a safe haven for young women in similar situations to yours. She does all she can to explain what an abortion actually does to your body, and she tries to help connect young unwed mothers and others who can't care for their babies after they're born with adoptive parents. She's the one that Gil and I have been working with for the past year, with not much luck. But now we've got you." Noelle barely caught the slight upturning of the corners of Abby's mouth in the half-light.

"You think she can help me? Help us?"

Abby nodded. "I do, and she thinks she can too." She unbuckled her seatbelt and pulled on the door latch. "Let's go."

It was much colder out here in the country than it had been in the city, with all the buildings around to block the wind. Noelle braced herself against the chill and followed Abby up the whitewashed wooden porch steps, her full bladder almost forgotten in the tension of the moment. She wasn't sure what would happen when she walked in that front door, but she knew she was right where she was supposed to be. She would find help and support here to protect the life of her baby.

Abby knocked on the door, and minutes later it was opened by one of the most beautiful women Noelle had ever seen. She was slightly older than Abby, her dark auburn hair showing a few streaks of gray. She had shallow laugh lines around her eyes, and her ruby-red lips were upturned in a welcoming smile. She opened her arms wide, and Abby accepted her hug before pulling away and introducing Noelle.

"Hi, Noelle. I'm Marcy," the woman introduced herself, although Noelle had already guessed her identity.

"Hi," she said shyly, looking down at her feet and trying very hard not to do a pee-pee dance.

"Abby's told me a lot about your situation, and I think we just might be able to help you."

"Could I...Do you think I could use your bathroom first?" Noelle asked.

Marcy's laugh was light, musical. "Yes, of course. It's right down this hallway. I'll show you the way."

Noelle took her time in the bathroom. She heard Abby and Marcy talking out in the hallway, and she knew they were talking about her. Why wouldn't they be? She and her baby were the reason they were here. Still, it made her feel a little like a project, and she didn't exactly understand the dread sitting like a lead weight at the pit of her stomach, when just moments before she had felt so safe and comforted.

She stared at her reflection in the mirror and was amazed by how pale and disheveled she looked. She'd always taken such care with her appearance, but now there didn't seem to be any point. She was a used-up has-been with a baby. *A baby, and it's going to be Abby's baby.*

Next to the bathroom mirror someone, probably Marcy, had taped a chart on the wall showing how babies develop week-by-week. She did a quick mental calculation and counted back to her conception date, which wasn't hard, considering it was the one and only time she'd ever had sex. Sixteen weeks ago, which, according to the chart, put her at eighteen weeks pregnant. She was already in her second trimester. Her baby was just now the size of a small sweet potato, and its ears were forming. In fact, the information on the chart said that the ears were probably working now.

"You can hear me talking to you now?" she whispered. "This is some mess we're in, huh?" Noelle sighed. "But it's not your fault. None of this is your fault."

A knock on the door was followed by Abby's voice saying, "Noelle, is everything okay?"

She nodded involuntarily. "Yeah, Abby, everything's fine."

She splashed some cold water on her face, dried her hands and face on the fluffy olive green hand towel hanging on the rack under the chart, and slowly opened the bathroom door.

Abby watched Noelle emerge from the bathroom, and she couldn't help but notice the change in her. Something had definitely happened to her in that bathroom, something more than just bladder relief, but Abby had no idea what it was. She turned to Marcy, who was smiling at Noelle. Marcy turned her head just enough to meet Abby's eyes with her own, and she nodded almost imperceptibly. Marcy knew what was going on with Noelle. She'd obviously seen this before.

"Noelle, honey?" Marcy said. "Do you know how far along you are?"

Noelle blinked at them both and nodded slowly. "Yes. On the chart in there, it said I'm right at eighteen weeks, but I don't understand how that can be, since I just had sex sixteen weeks ago. How could I be pregnant before I even had sex?"

Marcy laughed. "That's standard medical practice. Doctors had to find some way to measure a baby's age, in case of problems during the pregnancy. The actual date of conception was often quite difficult to detect, but the start date of the last menstrual period was much easier to remember. Because they knew that most women ovulate halfway through their menstrual cycles, which, on average, last twenty-eight days, that's how they came up with the extra two weeks. Now there are scans that are much more accurate in detecting a baby's real age, but the LMP method of pregnancy dating persists. Forty weeks total is what everyone says, and that's adding in two weeks from the start of your last period."

Noelle nodded, although she still looked a little confused. "So that's where they get eighteen weeks from. That makes more sense, I guess."

Abby glanced at Marcy out of the corner of her eye. Eighteen weeks. That meant they could probably find out the baby's sex. She knew Marcy had a 4-D ultrasound set up in one of the bedrooms.

Marcy must have been thinking the same thing, or maybe it was just standard procedure for her to ask, "Would you like to see your baby? Hear the heartbeat?"

Noelle looked nervously from Marcy to Abby and then back down at her feet. Abby gave her what she hoped was an encouraging, rather than a pushy nod and a gentle pat on the back. Relief flooded through her heart when Noelle nodded her assent. Her heart skipped a beat, and she couldn't stop the excited smile. They were going to get to see the baby!

As they walked down the hallway toward the room with the ultrasound machine, Noelle heard other people talking, and she realized that they weren't alone in this place. She peeked into rooms as they passed, and she saw several other girls—some her age, some slightly older. It even looked like there were a few who might be younger.

How many other girls are there in this house right now? Do they all live here?

When they got to the ultrasound room, Noelle pulled her pants down to just below her growing belly, as Marcy instructed, and she lay down on the cushioned exam table. The goop Marcy squirted on her was cold, and even though Marcy warned her that it would be, it still startled her. She felt suddenly nervous and reached out a tentative hand to Abby, who gave it a comforting squeeze.

"All those girls I saw in the hallway—do they all live here?"

Marcy nodded, her eyes focused on the ultrasound machine instead of on Noelle. "Some of them do. Some just stay here to help me out with the girls who are overnight guests. I guess you could say they're our hospitality committee." She chuckled. "You can meet some of them later, if you want."

"Okay." Noelle wasn't quite sure why she would want to meet any of them, but she didn't want to seem rude.

Within minutes, Marcy had the machine up and running, and Noelle saw and heard her baby for the first time. Tears sprang to her eyes at the sight of that tiny human inside her. It wasn't just an unformed mass of cells, as some tried to believe. It looked like any other baby she had ever seen—only smaller.

She gasped and clasped a hand over her mouth, looking over at Marcy, who gazed down at her and smiled. "Do you want to know the sex?"

"You can tell that already?" Noelle asked.

"Yes, of course. It's pretty clear here. She's not shy about showing us her stuff."

"She?" Noelle said, and she felt Abby's grip tighten on her hand.

"Zoe," Abby breathed, feeling tears form at the corners of both eyes. She tried to blink them away.

"Zoe?" Noelle said, looking up at her, brow furrowed in confusion.

"Zoe means life, and you're choosing life. I've always liked that name. It's been at the top of my baby names list for years, and it seems so perfect for this situation."

"Now wait a minute, Abby." Marcy's tone held a note of caution. "We don't have anything written down or signed. All we have, at this point, is a verbal agreement. I don't think you have much of a right to start naming Noelle's baby."

The words stung more than Abby wanted to admit, but Marcy was absolutely right. They had no written agreement. Nothing was signed or filed. This baby was not yet hers. Noelle had every right to name the baby herself.

"I'm sorry," Abby said, gazing down at Noelle.

Noelle shook her head. "No, that's okay. I did say you could raise my baby. You can give her a much better life than I ever could, and I love the name Zoe. You're right. It *is* perfect."

Abby squeezed her hand again and gave her a grateful smile. Then she turned her attention back to Marcy. "How soon can we have the papers drawn up and signed?"

Marcy laughed and shook her head as she removed the small photos of Baby Zoe from the ultrasound printer. "Abby…"

"Please, Marcy? You know how long I've been praying and waiting for this. I don't want to wait any longer."

Marcy's eyes were playful. "Well, you'll have to wait at least a few months longer." She nodded her head in the direction of Noelle's belly.

Abby executed a perfect moue. "I know that, but I at least want it down on paper as soon as possible."

"Well, tomorrow's Christmas Eve, so I don't know if any government offices will be open. We'll probably have to wait at least until the day after Christmas, which is good for us, because Noelle will already be eighteen then."

A knock at the door interrupted Marcy's speech. It was followed by the hasty entrance of a tall, thin girl with long, straight black hair pulled back into a ponytail. She looked embarrassed to be there.

"Uh, Marcy?" she said.

"Yes, what is it, Jana?"

"There's a couple downstairs—a man and a woman—they say they're Noelle's parents, and they're demanding to see her right now."

"My parents? How did they find me here?" Her frightened gaze caught Abby's. Abby shrugged and frowned. She had a suspicion they'd gotten the location, and possibly the directions, from Gil. He'd think it only right to tell them where their daughter had gone, even if that meant he was making himself an indirect accomplice to legalized murder. She'd have to have a long talk with him later.

Marcy sighed as she switched off the machine. "Tell them we'll be there in a minute." She turned to Noelle. "Are you okay with this?"

Fear jabbed Noelle's heart like a switchblade. *No, I'm not okay with this. Why would I be okay with this? My parents? I don't want to see them. They'll just drag me back home...and to the clinic in a couple of days.*

She turned pleading eyes in Abby's direction, but Abby wasn't looking at her. She was staring straight at the doorway the girl had popped into to deliver her news before popping right back out.

"What are we going to do?" Abby asked, looking to Marcy for help, her voice cracking with anxiety.

Marcy shrugged and shook her head. "There's not much we can do except get out there and see what they want."

"They want me," Noelle said as she stood up and trudged toward the door. "They want to kill my baby."

Marcy put a protective hand on her shoulder. "Then we won't let them do that."

Noelle nodded and let the older women lead the way out into the hallway and back into the foyer she had passed through for the first time not long before. Her parents were waiting in the sitting room to the left. As soon as Noelle's mother saw her, she sprang from her chair and lunged toward her, clutching her shirt sleeve in her clenched fist.

"Come on, Noelle, it's time to go home," she hissed.

She tried to back away from her mother's grasp—and the fierce look in her eyes—but she was unable to move. All she could do was stand and stare, tears threatening to break through the surface at any moment. Fortunately, Marcy came to her rescue by physically removing Mrs. Matthews's hand from Noelle's arm.

"Excuse me, but my name is Marcy, and I am the owner of this house. May I be of some service to you?"

Noelle's mother's laugh was sharp and mirthless. "Yes, you may be of service to me. Kindly tell my daughter to leave at once, get in the car, and go home with her father and me."

"I'm sorry, but I can't do that. Noelle has made the decision to stay here until the adoption papers are finalized."

Noelle blinked. When had she made that decision? She felt a twinge of guilt at the knowledge that Marcy had just lied to her mother in that way, but it was true enough that she didn't want to go home with her parents.

"I'm afraid my daughter has misled you, as she has so many other people before this. There will be no adoption."

For one glorious moment, Noelle thought that maybe her parents had changed their minds after all. Maybe they would support her and Zoe and let them both come back and live in their house, no matter what the church might think about the music minister's daughter having a child out of wedlock. But one look at her mother's unwaveringly stern facial expression, and her cold, dark brown eyes told Noelle that no such plan was going through her mother's mind.

"No," Abby interjected, "there won't be an adoption, as far as you're concerned, because all you want to do is kill this baby. You don't care about your daughter's feelings or your own grandchild's life. And, while we're on the subject of life, you're putting your own daughter's life at risk by pressuring her to go through with this abortion."

"What are you talking about?" Noelle's mother snapped.

"Do you know how many girls try to commit suicide following an abortion? They can't live with the knowledge of what they've done. Ask anyone here." She waved her right arm in the air, indicating the doorway, where four of the young women Noelle had spotted on her way to the ultrasound room now stood watching. "How many of you have had an abortion?" They all raised their hands, as did Marcy, Noelle noticed with some shock. "And how many of you tried to commit suicide after that?" Two hands went down, but Marcy's hand stayed up, as did those of two of the girls in the doorway. More than fifty percent. Not very good odds, as far as Noelle was concerned. "Is that what you want for your daughter?" Marcy asked.

"I don't see what business this is of yours."

"Oh, this concerns me a great deal, because I care about what happens to Noelle and Zoe."

Noelle saw the confusion written all over her mother's face. "Who's Zoe?"

"Zoe's my baby," Noelle answered.

"Your baby?" her mother scoffed. "You named it?"

Noelle nodded.

Mrs. Matthews turned to her husband. "Well, it's obvious the women at this center have completely turned our daughter against us. I think we're done here."

"Mom…please."

Her mother whirled back around and threw daggers with her eyes. "Don't call me that. I was trying to give you one last chance to come back into the family, but you've made that impossible now. I told you earlier, back at the house, if you choose to go through with this plan, then you're no longer our daughter."

The chill Noelle felt in the air didn't come from the fast-dropping temperatures outside. She waited for the tears to flow, but they didn't. She felt no sadness or pain now, only impassivity.

Marcy took a step toward Noelle's mother. "You're right. We are done here. Please leave this house now, and your biggest worry should not be the fact that you have a daughter who had sex and got pregnant outside of marriage."

Mrs. Matthews stood silent, giving her husband a chance to speak for a change. "What do you mean?" he asked.

"She means this," Abby said. "If you give us anymore trouble, if you try to stop this adoption from going through in any way, then we will tell the whole community about how you would rather your daughter commit murder than you having to admit that you have a daughter who doesn't fit within your ideal church standards."

"Abby," Marcy cautioned, shaking her head slightly. "That's not quite what I was saying. There are confidentiality agreements to consider."

"Well, it's what I'm saying. I don't care about any confidentiality agreement." Abby stuck her lower lip out in defiance.

"You can't do that to us. It's blackmail," Mrs. Matthews exclaimed.

"You're darn right it's blackmail. I'll do what I have to do to save an innocent baby's life—and to save any young girl from experiencing the horror of abortion like all these other young women did."

Mrs. Matthews put a strong hand on her husband's arm. "Let's go. Now."

He nodded and followed his wife out of the house, giving Noelle one last, long look. It was hard for her to read his eyes, but she thought she saw sadness there. Or maybe she only saw it because that was what she wanted to see.

When her parents had gone, all the other women in the room surrounded Noelle with hugs and reassuring pats on the back.

"What have I done?" she asked no one in particular.

"You've done what you had to do to protect Zoe," Marcy told her gently. "You acted like a mother."

"But I lost my relationship with my parents."

Marcy shrugged. "They'll come around, and if they don't, you have a whole new family now."

Abby circled an arm around Noelle's shoulders and pulled her in close. "That's right. Gil and I will adopt you as our own, just like God adopted all of us who believe in His beautiful gift of salvation through Jesus Christ as His very own children, now and forevermore."

"You can't adopt me," Noelle protested. "I'll be eighteen the day after tomorrow."

Abby smiled. "Who said it had to be a legal adoption?"

"Speaking of," Marcy interrupted. "Abby, why don't you and I go upstairs to the office and start drawing up some papers to make it legal for you to adopt Noelle's baby, and don't forget to call Gil and let him know what's going on. We'll need his signature on these papers too. And, Noelle, why don't you go upstairs with Jana? She'll show you to a guestroom you can use for the night. I'm sure you must be tired."

Noelle smiled weakly. "Yes, I am. It's been a long day. And you still need me to cover the early shift in the morning, right?"

Abby laughed. "Oh, I forgot all about that. I'll see what I can do about it. If nothing else, I'll cover your shift. You deserve a little break. Or maybe I should call Joe and tell him not to bother going in—just give everybody the day off. It is Christmas Eve, after all, and we've really got something to celebrate now, don't we?"

Noelle's smile got a little wider as the truth of Abby's words washed over her. "Yes, we do. We've got Zoe."

Gifts

Jeanette Hanscome

Aunt Sheila's apartment was not nearly large enough to support the aroma of so many scented pine cones, a real Christmas tree, and a live wreath. But it was Christmas Eve, so I enjoyed it while I could. In an hour I would be at the Main Street Hotel where fear of upsetting a guest's fragrance allergies meant a holiday decked in pretty plastic with only hints of cinnamon.

I tied a red and silver bow around the lumpy rectangle wrapped in snowflake paper—the last present in my 12 Days of Christmas gift box. *Okay, God, who do You want me to give it to?*

Aunt Sheila appeared in my bedroom doorway. She blew her nose into a wad of cheap tissue. "Don't worry, I'm not sick. I just heard one of those soppy Christmas songs." She swatted a stray tear.

"The one about the boy trying to buy shoes for his dying mother?"

"No, the one with military families sending Christmas greetings." She blew her nose. "It should come with a disclaimer."

"Thank you for shielding me. I just put my makeup on." That song tore me up every time.

My aunt sniffed and watched me adjust the bow until it was perfectly centered. "I love that you still wrap presents instead of using gift bags, Justine. That is a lost art."

I tucked the card beneath the ribbon on the underside of the package so it would lie flat. "I refuse to buy gift bags."

She tossed her tissue into my trash can. "Speaking of gifts, may I please put the one that arrived yesterday under the tree for you? I'll even rewrap it so it looks as pretty as that one."

My heart wrenched. "No." I shoved my wrapping supplies aside. "I told you. I'm dropping it off at the post office as soon as I get off work tonight. It's small enough for the drop box."

"Justine, he's your father."

"Step-father. And he's only trying to suck up."

"Please don't say suck up. It's crude, and very out of character for you."

"It's not out of character if I say it." I attempted a snarky smirk, but I could still taste the bitterness of my own words on my tongue. I detested the side of me that emerged when Mom's second husband, Jason, came up in conversation—the man who duped me and Mom into thinking he wasn't like all the others, the man who solidified my decision to take a vow of life-long celibacy. I even had an old-spinster hat stashed away for future use and pictures of the cats I planned to hoard in a tacky-in-a-charming-way apartment. At thirty-one, it would be a while before eccentric was considered cute, but it helped to prepare.

My aunt let out a frustrated sigh-groan and followed my unnecessary rush to the living room. We both knew I had plenty of time. It took less than ten minutes to get from our front door to the front desk at the hotel. I saw only one drawback to my life in this small Bay Area community—the apartment that Aunt Sheila and I shared was too conveniently located. Neither of us could avoid unpleasant topics with, "Oh, wow, with traffic and everything, I should really get going."

"Well, I think you're being silly. I'm not telling you to invite Jason to Christmas dinner, just accept his gift and call him to say thank you. E-mail him even! Your mom has clearly forgiven him. Why not you?"

Christmas spirit smothered. Thanks, Aunt Sheila. What could I possibly say to that? I opted for the actions-speak-louder approach and snatched the grocery-bag-covered box off the bar to toss beside my tote bag. A childish temptation to shake it came over me. Jason gave the best gifts. He always knew exactly what I wanted. I dropped it on the couch then found a safe nest in my tote bag for the gift I'd wrapped in my bedroom.

"Remember, seventy times seven." Aunt Sheila used her Sunday school teacher voice for emphasis.

I mimicked it. "I know the Bible verses." *All of them, which doesn't help at all.*

"Well, Honey, try applying them."

I turned to face the aunt who took me in when I crushed my mother's heart by dropping out of college and breaking up with one of the few nice guys that the McNally women had encountered in three generations. The aunt who believed I could do more than man the front desk of a hotel that only still existed because it bore the label *historic,* was nestled in the cutest area of Danville, California, and provided the perfect setting for weddings, teas, and significant Jane Austin anniversary galas. The aunt who had a perfect man picked out for me at church: Steven with the sweet hazel eyes. She did all this over-the-top decorating for me, knowing that as a kid I only got a loved-to-death artificial tree, thrift store Advent calendars, and cranberry candles if Mom's workplace did Secret Santas. Her life had been just as rocky as mine and Mom's, yet she still cried over emotionally manipulative Christmas songs. No wonder I couldn't think of a good comeback.

She rescued me from awkward silence by speaking first. "Justine, you are such a kind, generous, strong young woman. Don't ruin who you are by becoming bitter."

Suddenly I didn't need a song to make me tear up. "Mom doesn't know the whole story."

"Maybe she knows more than you think. Besides, Jason is reaching out to *you.*"

I let the spicy air calm my cluttered mind. I couldn't decide what scared me more, the idea of becoming bitter or forgiving Jason and getting burned again. I also didn't want to be a person who could be bought with a trinket.

I picked up the box and slung my tote over my shoulder. "Tell you what. I'll think about it."

"Think hard."

"I need to go to work." I would kill time on the way by stopping for one of those holiday coffees that would be gone come New Year.

"And pray."

"Merry Christmas, Aunt Sheila." I swung the door open, careful not to knock the wreath from its hanger. The outdoor twinkle lights performed their Merry Christmas dance in the late afternoon haze.

"I'll meet you at church," she called.

Church would definitely be a good thing. "I get off at nine, so I'll be a little late."

The snowflake-covered corner of Gift #12 brushed against my arm. How would I feel if I handed it to someone and they shoved it right back in my face?

I took the steps down to the sidewalk as quickly as I could without tripping, wishing I had the courage to heave Jason's guilt gift into the bushes.

This is not the same thing.

I dropped a dollar into the tip jar at Full 'a Beans Coffee & Tea and stepped aside to wait for my Christmas Eve indulgence. Meg, the girl making my gingerbread latte, handed a steaming cup to a woman who clearly liked faux fur and animal prints.

I was envying the woman's ability to get away with such an ensemble when she said to Meg, "What a pretty pin you have on."

"Thank you." Meg touched the angel on her apron. "It was a gift."

"Your friend has good taste."

I turned toward the clearance table and pretended to be interested in a mug shaped like a snowman's head. Only at Christmastime and at Disneyland would I even consider drinking out of a head.

"I don't even know who it came from." Meg lowered her voice a little, but a lilt still came through. "Someone left it for me a few days ago and didn't sign their name. It totally made my day."

Yes! Thank you, God.

Meg had received Gift #8 from my 12 Days of Christmas box. I chose her because she often looked tired and talked about juggling school with two jobs. All that, and she still remembered that I liked cinnamon on all my coffee drinks.

"Gingerbread latte for Justine," Meg called after exchanging politically correct holiday greetings with Fur Lady.

I bit my lip to erase the I-have-a-secret smile trying to escape.

Meg handed me a cinnamon shaker with my latte. "I saw someone swipe the one from the bar and take it to her table."

"Thank you." I gave my drink several good shakes of cinnamon and handed the container back to her. Meg's eyes looked bright, not like last week when I popped in for a quick caffeine infusion before work and overheard her tell the cashier that her boyfriend broke up with her via text. Watching her fight back tears as she prepared an espresso for a man who couldn't get over the inconvenience of standing in line let alone see her pain inspired me to give her the angel pin with four red and green stones on each glittered wing. It looked perfect on her. I snapped a lid onto my cup. "Are you enjoying the break from classes?"

"So much! I passed that awful calculus class. I've never been so happy to get a 'C' in my life."

"I hated calculus." It had been ten years since I dropped out of school mid-semester, one year short of my Social Work degree, and I still missed college. Even calculus.

I missed Alex, my too-good-to-be-true boyfriend. I missed him slipping his leather jacket around my shoulders when I got cold, and the way he gave stink-eye to anyone who treated me like less than the Queen. I missed his twin sister, Amy, who sent those annoying forwarded e-mails with dancing smiley faces. She called me in tears after I broke up with her brother. But that's what happens when someone else's actions send you running and the campus is too small to avoid bumping into each other.

I swallowed memories of Alex with a swig of gingery coffee. It didn't work. "Merry Christmas, Meg."

"Merry Christmas." She smiled and waved. The stones on her pin sparkled, making her blue-grey eyes gleam. What would Jason's eyes look like when he saw "Return to Sender" stamped across the gift he sent me?

Forget about him. Concentrate on the gift you plan to give away. I had found the pretty ceramic cross with *Grace* painted in gold at a thrift store. It could go to either a man or a woman, as could the card, containing references to 12 verses about God's grace.

I started the 12 Days of Christmas tradition the year after receiving an anonymous box of packages. The year I received the box, I had just thrown my future off the Golden Gate Bridge and moved in with Aunt Sheila because I couldn't face Mom. At first I thought Alex sent it in an attempt to win me back, but the handwriting on the card didn't match his signature boxy printing.

The instructions said to open one gift per day between December 13 and Christmas Eve. Each package included a card with a Bible verse that left me wondering how this mystery person knew what was going on in my heart that day. None of the presents contained anything fancy—a pack of four pretty pens on Day 4, three pair of fun socks on Day 6, a box of ten fancy chocolates. Then I un-wrapped the final gift. Inside a red satin box I found half of a sterling silver friendship heart on a chain. The half-heart had a pair of praying hands in the center. The card included 12 verses about God's love for me, and the note, "I promise to pray for you every day." I still wore the heart daily. I kept all the cards in a special box in my room. Sometimes I caught myself wondering if the anonymous giver still prayed for me.

The next year I decided to pass the joy on to someone else. Like the gifts I received, my packages contained inexpensive presents and a card with a Bible verse, except for the one for Christmas Eve, which was extra special. I had so much fun with my first act of secret giving and finding creative ways to tie in the numbers from the 12 Days of Christmas song that I made it a tradition. This year I changed it up and gave each gift to a different person. Most of them went to people I knew just well enough to recognize they needed a lift, like Meg. A couple of them went to strangers, like a frazzled mom I ran into in Target on Day 1. I knew she needed the gourmet chocolate bar wrapped in silver bell cellophane and an encouraging note when I saw her in line bribing her screaming toddler with organic crackers. I reached into my tote, prayed that she wouldn't accuse me of being a stalker, and held the gift out to her. *"Excuse me, but you look like you could use a treat. Merry Christmas."* She hesitated, but she took it.

Today's gift needed to go to someone who needed a reminder of God's grace as much as that desperate mother needed chocolate.

My phone chimed as I pulled into the Staff Only parking lot behind the Main Street Hotel. I sipped my drink and checked the text, expecting to see one from Aunt Sheila, sharing a story she read online about a man who died shortly after sending an estranged loved one a Christmas gift.

It was from Jason.

Justine, please let me know if you received the gift I sent.

My fingers quivered with the impulse to reply while my mind screamed, *Don't!*

Your Mother has forgiven him. Why can't you?

I wiped whipped cream off my lips.

I don't know. If those who think I'm a nice person only knew.

I'll admit it: there were times when I felt like an unreasonable brat for holding onto my grudge against Jason. I knew girls who had far worse complaints than mine—true horror stories. Jason, who felt more like a real father than the man whose name appeared on my birth certificate, had never laid an unloving or inappropriate hand on me. Unlike the many boyfriends who came between Mom's first marriage and him, Jason was faithful, un-addicted, a Christian, and had a good job. But losing that good job and attempting to start his own car repair business only to have it fail put him in debt up to his hair follicles. As Mom and I learned, desperation can push a person to do unbelievable things.

It stung enough when he slowly drained the bank account intended for my college expenses not covered by scholarships. He had already depleted his savings, so I knew it would be a while before he replaced my funds as promised. Then Mom's mother died and left her a set of 100-year-old wedding china. Grandma left me an emerald bracelet.

One weekend I went home and Jason asked for the bracelet. *"I suggested to your mom that we get the china appraised for insurance purposes. How about if I take your bracelet, too?"*

I'd wondered if it had more than sentimental value, so I gave it to him without a word to Mom.

Mom called a week later.

"Jason sold Grandma's china to an antique dealer. We didn't even discuss it; he just kept making excuses for why he hadn't gotten it back from the appraiser yet."

Mom was so devastated that I never mentioned the bracelet.

Mom left Jason. I cried with Alex then slowly pulled away from him. If Jason could turn out to be a lying thief, so could my boyfriend. Clearly the McNally women attracted only creeps, and the best way to break the cycle was to stay away from guys.

Fast-forward a decade and Jason was back in Mom's life, supposedly "a different person."

How much longer did I expect to avoid him?

I checked the time on my phone. Ten minutes until I had to be behind the reservation desk pretending to look busy on a day when no one booked hotel rooms. This was not the time to wallow in the past.

Maybe I could give Gift #12 to Lydia, my boss. Her high-maintenance in-laws were in town for Christmas.

Lydia grabbed my arm before the jingle bells on the hotel entrance had a chance to stop tinkling. "Good, you're here."

"Am I late?" I checked the garland-draped grandfather clock in the hotel lobby. I still had three minutes.

"No, but the Murray party is due to arrive in an hour. This place isn't anywhere near ready." Her voice cracked.

I dropped my coffee cup into the trash by the door leading to the hotel restaurant. Who were the Murrays and what were we getting ready for? "Did I miss something?"

Then I remembered the woman who called in hysterics the previous week, begging for a place to have her family Christmas Eve gathering. Her high-end address couldn't keep her washing machine hose from bursting while she was at work and flooding half the first floor, including the living room and two guest rooms. She reserved the Garden Room for dinner, and our two nicest suites for out-of-town relatives.

"I thought this reservation was the answer to your Christmas prayers."

"Yes, until a family dinner became a theme party complete with costumes and a request for appropriate décor, a fun twist the hostess decided to throw in at the last minute. I drew the line at a special menu and asking their waiter to speak in a British accent." Lydia shook her hands at the ceiling as if the chandelier was the one at fault. "And I thought my sister-in-law was difficult."

I refrained from spouting off a snotty comment about wealth and entitlement, another bad habit that Aunt Sheila considered out of character for a sweet woman like me. Working for Lydia and serving guests at the hotel had shown me that not everyone with money acted like the girls I went to private school with back in my scholarship kid days. "So, what's the theme?"

"A Christmas Carol."

"With costumes?"

She straightened a pair of red candles. "Yes."

"Who throws that together at the last minute?"

"Brenda Murray, apparently."

One of the waitresses whizzed past us with a tray of glasses. She swerved to avoid a life-sized nutcracker. The aroma of turkey and sage stuffing drifted in from the kitchen. *Brenda Murray.* Why did I feel like I knew that name long before taking her reservation?

Lydia pressed her fingertips to her forehead. "I gave too many people Christmas Eve off. What is wrong with me?"

I touched my boss's arm. There was no telling her that the Murrays could not expect much on short notice. What a guest wanted, a guest got if we had it. Lydia's tension told me that she definitely needed the gift in my bag. "Calm down, okay? I'm assuming they don't expect the staff to dress in costume unless they plan to provide them. This place already has a Victorian theme. The Christmas tree in the Garden Room is perfect with the simple ornaments and red balls. The one in the lobby looks like it belongs in a magazine. You can switch the music in the sound system to the Classical Christmas collection, and I'll see what decorations we have in back."

She squeezed my hand. "You're amazing!"

"I can even help serve."

"Would you really?"

"I was a waitress in college. It'll bring back memories." Memories of meeting Alex, who came into Denny's every Tuesday night with his Bible study group. He always ordered the same thing: a patty melt with extra crispy fries and a Sprite, easy on the ice. He dipped his fries in barbecue sauce instead of ketchup. "Where is the fat red ribbon left over from decorating the front desk?"

"Probably still in my office."

I stashed my tote bag behind the desk, propping it carefully so the gift wouldn't fall out. Jason's box still sat on the passenger seat of my car. Maybe someone would steal it.

An hour later the Garden Room didn't look exactly like a page out of Dickens, but with the help of a candelabra that I found in the back room and decorated with the ribbon, a fake old-time lamp post, and dim lighting it came pretty close. Memories of Alex suddenly got pushed aside by thoughts of the first Christmas with Jason, when he took me and Mom to San Francisco to see the musical *Scrooge.* I was twelve and, other than an abridged performance of the Nutcracker in the fourth grades, I had never seen a major stage production. Before the show he took us to dinner at Boudine's and to see the giant Christmas tree at Union Square. We watched the skaters, and he said we'd put skating on the list for next year. He was the first man in Mom's life to keep a promise like that.

I really can't deal with so many memories in one night, God. I have a job to do.

The jingle bells on the front door tinkled. A pretty middle-aged woman in a Dickens'-era ball gown rushed through the hotel entrance clutching the hands of twin Tiny Tims. Her smile masked frantic eyes; a look that only one who'd been trained to impress could manage. This had to be Brenda Murray. I took my place behind the reservation desk in case the young man and woman following her were relatives needing a room. The couple's working-class garb gave away their roles as Bob Cratchit and wife. They looked so familiar. Mrs. Cratchit took the boys from the older woman and walked them past the reservation desk to the Christmas tree. *That smile. I know those rosy cheeks and big brown eyes.*

My stomach did a cartwheel. I felt a sudden desire to hide under the desk but faked a welcoming smile instead. "Merry Christmas. May I help you?"

"Yes," the woman in the ball gown answered from across the room. "We're the Murray Party. Part of it anyway."

Mrs. Cratchit knelt in front of the twins, her back to me. She adjusted their costumes and whispered a gentle warning about not using their pretend crutches as swords.

It can't be her. It would be too weird.

"Um, yes." I prayed for my voice to stop quivering as I pulled up the reservation. "The Garden Room is ready, and your guests can check into their suites any time."

"Thank you so much. You saved our Christmas." She walked up behind the younger woman and touched her shoulder then pointed toward the Garden Room. "Amy, look, they did a lovely job."

Amy. It is her.

The details rushed back to me. In college Alex's sister Amy dated a guy named Kevin Murray. He went to a different school so I hardly ever saw him, but they were already talking about marriage. Once, while waiting for her in her dorm room, I took a phone message from Kevin's mom. *"Tell her Brenda Murray called about Thanksgiving."*

The twins had her eyes.

God, no, please. I cannot spend Christmas Eve serving my ex-boyfriend's sister.

Lydia's tense face reminded me that I had volunteered to do exactly that.

I wished for a fever, a violent onslaught of food poisoning from my latte, anything to get out of this event. Maybe Aunt Sheila really had been sick earlier today and I caught her cold. I coughed. I swallowed, hoping to feel pain. Nothing.

Amy followed her husband and Brenda to the Garden Room without giving me as much as a glance. Soon the whole Murray clan would be here, forcing me to follow through on my offer to play waitress.

God, is this my punishment for refusing Jason's gift?

I knew Lydia needed me to do more than stand paralyzed in the waitress station. The Cratchits, Scrooge, Jacob Marley, all three Christmas ghosts, and an array of beautifully dressed party guests had just ordered drinks and appetizers. A harp duet plucked out "God Rest Ye Merry Gentlemen" over the sound system. *Let nothing you dismay.*

Really?

Beth, our newest server, grabbed a tray of water and looked at me like she wanted to ask, *Are you going to bring the rest?* Lydia flew past the little nook, stopping just long enough to poke her head in.

"Justine." Lydia did not sound happy. "Does your offer to help still stand?"

I grabbed a glass and filled it with ice. "Yeah, sorry."

She stepped into the waitress station and leaned against the counter. "What is going on with you all of a sudden?"

The glass in my hand felt like a giant weight. My mind raced. She needed an answer.

"Are you okay?"

I set the glass down and did a thumb thrust over my shoulder. My words sounded lame before I got them out. "My ex-boyfriend's sister is in there."

"And?"

"And . . . and it's really awkward."

Her eyes told me how quickly I'd gone from amazing to immature. She reached for a tray and slapped it down in front of me. "Listen, I don't mean to minimize your angst, but for tonight that woman is a customer, okay? If she is rude to you, be polite and let it go as you would for anyone else. If you need to fall apart later, I'll be right here." She smacked my back. "Get out there, girl."

I sucked in my breath and blew out slowly. "Okay."

Amy had never been the type to be openly rude. At the very worst she would ignore me or send pitiful glances my way. After all, Alex probably had a gorgeous wife and at least one child by now. I filled the glass with water and added it to my tray, pasted on a smile, and forced my feet into the dining room.

Too bad I'd never required an extreme weight loss, making me utterly unrecognizable.

I dodged one of the Tiny Tims on my way to the table. The other one sat beside Amy, dipping his straw into his water glass, holding it up, and watching drips hit the table. She took the straw and moved the glass out of reach. Those across from her still needed water. She would know me in two seconds. I'd barely changed my hairstyle since college.

I avoided making eye contact by remaining sideways, but Jacob Marley's chain almost tripped me. I steadied myself before setting one water glass down then another. Again, Amy had to tell one of her boys to stop playing with his water.

Good, she's too busy to notice me.

I set the last glass down and made my escape.

Back in the waitress station, I let the empty tray fall on the counter and leaned my head back, releasing my relief. *Thank you, God. I did it.* Then I heard it; the does-anything-ever-get-her-down voice from a decade ago. She was right behind me.

"Justine McNally? I thought that was you."

Exhale. Good girl. Did she sound mad? Not at all. I gathered the courage to turn. She didn't look mad either.

"Amy?" I said it as if I'd just made the connection.

I waited for her face to contort into a glare. Instead, Amy's smile spread until her face lit up just as I remembered. She picked up her skirt and rushed over to me, right there in the waitress station. She threw her arms around my neck, pulling me into one of her perfect hugs. "How are you?"

"Good." *Liar.* Her hug dissolved the years. We might as well have been back in the Student Union grabbing lunch between classes.

She squeezed my hands. "I can't believe this."

Believe me, neither can I.

"You look great."

That's my cue to say something.

Strands of dark hair had escaped Amy's bun. A silver chain above her collar gave away that she'd forgotten to remove her contemporary jewelry. She'd probably noticed it in the parking lot and stuffed into her bodice. The tiny frame I remembered had filled out, but she was also the mother of twins. Even in a poor woman's costume with hair that refused to behave and the wrong jewelry, she looked as adorable as ever.

"So do you."

She smoothed her skirt. "Aren't these costumes fun? My mother-in-law made them all. Designing period outfits is Brenda's retirement hobby."

Yes, let's talk costumes. Anything to avoid the elephant. "They're incredible. I feel like I got sucked into a movie."

A very strange one.

"So, how long have you been working here?"

I got the job a week after moving in with Aunt Sheila. She knew Lydia through a book club. I didn't feel ready to be out in public, but Sheila insisted I needed the distraction. I wasn't about to confess to any of that.

"Oh, for a while. What are you up to?" Surely she was doing something far greater than working in a hotel. She'd majored in design.

The twins ran over and barreled into their mother. She wrapped one arm around each of them. "Mostly chasing after these guys."

The boys looked up at me with their dancing brown eyes. I grabbed a glass and filled it with Coke, completely forgetting the ice. "They're adorable. How old are they?"

"Four in February. Peter is wearing the red cap and James is in the green." She rubbed each of their heads. "Boys, say hello to Miss Justine."

They greeted me in stereo then she released them to go back to the table.

Amy patted her stomach. "We're expecting again. Only one this time, I hope."

"Congratulations." *I picture what Alex's kids might look like?*

"Oh, I wish you weren't working. I'd invite you to join us for dinner."

Had she suffered a head injury and forgotten what I did? I sneaked a glance at the table scene—the adorable twins already removing their caps, girls in ringlets, dresses adorned with ribbons, people laughing and attempting to act like their characters. If I hadn't freaked out, Alex would have asked me to marry him. The signs were all there. I could have been Amy's sister-in-law. Those beautiful little boys would be calling me Aunt Justine instead of Miss Justine.

I set the Coke aside. "Well, maybe we can chat after everyone has eaten." *Are you nuts?*

"Yes, let's do that. And refill our drinks a lot so I get to see you."

Before I could say, "Okay," Lydia waved me over. Amy gave me another grin and returned to her place beside Kevin Murray, who scratched at his high collar.

Lydia pulled me aside. "Everything okay?"

I nodded, sneaking a glance at Amy tying napkins around her boys' necks so they wouldn't mess up their suits. "Fine."

"Good. Can you find the light for the piano? They plan to sing Christmas carols after dinner."

"Please say you don't need an accompanist, because I don't play."

"No, Brenda plays. Carols are her Plan B. Originally she wanted to reenact Fezziwig's ball."

By the time we served dessert, I had accepted the Garden Room as my home for the evening and Amy as a guest who no longer needed to be feared.

"Mom," she said to Brenda after thanking me for her turkey dinner, "this is Justine, a friend from college."

I balanced my tray with one hand and shook Brenda's hand with the other.

When I served dessert she introduced me to the Spirit of Christmas Past, also as her friend.

Breaking up with Alex had doubled as cutting Amy off. Some friend.

I managed to squeak out, "Nice to meet you" as the woman tried to shake my hand and adjust her slipping wig at the same time.

The minute I set down her pumpkin pie, Amy's boys shot up in their chairs.

A jolly male voice boomed "Merry Christmas" in a bad British accent. Every head in the room turned to see the figure in a majestic, flowing gold-and-white-trimmed red robe and long white beard. In his arms he cradled a gigantic red bag.

"Santa!" Peter shouted.

"No," Brenda corrected, "That's Father Christmas."

Brenda directed every child in the room to find a place on the bright red rug in front of the fire place. Amy settled her boys into their spots, but instead of staying to watch what happened next, she started following me.

She stopped long enough to say something to Lydia then caught up with me.

I wiped a blob of something sticky on my apron. "Can I get you something?"

She shook her head. "Lydia said you could take a break." She pulled me into the lobby, worry taking over her cheerful face. "I could probably get away with not telling you this, but it wouldn't be fair." She looked over her shoulder at the scene in the Garden Room and whispered, "Alex is here."

"What?" My knees almost gave out. *This is not funny!*

"I'm so sorry. I was so excited to see you that I completely forgot he was coming."

Father Christmas took a present out of his bag and called a little girl in a green dress over.

I instinctively backed up, looking around for the man I still couldn't get out of my mind. When had he sneaked in? "Where is he?"

Amy pointed toward the happy cluster by the fireplace. Father Christmas handed the little girl a box wrapped in plaid paper. He patted the little girl's head and called for the next child. A chill shot through my heart.

"The guy she originally hired got sick." She rested her forehead in her hand. "And to think my biggest concern was that the twins would recognize him."

My eyes remained frozen on the man by the fireplace, picturing the face I once loved underneath that snowy beard. "Is his family here too?"

Amy shook her head.

Good. Seeing his wife would put me over the edge. "Oh, of course not. His kids might give him away."

"Alex isn't married."

Something in my cried out, *He's free!*

What was I thinking? Free? I'd probably ruined his ability to have a decent relationship. I fumbled for words, any words. "That's too bad. He would make a nice husband and a great dad."

"Yes, he would." Alley folded her arms and watched Father Christmas reach into his sack. "Too bad he never got the chance to be one."

A lump rose in my throat as I watched the nicest guy in the world pat Peter on the head and send him away with a rectangular box.

She looked at my face. "I'm sorry. That came out all wrong. He just never found the right person."

"No, I'm fine. It's just . . ." A sigh came out way more dramatically than intended. I wished for a chair to sink into. "I was so stupid."

Amy elbowed me. "Yes, you were." She leaned against the doorframe and watched her son tear the wrapping paper off his package. "Hey, Justine, maybe this is none of my business, but I think Alex being my twin gives me special privileges."

I prepared myself for what I knew was coming.

"Why did you dump my brother?"

Dump. Now that I didn't expect. That ugly word drove home what I'd done—tossed a wonderful man aside like junk.

"He really loved you."

I looked around for Lydia. How long of a break had she approved? "I know he did. I loved him too."

"You were perfect for each other."

We really were. Our backgrounds couldn't have been more different, but in every other area we fit like a puzzle.

"It's like one day you two were making us all sick with how cute you were, and the next you needed space. It didn't make sense."

No, it didn't. Ten years later it made absolutely no sense at all. I spilled out my only defense.

"Did Alex tell you what my step-dad did?"

"That he stole some things from you and your mom? Yes. That's horrible."

Father Christmas pulled up the hem of his robe to keep from tripping on it and revealed that he'd forgotten to take off his tennis shoes. At least the stripes matched his robe. "That's why I broke up with Alex."

"And what your step-dad did was Alex's fault because…?"

Reality, along with the shift in sweet Amy's tone, hit me like a punch in the stomach. Of course it wasn't Alex's fault. The need to be understood shoved aside the onslaught of remorse. "Jason—my step-dad—was the first man that really cared about me and my mom. My dad never came around, and before Jason every relationship that Mom had turned into a disaster. She used to joke that collecting losers was a family tradition."

Amy let out a laugh but looked at me like she felt sorry for doing it.

"Jason did everything I imagined a dad would do: helped me with my homework, took us to church and lived what he learned, got teary when he saw me in my first prom dress. Then he started having financial problems." I told her the rest.

Instead of an outpouring of sympathy, Amy said, "I still don't understand what that had to do with Alex."

I watched Father Christmas give James a big hug and lift him up off his feet. My lip trembled. "I didn't want to wait around for Alex to fail me, too."

She shrugged. "Alex is just as capable of failing you as anyone. Face it; we humans are masters at letting each other down. But he would never hurt you on purpose."

No, he wouldn't.

"Alex thought you were the one God had in mind for him."

"I thought the same thing." Tears started to trickle before I had a chance to feel them coming. "He must hate me."

She shook her head. "He never hated you." She toyed with the chain around her neck. "Okay, I confess, Alex was crushed. He never expected you to treat him like that, and frankly, neither did I. I felt ditched, too. You were like a sister to me. But one day I felt God nudging me to pray for you. So that's what I decided to do."

My tears trickled faster. "I'm really sorry, Amy."

"I forgive you. And I know Alex would say the same thing." She twisted her chain then let go. She smiled and held out her arms. "Oh, come here. Please don't cry. It's Christmas!" She wrapped me in another tight hug. "Justine, I can be such a dork sometimes. I shouldn't have brought this up tonight."

The fact that I needed to get back to work forced me to pull myself together. "No, I'm glad we talked about it."

She rubbed my back and gently pulled away. She patted her pockets. "I can't believe that with two preschoolers I don't have tissue."

I swept my fingers under my eyes. "Modern tissue wouldn't go with your outfit."

"True." She squeezed my shoulder. The thunder of pint-sized feet brought our tender moment to an abrupt halt.

"Mommy! Look what Santa gave me."

I turned to hide my tears from Peter as he held out a small old-fashioned electric train.

"Wow!" Amy knelt in front of Peter and admired the train. "It's the one you wanted."

"Open it, please!"

"Let's wait until we get home."

James sneaked up from behind and thrust a remote control sports car in front of Amy's face. "I got this."

Amy popped her head back in surprise. "Whoa, that is so cool!"

She was the best mom I'd ever seen in action, clearly in love with her kids.

James leaned on Amy's shoulder and rubbed his eyes. He stroked her neck, taking hold of her necklace.

"No, no, James. That needs to stay hidden." She looked up at me. "It's not authentic. Brenda would have a fit."

"I figured."

James pointed to Amy's chest. "That's Mommy's special broken heart."

Amy's face reddened a little. "That's right; it's special to Mommy." She kissed her little boy's cheek. "Leave your toys here and go see what your cousins got."

Mommy's special broken heart? I focused in on Amy's chain. Sterling silver.

The boys took off. Amy propped their gifts against the wall. I wrapped my fingers around the half-heart dangling against my sweater.

"Amy, can I see your necklace?" I stroked the praying hands on my pendant. "Please?"

Amy's eyes protested but only for a moment. She took a step closer and pulled the necklace out of her collar. At the end of the chain hung a silver half-heart. Mine had cracks on the left; hers had cracks on the right. The part of me that had watched way too many Hallmark movies with Aunt Sheila wanted to press my half against hers, forming a perfect fit. Instead I stated the obvious. "You sent me the Christmas box."

"Yes." She nudged my arm. "It was supposed to stay a secret forever." Amy threw up her arms and giggled. "Oh, well, secret's out. Thanks a lot, James."

Tears almost started up again. "I can't believe you did that after how I acted."

"That's what happens when you start praying for someone you're mad at. I figured you had to be going through something major to leave Alex."

More like temporary insanity.

"But, the handwriting...." I would have known Amy's loopy cursive.

"I paid my roommate a dollar per card to write them out for me."

I wiped my cheeks, dreading what I must look like, overcome with the desire to tell her what a difference her generosity made and share stories of what it inspired. "I didn't just dump a great boyfriend; I let a sweet friend go, too."

She draped her arm around me and squeezed. "We make crazy choices when we're hurt and scared. Your step-dad did something he probably regrets now, and so did you. When I get a chance to fill you in on the last ten years, you'll see I've had my share of regrettable moments. That's why we need forgiveness and grace, from God and from each other."

Father Christmas set aside his empty red sack and pulled a bundle of candy canes from the pocket of his robe.

God, I will never stop being sorry.

"Remember, he's still single." She winked.

"Oh, come on, what am I going to do? Ask to get back together?"

"You should probably start with, 'I'm sorry.'"

"Yeah, probably."

For a moment we both just stood there, watching one kid after another hug Father Christmas.

She cocked her head toward mine. "Alex was such a good sport to agree to hide in one of Brenda's suites until the party ends."

Father Christmas shouted a final Merry Christmas. Brenda took her place at the piano and called everyone over to sing carols. How would I ever keep my mind on work with Alex upstairs? "I'll make sure Lydia sends him dinner."

Amy picked up her kids' toys. "Brenda told him not to show his face in the lobby until nine o'clock, and he must be out of costume." She gave me another quick hug. "I better let you get back to work. Don't let me leave without getting your e-mail and phone number."

She stopped at the door to the Garden Room. "I don't really need to say, 'Hint, hint' do I?"

Amy waved to me before ushering her sleepy boys out the door. I waved back, sneaking another glance at the grandfather clock.

Lydia kicked off her shoes. "Thanks so much for your help, Justine."

I forced myself to look at her instead of at the clock. "No problem."

"No trouble with your ex-boyfriend's sister?"

"Not at all." I watched the stairs and the elevator door.

"You owe me the whole saga after Christmas." She headed back to her office.

I had been expecting him, but my heart still jumped when I saw Alex exit the elevator with a garment bag slung over his arm. The absence of his fake beard revealing a more distinguished version of the face I knew. His dark hair had receded just a bit. He rubbed his chin, peeling off remaining flecks of adhesive.

I stood frozen beside the reservation desk, rebuking the voice in my head telling me to forget it. *No, this is my only chance.*

"Alex?" I sounded like an eight-year-old.

He looked my way, stopping by the giant nutcracker. I pushed away my unrealistic desire to have him rush over and envelop me in his arms, carrying on about how long he'd dreamed of this night.

"Justine. Hi." He stayed put. "Amy told me you were here. I saw you earlier but . . ."

"You had a job to do."

He rubbed his face again. "Yeah."

"You make a great Father Christmas."

He laughed. "I would only make such an idiot out of myself for James and Peter."

We exchanged awkward acknowledgements of how great each other looked. Then silence opened the door for what I needed to get out. I willed my feet to move his way and my voice to work properly. "Alex, before we get caught up in so-what-have-you-been-up-to-since-college small talk, I need to say something."

He draped his costume over a chair. "Okay."

"I am so sorry for hurting you." I'd planned to pour out my reasons again, but covering an apology with excuses didn't feel right anymore.

His lips turned up at the corners. His eyes smiled. "You're forgiven."

I wanted so badly to bury my face against his chest. Instead I looked into his gentle eyes. "Thank you."

"I know what happened with Jason really affected you."

"It did, but I should have trusted you."

He reached out and took my hand. If felt wonderful. "Things are good for you now though?"

As long as this lasts, things are perfect. "Yes, much better."

He smiled. "Good."

The question of what to say after that brought us back to the small talk. He wrote for the local paper, just like he'd always wanted to do, leaving me feeling like an under-achiever. He and Amy and everyone else I knew had moved forward while I stayed stuck, held prisoner by resentment.

"So, how is your aunt that you always talked about?"

"Sheila. She's great." She would be crazy with joy right now. *That's right, Aunt Sheila!* I looked at my watch. "Oops, I'm supposed to meet her at church in, um, five minutes ago."

Alex picked up his garment bag. "I should let you get going."

No, please don't let me get going. She'll be thrilled if a say I skipped church for a guy.

"It was great seeing you." He started toward the door.

I called out to him before he could get away.

He looked over his shoulder in the way that always made me melt. "Yeah?"

"Would you like to…" I swallowed the *start over* trying to fly out of my mouth. "…get coffee or something sometime?"

He brushed something off his garment bag then looked back at me. "That would be nice."

"I know a great coffee place near here."

"Full 'a Beans?"

"How did you know?"

"I always thought it seems like a place you would like."

I hurried to my car, dying to squeal, "I have a date the day after Christmas!"

Jason's present sat abandoned on the passenger seat. The sight of it snuffed out the thrill of a second chance. Why did it suddenly feel like Jason and I had a lot in common?

I hadn't stolen anything. But I had hurt two people deeply. One of them prayed for me and sent me presents. Even the one I wounded the most cruelly forgave me.

Your step-dad panicked and did something he probably regrets now.

The package sitting beside me and an ignored text message cried out that he did.

I picked up the package and set it in my lap, moisture once again stinging my eyelids. I pulled at the packing tape.

Not yet.

I found a safe place for the box on the floor and covered it with a sweatshirt. I dug my phone out of my tote bag and pulled up

Jason's text. My fingers shook so badly that I had to delete three mistakes before finally entering *"I got it. Thank you"* and hitting send.

I wiped the last of my tears and slipped the phone back into my bag. Snowflake wrapping paper glittered under the street lights. *My gift.* In all the drama I'd forgotten to give it to Lydia. I grabbed it; then I put it back.

It took twenty-five minutes to get to his apartment according to the GPS on my phone. By the time I drove back, I would miss church. Aunt Sheila might turn the Christmas Eve service into a prayer vigil. *She'll be okay. It's worth it.*

I hugged the package to my chest to protect it from the damp air as I searched for apartment #114. The porch light was on. Multi-colored Christmas lights outlined the door. *He's home.*

I approached the door with my mind ping-ponging between fear and release, my heart racing so fast that I thought he might find me passed out on his welcome mat in the morning. Still, I managed to crouch down, lay the package on the mat, and stand.

I rang the bell and hurried away, wishing I could be there when Jason opened the anonymous package and saw the ceramic *Grace* cross, and the words on the envelope: *You're forgiven.*

Aunt Sheila sat at the kitchen table with her hands around a Santa mug. The tree lights were on and the Christian radio station's 48 Hours of Christmas. She had changed into her slippers but still wore her red shimmery sweater.

She sprang from her chair when she saw me. "There you are!"

"Sorry I missed church."

"Are you okay? I called the hotel, but Lydia said you'd left." She got up and rushed over. "Your eyes are red. What happened?"

"I'm fine." I smiled. "Really, I am. I'll tell you all about it later."

She looked me over. "If you say so."

"How was church?"

"Beautiful. The bell choir played, the worship team performed a song that made me cry so hard that I can't even remember the name of it, and I saw Steven."

"Steven?"

She swatted my arm. "Don't give me that. He is good-looking; you have to admit it."

I allowed myself a laugh before jumping to the more serious part. "Yes, he is. But, to be honest, he's not my type."

She ushered me to the table. "Do you have someone better in mind?"

"Actually, I think I do."

"Really? Someone has been keeping secrets."

"This is kind of a new thing."

"Tell me."

"Not yet." I didn't want to jinx it.

"Oh, fine, be that way. But I will get it out of you by the New Year." She patted the tabletop with her fingertips. "Sit down. I'll get you some cocoa."

"I need your help with something first."

I went back to the table by the front door to retrieve Jason's package.

Aunt Sheila put her hand over her heart. "You didn't send it back."

I shook my head.

"Would you like me to wrap it up pretty for you?"

I looked down at the box in my hands. Jason had probably opened my gift by now. "No."

"What do you need from me, Honey?"

I found the place on the couch near the tree. "Sit with me while I open it."

She sat next to me, not saying anything. I carefully picked at the tape until it came loose. From ages twelve to twenty, I looked forward to Jason gifts more than any others, but tonight I didn't care what was inside as much as the peace I had in letting go of hating him.

Inside a bubble wrap-covered white box, I found a bed of tissue paper surrounding a gold jewelry box with ice skaters etched on the lid. I'd admired one just like it in a store the night we saw *Scrooge*.

"How lovely." Aunt Sheila touched one of the skaters.

"I wanted this. I never said anything, but Mom could barely peal me away from the window." I lifted the lid. The one I remembered played "Winter Wonderland." The first notes barely rang out before I almost dropped the jewelry box.

An emerald bracelet sparkled against the black velvet lining.

"Oh, Justine."

I touched it to make sure it was real, examining the emerald in the center of an antique gold heart, and the diamond flecks and swirly etchings that made up the chain. "How did he get it back?"

Or did his conscience restrain him from selling it in the first place?

"I imagine the two of you have a lot to talk about, don't you?"

I searched for a note. I checked under the flaps of the packing box and every inch of the wrapping.

Aunt Sheila caught my hands. "Honey, doesn't the gift speak for itself?"

"I guess it does."

I took the bracelet out of the jewelry box, aching to put it on but unable to take my eyes off of it. Did he replace Mom's china, too? Obviously, she'd forgiven him with or without it.

I rested my head against my aunt's shoulder. She wrapped her arms around me.

"Feels freeing to let go of the past, doesn't it?"

I nodded. "I forgave him before I opened the present."

"I kind of sensed that."

"So, I've been thinking. Do we have room for one more guest for Christmas dinner?"

About the Authors

Kathi Macias - Kathi (www.kathimacias.com) is a multi-award winning bestselling author of more than 40 books. A wife, mother, grandmother, and great-grandmother, she lives in Southern California with her husband, Al.

Kathy Bruins - Kathy believes everyone has a story to tell. She walks with her clients and tells their story through her writing. She recently had three books of her own published: *A Season of God's Daily Influence – Book 1*, and a new Amish fiction series called *Aaron's Quest*, and *Vallikett's Journey* (collaborative), She also has written a Bible study *Psalms: My Sentiments Exactly* that teaches about the different genres of the psalms and how they relate to our emotions. Her speaking topics include writing book proposals, ghostwriting, creating dramas for church use, Spiritual Spa Day (Event), prayer, leadership, and cancer. For more information, please visit www.kathybruins.com.

Jessica Ferguson - Jessica Ferguson is a freelance writer, author and co-editor of *Swamp Lily Review, A Journal of Louisiana Literature & Arts*. She is a staff writer for Southern Writers Magazine, specializing in author interviews. Jess is the author of a romantic suspense called *The Last Daughter*, and a romantic comedy entitled *The Groom Wore Blue Suede Shoes*. Her short fiction, *If You Believe* and *A Child Was Born* are in

Christmas anthologies. Her nonfiction has appeared in newspapers and magazines in Louisiana and Texas and she has taught Basic Nonfiction classes through Leisure Learning and Continuing Education Departments. Jess is the founder of the East Texas Writers Association in her hometown of Longview, Texas. She's involved in a number of writer's organizations and served two years as president of the Bayou Writers Group in Lake Charles, Louisiana where she lives. Helping others find their passion, get published, complete a novel, sell a short story or just solve a writing problem – according to Jess, that's the thrill of being in this business. Check out her blog at jessyferguson.blogspot.com

Christine Lindsay - Christine was born in Ireland, and is proud of the fact that she was once patted on the head by Prince Philip when she was a baby. Her great grandfather, and her grandfather—yes father and son—were both riveters on the building of the *Titanic*. Tongue in cheek, Christine states that as a family they accept no responsibility for the sinking of that great ship. It was stories of her ancestors who served in the British Cavalry in Colonial India that inspired her multi-award-winning historical series *Twilight of the British Raj. Book 1 Shadowed in Silk* and *Book 2 Captured by Moonlight*. The final installment to that series, *Veiled at Midnight* will be released August 2014. *Londonderry Dreaming* is Christine's first romance which is set in Ireland. Christine makes her home in British Columbia, on the west coast of Canada with her husband and their grown up family. Her cat Scottie is chief editor on all Christine's books. To connect with Christine please drop by her website **www.ChristineLindsay.com**

Marcia Lee Laycock - Marcia's writing began in the attic of her parents' home where she wrote poetry and short stories for her dolls. She says they never complained so she kept it up. Since those humble beginnings, her work has been published in magazines, newspapers and anthologies in both Canada and the U.S. and has been broadcast on radio across Canada. Marcia's work also appears frequently on the world wide web. She currently writes a regular devotional column, *The Spur*, which appears in publications across Canada and goes out by e-mail to avid readers. Marcia's work has won many prizes, garnering praise from notable Christian writers like Janette Oke, Mark Buchanan, Phil Callaway and Sigmund Brouwer. She has published two devotional books plus four ebooks and won the Best New Canadian Christian Author Award for her novel, *One Smooth Stone*, published by Castle Quay Books. The sequel, *A Tumbled Stone* was released by Word Alive Press (www.wordalivepress.ca) and was short-listed for an award at the Word Awards in June 2013. Marcia's latest releases are a third expanded edition of her devotional book, *Spur of the Moment* and a Christmas novella released by Helping Hands Press. To learn more about Marcia's writing and speaking ministry visit her online at: www.marcialeelaycock.com

Marcy Weydemuller - Marcy lives in northern California. She writes fantasy, historical, and contemporary stories, and has published two poetry collections, *Summer Sketches* and *Wind Sifting* and received the 2006 Mount Hermon Poetry Award. She teaches poetry, fiction and non-fiction workshops, both in person and online. Marcy has a BA in History and Sociology, and an MFA in Writing from Vermont College of Fine Arts. She is also a sought-after content editor for many award-winning and multi-published authors. Visit her at www.marcyweydemuller.com

Ruth L. Snyder - Ruth was privileged to spend the first 10 years of her life in southern Africa where her parents served as missionaries. From there her family moved to Canada, settling in Three Hills, Alberta. Ruth enjoyed her years as a "staff kid" at Prairie and is grateful for the biblical grounding she received there. She now resides close to Glendon (the pyrogy capital of Alberta, Canada) with her husband and five young children. Ruth enjoys writing articles, devotionals, short stories, and Christian fiction. She is a member of The Word Guild and The Christian PEN. Ruth currently serves as the President of InScribe Christian Writers' Fellowship. Ruth's children have taught her many things about living with special needs. She is a strong advocate and spent several years serving on the local public school board. Ruth loves her job teaching Music for Young Children. She is fascinated by children's imaginations and enjoys helping young children learn the basics of music through play. In her spare time, Ruth enjoys reading, crafts, volunteering in her local community, photography, and travel. Several years ago, Ruth and her family traveled through 28 States in 30 days! Find out more about Ruth and her writing at http://ruthlsnyde

Sheila Seiler Lagrand - Sheila lives with her husband Rich and their two dogs in beautiful Trabuco Canyon, California. She enjoys serving at her church, Trabuco Canyon Community Church, doodling, cooking, and most of all, spending time with their children and nine grandchildren. She has lived her entire life in southern California, except for a year spent in French Polynesia as she conducted dissertation research. She doesn't understand boredom and is passionate about words, their power, their beauty, and their care and feeding. She earned her doctorate in anthropology at the University of California, Los Angeles. As an undergraduate at the University of California, San Diego, she studied anthropology and literature with an emphasis in writing.

Sheila is a member of The High Calling. As a young woman she published poems in dozens of literary magazines. Her academic work has been published in anthropology journals and she contributed a chapter to the book *Fieldwork and Families: Constructing New Models for Ethnographic Research.* More recently, her work has appeared in *Wounded Women of the Bible: Finding Hope When Life Hurts, Paul's Letter to the Philippians (BibleDude Community Commentary Series),* and a few volumes of *Chicken Soup for the Soul.* She has work forthcoming in *Soul Bare.* She is a contributor to the collaborative serial romance novel, *The San Francisco Wedding Planner.* The characters from *Yankee Doodle Christmas* live on in *Remembering for Ruth,* a serial novel being released in 2014. Keep up with Sheila at her website, sheilalagrand.com.

Peggy Blann Phifer - Peggy Blann Phifer is a retired executive assistant after working twenty-one years in Corporate America. She resides with her husband of (almost) 25 years in Clark County, Nevada. Peg is also an avid reader who has been known to panic if she doesn't have a book to read. She enjoys handcrafts of all kinds and her home shows off some of her work, though most end up as gifts to family and friends. To See the Sun is Peg's debut to the world of fiction writing.

Anne Baxter Campbell - Anne is a Christian wife, mother, and grandmother who enjoys writing and boosting other writers. Anne is also a speaker and the author of *The Truth Trilogy,* historical novels set in the first century AD. You can find out more about her on annebaxtercampbell.com.

Mishael Austin Witty - Mishael is a professional editor and the internationally bestselling author of *Shadows Of Things To Come*, a Christian thriller/suspense novel, and *Believe In Me*, a sweet contemporary romance / women's fiction novella. In addition to these books, she has newly released a zombie fairy tale, *Campanula*, which marks a departure from the usual for her, but it was great fun to write, and she already has plans for another. She has, to date, published two short stories with Helping Hands Press: *Protecting Zoe* (Kathi Macias's Twelve Days of Christmas, Volume Eleven) and *The San Francisco Wedding Planner, Volume 1: The Initial Consultation* (a story that was written with the series's five other authors). She is currently hard at work on her next installment of that series, which will be released in either May or June 2014. She lives in Louisville, KY (where most of the action of *Campanula* takes place), with her husband, two cats, and two daughters.

Jeanette Hanscome - Jeanette is an author, freelance editor, writing mentor, and busy mom. She has written four books, as well as hundreds of articles, devotions, and stories for magazine, including *Guideposts*. Jeanette is a regular contributor to Standard Publishing's *Encounter—the Magazine* and LifeWay's *Journey* devotional. She had the honor of co-authoring *Running with Roselle* with blind 9/11 survivor, Michael Hingson. Though she has been visually impaired since birth, Jeanette refuses to allow her limitations to hold her back from doing the things she loves. When she isn't writing, Jeanette enjoys teaching writing workshops at conferences, online, and in the community, cooking and baking, and knitting and crocheting gifts for those she loves. She is the mother of two wonderful sons. Read more about Jeanette on her blog and website jeanettehanscome.com.

Made in the USA
Charleston, SC
10 May 2014